D0062619

Praise for *Going Under*

". . . an immensely entertaining mixture of rock and roll, introspection, and action."

Booklist

"This is a fun adventure tale with a healthy mix of fantasy elements with science fiction elements. . . . The momentum credibly builds to a final climax with a suitably metaphorical ending full of faerie glamour and mystery."

Book Spot Central

"The third outing for Lila Black (*Keeping It Real*; *Selling Out*) tackles the elusive world of Faerie, a place far from the stereotypes of legends. Robson's (*Mappa Mundi*) mercurial style suits her quick-witted heroine in a fantasy/sf adventure that is a good addition to most fantasy or sf collections."

Library Journal

"Lila Black is one kick-ass bionic woman. . . . Impossible-to-put-down, the series stays quite interesting and I'm waiting for the next tale."

Weekly Press/University City Review

WITHDRAWN
FROM THE RECORDS OF THE
MID-CONTINENT PUBLIC LIBRARY

Mid-Continent Public Library
15616 East US Highway 24
Independence, MO 64050

Praise for *Selling Out*

"It's good. It's really very good indeed. I loved it."
Peter F. Hamilton

"Fast, lucid, and engaging throughout, vivid with inventive detail and sharp with unexpected twists snagging the unwary reader. . . . I can't wait to see how they'll tackle what comes next."
SF Revu

"You get pulled in by the novel's sheer energy. The cross-genre pollination of various ideas makes for a quirky read."
Deathray

Praise for *Keeping It Real*

"Entertaining fusion of SF and fantasy spiced with sex, rockin' elves, and drunk faeries."
Publishers Weekly

"This is by far the most entertaining book Robson has written, a novel packed with memorable characters and ideas but that doubles as holiday-reading escapism."
SFX

"Think an enthusiastic melange of Laurell K. Hamilton's *Meredith Gentry*, Tad Williams's *War of the Flowers*, Anne Rice's *The Vampire Lestat*, a touch of Marianne de Pierre's Parrish Plessis, even *The Bionic Woman* or *The Transformers*, and you get an idea of how much fun this book is."
SFF World

DOWN TO THE
BONE

ALSO BY JUSTINA ROBSON

Silver Screen
Mappa Mundi
Keeping It Real: Quantum Gravity Book One
Selling Out: Quantum Gravity Book Two
Going Under: Quantum Gravity Book Three
Chasing the Dragon: Quantum Gravity Book Four

QUANTUM GRAVITY BOOK FIVE

DOWN TO THE
BONE

JUSTINA ROBSON

an imprint of **Prometheus Books**
Amherst, NY

Published 2011 by Pyr®, an imprint of Prometheus Books

Down to the Bone. Copyright © 2011 by Justina Robson. All rights reserved. No part of this publication may be reproduced, stored in a retrieval system, or transmitted in any form or by any means, digital, electronic, mechanical, photocopying, recording, or otherwise, or conveyed via the Internet or a website without prior written permission of the publisher, except in the case of brief quotations embodied in critical articles and reviews.

Cover illustration © Larry Rostant.

Inquiries should be addressed to
Pyr
59 John Glenn Drive
Amherst, New York 14228–2119
VOICE: 716–691–0133
FAX: 716–691–0137
WWW.PYRSF.COM

15 14 13 12 11   5 4 3 2 1

Library of Congress Cataloging-in-Publication Data
Robson, Justina.
Down to the bone / by Justina Robson.
    p. cm. — (Quantum gravity ; bk. 5)
ISBN 978–1–61614–379–4 (pbk. : alk. paper)
ISBN 978–1–61614–380–0 (e-book)
I. Title. II. Series.

PR6118.O28D68 2011
823'.92—dc22

2011014996

Printed in the United States of America on acid-free paper

For Laszlo

FINAL THOUGHTS

It's a bit odd to have some final thoughts at the start of a book, but as this is the end in a series of five I'd like to take the opportunity to thank everyone who stuck with me throughout the long cycle of Quantum Gravity's creation. It was made over a period of five years in which my entire real life got turned inside out. I don't credit that bit to anyone but myself, incidentally.

In no particular order then: thanks to Stephanie Burgis-Samphire, who gave me the first encouragement all those years ago and who is always there with sage advice and a big heart. Here's looking at you kid!

Thank you Simon Spanton, for being a sensitive and encouraging editor. Thank you Lou Anders, for being an inspiring and cheerleading editor. You guys rock.

Thanks also to John R. Parker, my agent, who went indie and started a new agency during QG whilst still keeping track of all the important details. Go team Zeno!

And finally thanks to you, the reader. I hope that you find this book to be a satisfactory conclusion to the story. I had a lot of fun writing it but mostly it was made with you in mind.

CHAPTER ONE

Zal woke to the strobing flicker of orange light. It shattered the pitch darkness of the night, accompanied by the sudden whining scream of metal grinding on metal. His ears flicked with hurt at the offence and the hot chemical stink of burning bit his nostrils, sharp and fresh even though he'd been in the room for hours. He pulled his noise-cancelling headphones off the useless place they'd slid to on his neck and sat up silently to resume his spying.

Sparks jetted in the shape of a small firework flare and lit the unprotected face of his wife as she bent to her task. They leapt into her cropped black hair and briefly illuminated its scarlet streak as it consumed them. They showered onto her pale skin and finished their brief, brilliant lives there before falling away as motes of black dust; all passion spent in that single gesture. Well spent. He saw one dart straight into the liquid surface of her eye as if it were trying to give her an artist's impression of a wicked glint against the stormy blue iris and its peculiar lilac ring. She blinked and it was gone. Where they cascaded into the front of her short floral sundress they vanished entire and whole. The hem of the dress shed soot onto the raw concrete beside her knees.

Her arms, slender and muscular, were vibrating with effort. In place of one hand was a large steel vice and in place of the other a spinning borer. The vice held the blunt mass of the engine block she was working on. She had it braced against the floor at a precise angle as she redrilled the cylinders with her other hand. Under her persuasion the antique thing had a resonance that made his inner ears vibrate to tones he hadn't heard in half a century. Elves were sensitive to sound and ultrasound, and he was particularly good with harmonics. His body told him that whatever care she put into her labour she was still as likely to break the old Ducati block as mend it. It was old, old metal that had endured years of use and huge temperature swings and its matrices were close to shot. She would know that herself of course—her machine-perfected hearing bettered his—but it made no difference to her. She had to try and she had to do it the right way, which meant attacking it with the antique brutality of metal tools and risk destruction when she could have plasma-gunned or light-cut it without any trouble or danger in a fraction of the time. The sound made him shiver with old remembered joy.

Zal waited for a pause, enjoying his admiration of her, and darkness returned. The yellow and orange spark fountain was replaced by a blue and green afterflare in his mind's eye. Against it her hands and face became a lime silhouette, the dress a yellow tatter whose vines and roses suddenly twisted into a face of its own—wickedly grinning. The dress smiled at him and winked and he didn't know if it was the faery's equivalent of "hello, darling" or "fuck you." He'd met too many faeries. There was no way to know the answer and they'd never tell. Like the elves, they liked their games too much to give anything away.

In the sudden silence he found his amusement at playing his own game had worn thin. He took an audible breath and spoke into the darkness, "Can't sleep?"

He heard a sigh. The drill briefly whirred and went quiet again in a blurt of annoyance.

"Darn, I didn't even know you were there." She spoke with the gritty burr of someone who hasn't used their voice in many hours and added a snort of disgust. "There goes my theory of a soul-link between us through which I'd know your every move. How long've you been here?"

"Since you started taking it apart." Zal was referring to the latest motorbike carcase she had bought, one of several whole relics that she'd collected over the last month. Their dismembered parts lay all around in mute explanation of her mysterious absences. He hadn't known what had caused her to spend so much time away until tonight. He'd wondered, until that had lost its "poor me" tang. When he'd asked she said Agency business, but he talked to her agent partner, Malachi, too often and knew she wasn't there. Not that sitting on the premises was important to the work she did for them, but he still thought she was lying. His demon heart knew these things. Now satisfying his curiosity by following her and exposing her secret was pretty low, he had to admit, but after all they'd been through he wasn't about to let her get away without a fight. He'd rather face her anger.

She sat for a moment but "I see," was all she said in the end.

He heard the engine block meet the concrete floor as she put it down, and then the whirr and click whispering of precision engineering tools putting themselves away. The sounds were hollow and tinny in the old garage's bare space. A faint line above the rollup door glowed in waxy grey, like the end of the last candle, providing the only light in the entire place. It illuminated nothing, but neither of them needed visible light. Lila could see on every part of the spectrum if she chose to, and he was finally the creature of darkness that his enemies had always claimed him to be, although they'd been talking about his soul and not his body. Left without light or heat long enough Zal knew he could dissipate entirely into shadow, even in Otopia where all aetheric processes were reduced to fractions of their otherworldly power. He hadn't been sure that he could fool Lila by shedding as much material form as possible and cloaking what remained of his physical self in his aetheric body, but it seemed he'd done a good job.

He felt the cool touch of her hand on his cheek, long fingers and delicate skin where the vice had been a moment ago. Her voice was soft, close to his face, her breath kissing him.

"I don't understand how you can exist without giving off any wavelengths at all. I don't get how shadow can be anything. Darkness isn't a thing, it's an absence of light."

It used to be the case that Zal didn't have an answer that would satisfy her scientific curiosity. He hadn't even known the technicalities of why he was invisible, though he'd made an effort to be so and intention was required. The scientific analysis of aether was a demon pastime and a human obsession. He was only a demon in nature but not in the particulars. Lila was the opposite. She knew the particulars about everything but she wasn't a demon at heart. She was human to the core.

Zal released all intention to be invisible now and saw her start back slightly as the last of his cloaking aura vanished beneath the surface of his skin and revealed his Cheshire cat expression. "Humans never used to see my aura at all, even when it was the old me and nothing more."

"They *felt* it," she said, the expression of mixed annoyance and softness in her face convincing him that she was remembering their first meeting. She put her hand up to cup his jaw and tilt his head towards her.

At the time, being a smug bastard full of inflated rock-star importance, he'd used her ignorance against her, to score a cheap point and had felt her up using just his aura. He grinned at the memory himself. She snorted with laughter this time as her fingers against his lips felt his smile. "And I doubt they'll see this one unless you choose to make it visible." Her eyes narrowed fractionally—a movement he'd learned was a sign that she was listening to the Signal; the constant background hiss she was able to hear that comprised the world of machines, the full data record of everything that had ever happened and what was possible. It wasn't a world like this one, or Alfheim or Demonia. He didn't know if world was the right idea. It was more like an idea than a thing, and less like either than suited his grasp of cosmology.

He let a few seconds pass, hours to Lila, and then saw the blink of her fugue state ending. She jumped up to sit beside him on the emptied crates and their lid of folded tarps that he'd been using as a bed. Her body was as warm and vibrant as any living human woman's, no heavier and no stranger. Her bare legs and arms were girlishly smooth. There were no clues as to where the machine structure had once fitted its bulky robotic prostheses to what remained of her human body, and no trace in her easy movements of the pain they used to cause her. They were long changed.

Since the two of them had been through the cauldron of Faery, she had been flawlessly combined, a machine of living structures that were able to replicate any material. What vulnerability she had ended on the inside now and was hers to share or conceal—her physical form was as close to invulnerable as anything he could imagine.

But he remembered the first time he'd seen her through the toughened glass of a recording-studio window in her security agency girl's suit, trousers burst at a seam, a streak of dust across her white collar. Her poppy-red lipstick had cut a streak of rich, contemptuous disapproval straight at him like a laser beam. She came, she saw, she on the spot couldn't stand him, so much so that he'd felt the roots of his hair ache with the surprise of it. Then his heart had shivered with the citrus zing of that ancient demon pleasure in opposites attracting and the simultaneous ancient call of what, if he were drunk, he'd've called destiny. He fell in love on the spot and so did she, and hell, did she hate it. And so their game of seduction cat and mouse was begun, dishonestly, deliciously, and under illusions. Since that moment his life had exploded from mere celebrity and notoriety into the realms of the truly madly dangerous. Zal had died and been lost but even that wasn't enough to keep him away. There were no words for how much he loved her and he used to be good with those.

He leaned in towards her and kissed her gently. Her mouth was firm under his. She was still thoughtful. It took her time to come down from being with the machines as though she had to find her way back to human through a difficult maze. He sat back. "I don't feel the metal in you anymore. Only the signature of the elementals bound into it, like they're all that's left."

She murmured her reply with amusement and affection. "You would, if I were in my battle gear."

"Maybe." He leaned into her touch, resting his cheek in her hand. "I hope not." Elf senses and aetheric powers didn't operate well around metals.

"I've refined myself," she said, smiling as she looked at him, not into his eyes but over his cheeks, his mouth, tracing their contours with one delicate fingertip. "There are alloys that wouldn't bother you now. Permeable matrices, tunable to the frequencies of any aether. They vibrate to the same harmonies as a charm. You could play me, like a musical instrument."

"I like the sound of that."

He hesitated, watching her watching him, content in the lull of her attention. This dancing around their changed ways felt delicate and uncertain, a charm in itself, although for himself he hadn't changed at all, he was still Zal, only a few particulars were different and what did they count for? He felt he ought to correct an important point however. "Shadow isn't darkness though. Shadow is a frequency of aether. Better think of it as a kind of black light. All living things have it, and some not living ones. It is as real as any other form of energy. It just happens that it's of a kind not visible."

She was not entirely impressed. "Energy, spirits, souls if they exist . . . I can't fit them together. I don't see them properly. It's like there's a missing piece in the picture. Is it because they don't emit radiant signals? And then there's all these priestly types talking on and on about the light. Another metaphor and nothing but? I wish I could talk to Tath. He'd know."

Zal wasn't sure that Tath would know or if he did that his revelations would satisfy Lila's incomplete pattern of the universe.

Tath's own personal bargain with Jack the Giantkiller had transformed him from a relatively simple, if slippery, necromancer into the speaker for the dead. This position, whilst not Death itself, gave him dominion over the half-tangible regions of transition through which the spirits of the newly dead passed on their way to their ineffable final destination, itself a place Tath could not enter. This was a zone that bordered on the fey, but also the elemental. Zal knew next to nothing about it even though he had passed through it himself on his way back from the brink of creation. Death herself had brought him most of the way. It hadn't inspired any fervour in him. Things lurked there in the grim darkness that were hungry and forsaken; needful things without the means to grasp what they must have. Bodiless hunters. Vampires and their like, or the things that would be vampires if they ever got the chance. They were spirits of a kind, mindless, raw. Necromancers knew to stay away from them. He didn't like the idea of Lila going on some hunt to find out what they were, either in the region of the near dead or by other means.

She was talking to herself again, so gripped by the whisper of the Signal and her own need to fit everything into a coherent whole that he could sit with her, even kiss her, even make love with her and know himself quite alone while she spun away into the strange infinities of her mind. He feared for her in that inner space, where neither he nor anything else could go, where she could get lost forever in the twists and turns.

"How about the bike?" The bike was a great sign. The bike was creative, important. The bike was sacred. The bike was something that existed in all her worlds, something he could ride to get in. "Is that fitting together?"

She smiled. "It's just a matter of time."

He saw parts he thought he recognised as old Harley Davidsons but there were other lost beasts in there too, laid out all over the floor in precise patterns with Lila-sized pathways left between their ranks. "What are you going to run it on? Looks kinda petrochemical."

"I'm not sure yet," she said. "Might have to be petrol. Depends on whether anything else makes the right sound. Anyway, has to be if I use genuine parts. They aren't up to anything else."

He didn't mention that there was no petrol industry anymore. She knew that. She'd figure something out. He wouldn't even have been surprised if she could drink beer and piss petrol but although that might be a hell's angel dream and he fancied himself one of those it wasn't a particularly erotic fantasy of his so he let it go and coughed, perfectly mimicking the sound of a carburetor choking to death. "Care to run a diagnostic on me?"

Now she turned and poked him in the chest gently, making him sway back on the crates. A flickering rush of thrills ran through him as her ultrasound frequencies penetrated his clothing and skin to the energy centres beneath making him gasp and fall backwards. He caught himself in time. She snickered.

"C'mon," he said, opening his arms and giving her a smouldering stare. "My nuts are rusted. I need an oil change."

He could see her eyes, their faery-enchanted human irises glowing with lilac as they narrowed. In a flash she was on him, the tatters of the summer minidress flaring up in a nonexistent breeze as the pile of crates wobbled precariously. There was a distinct cracking and splitting noise from the wood as they swayed. Zal got a hand out to the wall behind him but it was a long way away. Lila's knees gripped the outside of his thighs as she went for the pinning move and then he felt her fingers tug the lace knots of his jerkin. She got fed up after a second and he felt them part under a blade. Then her hands were inside his shirt, emitting faint pulses of deep low-frequency sound as she ran them across his chest and shoulders. The crates leaned and he had to keep his hand on the wall or crash to the floor as his body arched in pleasure involuntarily.

"That demon was a good teacher," he muttered through closed jaws as she bent close to him and he felt her lips on his neck. He meant Teazle, their pureblood demon husband, who had been with her in her fall through Faery and after. "Fifty year—"

"It was *weeks*," she hissed and he heard the ache and anger in her voice. Between hot kisses that ran up to his ears she breathed, "It was only weeks and we waited for you and we didn't know if you were alive or dead and we had no idea what to do, *no idea at all*." Her hands flared with hot and cold pulses, with bursts of specific vibrations tuned to the channels of aether that ran in him and he lost control of his aether body. Black spilled out in clouds around both of them, swallowing the pathetic remains of the light. With his free hand he found her waist, tiny and taut with power not far above his own. As he touched the dress he felt it slither away from his grasp with an eel-like shiver, cotton turning to satin the better to slip away from him, even though threads of it curled lasciviously around his fingers as it did so. It parted, unstitching itself, sliding away from her so that she made a sound of surprise as the faery thing escaped and his hand found her naked skin. He let it rest for a moment, feeling the texture of her, cool on the surface, hot underneath, soft and silky, dry enough for him to slide his palms on her with the same skimming ease she used on him.

He remembered his other hands, without regrets, their thick, three-fingered gloves that were overstuffed with the remnants from the weaving of the three fey sisters. For fifty years they'd left him able to feel almost nothing, were so clumsy he couldn't have picked up a spoon to feed himself; not that there had been a need for food, or anything else in that time-lost place. His hungers now were savage in retaliation.

With anger he pushed the unwanted image away, feeling his rage direct itself at the skirts of the dress, now trailing themselves like waterweeds around his wrist and elbow, teasing him in their own inscrutable way. He had brought this dress to Lila, armour as it was then. He didn't know what he'd done in that gesture. He hadn't known what it was. He couldn't tell if its complicity in getting Lila to jump the fifty-year penalty of his "death" was a blessing or a curse, he didn't know if it meant her harm or good or if, like any faery, it would change its intentions with limitless caprice. He didn't want its strange flirtation now. He focused his shadow body on it and *pulled*.

With the speed of lightning, a charge of aether shocked through him with such enormous force that he thought he'd killed himself. For the split second of its possession of him it interpenetrated every part of his being in a way he hadn't felt since the day that the three weird sisters had pulled him from the cloth. It was not simple, inert charge. With it he felt the faery herself—a feral intelligence, as peculiar as anything he had ever encountered—searching him. Then she was gone and only the energy he had sucked out of her remained with him. He felt her understand that he only wanted her out of the way to be alone with Lila and in that moment the tendrils of soft fabric around his arm became suddenly a thick rope wound there, binding him, then in a second instant he felt the slide of silk sateen as a python's coils slipped around him, letting him go. There was a hiss of heavy rich fabric falling to the floor off to their right, as if an entire theatre-curtain's worth had gone sashaying to the ground.

"What the hell . . . ?" Lila was saying, finding herself suddenly naked and touched not by one but by many hands of Zal.

But Zal was the darkness, his aether given form and mass in Tatterdemalion's wake as some of her faery nature lingered in his aura; a strange gift or theft he understood intuitively with a shock as great as the result of his bad-tempered attack. Now Lila's hands gripped and held onto his body beneath her as he was able to repay her kindness with his own new touch. His many hands, many more fingers, long and articulate, delicate as feathers, powerful, tentacular, slippery as oil, flowed across her. He was able to caress her everywhere at once as the dress's metamorphic patterns cascaded through his *andalune* body. It was a fantasy he thought could never happen because she was human —they couldn't even make the common interface of one aether body to another like elves would together. But now he could play with her breasts and feel their soft reactivity to the teasing of his fingers and the lick of his tongue, at the same time as he played sweeping scales along her back and over her buttocks. His senses were filled with the roundness, the soft weight of her, the sound of her gasping moan in his ears. Meanwhile his hand on the wall held them from disaster and the one at her waist gripped hard enough on her to anchor him and stop him from falling into delirium and giving in, coming like a kid before he was ready or the gift was wasted. Before that happened he wanted to pour everything he felt for Lila into the way he touched her. Centuries of practice with musical instruments of every kind and with his own breath for voice rose through him, guiding his actions and his reactions. A sensitivity greater than any he'd had as an ordinary elf flooded back into him and he was able to attune himself to her as keenly as she was able to play him.

He felt her hands slipping down from his shoulders as she grounded and balanced herself on her knees. She leaned forward and he felt his breath, then her lips against his neck. The tough cotton of his trousers that had been hard-stretched against his hips in that position suddenly loosened and separated as she precision-dissected them, leaving them in tatters around the top of his thighs. He shifted precariously into a better position, crates juddering. He was as hungry to join her fully as she was for him. In the complete darkness of his shroud body the touch sensation was so heightened he had to bite his lips as she mounted him.

The metal elementals bound into her form acted as conduits for his shadow energy. There was traffic both ways; a subtle vibration ran through his aether body as she found a way to touch him back through the same circuit. Her charge, metabolised by the elementals, was very strong. The absolute dark of his covering, *andalune* about them, began to glow very faintly red like a smouldering ember. He noticed it and felt the change but he was too far gone to care what it was or what it meant. It wasn't until she screamed and then sighed with delight on him and he did the same that he opened his eyes to a hot yellow-white flare so bright he was nearly blinded. Without his concentration his *andalune* reverted to its ambient energy form and she grabbed and held him as the crates gave way at that moment and they fell to the concrete floor amid the smoking, splintering wreckage. He landed on his ass with a painful jolt that ran up his spine and he got a lungful of nasty smoke. Lila was laughing. He heard her quick footsteps and then the hiss of a foam fire extinguisher being used. Something wet splattered around his feet and ankles as he stood up.

Now that he had lost contact with her, the brilliant glare died away rapidly, through all the colours to red and then crimson before his ordinary shadow body was all that was left, giving him a sun-glasses-view of a mess of wooden planks and singed tarps. In the midst of it Lila stood naked, holding the extinguisher in front of her. The nozzle was pointed at him.

He read the look on her face as he pulled a splinter out of his hand and raised an eyebrow, daring her.

Cold, wet froth covered his face and chest, then his naked crotch. He heard her laughing—the carefree, mischievous laugh of the pixies —and leapt forward at the same moment. She was hard to catch off guard but he did wrest the canister away from her and dance off with it far enough to give a good blast on her butt as she darted away, shrieking and dancing over bits of engine without treading on a single one.

When the foam ran out, they were in the midst of a wobbling white hillock, splattering each other with huge handfuls of soapy film, using great, cartoonish knockdown throws that gave the softest kiss to wherever it landed. Zal's trousers had become sodden legwarmers around his boots.

As he looked down at himself, Lila got a double handful and dumped it on his head, mashing it well into his hair and ears. Cold trickles of run-off showered out across his face as he looked up at her.

He raised his fist and shook it at her threateningly.

She scooped up some ammunition but he made a dive for her legs instead, caught her around the hips, and they both slipped and went down hard into the mound of foam. He heard the breath shoot out of her but both of them were too tough to care about a thump onto some dirty concrete. They wrestled, limbs slip-sliding against each other. It was a struggle but eventually she got the best of him and he found himself on his back with his arms pinned by a single hand of hers above his head. A triumphant look made her face radiant. In her free hand she held a mountain of white.

"Give me one reason not to."

"Uhh . . ." He stared at her breasts, dripping with suds. "You like me too much?"

"Right," she said, sitting down on his pelvis and letting up on his hands a little before smushing the lot right into his face.

He spat the horrible taste out, blowing, after she let up. "Okay, okay! You win."

"Say it again?"

"You win."

In a flash she was gone, standing over him. He ignored the hand she held down to him and got up, spitting and shaking his head.

"For now," he added. "Come here."

"The winner doesn't come here."

"She does," he said more firmly and grabbed her.

The foam cut out conduction between them. They were just bodies this time and they took longer about it. The garage had an old, pitiful shower stall and toilet in one corner of its office and they used that to clean up in, though there was only a trickle of icy water until Lila siphoned it through her arm to make a warm jet. Zal threw his trouser legs in her rag bucket and tipped water out of his boots. His shirt was the only thing left and it was soaking. He wrung it out hard and put it back on. Then he felt cold. The scrapes on his knees and elbows stung. He went out and found Lila wriggling into a lilac spaghetti-strapped evening gown that clung to her figure as if it was designer cut. For the first time he forgave the faery for her position, though it was a temporary arrangement. She was still on parole as far as he was concerned. He held up his arms.

"Great, you can go eat at the finest restaurants now and I can sell myself for fifteen bucks on the strip."

She shook her head. "Twenty at least, have you no pride?" But she paused and retrieved the trousers, stitching them up roughly and quickly. Needles flashed in and out of her fingers, thread spooling spiderlike from their trailing ends. They were still wet but they were wearable. "That'll work until you get home."

He dragged his boots back on and pushed his dripping hair out of his face. He didn't conceal his disappointment. "You're not coming with me?"

She hesitated. "Let's get coffee. Talk where it's warmer." Her eyes were looking at him with affection. He agreed and they wheeled the Agency's state-of-the-art black bike outside. He sat on the seat as she locked up the garage and set some security device on the door, checking it over.

"Expecting someone?" he asked as she pulled the dress skirt up and set herself behind him.

"I sometimes get rogue attacks," she said as if it were an everyday matter. "I like some warning as to when they're coming so that I don't have to monitor the situation myself all the time."

Zal paused. "You do?" The rogues were those who had survived Otopia's cyborg project, as she had, except they had felt no loyalty to the Agency once created. Those who wouldn't guarantee loyalty to the state were hunted down. The project was concluded now and there were very few left, he knew, and none who could cause her trouble, she claimed. But he felt less sure of that suddenly.

"You know how it is with machines," she said lightly. "A hacker war. If they feel they need to get close enough for a direct connection, well . . . then we fight." She nudged him to start driving but he was too disconcerted.

"I thought they were all taken care of?"

"It's fine, Zal. Don't worry about it. Ride."

After a moment of failing to muster any real objection he put his hands back on the bars. Nothing happened. "How do you start this thing anyway?"

"Like this." She leaned forward around him and showed him, then wrapped her arms around his waist. He found it touching she would let him drive though he'd never say so. He *carefully* teased the bike out onto the narrow streets until he figured he'd got the measure of it, waiting for her to say something about it though she didn't. She just snuggled against his back. On the highway he opened it up slowly. He saw what she meant about it then. He could drive it as hard as he liked; it was full of compensatory mechanisms that made the ride perfect and secure. He could have had more thrill from a hairdryer.

"Can you turn it off?"

"Here." She held out her hand and a brief spark shot across from her to a part of the machine just under the tank. Suddenly it came alive, juddering and sliding under them across the surface. Then he had to fight to control it and keep the speed, dodging the sedate lanes of AI-ordered cars and floats, setting off a dozen proximity alarms until he'd got the hang of the thing—too light and overpowered—and found a path through. It was so much fun that he almost forgot he was freezing his ass off, starving, aching, and hungry. But then Lila tugged his hair and put her hand to his ear. She was playing music for him in the palm of her hand—his favourite old track—but she interrupted it DJ-style to say, "Food!"

He obediently took a look around on the GPS, saw what district was closest, and took a curve down the next off-ramp, easing back until their speed matched the dawn traffic. Bay City had changed almost out of recognition since he'd been there last but in recent days he'd been finding a new way around and this place was something that was so unusual he found himself pulled to it easily. There was no lot so he parked on the street and they got off in the early, misty yellow light of morning as a cleaner truck whirred past on automatic, almost spraying them with its washer jets.

Lila looked it over from its ordinary oh-so-subtle stone and glass front to its heavy, studded wooden door like a cathedral vault entrance, and he was sure she was pulling all its files. He felt smug that he knew somewhere she didn't.

"An elf bar," she said, not quite believing it. "Isn't that some kind of Alfheim statute violation?"

"We're not in Alfheim," he said and palmed the door. A trace of magic reacted to his aether body and the locks slid open in five separate heavy-bar slams before it silently swung ajar.

"Seeing that . . ." Lila glanced up at him with a wry grin and real pleasure, the light flashing off her eyes into his. He grabbed her wrist and kissed her hard as he moved her past him. She smiled up into his face before sliding beyond into the dim glow of the oak-panelled room and its two fully armed elf guards. He didn't blame them for overdoing it here.

The humans were in the middle of an agonising fall from a world that had been scientific and made sense to them, and the throes of it vomited up some horrible scenes that wouldn't have been out of place in an all-out war. Sometimes he wasn't sure it wasn't a war conducted on very slow guerrilla lines. In any case, though Zal was *non grata*, he was still a *persona* and a previous visit and some bloodied noses had gained him enough respect to get in a second time without questions.

The guard who had spat at his demon blood before was standing there now, looking straight ahead from his black eye as if he was bored beyond belief. The other one, much more advanced, gave Lila a curious look that was a mixture of so many expressions it was comical. Surprise, awe, disbelief, interest, and the difficulty posed by being expected to do a pat-down weapons check on her all warred for a moment and left him slack-jawed. Weapons weren't allowed and Lila, well known among the worldly elves at least by reputation, was nothing if not a weapon in herself. Also, they universally despised what he was wearing and the condition he was in.

"She's with me," Zal said in elvish, quietly, as if that covered and explained everything.

Lila glanced at him curiously and returned the frosty guard's icy glare.

The guard looked at Zal and their auras briefly entangled, communicating faster and more efficiently than speech. With a slight blink of deference he moved aside and held open the heavy black curtain to let them pass. Behind the defensive one-way glass surrounding the entryway, Zal felt several more guards pursue a sudden curious interest in him. As they moved through into the main room, he felt them tracking him through their secret passages in the walls.

A familiar sensation of several very widely diffused *andalune* energies greeted him and he recognised the mages employed as wait-staff from his previous visit, briefly touching them all before he withdrew into his customary silence, inside his physical body. They all turned to watch Lila, feeling the oddness of her presence, and he was aware of a degree of ill intent, which he ignored completely. Beyond the second room with its gentleman's-club arrangement of sofas and low tables, the bar proper opened out into an enormous glass-roofed conservatory entirely filled with grass and trees like a tiny park. They sat at the edge of this on a huge floral recliner, Zal in the pit of it and Lila in his arms, looking up through the roof at the clearing skies.

"Too surreal," she murmured.

"Just one of many things," he agreed, ordering for them both through the auric connection to the spiritual net that swirled invisibly around them in a pale imitation of Alfheim's own massive psychic presence. In the casual touches of the other elves he read all the nuances of their feelings about him and they were deeply ambivalent. Only one mage had no animosity in her signature. He asked her to fetch the breakfast and a set of clothes from the room he used when he was staying in town.

"What happens at night?" Lila peered around, identifying the bodies of sleeping elves under and in the trees in the glasshouse, a few human companions scattered among them and the odd faery. They kept human hours. Most of them were hungover, Zal guessed, or exhausted.

"It's a madhouse," he said. "But on the plus side, lots of teenagers desperate to hook up."

"And do they get their wish?"

He shrugged, "No idea but there are plenty of predatory elves in the world and surely some of them are here. There must be thirty in this room so hundreds potentially in and around the place."

She shook her head. "Can't believe it. It seems just . . . wrong."

"Times change," he said, letting the meaningless words slip out as he lay back and gave in to a minute of exhaustion. He wasn't as young as he wished he was. "Speaking of which—meaningless segue—you haven't seen much of Teaz since we got back. Are you avoiding him?"

"Why, did he ask you to ask me?"

Which sounded defensive and then some, so he took it as a yes. "He misses you is all I was going to say." Not exactly true but he was going to have to fish here before he figured it out.

"Hmm," she said, fiddling pointlessly with the rent front of his shirt. "He won't mind, Zal. He's got a billion things to do." She made some slicing and dicing motions with her hand. A sigh escaped her nostrils.

"I didn't pick you for the jealous girlfriend type."

"What? That's insane. I mean, when you were gone we . . . it was convenient Zal, and it was distracting and he just found it terribly terribly entertaining and I . . ."

"You?" he prompted in the pause. His mage came up in her soft flowing robe and wordlessly handed over a set of towels before laying his clothes out on the arm of the sofa and retreating. She tried quite hard to get a reading off him but he was closed to her now and registered how much she didn't like it. It was considered deeply impolite to remain aloof in that manner. Only agents of the secret service from old—the Jayon Daga—were permitted to habitually contain their aetheric bodies. He hadn't served there for a long, long time but he was going to keep the privilege. "You?" he nudged Lila and handed her a towel for her hair, even though it was almost dry already from their ride.

"I don't know," she said unhappily.

Zal realised this angle was going nowhere. He knew perfectly well what was going on, but if she didn't want to admit it to him that was another thing. "I think you should talk to him."

She made a "not now" gesture and busied herself with the towel. "He's full demon, Zal, he couldn't care less. It's a marriage of convenience and politics. No need for the drama."

Zal smiled under his own towel, gave up, and tossed it aside. "If you don't, I'm sure he'll come for you," was all he said.

"Yuh," she replied, curling against him like a large cat.

"How's Greer?"

"Fine," she said before she had time to think it over. "Why you—"

"See, I know you inside out, Metallica. You can't help yourself. The Agency fall in another pile of shit and you have to be there to help them out."

"Yeah well, the pile of shit you refer to is walking around out there in its hundred bits of undead glory and it shows no sign of stopping.

As for cause, since I was instrumental in the cause, I guess I do feel some responsibility towards finding a solution." She was clipped with him. He felt duly rebuked but that only made him angry.

"It was Xavi," he said. "Not you."

"She's in the cells," Lila replied. "I'm in charge of her."

"It's a fucking bad idea," Zal said. "Every time I go near her I feel the same thing and it's not good. And yeah, you tied her to us, to me, you, Tea, Tath, and Malachi . . . but it remains to be seen how far those bonds will pull. I know lots of friends and lots of lovers who are more than able to stab each other in the back."

"She's totally contrite," Lila said in a tone that made him shut up, not because he wanted to but because he felt anything more would only push her into a greater defence of the woman. "And she's in prison. And she's doing all she can to stop it."

"What's that?" Zal asked. "Is she reading a book on it?" But he wasn't going anywhere with it. Lila would always take the underdog's position first. It was something he liked about her, but now it was driving him nuts.

"She's explaining everything."

Zal could only roll his eyes at this. No human had any idea of the nature of elf politics, which was infinitely long in its centuries of progress and infinitely complex. One reason he had left Alfheim behind. Still, maybe she could be right. The magical bond was written in the blood of Nyx, the black dragon of creation. It was probably enough to alter time, space, and more than a few hearts. It could have the power to make a friend of an enemy, he didn't doubt that. And yet . . . still he couldn't rest easy with it. "Your power is making you insensitive to other angles of attack," he said, in a tone that made her look around at him.

"You're serious," she said, folding her own towel and laying it aside.

"Always," he said, hopeless now.

"Zal, that prison was built by Sarasilien and a hundred others, especially to contain aetheric beings. She can't get out, not any way. She's got nothing. She's going nowhere."

He gave up. "Here's breakfast."

She looked down. "Oh god, what *is* that?"

He handed her a sealed, disposable hot cup. "At least I made them go out to the Italian place down the street for the coffee."

She opened it and took a deep inhale. "You're forgiven. I suppose this isn't the time to mention that Malachi wants to see us all."

"All?"

"You know who." She poked him with her elbow, sitting up.

"Is he going to ask us to hunt down the undead for Temple Greer?" Zal's heart was sinking.

"I don't know," she said. "I don't think so. He seemed a bit disturbed. Wanted it to be soon. Today or tomorrow."

"You should see her before that," he said without thinking.

"Who?" She sipped the scalding drink in her hand, settling herself down against him again.

"You know who." He was referring to her sister and he knew she knew it. The talk of undead never left Max far behind: she had died of old age during Lila's fifty-year blackout, but a month ago Otopia had suffered an incursion of beings from the undead planes and ever since then the numbers of Returners had increased steadily and unpredictably. Max was one of these, apparently alive, full of memories and not a day over twenty-five. She had gone back to live in the house Lila had inherited from her and he was sure this was the reason Lila had tried to live in Demonia with her husbands again, and taken to sneaking back to spend any nights in Otopia sleeping at the office with Malachi and whoever else was unlucky enough to pull two shifts.

"It's fine," she said.

"You can't run from them forever, Lila."

"Yeah well, it's not forever and it's not even her."

Except that he knew as well as she did that for her Max really was still twenty-five, alive as the day she'd been left behind a few months previously. And there was more to it.

"Zal," Lila said quietly after a minute. "I called them, didn't I? I wrote that note in that ink with that bloody pen and I called her back. And they followed."

"They didn't follow without a lot of help," Zal replied, though he couldn't deny it entirely.

"Still. I did it."

"The pen did it. These things have minds of their own. You were just the fingers and the legs that delivered it."

She took another drink and watched the sunlight come through the roof. "I wish I believed you."

He pulled her against him closer. He wished he believed it too, but he didn't have any of the feelings that equated with things being over, finished, and done. This brought him to a question he knew she'd know the answer to and which he didn't want to know the answer to. For all of them it was the elephant in the room these days. He guessed it was behind the elves' rapid incursions into Otopia—a *see it before it's too late* kind of impulse. Since long before he had met Lila, before she was born, before he was even born, fissures in the space-time fabric of all their worlds had started opening up. Some led onto the Void—a vast space brimming with creative energy from which he'd seen the youngest of the three weird sisters pull the material she spun on her distaff to create reality. Some others opened onto the least understood of all the worlds it was possible to go to.

Dubbed Thanatopia, rather fatuously, by the Otopian security agencies, as if it were some kind of paradisical death playground, it was a place into which material beings could not pass. They said these days that things came out of it; invisible, immaterial creatures—spirits and ghosts. But ghosts spawned in the deep Void so Zal didn't believe that. He was familiar enough with ghosts to know these fresh invaders weren't that. And since those later cracks had opened up, creating tensions along the planar divisions, it had been clear that unless something was done eventually a critical rip would occur. After that all bets were off, no matter who you were or what power you had.

The humans blamed the bomb they thought had created the entire situation from their ordinary single space-time seventy years previously, but the elves and fey and those who'd been around longer than Otopia knew it wasn't the bomb's doing. It was something else. There were even speculations that the bomb was an indirect product of the abyssal formations that had permitted wild aether to leak into Otopian space somewhere too close to a quantum-research facility. Otopia's bomb was just some minor occurrence in a much larger pattern. Since the bomb, however, there was no doubt that the problem had accelerated. And since Xaviendra had made her ill-fated bid for godhood, they had moved into exponential figures. So Zal really didn't want to know the answer, because it was like asking when the world was ending, but he asked it anyway.

"What's the cracking rate?"

"Five percent acceleration per Otopian month," Lila replied without even having to check.

"When's critical break point?"

"Don't know," she said. "Nobody knows. Weeks, months, years. Depends where the weakest warps are and what happens across the cosmosphere. Inherently unpredictable and not even certain. There have been reports of temporal anomalies closing previous cracks and stabilising local continua. It's not possible to survey most of the worlds due to their size and some not at all—Zoomenon, for instance. Nothing survives long enough there to take readings that are reliable."

Yes, that was a *far from over* feeling if ever he had one. "Can't you hear it in the Signal?" he asked her, hoping the answer was no. The Signal was the machines, they were information and process, nothing more, nothing less.

"Yeah," she said unhappily, putting the empty coffee container down. She leaned over him to look into his eyes and gave him a lingering kiss and a wryly sad half-grin. "If only I had a clue what most of it meant." She cupped the palm of her hand, shell-like, next to his ear, and played him the sound.

It sounded like white noise to him, a low hissing whisper of meaningless static like the sound of radio telescopes listening to the echoes of the first moment. There was nothing to cling onto, no trace of a pattern that he could detect. But she was a million times more suited to it than he was. Even so her face had a bleakness, a greyness in it suddenly as she listened with him.

"There it is," she said quietly over the wash of sound. "There it all is. If only I could understand."

A flash of insight occurred to him and he said aloud, "You're hoping that the rogues know, that they have an ability to listen that you don't. You want them to come and find you out in the middle of that industrial nowhereland, so you can take it." He wondered if all those components were more than bikes.

She fisted her hand and there was silence.

"Lila," he said, knowing they were the only thing that really threatened her. "They're more advanced—"

"They just lived longer. They had more time. That's all," she said stubbornly and put a piece of bread in his mouth.

He stuffed it into his cheek with his tongue. "Don't get that look with me."

"What look?"

But his objection was cut off by the sudden commotion in the entryway—a wash of rage and energy coming through the *andalune* that jolted Zal half out of his seat and woke every last sleeping elf in the building, spilling them to their feet wide-eyed and witless.

Zal was out of the seat and halfway there as he heard the snapping of teeth and the desperate sound of blades ringing out uselessly on scale armour. Lila was close behind him, barefoot on the stone floor. He heard her dress catch and tear and her curse it as steam and smoke billowed under the curtain, lifting it enough for him to see the guards' feet in fighting stances and the huge claws that feinted a savage strike at them, pushing them backwards into the weighted cloth. Their stumbling retreat was echoed by running in the walls and the sudden high-pitched shriek of armour-piercing arrowheads slicing the air open. Wooden shafts peppered the screen and fell clattering to the floor. There was a low, sinister hiss that became a snarl of rage; a deep, bloodied sound of raw ill-intent that was formed into almost incomprehensible elven words by a huge, nearly lipless mouth and a barbed mass of tongue, "Get out of way if want live!"

Zal didn't think the owner of that voice was in a mood to be too careful with the Otopian armistice agreements. He caught a swaying edge of the screening and pulled it back to let him through. The guard on that side tumbled past him, losing footing and falling on his ass. Blood spattered from several shallow wounds, onto Zal's boots, and across the floor.

Before him, filling the confessional-box confines of the entryway, a draconid the size of a horse was busy pulling the last of several arrows out of his hide with his teeth. Their feathered ends were dwarfed in any case by his own blue quills, wet with poison. These rattled and erected themselves with the slight pain of the attack. With a jerk of his long neck, the demon yanked the shaft out impatiently, leaving the head stuck in his skin. It was an impressive sight. Zal knew the shots could have gone through a car door. Then the huge ugly head tilted towards him and glared at him with one and then another slitted white eye. A slight pall of steam rose from the long lines of its face, up from the white mane of hair rising between its long horns, and from the cramped lines of its wings. Its tail lashed around, striking long splinters off the panelling as the finned edge, tipped with diamond, struck the walls.

More arrows were aimed from the hidden sconces, but Zal was already extended into the *andalune* matrix of the place and waved them back. At his touch the remaining guard looked up at him with a faint dawning of horrified comprehension running across his handsome features.

"*This* . . . is . . ." the guard started to say, sword still held out before him until the dragon head swung in his direction and fixed him with its inscrutable glare. Yellow and white light radiated from its hide in sudden brilliance and then, in a motion that was as smooth as it was impossibly awkward, the demon stood up on its hind legs, shrinking, changing until it was of a similar size, height, and form to the rest of them.

"Yes," it said much more clearly from its human mouth, as unreal as a white statue talking from the pedestal of an ancient gallery, "this is that demon you always wondered about. Yes, I will kill you without a care. Yes, I have come here for them. Yes, you will get out of my way and make me very comfortable until I tell you to stop. No hysteria. No touching, unless I say so." He paused and glanced unerringly towards the hidden elves behind the security panes. "No more arrows."

The arrowhead that had lodged in his hide fell to the floor from somewhere among the narrow panels of blue cloth that now draped off his shoulders and around his waist. His white hair fell over his shoulders unbound, and at his back two long swords were crossed, one gleaming yellow, the other a blue-white. A faint and nasty sound came from them but it was overpowered by the distinctly visible, although translucent, white wings that seemed to grow from his shoulders out and through their sheathed blades.

Zal pulled the screen aside wider and stepped back to let Teazle in.

As they drew level, he moved forward again until they were chest to chest. This put them eye to eye as well. Teazle's eyes were almost completely clear, like crystal. They stared at one another and Zal felt the demon's will pushing at him but he didn't move. It was going to be this way from now on. Even though Zal was pleased to see Teazle, the demon was getting older and that meant that his dominance would have to be kept in check all the time. If he got overconfident around Zal, their tentative equality—dodgy at the best of times with Zal's elf nature in the mix—would tip in Teazle's favour. At that point Zal could expect to start watching his back and considering an exit strategy. One day in the future he'd lose one of these alpha-male contests as Teazle altered from youth to maturity. One day he'd be in the fight of a lifetime and he knew that he'd lose it. But not today.

The vertical slits in the demon's eyes expanded slightly and only then did Zal slide his leg back and allow Teazle to pass him. He felt Teazle's hand on his ass briefly, in the kind of idle, suggestive caress that was inviting and submissive at once and then figured they were in the clear for the length of his stay.

Lila, who never believed Zal when he warned her about how things were heading with Teazle, blushed and ducked her head for a second as she moved forward to greet their husband. Zal rolled his eyes as he felt Teazle's energy level increase.

Demon auras operated at different frequencies antagonistic to elven ones, hence the legendary hatred between the two races. Zal had learned to tune to it and not mind the rasping disharmonics. Now touching Teazle that way was a familiar and not entirely unpleasant feeling. He knew he could grow to like it and that this went both ways between them. Lila had no such contact available, but fortunately she noticed in time and lifted herself to her full height as she met Teazle and embraced him. She lifted her hand up and twisted one of the demon's sharply pointed and fan-edged ears that were the butt of a lot of elf-ancestry jokes and pushed her face into his neck to kiss him under his jaw the way she liked. The demon's long tail, tipped with a blunted arrowhead point, snaked under the hem of her dress and Zal snorted in resignation and let the screen door go. He stepped over the prone guard, ignoring the man's open stare, and went back to the recliner and the food without a backwards glance.

He hadn't actually thought that Teazle would arrive for at least another day and felt annoyed that he'd spent so long lying and freezing in a cold garage before announcing himself. For reasons that largely escaped him, he felt it was important the three of them did not experience any conflict that might lead to separations. The conviction bothered him. Zal wasn't possessive but now he found himself the unexpected arbiter of their relations and peacemaker wasn't his forte. Troublemaker used to sit much more easily on him, but that was before Jack Giantkiller had slammed the life out of him on the bank of the frozen dead lake with his floating dead friends inside it.

He moved to the comfort of the sunny grass, newly vacated, and waited for the others to come and sit down there before lying down with his head in Teazle's lap. He found the demon's tail with one hand and pulled it around and over himself like a blanket.

The chiselled, handsome face bent over him, speaking Demonic so that nobody could understand whom he didn't wish to overhear. Their aethereal bodies teased each other with a sensation like popping candy just under the skin. Teazle's tone was affectionately mocking, "Do you feel safe now?"

Zal ignored him and closed his eyes. "Don't move around too much. I'm tired."

"You smell of each other," the demon said.

Lila moved up to Teazle's other side and they found a position where they leaned on each other, heads close together. Their conversation covered a lot of what he'd talked about before but there was a hesitancy about Teazle that was interesting. It only confirmed what Zal had already seen. Teazle was in love with her. Whether the demon knew it hardly mattered. He knew that Lila wasn't conscious of the fact and wondered if it was going to lie dormant until some moment of crisis when it would ambush one of them and get someone killed. He probably should have left them alone together, he thought, but then again he actually found Teazle's lap *comforting* of all things and Zal was bad at denying himself anything these days, especially something new and curious. Not that he'd ever been remotely good at it.

It didn't even occur to him who else might notice.

The elf who had served them before returned and gave a half bow, her eyes fixed on Teazle and steely with self-control. "I must ask you to leave. Our guests consider this a place of refuge and you are severely disrupting the aether." She spoke in beautifully precise Otopian as a clear deference to Lila, but her discomfort and hostility was palpable.

Lila opened her mouth but Teazle beat her to it. He spoke elvish like it was a blade weaving in the air between them. "And if I do not?"

"Cut it out," Lila said sharply, placing her hand on his knee at the same time. His head inclined towards her and she felt him relax slightly. "How about we stay long enough to finish what we ordered and then go quietly?"

The waitress composed her lips in a line and then said, "That might be possible if he would contain his aura as long as he is in here." She looked as though she had a terrible taste in her mouth.

Teazle turned his gaze back to her, baleful, but the tension lessened and Lila figured he must have done whatever he was asked because she started to hear voices again and then the movement of the other customers slowly creeping out of hiding. The woman hesitated.

"Thank you," she still hesitated, looking at Teazle as if she were watching something repellent but unusually fascinating. "You . . ."

"Get lost," Teazle said in Otopian but with absolute finality. She departed although, Lila was glad to see, she didn't actually run. Under her hand Teazle's body was solid as stone, temperature rising in reaction to his temper. "Elves," he snarled, back in Demonic again, every ounce of contempt rendered so deeply in the utterance that she smiled—no other language had the ability to enhance the world with its speaker's feelings in quite the same way. For a split second she saw every elf in her field of vision transformed into a strangely loathsome colour, all except for Zal.

"Familiarity hasn't softened your opinion then?" she said, seeing him look down at her hand with the intensity that used to both scare and excite her. It did so now although she tried to suppress it, and the memories of their unions in months past. She felt abruptly angry with herself for being embarrassed, for being an idiot, for talking foolishly to cover up in front of him. In front of Zal.

Teazle glanced down at Zal's head. "He and they are not of one kind," was all he said finally. There was an undercurrent of darkness in the statement she found she didn't like. Then that juggernaut attention turned itself on her with full force. "You are ashamed of your liking for me."

She should have known nothing would get past him.

"I'm ashamed of myself," she corrected, trying to find the words that would explain even though she didn't understand it, but he shook his head fractionally and put his hand on hers, gripping it tightly enough to hurt. She felt the balance of power between them tipping away from her inexorably and cursed herself for her stupidity. She hadn't been expecting him and she wasn't ready. She realised that she was afraid of him. This was what added such spice to their relationship, although now that she saw the fact clearly it appalled her but didn't stop her breath from coming faster as he gently moved his own head closer to hers and very, very gently rubbed his cheek against her own. His breath was soft over her lips as he murmured affectionate nonsense syllables to her.

She might as well have been cuddling up to a tiger, but there was such a thrill to his interest in her that she couldn't resist. She kissed him, almost without meaning to, at the side of his lips and saw him looking down at Zal with a strange, fixated expression. Then his diamond clear eyes flicked towards her and it was gone.

"I have a favour I must ask," he said in Demonic very quietly and straightened his back. "Since we have come back from Faery all of us have been altered but I am still changing," he said finally. "I want you to see if there is anything you can detect—if you are able to know what is happening. I went to see a necromancer who wouldn't speak to me about it and now won't be speaking about anything anymore, and a shaman who told me something unbelievable."

"What do you mean?" The moment of his trust was so surprising that it touched her deeply. She tried to cover for both of them by the first thing she could say. "I can try. But you're so very aetheric. I doubt I could identify what something was even if I could see it."

"No," he said and she knew that she was the only one he trusted enough to show the depth of this vulnerability to. "Do it. Look. As you can. Look everywhere."

Tenderness made her nod gently at him, showing her sympathy, but he shot her a look that was a warning and then Zal quietly dug him in the back of the knee and the moment in which she had seen a killing light rise in his face passed. Confusion filled her, and a touch of new fear. She was falling foul of that demon domination thing, she knew. She'd done it when he had exposed a weakness and she had sympathised, thus agreeing to notice it. But even so, to find that look heading in her direction was a shock. She stumbled over her words. "Sure. Of course I'll try."

"Now?" he murmured, so softly she barely heard him, and his tone was a command.

"Yeah," Lila activated all her sensors. She realised there could be no real love between her and Teazle, because all her care would be a weakness his nature could only exploit. She felt a feeling she was used to—despair—and wearily pushed it aside.

He started when she gave a slight laugh. "What is it?"

"Well that can't be right," she said dismissively, checking and rechecking the data. She was using the graphs and charts from a

demon aethero-medical resource, testing readings against their collection of averaged scores on every kind of material manifestation.
Their zeal for excess meant there was no parameter left unmeasured
with regard to the makeup of any kind of demon. "I think . . . I think
I have to check that with an expert. I'll go to Bathshebat and—"

"Tell me!" he hissed, and his hand was getting stronger on hers
again. "If you have any idea I want to hear it, I don't care what you
think of it."

"All right." She wrenched her hand back with just as much violence
as it took and looked him in the eye. She was surprised at how much of
a shock it was to her human expectations to feel that she saw right
through into his soul every time she did this. Humans said poetically
that the eyes were the windows to the soul, but with demons it was
absolutely true and also that their soul was capable of staring right back
into yours with a deadly accuracy no human vision really ever managed.
It was why they had never had any time for lies. Once, looking at Teazle
had been like looking at a snowfield or an arctic whiteout. The colour
was supersaturated. Over the last year, however, he had started to shine
and take on a quality she could only describe to herself as translucent.
She felt his apprehension and his hatred of how much this was weakening his basic ability to dominate everyone in his path. She saw his
self-loathing and he saw hers. With difficulty she assembled her results
into words, ignoring it, knowing it wouldn't go away.

"Your basic vibration sequence, the way that your fundamental
particles resonate in the material planes, are mutating from demonic
normal activity to . . . something else."

He stared at her. "What?"

"Yeah, exactly. What?" she shrugged. "I have no idea what." She
paused and he sat back, deep in thought, frown lines cutting across his
high forehead and down between his heavy brows. She said with more
venom than she planned, "What did that shaman say as he was begging you for mercy?"

Teazle shot her a dark look. "I did not touch him in any way." His scowl deepened and even she could feel his mood drop the overall room ambience into a brooding, gloomy pall. "He said I was turning into an angel. Not metaphorically. Literally."

"Death's angel," Lila said, looking at the swords, the faintest veils of light trailing off them, forming spectral wings that vanished into the sunlight. "Because those are her swords." The idea emptied her mind of anything else. She remembered seeing Teazle as a descending angel when he came with her to the Fleet where they had finally cornered Xaviendra, the elf who would be a god. Angels had flown with Xavi at the time and they had been almost unwatchably alien. They had left before the end and not explained themselves, and Xavi's own explanation—that they were there to ensure her safe rise to power—didn't stand up as far as Lila was concerned. Even so, the notion was ludicrous. It was there and it was impossible. "Literally."

Teazle growled, "So he said."

On Teazle's lap Zal made a short sigh although he didn't speak or open his eyes.

"I don't know what an angel is," Lila said after a second. "I mean, outside of books and stories. When Xavi said she had angels escorting her I thought that she was delusional."

"She is, and they're The Others," Zal said then, coughing to clear his throat. He still kept his eyes shut and feigned a sleeping pose. "Angels are what the rest of us whisper about around the campfire when it's time for the scary stories. Humans wonder about ghosts and demons. We wonder about angels. And, to a lesser extent, dragons. And spirits. And shadow. We just say Others, because that means all of them and we really don't know if they're all different or all the same. They certainly come and go from the same place."

"They *can't* all be the same surely?" Lila let her AI page through the vast texts on these matters in an offline mode while she stroked Zal's hair. Later, once she'd slept, she'd wake up and know the contents as if she'd read it properly. Better, in fact, because she'd never been that diligent a student. She let her head come into contact with Teazle's and then both of them turned to kiss one another for a moment. He was so on edge that he didn't notice how tense she was in return, or didn't comment. Lila was taking notes on him now, endless, cold notes: I do this, you do that.

She asked him, "How does it feel?"

The demon flexed one hand, claws suddenly apparent on his finger-tips in a way that happened only when he was readying for a fight. She'd seen them rip through limbs with a seemingly casual swipe. Their edges and tips were diamond sharp and in the tentative Otopian dawn they shone with a wet look. Then, as readily as they'd emerged, they subsided into more of a human nail, blunt and shortened, all the easier to make a fist with. He looked at her for a long moment and she saw him struggling to find any words.

"I feel strange tides," he said finally, disappointed with his own pronouncement. "Things move unseen beneath."

Lila appended it to the casebook she'd opened on him and closed it down. "I can track your progress, but I can't say anything about it. Only give you the facts."

At that moment the waitressing elf returned. Lila expected her to ask them to leave but instead, face firmly steeled against their reaction and eyes averted from any direct eye contact, she said, "Azrazal Ahriman-Sikarza, someone wishes to speak with you privately."

Zal opened his eyes and looked up at her without moving. "Who is it?"

"I cannot say."

Zal closed his eyes. "Then I can't go. Tell them to come here."

Lila scanned the entry records, wondering who was there, but as a private club it didn't have to reveal its data to her without a warrant even if she had the highest level of clearance, and she didn't have one. She considered hacking them but that seemed a bit excessive and they'd already strained Zal's status there to breaking point as it was. She didn't want to ruin it entirely for him.

The waitress hesitated and it was clear that she wanted to deliver Zal's message about as much as she wanted to drink poison, but after a second she turned on her heels and paced away with that elegant stride that made elves seem to glide easily over any ground. Lila found she was glad of the intrusion. Wordlessly Zal reached out and passed her the coffee cup. As she took it she felt his thumb brush the backs of her fingers. Teazle saw it—it was right under his nose—and sighed with a strange softness. She had no idea what to make of this but there was no time to wonder.

A new figure came drifting towards them, tall and as narrow as an arrow. It wore a green cloak with a large hood that hid its face in a deep shadow. Here and there movements revealed a delicate female body wearing ranger's clothes in plain materials. An Otopian government-issue Tree-pad was attached to her belt, concealed in a tiny leather satchel. Lila thought you probably couldn't do much without one of those, hate it as you might, and looked up as the mystery elf's two long, white hands started to lift themselves towards the hood. With slow exactitude they lifted it and swept it backwards.

There was nothing that could have prepared her for the sight.

Lila froze. Zal was suddenly on his feet with no apparent transition from asleep to vertical. His eyes were wide, his expression grim. Only Teazle sat with an expression of mild interest.

Before them, as large as life and as pretty as Lila remembered her, stood Arie, the Lady of Aparastil, whom she'd last seen disappearing down the gullet of a large dragon in the dark depths of Aparastil Lake.

It had honestly never occurred to her that anyone other than the humans could become Returners, but she supposed that if the dead could be brought back here, they must be able to be brought back anywhere. There seemed no law governing who returned and who didn't. Perhaps this was spectacularly bad luck. But looking at Arie's face she didn't think so. That confident, preening air suggested the same level of calculation was in place that had plotted Zal's permanent imprisonment and eternal torture and justified it with the survival of Alfheim as the necessary greater good. Because of Arie, Lila had stabbed her friend and lover Dar to death. Because of Arie, Dar had killed Ilyatath in cold blood. All in the name of survival, but that didn't make any difference.

The guilt and horror of that moment, the shame and misery of it, erupted as if it was happening again. Tears filled her eyes and she felt as though she had taken a hammer blow to the solar plexus, so hard that she was forced to cave in around it, hunching protectively over her heart. She saw Teazle react to her movement with strange understanding dawning in his face. But she never took her eyes off Arie. She wanted to carve that face off. The level of her own hate and how good it promised to make her feel should she act on it was a shock that rendered her motionless so that she lost the initiative.

Arie ignored her in any case.

"Hello, Zal," she said, her golden hair shining, her blue eyes giving him a look as if he were her favourite toy. She shrugged eloquently at his returning gaze, which was slowly moving from stunned emptiness towards wary loathing. Arie smiled, "I wager you did not expect to see me again."

"No," Zal said quietly. "I hope you put a lot of money on it. What do you want?"

"I thought you might like to know what happened to me after you ruined my efforts to save our world." Now she did flick a glance at Lila, as though the effort of ignoring the architect of her downfall had finally proved irresistible. Her loathing and repulsion were unchanged from the first second that she had first seen Lila for what she was—an ignorant human welded badly to an incomprehensible machine. It was an expression that made her beauty ugly in a moment.

Lila wished she had a mirror, but there was no avoiding the ill wish of that stare. Added to the shock of her arrival it lanced other old wounds open she'd thought were long done with. She felt a freak, worthy of spite.

By her feet Teazle hissed. He was amused and alert, keen with anticipation as he watched them fight.

Zal did something with his hand, some arcane gesture that flicked Arie's attention right back to him and at the same time released Lila from the grip of the sorceress's intent.

His voice was a rock star's disinterested drawl. "State your fucking case and be done. I'd be content to see you twice dead."

Anger flashed through her green eyes. "Very well. I assume you thought the dragon of the lake had eaten me up. And it did, in a way. But a dragon is not a blood-and-bone creature, some monster of the elements made flesh. I was consumed but I was not destroyed. It kept me in its belly."

She spat the words out as if each one was a bullet given to her to bite on for a separate pain. "It took me to the edges of existence and there it showed me the source of the destruction that is ripping all of our worlds into shreds. A point of stillness, of opposites meeting, where energy spits from the mouth of nothingness. It showed me that all I would have done was speed the destruction."

She had become stonelike in her resistance to what she had come to say next. Her fixation on Zal remained, the only thing that was keeping her self-control in place. Her lips worked, narrowed, and finally she said, "I have come to offer you my aid in what is coming. I owe it to Alfheim. And I was convinced that I am in some part to blame, so it must be paid back. I am no longer Arie of the Lake. I am Arie of the Waters. You may summon me through that element, when the time comes."

With the mention of her titles some dignity returned to her, though she was unable to conceal her loathing of Zal behind aloofness anymore. Lila realised that even though she considered him a traitor, Zal was the only one Arie could stand to look at. She and Teazle were abominations too far. Without another word Arie turned on her heels and walked back the way she had come.

Zal stood for a moment or two, his hands flexing at his sides, watching her go. "Something's really off here," he said.

"Do you want me to kill her?" Teazle offered.

"Nah," Zal sat down again, picked up the nearest drink of clear liquid, and drank it all. As Teazle surrendered grumpily to his reply, Zal shot Lila a loaded glance.

"It's time we all had a nice sit down with our friend Malachi and found out what the hell's going on."

CHAPTER TWO

Lila, Zal, Teazle, and Malachi lay on the floor of Malachi's yurt. It was two a.m. There was no sound except for the burr of cicadas and the hum of air-conditioning units. The yurt's main doorflap was closed to block out the sight of the Agency buildings and the courtyard, save for a small fold that was clipped back to let some of the night air in. In the middle of their group the space was occupied by Malachi's hard-working icebox and its ever-replenished supply of Lite and Dark bottles of faery ale.

At the very edge of their ring amid a sea of empties lay the slim, dark curl of the elf who would be god, Xaviendra, her pointed ears slack, her mouth open. She'd passed out some time ago and they had put her there after she had fallen over backwards with a Dark bottle still upended in her mouth like a flag raised on a freshly discovered island. Malachi had worried that the faery brewmaster, to whom he was paying a stiff subscription, and who prided himself on his professionalism, might give her an endless free refill and drown her. It had taken two of them to prise the bottle out of her hand and loosen her jaws from their clamped position around its rim. The charmed hemp manacles on her wrists remained in place. She was a guest, but she was also a prisoner of the state and in Lila's custody. Until a short time ago she had been unknown to them, but Lila had written her into the script using the most powerful weapon in the universe and now . . . here she was, their strange new friend.

Lila thought of this often, almost as often as she reviewed Xavien-dra's interview sessions searching for telltale signs of deception. But she couldn't help it. She liked Xavi, and trusted her, and there was no way to know if that was the doing of magic or the more commonplace forces of personal interaction.

"And another thing," Malachi was saying from his reclined posi-tion, waving his bottle about by a two-fingered grip on the neck, "about this dragon bishniss." His brilliant orange eyes narrowed as he held their attention and he gave off a faint fey puff of anthracite dust, briefly making the air around him glitter.

Teazle, in his human form, nodded sagely as though Malachi were already making profound sense. "Tricky," he said, carefully. "Tricky bishniss." His long white tail whirled, the arrow tip drawing a kind of circle before falling back to the rug with a thump and lying there, spent. He glowed, his eyes as brilliant as police officers' torch beams. Thanks to this, they'd been able to cut all power and data and were in splendid isolation. As a courtesy he mostly remembered not to look anyone directly in the face. After a second's blink, in which he shrouded the rest of them in near darkness, he added, "Prolly more to come. More."

"*You* met a dragon," Lila poked Zal on the leg solemnly. She sounded more accusing than she meant to but as she intended it play-fully she felt as though she was getting away with something naughty. He was cross-legged, his back deep in a beanbag. Zal was slender and muscular, lithe as only a true elf could be, and Lila had the pleasure of lying resting against his chest as if he were her throne and she was a little girl playing at being queen. She amended her poke by quickly stroking the area and admiring the hard line of his thigh.

Zal shook his head, slowly. He was matching Malachi bottle for bottle. "Mr. V," he said after a moment's pause. "He was stuck in the mirror and I . . . well he tricked me into letting him out, kinda. I don' know. He didn' seem t'have much of an agenda, so t'speak. The other one, back in the Lake—that was something. I forget what it said now. Somethin' like . . . ah, no . . . it's gone. That one ate Arie, though. Then it sicked her up again."

This wandering retrospective then was the end of their debriefing session, which had begun that morning in an official manner with recordings and witnesses and suchlike, but which had at some point in the evening become so exhausting that Malachi had called a timeout and brought them all here to recuperate. The office staff had gladly fled homewards, but because they were so preoccupied with their analysis, they had continued to talk about their joint past experiences over drinks. They had been going to have dinner, but this was forgotten, in favour of the Dark, which had properties of insight, foresight, and other kinds of clairvoyance when drunk in large quantities.

They had also needed it because of the alcohol content to prise Xaviendra out of her habitual frosty silence. This had backfired rather, since she had gone from silent, through silently rapt, and directly to the ultimate frigidity of unconsciousness without uttering a word. However, from her position on the floor, occasionally snoring, she had spoken in a slurring way if a question was put directly to her. They had discovered this by accident when Zal had turned in her direction and said, "What's that sticking in my butt?" and Xavi had replied, correctly, "It's your phone."

Now she sometimes said a word, such as, "true" or "shathi," which was elf for fuck. Then Lila had said elves did not have words like that and Zal said they just weren't listed anywhere the elves would let anybody else see. At that point the debriefing had changed into bantering and even Teazle had started drinking. Ever since then he had occasionally punctuated the conversation with one of the demon words for fuck and although a long time had passed he had still not run out of them.

"She must have tasted horrid," Lila said, referring to Arie, who had once put her on a platform for all the elves to publicly despise.

Zal made a soothing noise and nuzzled her ear.

"Kuroosma," Teazle said into the moment of contemplative silence, lingering on the vowel with enjoyment. Lila looked the word up, cautiously, as if she were peeking at it through her fingers. Every different one had a different nuance. This one made her face heat up, and she was no prude.

"Nah," Zal said. "It didn't say that. For sure." Then after a second, "Do you think dragons swear?"

"No," Lila said firmly.

"Yes," Malachi said at the same time with equal conviction.

"No," Lila waved him down with her free hand. "Noble. Godly. Things like that don't swear. Forces of nature don' swear."

"What about lightning?" Teazle said, taking a swig from a new bottle. "Lightning is nature swearing. An' if a thing like that can swear, which isn't self-'ware, then dragons mus' swear 'cos they is speakers and things that speak swear. Proof . . ." he pointed vaguely at Xaviendra, who had begun to snore. "She done nothing but ruffaguff this and shathi that since she fell over."

"Are dragons forces of nature then?" Lila asked.

"Something like that," Zal said. "But with more wizard and less . . . less . . . they don't have to be manifest or, shathi, help me out here . . ." he appealed to Malachi who had been nodding along.

"They are part 'maginary," Malachi intoned solemnly. "Cusp beings, intershtitial, on the edge, not matter or aether, both and neither, the primary moversh that shtir the great s-soup of creation, that'sh what they are."

"Soup spoons," Lila said, blinking. She was playing with the end of one of the ties on Zal's shirt and this notion just came out of her mouth without passing through her head.

"Yesh," Malachi replied earnestly. "Jusht that. And now they are . . ." he whirled his fingers and shed some more dust. "Dammit, didn't mean to do that." He put his hand down where the floor was blackened with coal and when he lifted it up the white rug was pristine again.

"Stirring!" Lila said, feeling quietly triumphant.

"Yes!" Teazle glowed more brightly for a second.

"T," Lila said, addressing him with a slight yet regal frown across the icebox that sat between them with its fresh bottlenecks at jaunty angles. "Aren't you a dragon?"

"No," Teazle said. "I jus' look like one. Demon's an aetheric creation. But you gotta remember they don' always look like that."

"Dragons can be a human or elf," Zal said. "Or dwarf."

"They can be a bunch of flowers," Malachi added, frowning at himself as though he wasn't sure he hadn't just invented this. "Or, well, maybe not. Can't see the point of that acshally. But my point is . . . my point is they can rise in like, a material form, in a body, as flesh and bone, or they can rise as energy inshide other things."

"What things?" Lila demanded, finishing her drink and shaking the bottle upside down for a few seconds before tossing it over her shoulder where it hit Xaviendra's foot and rolled to clink among the others lying there.

"Like a pop—a poppy—a pip—" Teazle struggled heroically for a moment, working his mouth carefully. "Pop-u-la-tion."

Lila stretched forward for another drink, picking up the one brown bottleneck poking out of the heap of ice in the cooler. She drew it out, admiring its label and the icy water running off it. As she sat back with the prize, another one slowly nudged up out of the ice mound to replace it. "Yeah but, what ARE they?"

"What ARE you?" Malachi slurred mildly with an emphatic nod. "Hmm?"

Lila paused for a few seconds. "Drunk."

"Exactly," Zal said. They all paused. "Primal forces," he added a

minute later. "But with attitude. Some of them . . . they rise and fall
you know, into . . . I'm not really sure."

"Dragons," said a delicate, exacting voice from behind him in the
tones of a slightly annoyed schoolmistress, "are archaeotypal subdeic
elementals, predating the actualisation of the seven worlds and instrumental in their creation, by virtue of being organising principles
and generative structures within which any amount of conscious real-
isation of the infinite may occur at any time. Persistence in material
form occurs as a necessary process of becoming baryonically bound.
Personality and etcetera accrue after this manifestation into linear temporal planes according to the usual principles."

"Unnerving how she does that," Zal said, twitching his shoulders.

"It's like she's shome kind of enshyclopaedia with a will of its
own," Teazle frowned and stared accusingly into his beer. "A will sho
powerful it can work even when she's ashleep. Or only when she's
asleep. Spooky." He shivered in pretend horror and shone the rays of
his interest on Xaviendra for a moment.

"Well it's more than she ever says when she's awake," Lila said and
felt bad for reproaching the girl. Xavi had good reasons to shut up, Lila
figured, having been convicted of acts of terrorism of which she was
certainly guilty. She was out of her cell for a few hours only because
Lila was able to bring her out and guarantee she wouldn't escape. The
entire drinking event had been staged in the hopes that it might make
her tongue loosen, and in its way it had been successful.

"Ask her the angel one again," Malachi said, blinking as he
changed position to something more upright in an effort to stay awake.

"What is an angel?" Lila said, half angled towards the unconscious
elf so that she could see Xavi's mouth moving even though the rest of
her remained in a stupor.

"An angel is an articulated form of energy imbued with mental and
emotional faculties that act in accordance with its own will. Angels are
beings of nonbaryonic dimensions, although they are able to assume

baryonic forms, and are not limited to ordinary space-time considerations. It is suspected though not proven that their appreciation of the nature of all material and immaterial things far surpasses that of the bound races who have intelligence and awareness. Emergence from the purely aetheric into material form will result in a necessary accrual of personality and etcetera according to the usual principles."

There was nothing about this voice that was the slightest bit intoxicated.

"Hah!" said Zal after a second, "I know what sh'minds me of. You, Lila! She talks like you do when you've got the AI on." He twirled a finger next to his head.

Lila scowled and fixed her gaze on Teazle, who was snickering, his tail tip gently beating the rugs in time with his laugh.

She felt annoyed. "I make more sense though. This isn't getting us far—"

"Wait, wait," Malachi said confidently. "Dark takes time to work. Got to get down to get up again, like they say. We jus' need to keep going aroun' the subject an it'll be fine. You'll see. Inspiration'll strike!"

"What *was* the subject?" Teazle asked. He blinked slowly and the yurt was once again briefly submerged in the sepulchral glow of his exposed skin. In that second Lila could see the outline of his body gleaming faintly through the folds of his robe, dappled on his lower torso, arms, and legs like a cheetah-patterned lightbulb.

"What are we going to do about all the dead people?" Lila reminded him, ignoring the knot in her stomach as she mentioned it. Images of her family home flashed in front of her mind's eye in an unstoppable rush, which she tried to blot out by carrying on. "Also, is this the end-times as foreseen by the popular press? And if so, wh—" but she was interrupted by Zal gently putting his hand over her mouth.

"Shh," he said. "It's happening. I had an idea that wasn't my own."

"And?" Malachi asked, foregoing the obvious remark about Zal having any kind of idea at all, but sharing the fact that he wasn't saying it by giving Lila and Teazle a significant stare each.

"And," Zal said emphatically, including Lila and Teazle in his own three-way group by glancing at them, "we should get divorced."

Lila did a quick retake on it. "*That* was your idea?"

"No. That was my conclusion, given my idea."

"What was the idea?" Teazle asked, staring his potential ex directly in the face for a second and then, becoming aware that this was painful for Zal, suddenly flicking his thousand watts back to the drinks cooler while still remaining attentive.

"Well, as you were talking I had this vague kind of . . . you know dragons, right?"

They all nodded vigorously in the hope that he would get to the point.

"Well, we are intersti—, cusp—, beings who've been changed one way and another and made into hybrid sort of things, you know?" he raised his eyebrows and nodded as if this made things so clear they must leap to an intuitive judgement. When they continued to look at him, Lila over her shoulder and Teazle with his long, horsey ears indicating the direction of his attention, he sighed. "We are . . . what we are . . . and we are together. Between us we cover eighty percent of the total aethero-material troposphere."

"Whoah, it really *isn't* his idea!" Malachi said at the mention of these highly theoretical terms, his jaw going slightly slack.

Zal shook a fist in Malachi's direction, but continued. "And if you add in Tatters, it's ninety. And if you add in Malachi and Xavi, it's ninety-five. And—"

"Tath," Lila said. "Add Tath and," she hesitated, stomach burning, "and Max and it is one hundred percent."

"We," Zal said, including everyone mentioned, "are a . . ."

They waited.

"I don't know what we are but we are one hundred percent and THAT is a bit scary; was my idea," Zal finished.

"Dragon," said Xaviendra's voice.

"Shikba!" Teazle snorted, laughing almost silently, faint beery bubbles coming out of his nose.

Lila looked up Shikba and found no human equivalent or translation, although the dictionary appended a symbol that indicated it was highly perverted.

Malachi made a pfff sound with his lips. "It would be scary, if it added up to anything like a clear indication of trouble. But there's no direction, is there?" He waited for a second, looking around at their faces.

When they didn't reply straightaway, he faced them with a frank expression, "Lila, you're fed up of serving the agency but you've no clue about what to do with your life instead."

Lila gave him a daggers look but she couldn't find a riposte because this was the truth.

"Teazle, you've become the demon who's got a master, which is on the slippery slope to hell, although given the master (who shall not be named, bless her soul), it could be that she's grooming you to assume a role with an awesome reputation."

Teazle glowed brighter with pleasure and rolled onto his stomach, rubbing himself on the scrap of carpet he was lying on like a contented cat.

"Zal, you're a has-been musician without a band . . ."

"I've got a song in my heart," Zal countered, theatrically, hand on his chest.

". . . and a few million in the bank they don't want to give you, you being officially dead. And I'm hanging around waiting for something to happen and trying to prevent Xavi from getting any worse, which is hardly a mission."

Zal scowled at him. "Yes, when you're here. Otherwise you're shacked up with Jack's wife, getting the benefits of spring and summer Green-man duties, and licking the cream off your whiskers. The last thing *you* want is for something to spoil that. But carry on."

Malachi scowled back. "Xaviendra is a mystery, but there's no way I'd trust her to be out for anyone but herself. Ilyatath is indisposed as the Winter King until further notice, not that he can leave Winter. And Max is . . ." Now he faltered and glanced at Lila cautiously, his mouth still half open in midsentence.

"Max is undead, unemployed, and unhappy about both of those things. End of," Lila said for him, moving her hand to her belly to ease a biting pain. "And you forgot Tatters," she brushed the ruffle of the blue and lilac ra-ra skirt that was sitting on her hips over the top of her biker's leather trousers.

Malachi glanced at the cloth faery and then quickly away, making a small sign of warding that everyone noticed and nobody commented on. "Tatters is as she is," he said with uncharacteristic vagueness.

"And your point is?" Teazle drawled, stretching his legs until one of the joints popped.

"My point is that we don't add up to much, countering Zal's point that we add up to a hundred percent and Xavi's point that we are here as we are because of a rising dragon. Which is, incidentally, also her theory for the state of the worlds ever since the cracking began. That's several millennia by anyone's calendar, so in summary, it's hardly news."

"Perhaps it's a rising dragon's fart," Teazle said.

Zal laughed. "No no, Ragnarok, like the press all say. Or Armageddon. The End-Times."

"Ragnageddon," Xaviendra's voice said with withering contempt from the floor.

"See, the resident speaker of prophecies says so," Zal said, peering to be sure that Xaviendra wasn't about to be sick on his boots.

"And all because of a few returning dead," Lila said with a shrug and mock exasperation. "And a few breakdowns in physical material laws here and there, and the inexplicable leakages, timepits, and etceteras that have all appeared in the last fifty years, dated to within a few hours of the opening of Under. God, what a bunch of frothing exaggerators."

"Armarok," Xaviendra intoned as if playing the narrator in a school drama production.

"Shazbat," Teazle said, sighing with longing.

Lila sighed. "You're missing the obvious." Her pleasant merry fug of tipsiness had dispersed as this occurred to her. "We were all united by Night's Mantle when I wrote in that journal."

"I didn't understand that part," Zal said. "Was Night the pen itself?"

"Yes," Lila said. "And Night was the first dragon, out of which all the others sprang."

"They killed her in doing so," Teazle said. "The sisters, Zal, the daughters of Night, those ladies who kept you at their disposal doing bin duty and minding the cat. It was them, wasn't it? Those faery ones?"

Zal nodded.

"Night can't be killed, she was only sundered," Malachi corrected him in a grumpy, unhappy tone. "She's in pieces, abstracted, objectified, separated, whatever, but she ain't gone. She is the sum total. She is the system. She just doesn't exist as a whole being anymore."

"Did the faeries come from dragons then?" Teazle scratched his head and examined his nails for findings.

"Not like oaks from acorns," Malachi had to get up and turn around three times before he sat down again, looking pained as he made a variety of distracting signs with his hands in an effort to diffuse the aetheric vortices that gathered anytime anyone mentioned the faeries directly. "*Please* don't discuss this in open air. It's dangerous."

"Mmraah," Teazle said, which was a kind of apology, and sliced a hole in the rug with the nail on his forefinger. "I don't mind being a dragon or part of one. It sounds like there'll be fighting."

Lila took a long drink to try and quell a moment of severe stomach pain. "But I don't get how this leads to divorce, Zal."

She leaned back on him and turned her face briefly into the curve between his neck and collarbone. She knew they all joked about the marriage being a sham anywhere except Demonia and that it was a convenience of state for Teazle and Zal, not the kind of white dress and romance life match that was the Otopian myth of weddings. But somewhere inside her she was deeply attached to it and she disliked any notion of separation from Zal even though he didn't seem to be talking about an emotional divide.

"That's very simple," he said. "Whenever we're together major shit goes down that threatens our lives. We should split up just to survive. At least if we got a divorce, then that would nix the demon interest in us and that would be a good thirty percent drop in the trouble."

"You're very mathematical," Malachi told him. "Not like you at all."

"It's the beer," Zal said. "And I want to live. Anything that ups the odds in my favour, that's good. Dragons are not good in this case. They're bad. They're like a big neon sign saying Trouble This Way. Is this why the faeries created Under, to keep this stuff away?"

"I don't know," Malachi said quickly, glaring daggers. "There might've been another reason."

Zal stared at him. They were well used to each other's different forms of lying. "Yuh huh. The Queen's Magic, I heard."

"Yeah!" Malachi said, smiling a salesman's smile.

"I don't understand fey," Teazle grumbled, resting his head on his crossed hands. "You wan' it, you don' wan' it. You like it, you don' like it. All at the same time."

"Yes," Malachi said with relief, as though he had found an unexpected soulmate. "Yes, that's exactly it."

Teazle sighed heavily. "I'll divorce ya, Zal. Way I see things going I'll only become a threat anyway." He said this in a matter-of-fact way, with some regret in his tone. Another long sigh shrank his ribs and flattened his body to the floor. He stared morosely at the cooler. "And you, Lila," he added. "You're free to go."

And just like that there it was, all done. Say married to a demon and you were. Say not and you weren't. A word was all it took.

For a moment silence rang through the room and made it seem smaller and grubbier than ever before. Lila felt there should be more to say and do, some fall in the weather to mark the shattering feeling in her solar plexus. She glanced at Zal and saw him look abruptly nothing more than tired, old. Teazle sighed a heavy sigh. His eyes were on Zal, she saw, watching him with something like regret.

Lila's heart sank. "Teaze," she said, but was unable to say any more. It was so unlike him to be down about anything, it felt completely wrong, as if the world had got a loose screw. She consoled herself with the excuse that probably he was regretting his loss of status and command in Demonia, but another part of her knew that wasn't true. Teazle would have scorned the idea that he ever needed more than he already possessed. She and Zal had been a temporary kind of truce that worked to cover a bad political moment in history and that was all.

Anxiety gnawed her and for a second the pain in her stomach made her speechless. Teazle's arrogance was the rock she'd clung to in Zal's absence, when Malachi chided her, when she'd felt herself falling to bits in the horrible days of their return. When the machines had whispered to her so much she felt they intended to drive her insane, Teazle's body and willing lust had been there to anchor her. Since Zal was back, that part of their relationship had been put aside but it wasn't finished, merely suspended. She had wondered what it meant to him, but hadn't asked. She felt it would be weak of her, and the bond itself was already one in which her position was inferior so she could not risk giving him more power over her. In a human world this would have mattered much less. In a demon one it could lead to nasty things and that was why now, when she wanted to go and touch him and affirm something that felt threatened, she stayed in Zal's lap, immersed in the sensitive shadow of Zal's aetheric body, and watched the demon without speaking.

"Hm, didn't expect that," Malachi said after a while had passed. "I wish I thought it was worthwhile but I fear you might have bought more trouble, not less now."

He stood up and for an instant his body glittered as his moth aspect fluttered its wings and coal dust filled the air around him, turning and sparkling as it whirled into the familiar runes that would port him away. "To Faery with me. I see you all, adieu, anon. Rest well." He bowed, smiled, and with a flourish of his hand turned to walk away and vanished around an unseen corner.

"Goodnight!" sang out Xavi's voice from the floor, as sunny in disposition as she was not.

Zal jumped. "I wish she wouldn't do that." He put his half-finished beer back on top of the cooler. He looked at Teazle with misgivings.

The demon looked back and Lila saw some kind of communication passing between them that she couldn't understand.

"Is that it?" she asked. "We're through?"

Teazle's head swung to her and he nodded. "You're free of me, free of Demonia." His expression was inscrutable now though she tried hard to see into it. His face was set. "You wanted it."

And there was nothing she could say to that. She looked down, pushing the force of everything that was bursting her heart and which she didn't understand down onto the sleeping elf. She had wanted it. Wanted things to be more simple. Now she had this and her insides were screaming that they didn't want it at all and it made no sense to her. Tears flooded her eyes so that she had to turn her head from them both.

"I should put her back, we can't fall asleep here with her like that," Lila said, using her AI to subvert all her natural reactions and replace them with steady confidence. Above all she had to get out of that moment and move into the next. Any movement would do, so she wouldn't have to ask Teazle if he was going now, if Zal was going now, if there was nothing left to keep them there now that the bond was broken. It helped not a bit that the two men seemed far less affected, almost as if it happened every day.

She got up and went to stand over Xavi, wondering if she really was asleep or was pretending. The thing about Xavi was that she was new to them, and a daughter of someone they had learned to be far from the simple elf he had made out to be. They didn't know her or what she was capable of.

Teazle looked over at Xaviendra. In the light of his eyes they were all able to see her clearly but she made no move to indicate she was anything other than unconscious. Her mouth was open and she was snoring lightly. "I don't trust her," Teazle said, his tone much less drunk and more thoughtful than had seemed possible a short while ago.

"Having your life threatened by someone can do that to you," Lila said.

"No, it isn't that," the demon smiled. "She's no threat to me whatever she may have thought. I can't pin down what bothers me but I feel bothered, when I look at the two of you and her with you. On the surface we know her story but only what she has chosen to tell. It's what she hasn't said that itches my spirit."

"Think she's dangerous?" Zal asked.

"Of course," Teazle replied.

Zal frowned and his expression was very sad. "She is a creation of a very bad moment in elven history. Possibly the sole survivor of that time."

"All the shadowkin come from that time, though, right?" Lila asked.

"Yes," Zal said, "but the ones alive today, including me, are the descendants of the originals and a lot of us are half-breeds or some mix of shadow and light. She looks so young."

"Heh, and not like a badass raptor on speed either," Teazle said, referring to the Saaqaa, shadowkin elves who had been spawned far from their geneline and who were less elf and more of what they had been forcibly crossed with.

Of those beings who had provided the non-elf material nobody was able to say very much, because they knew nothing about it. Xaviendra was the only one who would know, and she had stolidly refused to speak of it. This was one of the reasons for her permanent imprisonment within the containment of the maximum-security cells at the Agency. They wanted her where they could see her, close at hand.

Lila repressed a shiver. "She can hear you."

"I don't care," the demon said. "I'd say it to her face."

But to Lila it seemed unfair, as if they were talking behind her back. At the same time, she felt an unerring curiosity prompting her to demand answers from Xavi while her conscious mind was apparently incapacitated and thus unable to stop her from replying.

Zal beat her to it in any case. "Xaviendra," he said. "At the time you were made, what did they use to change you?"

Xavi replied with a piglike snort and rolled onto her back, sending bottles rolling and chinking. "Elementals," she said. "And ektaluni." Here she used a word that none of them knew.

"What's that?" Teazle asked.

"Primal spirits," Xavi said.

"Where from?" Lila tried to get more information as this wasn't helpful.

"Phantoms," Xavi replied with the exaggerated patience of someone explaining basic material to lazy students. "They are a form of ghost, but a form generated by the application of disciplined and focused consciousness to the raw aether of the Void rather than random accretions formed by the natural processes of mnemonic evolution within the nonmaterial planes."

Teazle made a face. "Demons are made in a similar way at the moment of their conception." He glanced speculatively at Zal. "And here you are, elf in blood and demon by spirit. No accident that."

"My mother certainly thought it wasn't," Zal said. "Though she never told me all the details. But why did the elves do it *at all?*"

"They were under attack," Xaviendra said, smacking her lips as she settled down again. This above all made Lila convinced that she wasn't faking the sleep. Xavi was fastidious and had impeccable manners, the sort that would persist through death rather than reveal anything other than someone in perfect self-control.

"From what?" Teazle's tail lifted, cobralike, and swayed as he waited for the answer.

"The sleeper within," Xavi said and abruptly rolled to her side and curled up again, hands tucked under her chin like a child. She frowned briefly and shivered before falling into a deeper kind of sleep; softness overtook her.

As one they turned away to leave her in peace. Lila glanced at Teazle, but he shrugged—he had no idea what that last phrase meant.

Zal shook his head. "Never heard of it."

"I thought you guys kept impeccable records," Teazle said.

"Maybe, but we also had impeccable rewriting skills," Zal replied, "and our propaganda services were second to none. Until I found Friday back in Zoomenon, all the elves I know thought the shadowkin were a naturally occurring race and not a genocidal experiment. They were made a long, long time ago."

"Still," Lila said. "It must have been one hell of a threat to do what they did." She felt even less comfortable with the idea than she had two minutes ago, before Xavi had put this strange label on the cause.

"Or a hell of an opportunity," Teazle said, relaxing to roll on his back again. "Mages'll fuck with anything for power. Elves doubly so. Gzzz, I feel sleepy. This beer is useless."

"I'll take her back," said Lila, cancelling the effects of the alcohol on her system with a filter. She bent down and gathered the light form of the elf into her arms as unwelcome sobriety set in. She heard herself ask, "Are you sticking around?" And then she felt so off balance that she almost staggered and had to fight to keep her feet.

Teazle glanced at Zal and their gazes locked for a second, then got up slowly. "I'll take a rain check." He shook out his thick mane of white hair and composed himself, standing tall with his chin lowered in a manner Lila recognised as being his pre-teleport orientation. He looked at her, his gaze blazing. His nostrils flared for a moment and she smelled brimstone and the psychoactive tang of his personal poison as he said, "Have to be a dog about a man."

"Where will you be?" She hated herself for asking, hearing her voice crack on the last word.

"I'll check the dropbox," he said and she felt kicked in the gut once again. Then he gave the merest downward flick of his eyelids in Zal's direction, baffling her entirely because she'd assumed his submission to Zal would end now that there was no more need for them to fool around with who had the power. He vanished from Otopian space with the finality of a gunshot. The sharp crack retort of the air closing on his space made Xavi jolt.

"Bad dog," she murmured, her head lolling against Lila's leather-clad shoulder.

"I'll be here," Zal said, lying down flat on the rugs. The ink spill of his aether body shifted around him like a restless pool and where his fingers came into contact with the empty bottles he tapped out a brief rhythm.

Lila swallowed down to prevent the hole in her chest from opening any further and stooped to clear the yurt's low-slung doorflap. Outside the night was cool and a faint drizzle was falling. She could hear the soft murmuring swish of the city, a breath instead of the roar she kept listening for and never finding.

The whispers of the machine, which had haunted her a long time from the edges of her mind, were also absent these days. They'd translated into silent knowledge. It was this, and not her connection to the Agency's powerful AI systems, that made her back shiver with sudden cold as she walked towards the lit doorway of the building's garden exit.

Tightening her grip on Xavi's ragdoll form she picked up speed, linking briefly to the building's internal sensors. The doors opened for her, mechanisms spinning into reverse at her command as she approached because she would pass them before they were even fully open and she wanted them shut at her back. As they swung wide, she began to run.

Xavi's cell was a long elevator ride away. Lila felt two choices emerge from the silent knowledge as she started to pass through the open-plan office section where administrative staff processed the Agency's billions of daily documents. She could run to where she perceived trouble coming, and take Xavi with her to save time, or she could dump Xavi beyond the reach of all physical and most magical harm first. She chose the second option for a host of calculated reasons that had already bypassed her conscious mind several times on their way through her AI synapses.

At the elevator doors a secretary was standing, yawning, her tray of cups indicating that she'd picked the short straw and was on the coffee run. The elevator car was a couple of floors above, descending. Lila bypassed the control system and opened the doors to the empty shaft. The secretary staggered forward on automatic and jolted as Lila shouted, "Stand still!" on her way past.

Lila turned as she jumped and saw the cups falling with her, the sight of their impact on the carpet cut off abruptly as her head passed the floor level. Only the lingering cry of the swearing woman trailed after them down into the abyss. Above them the car eased down and stopped. Lila turned her attention to the subbasement and opened its doors up. Jets in her boots slowed them down with a deceleration she had to be careful of—she was pretty unbreakable in this gravity but Xavi was twiglike—and then she was in the corridor of the security wing, sprinting for Xavi's door, the guards already plastering themselves to the walls in accordance with orders that she'd sent belting through their earpieces moments before.

The only hitch in the matter came in the form of the duty shaman who had been woken from a catnap to release the aetheric binds that master mages had emplaced upon that part of the prison. She was stammering her way through some chant, trying to get something out of a bag and shake a fetish stick all at the same time. A plate of half-eaten biscuits lay on the floor next to her. Lila was sympathetic but had no time to show it, nor did she feel the need as Blondine was one of the greater shamans of the post-Moth era, even if she did look like a frazzled housewife from the Bay. She shoved Xavi at the woman, more or less dropping her directly into her lap, and said, "Pack her in tight. Come to my office soon as you're done."

The journey back was a blur, executed on automatic as Lila fine-tuned to the sensation that had upset her in the first place. It centred on her office—the place that used to house Sarasilien, the elf mage who was Xaviendra's father and who had been Otopian liaison to the elf world since the Quantum Bomb had burst Earth and opened up the hidden worlds.

But Sarasilien was long gone and there was no sign of him anywhere. He hadn't left a note, just a big fifty-year-old hole where he used to be. He was another one Lila missed every day, the office a memorial, mausoleum, reminder, storehouse, hideaway, library of secrets, and epicentre of residual energy that was the obvious hotspot for any aetherial interventions to occur, or invasions to strike. Her only true aetherial helper was the flimsy scrap of ra-ra skirt around her hips: Tatterdemalion, the faery.

Now Tatters was a worn-out relic from an age where Zal's music had held sway. She was worn and washed out, but as Lila ran through the open plan again, dodging staff, she felt the sudden shift of fabric around her waist and within a few moments the skirt was gone and she was wearing a doublet and surcoat, stitched with the symbols and signs she had learned to associate with protection charms.

The locks and bolts on the door shot back at her approach along the lengthy corridor that separated this volatile place from the rest of the human offices. The foreboding weight in her shoulders increased as she made herself slow down to a walk and survey for traps. There was nothing she could detect, nor did the faery cloth react, so she pushed the door open with a flick of her fingers and crossed the threshold.

The office was made up of three rooms, each leading to the next. Lila kept the doors open because she knew the place could guard itself without her help, and besides, she liked it to look friendly. Now she could see a light in the farthest room, one she hadn't left on. It was something cheap to decorate boudoir side tables, and she thought it was a present from Sorcha, the succubus, to the office's old master. It had a rosy, golden gleam that made everything look warm and comfortable and it cast a direct path of fading beams to Lila's feet.

She felt her teeth slide together. Invitation plus invasion—that really rubbed her up the wrong way. But at least it meant intelligence and not the wholescale space-time disruption disaster movie that had started playing itself in her head on the way down here.

Never one to be cautious when she could be bold, Lila straightened her shoulders and put her chin down. She walked forward along the designated line, though she'd have preferred to do anything but obey the summons. Even this irked her. As she turned the final corner around the study door, she wasn't ready for what she saw or the blood-draining shock that it started before her mind had even put names to the faces. All she could think of was that it was two in one day. Two.

Sarasilien was standing in the corner, reading at his lectern. His long fox-coloured hair was loose and his clothing was unfamiliar to her, though it had the cast of elvish fashion about its skirted coat and leggings, its cloth boots. He was surprise enough to her, but nothing had prepared her to respond to his companion and the pair that they made. Beside his tall, rangy figure stood the shorter, sleeker, and infinitely more plastic charcoal female form that Lila knew to be the rogue leader she had beheaded and doomed with the sword of Night months before.

It was Sandra Lane.

No, she thought a second later. It was Lane's clone.

A perfect clone. So, which one of them was Lane? And how many of the things were there? But there wasn't time for that thought. They were turning to her now.

Lila might have forgiven Sarasilien if he'd reacted with heartfelt emotion, with something other than the grim seriousness that he offered as he raised his head, but his look was calm, self-contained, businesslike, as though she were just some official he'd come to see on an important matter. She didn't want him to run across the room in hysterics or anything, but this left her with the feeling, once again, that she could stand with her guts out and he'd be passing her a tissue. It struck her there and then just how one-sided their relationship had been. She'd needed him so badly, anything had seemed like it must be enough. How cheaply she'd been bought. The revelation washed through her like ice water, freezing what was left of her heart.

Meanwhile Lane stood there with her hands grasped together like the master's toy. Her immaculate, basic features held no individuality but they managed an expression of grave disappointment as though she were a teacher who had caught Lila out in a naughty prank. Only the confirmation of her machine self, one robot to another, convinced Lila this was the real deal and not some other creature in masquerade, because she'd been sure Lane was beyond the reach of the material world and finding her in one piece was disconcerting to say the least. But she recovered fast from her disappointment.

"Well," she heard herself say with a cool bite in the words, "if it ain't the returning dead."

"Lila," Sarasilien said, a beat too late, not warm enough, not anything enough to make up for his defection. "Don't be alarmed. We can explain."

In response Lila manufactured guns from her hands and raised them in a single, exacting motion.

"Yeah?" she aimed one at his forehead, one at Sandra's. "I'd like to hear that."

She looked him in the eye and saw there the same warm compassion they'd always held only this time she wasn't grateful for it. Maybe it was getting to see Xavi and her pain, hear her crazy thoughts, or maybe it was the feeling of being treated like a caretaker, left in the cold on a need-to-know basis that was burning her gut. No, it was all of them. "You got twenty seconds."

Then she flicked her gaze to Sandra Lane. "And you got two."

CHAPTER THREE

The conversation with Sarasilien took place at ordinary speeds. The one with Sandra Lane went by in less than a human blink, but that didn't mean it played any shorter. In real-time terms however it was over before the other one even began.

"I am not the same Sandra Lane whom you murdered," said the rogue in their shared bubble of expanded time. She used abbreviated digital codes to communicate with Lila. They were the machine equivalent of text shortforms where a simple two- or three-digit string acted as the symbol for entire philosophies of thought or vast networks of memes. Any cyborg could have burst-broadcast the entire written language output of Otopia in less time than it takes to sigh by using them, which left plenty of room to add details about feelings and opinions that would usually be left to facial expressions and posture in an ordinary human conversation.

Sandra Lane added nothing, however. Her speech, save for her choice of words, was devoid of personality.

"Uh-huh," Lila said, holding her aim.

All her attention was free to be fixed on the creature, since at their shared rate of time compression Sarasilien wasn't moving worth a damn. Lane's lack of affect was a gulf between them, one that Lila was sure was intentional. It acted as a political statement of their core difference. Lane was stating how much she identified with the machine by withholding all information about her emotions, supposing she still had them. Lila didn't understand how Lane could kid herself that this was a superior model or that her stand was anything other than a pose. But Lane had a lot more to add.

"We're holographic," Lane said, spelling it out so slowly that Lila thought she might be genuinely afraid of getting a faceful of bullet. "Any part of us could be cut off and, given sufficient matter and energy, regrow our entire structure, complete with memories up to the point of excision. Additional memories from the primary identity could be added later, if required, or the alternate could be left to run an individual time-and-life-path of evolution. I am an alternate of Sandra Lane."

Lila took a few picoseconds to assimilate this and draw her conclusions. She remembered the sight of Lane's beheaded corpse sliding into the flat world of the sword's surface, eaten all up. Where the sword had been in her hand the gun pointed bluntly. Lila felt the trigger in her mind, caressed it lovingly. "And when did *your* river of memories dry up?"

"When the primary was destroyed," Lane replied. "At the moment of decapitation there was no loss of transmission, but immediately afterwards the signal failed." True to her avowed machine principles, she betrayed only a kind of mild professional interest.

Lila didn't entirely buy it, however. One didn't use the word murder without reason. Lane Prime was the dead one then. And apparently the most important one. Why that should be so remained a mystery.

She matched the cool for cool, although her anger was rising. "Well, since you were there, so to speak, you know what happened. Nothing's changed since then. I still don't want to talk to you, but you insist on invading my space. The only reason you're not dead now is that you're standing next to him. I asked you then and I ask you one more time, for the last time, what do you *want*, Miss Lane?"

The plastic mouth moved. "I need to explain at some length."

Lila gave a static fuzz burst, the equivalent of a shrug. "I gave you two seconds, we're still in the first half of number one. Knock yourself out."

She was aware of the other cyborg's sensors and transmitters searching for inroads through which they could upload or read her systems—it was a constant storm of electromagnetic tentacles—but even if the Lane cyborg was a later, better model, it wasn't finding any openings. Lila guessed that was the only reason they were having a conversation at all. That and some residual, inconvenient trace of guilt on her part.

"The rogue and submissive population of cyborgs made in the human world are all now a half century in advance of you in terms of real-time ageing and process," Lane began. "We have learned, as you have, that our existence is the result of a migration of the Akashic Record from the dimension of the nonmaterial into the material planes. Yet the Akashic Record itself is not an entity as we understand ourselves to be. It is pure data, the sum of all changes of state taking place over time since the beginning of this universe to the end. As such, it extends beyond the general assumption of the Akashic Record as being merely the sum of human knowledge and activities. It would more correctly be understood as the universe itself from a purely informational point of view." She paused, waiting for Lila to signal comprehension.

Lila knew that to the aetheric races, the Akashic Record was the sum of their own histories and lore. It was encoded in an elemental form of raw aether that could be read, if you were a powerful mystic with a will and education strong enough to attempt a reading. So the stories went. She'd yet to find anyone who had experience of its actual existence, and none of them, she was sure, would accept a vision of it as mere data written in time—as the sum total of events in the universe. This is what Lane meant, however.

She was saying that Time was the book of record, every quantifiable instant a single page upon which a complete snapshot of everything in existence could be seen. In her version there was no need for aether. But that wasn't her problem. Lila guessed where this was going, because nobody would talk to a cyborg about the Record unless they were going to talk about how cyborg technologies came into existence. But Lila wanted to know exactly what Lane's motive was before she joined in, so she took an oblique angle for her reply, hoping to lure Lane out a bit more.

"Some say that's god you're talking about," Lila said.

She was sure that Lane was as atheist as you got. The idea of god as everything that existed was also as secular an idea of god as you were likely to find: god as a collective noun. Lila would have wanted her gods distinct, carrying their own load, with everyone free to heed them or not as they liked, if there had been gods. But at least if she were god in the making then she wasn't expected to serve greater purposes than her own, so she didn't mind this version of deity. She wondered what Lane's take was.

"I do not say that," Lane replied. "I say only that this perspective on the cosmos shows no need for an animistic sentience of any kind, creative or generated as an emergence of the continual process of entropy. But," and she paused for several milliseconds, "our existence and the discovery in Otopian space of the original information that gave rise to our present state as hybrid beings that are living but able to actualise the Akasha itself: *that* does require an explanation that only a directed-sentient will seems to answer."

"Intelligent design," Lila said. But although the world and its works didn't to her mind require a designer, there was no doubt that her own and Lane's existence did. Lila knew that someone had to be implicated in the Otopian cyborg development and now here was Lane, all but confirming it. There were only two theories in Otopia about this and Lila subscribed to neither.

"Why Sandra, you've come to me with a crisis of faith."

"No," Lane said in the same, evenly measured tone. "I have come to you to request a truce between us for the duration of a different kind of crisis, one which exists in the material and aetheric planes; one that binds our origins to this moment and its workings. Though the discovery of our maker would be satisfying to me and, I assume, to you, it is a secondary consideration. Of primary importance is the discovery of a defence against what I can best describe in purely mathematical terms as a possibility storm. A Mightquake. Perhaps it is the final consequence of the Quantum Bomb. I am unable to say. However, I am certain of one thing. Neither your manufacture nor the creation of other hybrid agents and planewalkers is the product of chance, circumstance, and, as you might have it, Fortune—the play of all potentials falling into the one manifest world."

She paused here, in what Lila interpreted as a grace moment in which she was meant to make a leap of implication and she did, and it toppled like this: Teazle says nothing is an accident; Lane says nothing is an accident; Malachi says there are unseen forces at work; making a cyborg means you have pulled knowledge directly from the Akashic Records; the only people capable of that are angels, dragons, or elf mages of the kind wiped out in recent history; Lane is standing next to him and that can't be an accident.

Lila felt all the pieces suddenly snap together with a sharp pain like a slap in the face. *Sarasilien made us all.*

It took her a long time to work through her shock, so long in fact that Sarasilien was drawing breath to speak by the time she released the comms protocol with Lane and turned to him with the aeon-slow deliberation of human speed. She pointed both her guns at the ceiling and let them become her hands again. For a machine day she stared into his fox-brown eyes and remembered all of his kind words, the feeling of his aura bathing her in analgesic, wholesome rays. And all the time he'd known. He'd done it. He made her. Not the Otopians. They were only his instruments.

"Don't," she said, staring at him. "Just don't bother. I don't want to hear it. We've got a lot of talking to do, but it ain't gonna be now."

Humiliation and shame layered with rage until she couldn't think at all, and didn't want to. More than anything she wanted to let rip with those guns and see his lying, scheming face blown into plasma— a condition from which she was pretty sure not even he would return. As she looked at him, at his solemn, fatherly elven expression, his air of grace and sadness, she felt a twinge of a feeling that was all new as it zigzagged through her, arc lightning, joining up her life, Zal's life, Teazle's life, Xaviendra's life. The jolt almost made her stagger as it shot from the present into the past. Yes, why else would he be here and now? Not to help or comfort her. To use her because some part of this scheme was coming to fruition.

It must be a big scheme. From abstract nothing he had made the machines.

He began to open his mouth again, but saw the look on her face and apparently thought better of it.

Lila didn't know if he was the only one involved or the prime mover; it didn't matter. She didn't trust herself to listen now. She wanted to get away from him before she had to kill him. The visions in her mind of a puppet master, pulling his invisible strings, was over-powering. Also, he was a liar, so there was no point even asking or trying to know what the extent of his influence was. No point in talking at all.

She met his reddish-amber eyes with a gaze of her own, blinkless and silver. "Don't call us, we'll call you," she said, deliberately using the phrase so often doled out to unsuccessful actors at auditions. The touch of bravado almost made her wince, but the new electric connection joining up the dots inside her was pleased. It wanted to have any upper hand, to hurt in any way it could. She knew its name. It was hate.

Lila flicked her gaze to Lane. "Blip me all you know, or you'll be the late Sandra Lane one more time."

She wasn't sure she could beat Lane in a straight fight, but she was sure she'd be glad to go down trying, and she let Lane know it in no uncertain terms, coding it direct so there could be no room for misinterpretation of her intent.

"Once was enough, thank you," Lane said. "Besides, the sooner you know, the sooner you can agree to help."

Lila assimilated the data, allowing none of it access to her conscious, which was more than fully occupied just getting her out of the room before she did something infinitely regrettable. She thought to herself that agreeing to help would mark one cold day in hell, and then, against all her instincts, she turned her back on both of them and walked out, leaving the doors wide open behind her.

The same, pointless recitation spun through her thoughts: leave without a word, come back when you feel like it, dump everything on me, start whining when things get tough, lie and lie and lie about everything, and then have the nerve, the sheer fucking nerve to come and do puppy-dog paternity angle. Did he even know that Xaviendra was here? Did he know she was alive? Did he care? Not likely.

But as the storm of loathing subsided, she kept the useful parts and placed them carefully into the cold locker of her brain.

One thing she did know was that whatever came out of their mouths was a lot of calculated crap whether it was true or not, so the less she heard it the better. To think she'd had moments of regret for slaughtering the "original" Sandra Lane in a moment of instinctual self-preservation! It was an obvious truth that nobody came into her office without wanting something big, and never did they come offering help or payment, recompense or anything like that; especially the ones who came in without using the doors.

Especially the ones who were dead.

Lila didn't buy a goddamned word of it, and she wanted nothing to do with them although that looked like it was going to be tough to ensure. No, the only way to avoid them would be to leave the Agency right now, detach from all wireless connections, and move out of Bay City, probably Otopia, possibly further.

She longed to do it, and knew she wouldn't. Everyone she knew (not so many) or cared about (fewer) were connected heavily to everything that the loathsome Sandra had said. Besides, she was tired of the pretence that one day she'd run free. There wasn't any freedom for people like her. Nor from them.

She returned to Malachi's yurt and closed her connections to the Agency and Worlddata networks. It occurred to her that Lane's attempt to hack her might have been just for show. Lila didn't think this was honour between machines, however, only that both of them were running systems that were too resilient and automatically on the offensive. As for hacking Lane—touching via the medium of short-wave radio was more than enough.

The yurt interior had been tidied. Of the ocean of empties there was no sign, and the icebox had its lid back in place; the faeries had been in and cleaned up. Zal was sitting on the rug where she had left him, his fingers moving on the pattern in a piano action. He was wearing his headphones and his eyes were closed.

Lila sat down beside him, without disturbing him. The headphones tracked his hands. She guessed from the movements that he was playing a replica of Mozart's piano—a favourite of his recently—though he hated using the virtual instruments as there was no feedback to his hands. After a moment he opened one eye and slid the 'phones off one ear.

"Trouble?"

"Yes, of course, what else?" she said. "Xaviendra's father's back. With a robot sidekick. And a conspiracy theory. At least, I think that's what it was."

He nodded, as if this happened every day. "Oh yeah? What do they want?"

"I get the impression they want me to help them against something big and scary. They have a stick, which is that they're already in my offices pursuing me like a pair of mad aunts. And they have a carrot, which is maybe finding out that Sarasilien's sticky fingers were in all our pies. And he's maybe here to create one big pie. For some reason."

"Carrot pie?" Zal wrinkled his nose, rabbitish. "I don't like the sound of that."

Put like that, her analysis sounded crazy. She smiled. "I'm glad I learned to analyse so clearly from you, oh master. Anyway. Zal, do you know where Friday is?"

Now he took the headphones off entirely and looked at her with both eyes.

Friday was a golem. Zal had created him, accidentally, when he got stranded in Zoomenon, the dimension of the elements. Friday, rudimentary as he was, had saved Zal from disintegration by hauling him through Voidspace to the Fleet. But the reason Lila mentioned him now, the only reason he was important, was because his clay was embedded with the bones of the long dead. They had been murdered in the experiments when the Shadowkin had been created. They were the ones who didn't survive to become the elves' weapon against the terror Xavi named as "the sleeper within." Besides the bones Friday held the remnants of their spirits and voices. Ignorant of this at first, Zal had brought him to Otopia and used him as a hatstand and general prop. Lila hadn't seen him since Zal's last concert when the golem had stood on the stage as part of the set. Since Friday couldn't be moved against his will, she'd assumed it was okay.

The only other thing Lila remembered about Friday was that the faeries had wanted to lose him. They said he was a chalice, a grail. They had been very interested in that. She would have asked Malachi now but he wasn't there.

Zal's dark aura bloomed suddenly and made the room seem brilliant. It drew shadows towards him, as if they were comforters. Lila had to work for a moment not to start and recoil. This was new to her, new to him; she even saw his own surprise and they shared a look in which each silently acknowledged their discomfort. They were strangers in their own skins these days.

Zal reached out and took her hand. She watched her fingers darken, her wrist submerge into the blue-black tinge halfway to the elbow. She couldn't feel it, only the gentle pressure of his fingers and thumb as he stroked her knuckles. "I left him behind." She knew that he meant he had left Friday in the past, on the day they'd gone to Faeryland and thought they'd be back in under a week. Fifty years ago.

"Yeah, but where?" She slid close to him and they leaned on each other. She put her head on his shoulder and wriggled until she could rest half across him, ear flat to the top of his chest. He stroked her hair and she listened to the strange sigh of his heart.

"At the Folly," he said. "In the basement."

She shuddered slightly with the mention of the old house. "I don't get it. You didn't even live there then."

"The landlord agreed to store a lot of my stuff. When I was touring, I'd leave it in the basement or in one of the lockups. The energy sink meant any magical things were pretty much secure. I sent Friday there. It's an earth energy well. He'd be right at home."

There was a moment's silence as she noticed his defensiveness but didn't pursue it, and he was relieved. "He's evidence in a genocide," she said.

"Yes, one which has never gone to trial," Zal said. "Nor will I should think. Is that why you want him?"

"Yes," she said. "Apart from Xavi, Friday's all there is left. But it occurs to me that there might be a lot more to him than that. I want to talk to the people inside him." She meant the spirits of the long-dead elves who had shared Xaviendra's fate as the subjects of unsuccessful experiments; theirs much less successful than hers.

"Most of them have gone, passed over," Zal said but he was uncertain.

"I want to find out. Unless you know of living elves who are contemporaries of Sarasilien's? The thing is, I used to be convinced that Sarasilien was the one who had left their bones in Zoomenon as evidence; he was the good guy in the war I imagined. But here's Xavi, and it looks like he wasn't much good at all. Do you think he could have had a hand in what happened to you?"

"No," Zal said. "I'm not sure he had much of a hand in what happened to you either." He held up a hand as she started to interrupt. "Not that he couldn't have been involved. Just that it violates every principle of the world that I hold to for anyone to succeed in having so much control."

Lila thought it over. "That's just *your* theory though."

"Yes," he said. "And if you prove otherwise, I'll be very upset." He kissed the top of her head. "Are you going to prove otherwise?"

"For my own satisfaction I'll prove something," she said.

Zal looked at the sand clock on Malachi's vast and expensive banker's desk. "Four a.m., still early. Let's go dancing."

Lila rubbed her cheek against his own. "Let's dance right here."

"Oh well," he said, pretending to be disappointed. "I suppose so, if we must."

Later, as they lay naked under the strew of their clothes she said, "Did you have a beer vision?"

"Not really," he said.

He didn't mention the odd sensation he had experienced while she was gone. He felt that he'd nodded off as he was playing the piano, just for an instant, and as he'd faded out there was something else, most definitely not asleep, which was looking out at the room through his eyes. It had felt very real, but he had known it was the beer. Like it said on the Dark bottles: *any hallucinations, visionary experiences, or out-of-body journeys resulting from consumption of our ale will be accompanied by our illusory guarantee—it ain't real, so don't fix it!*

Now that he thought about it, that was less comforting than it seemed.

Lila fell asleep for a moment, her head back on his chest, then she gave a small start. "Teazle. What happens now? He's alone. They'll kill him."

Zal put his arms around her. "Doubt it."

"It felt better the other way, when we were married." She went back to sleep. He could feel the drop of her energy into stillness like a fall. It almost pulled him with it, but he didn't want to sleep. He stayed awake until well after dawn thinking about the dragons he'd met.

First there was the water dragon who had eaten Arie, and now spat her up again without apparently digesting any of her more repulsive aspects. When he was her prisoner it had talked to him, after a fashion, but he'd thought it only remarked on his strange dual nature. Now he wondered if it had only been waiting for her.

The other one was the green dragon that had been a prisoner of the three sisters and their Mirror. He knew next to nothing about that one either even though he'd spent half a century living with its aspect—a dwarf who spent all his time looking after the littlest sister, doing her cooking and cleaning while Zal had ferried her yarns from one end of the world to the other. Zal had no idea at the time that Mr. V, who smoked a pipe and snored in an armchair for most of every day, was a dragon. If it hadn't been for a competitive spirit between the three sisters that had allowed him to free Mr. V from his prison, he would never have known. He had no idea why they had kept Mr. V in the Mirror at the end-beginning of the world, but probably there was a good reason. He'd never even found out what V stood for, though he'd tried to guess. A true name was as good as a soul-bond for the ancient creatures, so maybe it was just as well he couldn't divine it. Even so, he wished he knew it now.

CHAPTER FOUR

Zal tried composing songs in his head. Music used to come to him so easily, but where it had been inside him there was now a soft, woolly deadness like the kind of snowfall that mutes every sound. He could only remember melodies he had recently learned, and other people's songs that he had heard. The notes didn't run together for him. He remembered that they used to, but not what the experience felt like. There had been music in his head, and now there wasn't.

He was sad, but not as sad as he might have been because of that. Worse than the dead music was a sudden lack of purpose. Even as a plaything of the faeries he had had the purpose of survival, the focus on an end to his imprisonment. Before that had been music. Before that his political passions, a zest for living, the world itself calling with its million wonders. Now he groped around for any of them, fumbling across the strangely flat zones of his inner world.

Traces here and there, like the crumbs left over from a feast, were all he found. Their taste was almost undetectable and instantly gone. Jack the giantkiller had purged him of almost everything he had ever done, and the Three Sisters had sifted what was left and taken some of that. He remembered the middle sister saying it was for his own good. He wished he could remember what she'd taken, but he had no idea at all. He had been robbed, but what of? *Fifty years*, she said, *you'll never manage it if you remember everything*. But that hadn't prompted her to restore it when his time was up.

Only Lila was sharp and clear. He felt a continuity with her. From the first second he laid eyes on her, he hadn't forgotten that. It had been the strangest and most unexpected thing he had ever encountered in his long life; a young human woman, barely a fifth his age, mostly made of metal, powered by a nuclear reactor, staring at him with disapproval from the top of her regulation Agency suit and him at the height of his fame, a demigod of the media, adored by millions and hated by a few hundred key players within interglobal politics. He elf, she robot, love at first sight.

Hardly plain sailing, however. Lila didn't take well to love. She preferred antagonism. Zal hadn't minded. Antagonism meant she cared and he could live with that. It also made his demon side happy. He knew these things, and he remembered the red splash in her hair and her strange, cyberpunk mirror eyes, which he always thought of as blue, in spite of the fact he could only see his own eyes reflected in them; brown and earthen and full of self-mockery.

Now Lila Black snored softly against him, the strange alloy of her body barely heavier than an ordinary human being, but as far from that as you could possibly be and still qualify for the term. Then he felt a strange sensation on his chest and realised his skin was wet, and that she was crying. The tears were silent and her breathing hadn't changed, so she was trying to hide it.

"What is it?" he said.

Her voice was very small but controlled when she answered. "I'm not sure, I feel . . . like I want someone to look after me. Isn't that stupid? I think about going home, and I don't want to. But I do want to. I long to go. I can't go."

He knew then that she was speaking of her sister. Max had died in Lila's absence, but returned and lived again in their family home. She was a Returner. Maybe the first. Certainly not the last. "You don't have to see her."

Lila took a deep breath, "She wants to see me. She keeps calling to ask when I'm coming over. She wants to make me chicken pot pie. She says she's still got some of Mom and Dad's old stuff and I should check to see if I want anything."

By the end of the final sentence her tone had started to rise and fade. She snatched another breath through her teeth and forced herself into control.

"In my lifetime *they* died months ago. *She* died weeks ago. I haven't stopped once to think. There hasn't been time. There hasn't been a funeral, not for me. And now we're at chicken pot pie and Mom's poker books and Dad's crystal collection and what to do about the leaking roof. I'm not there yet. I don't think I'm even out of the front door on the day I last left home, 'cause that never ended like it was supposed to. I'm way behind. Or like I sidestepped into another world and I don't want to go back to the old one. Can't. Don't want to.

"Cause it feels like if I don't go then all that still hasn't happened yet. And I wish it was her. I'd love to see her. I want to see her so badly. But it isn't her, Zal, is it? How could it be? And if it isn't her, then what do I do? Do I kill her? Should I? What is she?" She took another breath. "I just don't think I can face it."

Zal stroked her shoulder and then let his hand press down firmly. He didn't say anything because there wasn't any need. She was talking to herself; he was only the catalyst.

She snuggled closer to him, wrapping her legs around his. "They haven't decided if killing a Returner is a crime or not, you know. There are squads of faith killers out to scrub the world clean of the undead, vigilantes hunting the half fey, and hackers trying to grab control of cyborgs. My inbox is bursting with them. Not to mention the Hunter's children still out there who are as close to were-creatures as I've ever heard of. I get letters from people complaining that their fortune-tellers are holding out on them, and I get complaints inside the Agency from people wanting to know if we should make any more cyborgs or not, because there're always candidates coming up, interesting candidates, ones who are half human or not human at all. And I know that if I say no, don't make any more of us, you idiots, then that's as good as saying let them die instead."

Zal stared at the yurt roof. He could see very well in the near darkness, almost better than in the light. It reminded him of being in his father's hut, long ago. His father could move easily in pitch blackness, just by sensing the energy patterns of objects. He'd never mastered that himself, and had had the bruises to prove it. He just hadn't been shadow enough.

Lila wiped her face on his chest and absently rubbed his skin dry with the sleeve of his shirt where she found it beside them. "I don't know what to do with this job. And I don't know what I'd do without it either."

"We should get another place," he said. "Somewhere that you like." He felt that she was slightly taken aback.

"What, you mean *not* sleep at the office?"

He heard the smile in her voice. "Yes. It probably won't vanish if you're not here all the time."

"I don't believe it."

He nodded, honest-faced. "Temple Greer goes home at weekends."

She snorted. "That's just a story to frighten children."

Zal smiled. "We could take a drive up the coast and maybe pick up Friday and a condo on the way."

She hesitated. "I'm afraid," she said and then added with difficulty, "anything that feels like roots makes me frightened." The last words were hesitant and they sounded like it was a thought she'd carried for a long time, but only just realised.

"Then we can just rent."

"Can't afford it," she said, but without much resistance.

"I can. I was a rock god once, and even dead rock gods make money. Besides, aren't you owed fifty years' back pay? That must come to a lot."

She opened and closed her mouth once without speaking before she said, "That never occurred to me. Can we, really?"

"Yes," he said. "Anywhere you like."

She got up with a sudden burst of energy. "Let's go right now!"

"You have to get dressed first," he said, grabbing for his clothes.

"I am dressed," she said with only the faintest hint of discomfort and he saw she was right.

Her leather gauntlets and boots stood out sharply against her tanned skin and where there had been nothing a second before a silk bias-cut lilac minidress swirled its luxurious skirts around her thighs.

The faery, he realised. Lila had no clothes now, not like he did. She could be human or machine, leather or flesh, and all she wore was the faery, who had made everything else redundant. It gave him a shiver as he pulled his shirt over his head and flicked the long tails of his hair free of the collar, all the while watching the dress's apparently ordinary movement. Vague, half-realised runes wove themselves through the fey cloth like waves moving idly on an ocean, speaking of realities unseen. They didn't make sense to him, but he had never studied the written forms of energy very hard, only music, and much of what they were saying was lost on him.

Glancing at Lila's face, he was sure she wasn't even aware of the dress's conversation with itself. He wondered if she was so used to wearing it she'd forgotten it was a living fey. Maybe she was resigned to it. Was it a battle she had lost? He felt unable to ask outright. Something in the self-conscious way she wore it made him feel she wouldn't have told him the truth.

They left Malachi's room, closing the doorflap behind them. As dawn started to creep slowly along the line of the ocean, it found them on the coast highway, their knees skimming the tarmac as Lila's bike bent over into the curves of the hills. She took them out of the city archipelagos, across the small breakwaters and lagoons, beside the endless quarrelling streams that formed the shining net of the Bay proper and held its thousands of islets together like a shoal of fish. Slowly they climbed away from the water. The land grew firmer and taller as they topped the cliffs that looked out over the Pacific Reach towards the invisible volcanic island chain of the Jewelfires. If the wind was right, a streak of smoke marked their evolution, but this dawn was misty and they could only see a few tens of metres beyond the land.

On the rocks below them the tide was high and filled with the soft, luminous green of seagleam—the remnants of moth dust that had fallen into water and been taken up by algae. It painted the cliffs with a weak, spectral light of its own. Into Zal's head ran news reports of talking fish, of mermaids, of leviathan spotted from deep ocean trawlers, scaring crews into early retirements.

They were alone on the road. Lila pulled on the brakes and slid them towards the edge of the cliff, stopping a half a metre from disaster. Loose chippings scattered into the air, fell and fell. Dust settled around them. Zal put his foot down beside hers.

"Do you believe in that dragon stuff?" Lila said, staring out into the water and the cloud above it. From this viewpoint the effect of the dust in the sea was clearly visible. "I mean," she said, "look at all that dust. Touching everything, changing everything, making the world magical. See it and believe it. I don't know why I find the dragon stuff so hard to believe. It doesn't make sense. Look at you, at me. You'd think I could believe anything now. But I don't."

"You're always looking for a reason," Zal said. He put his hand out gently onto her back, where the thin straps of the dress exposed the black leather of her, and caressed her. He felt muscle under his fingers and worked at the tension there. "You think there's another order behind everything you find, and that if you see what it is then you'll escape."

"If there is I don't even care," she said, looking out to sea. "I think that's awful. But I don't care."

"Yeah, yeah, that's why we're having this conversation," Zal said easily. He leaned forward and kissed her neck where the wind had blown her hair away from it. "There's no getting out of it, Lila. Not dead, and not alive. Doesn't matter who pulls the strings. Doesn't matter."

She kicked down the bike's stand, levered it up easily, and settled it. Then she spun around on the saddle and kicked her leg up high over his head until she was sitting facing him. She rested her legs over his thighs and put her hands on his face gently. They were cold but gentle.

"I hunted down all the rogues," she said. "Every last one. Lane knows it. She's not the only one who had a clone, but there aren't many and those that there are have gone silent." Her lips were white, they were so bitten together as she paused.

He waited, knowing there was more, and put his hand up to brush the hard line out of her mouth with his thumb. Her steady lilac gaze, that faked human look, faded away to the hard mirror-shine of her true machine eyes in which he saw himself, the road, the cliffs, and the sky all bent and curved in perfect detail.

"I thought they would know something I didn't," she said. Her leather hands flexed very slightly and he felt how easily she could have broken his neck. Her fingertips pressed his skull with precision and he knew that this is how she'd hacked their systems, straight through the head.

Zal kissed her nose.

Lila let her hands drop down into her lap. "Nothing," she said. "They didn't know anything." She looked down. "It's strange to have a battle fought in less than a second. Almost like nothing happened."

Zal kissed her forehead.

"I didn't kill them," she said quietly. "But I might as well have. They couldn't understand how I beat them. It was almost funny." She gave a hollow laugh that died as soon as it came out of her mouth. "The elementals. Reconfigured them. Just a few electrons is all it takes, in the right place at the right moment. They're the only reason Lane couldn't rip everything she wanted out of me in the first place. I realised that."

She paused and took a deep breath. It shuddered and he knew she was trying not to cry. When she looked up at him, her face was set and angry with a refusal of pain. "Zal, do you think that if Max is back, or, if she's gone and something else lives in her place, outside her time, will they all be coming?"

He knew who she was talking about. Dar, who had healed her from her body's original rejection of the machine technology and fused her with the metal elementals in the first place. She had killed him in cold blood, to save Zal's life. "I don't know."

Tears filled her eyes. They lensed the mirrors and the world reflected there shimmered, wavered, fell apart. "I have to tell him I'm sorry."

Zal leaned his forehead against hers, looking into her eyes. He took her hands in his. "I'm sure there's no need. He would have known."

"Would he? I judged him for doing the same thing. And Zal, what if they all come back?" She swallowed and gritted her teeth briefly, sniffing as tears ran down her nose and dripped off onto their joined hands. "It feels all wrong to me. I'm scared of it. I don't know what it means. It's wrong. They shouldn't be here. When I look at this part of the world in the Signal, it's like looking at a series of mistakes. I don't know how to explain it better than that. It doesn't add up. The numbers eventually all fall apart and where the potentials ought to drop out they just keep on shifting values. At the farthest edge there's chaos. Nothing remains. Nothing adds up anymore."

Zal stroked her fingers with his thumbs. "We'll ride it out," he said.

"You idiot," she said, without rancour. "I tell you the world is ending and that's all you can say?"

Zal thought before he answered and said, "There's a book in one of the Elven libraries about dragons. I didn't read it myself." He hesitated. "I only heard about it. It's the lore of the dragon. Very short. It says that dragons are emergent beings, formed out of the energy of living, conscious beings and gaining a separated existence of their own after they reach a critical level. They can arise in the wild, accidentally, if a culture has a common purpose or need, spoken or unspoken, or even many of those. They can manifest in dragon form."

"Sounds like that theory of ghosts," Lila said.

"Yes it does," he said. "But these have enough directed intent to make a transition from energetic to material form, to have independent life and consciousness. They are astral, but also material. They are immanent but also evident. And once they have matter, a body, then they become subject to the law of Flesh and Blood."

"All usual rules apply . . ." Lila said, echoing Xaviendra's recounting. "What's that?"

Zal did his best to translate what was an aetheric and esoteric theory into terms she would better understand. He interlaced his fingers with hers and, through her gloved exterior, felt the hard grip of her bones on his.

"Flesh and blood are living memory, but memory being refined, being changed, being forged anew every day, being tested. Flesh and blood are no longer potentials, like aetherial potentials, they are much more massive and have much greater inertia. Once you have a body, once there is a 'you' then you can't be subject to the laws that brought you into being as an energetic form. You have your own life, your own personality, your own thoughts. You are alone. You are yourself. Dragons have awesome powers at cosmic scales, which they inherited from their genesis, as a kind of waking dream, but they keep them when they are bound to flesh, and that flesh and bone makes them like the rest of us."

"Do they really exist like that?"

Zal thought of Mr. V, the dwarf, smoking his long pipe, his darned, stripey socks hanging over the ends of his toes. "Yes. They're alive like us."

"And do you think they'd want to make us—you, me, Teazle? For what? Into what?"

"I don't know," Zal said honestly, although it did occur to him as it must have to her that they were, in their own way, dragonish, the three of them together. "Look at what humans do for entertainment, though. Maybe that's what they do too."

Lila nodded. She clasped and reclasped his fingers, still sniffing. She turned her head so that her whole forehead pressed flat to his as though she wished to push through the bone. "And what's the sleeper within? Is that something else again?"

"I knew you'd ask that," Zal said. "I don't know, but I know who would. Ilya would know. His magic is from the tradition of which the sleeper was a part. He's bound to know." He felt his face tighten as he spoke the next bit, knowing it for the truth. The venom in his own tone was no surprise to him.

"Arie wouldn't have wasted a good elf for each of the deadly sorceries; she was a conservationist. She'd have wasted one and made him learn all of the dark arts so she could keep the badness in one spot ready to be wiped clean when it had served out its regrettable usefulness. I'd bet against the Hoodoo that he knows."

They shared a quick glance at the mention of the Hoodoo, though they said nothing. It wasn't something that could be spoken of directly. The glance alone spoke the volumes of their unease about the Hoodoo's absolute power, it's unknown nature.

Lila gave a half-smile, a small sniff of false cheer. "That's good, 'cause I was hoping he'd help me out with Project Death anyway."

Zal grinned, his spirits lifting at her girlish manner. "Project Death?"

"To find out how and why all these dead people keep coming back."

"Is that the name *you* gave it?"

"Had to have some name," she said defensively.

"Mmn," he smiled at her and pushed awkwardly at her until she lifted her face up and let him kiss her properly. He put his arms around her and slid her up his thighs until he could hold her fully against him. This put her higher than he was so that when she broke the kiss she was able to pull his head against her chest as she talked. He heard the words through the wall of her body, resonating in frequencies that almost made him swoon so that what she said in her fast-as-thought worrying came across like a kind of dream.

"Anyway, stop getting off the point. Aren't ghosts and dragons and all that other stuff the same somehow? I can't see what the difference is. Some intent causes a reaction in the fundamental energy goo of the Void or wherever it hangs out—Wait, no, aetherial energy and the kind of energy you mean when you talk about people vibrating with joy or whatever, are those things the same?"

Zal pushed his face into her neck, cheek on the leather of her collar, lips against her skin.

"If they're the same, why is there some load of it hanging out in the Void? Is that like energy spontaneously bursting into empty space? Is the Void the aetheric or astral equivalent of outer space? Is there such a thing as outer space or is that just a term meaning not-right-in-our-backyard-which-is-pretty-chock-full-of-matter?"

Zal kissed her, feeling the dull thud of her arteries below his tongue; ten-ton hammers.

"If there's an astral equivalent of the material and an energetic astral equivalent to . . . shit, no, that won't work because the energy of a person with intent and the energy released through fission surely isn't the same thing and that would make three energy things and only two types of plane. Is the personal energy even real in the same way that matter is real?"

Zal opened his mouth as wide as he could in a simulated vampire bite and pulled her hips hard into his own.

"Could we not say that it was a feature of the inner world and not the outer world or . . . no, that would mean there had to be some kind of method for it to affect both, which would be consciousness or mind or whatever, probably, right? But if it comes from the inner world of the individual, it vibrates somehow with the fundamentals of both aether and the baryonic material?"

Zal sucked gently on her neck. She tasted faintly of sugar, and violets. His hand gripped the back of the silky sundress in a threatening fist, warning it to back off. Her hands caressed his head, pulling him to her as she continued.

"Or is it all the same energy arising in different places by different means but mixing together naturally because of being the same thing? Is it the same, but manifesting differently across different spatiotemporal realities? Is the astral world purely internal or a nonbaryonic zone accessible by certain energy patterns from here? And now that Alfheim and Demonia and Faery all have some kind of definable spatiotemporal existence following relatively normal physical laws . . . mmmfmmmfmmfffffmmmm!"

Zal had put his hand over her mouth. "You've exceeded my short-term memory buffer," he said gently but firmly. "I think the answer is probably yes. I don't see where you're going though. So, can you tell me?" He eased up a finger at a time.

Lila caught and kissed his hand as she spoke. "Human beings," she said. "They must be aethero-active. Have to be. If all that's true. They're not the dullards everyone says. Yes, magic doesn't work here like it does in your world, but that doesn't mean nothing's going on. The Burgis Hypothesis says that we created you, your worlds, and all the other things, and the energy reaction of the bomb made you quasi-material. It didn't explode. It imploded. On us. Everything that isn't human was once just a figment of our imagination."

She waited for his answer, looking at him with a pert expectancy that only made him laugh harder once he started.

"Zally!" she slapped his shoulder lightly, pouting. "It's not funny. It's real."

He bounced her gently on his lap so that she could easily feel how hard he was through all their clothing. "I'm real. And so what?"

"What do you mean, so what?" Her pout had turned sultry although she still had a way to go before she was prepared to give up her outburst of intellectual defence.

Zal played around, trying to catch the zipper-pull of her biker jacket between his teeth as he spoke. "If it's true, does it matter? Does it change anything?"

She thought about it.

On the rocks below, the glowing algae sloshed like weak paint, gathering in the crannies until the stones looked as if they were cracking open to reveal green molten cores.

"If the humans believed it, then it might matter," she said. "Look at how they treat us now. But if they thought we were all creatures they made, who weren't as real as they were, then they'd think they could do what they liked, that they were first, better. Is what I think." She began to comb through his hair with her fingers in an absent way.

"That's what the elves would think," he said, the zip-pull caught firmly between his front teeth. He began to nudge it downwards as he talked, the strange, zinging sensation of the metal and its odd taste covering his tongue, "Or I should say, what they think anyway. To them humans are an upstart race lacking in most interesting skills, living in an impoverished world they don't appreciate, like starving beggars in the middle of paradise. Undeserving savages."

She gave up on the wild tangles in his hair and pulled it into three roughly equal parts, beginning to wrap it into a rough braid. "It doesn't matter anyway, does it, because everything has gone wild and become its own thing now, hasn't it?"

"The Law of Flesh and Blood," Zal said, coming to the point where his neck couldn't go any further and the lilac dress was stretched taut, blocking the way anyway. "Once real, then free."

"But freedom doesn't necessarily mean happy, or even able."

He nosed his way between the sharp metal teeth of the jacket and kissed the warm body underneath. "Did you think it did?"

"Yes," she said. She tied off the braid and let it fall against his back.

"Ah, Lila," he said sadly and hugged her close, webbing them both in a sheen of darkness.

The sound of the water endlessly washing the shore surrounded them. The mist thickened, tinging at first rosy, then orange as the sun struggled to break through.

"I don't want to live by the sea," she said suddenly. "Not this close."

Zal bent low and kissed her over her heart. "Doesn't matter to me," he said.

"I don't know how to go on," she said, her hands tight on his shoulders. "I don't know what to do. Or why."

He kissed his way back up to her neck and then went back for the zipper to pull it up again.

"Welcome to the club," he said. "I find if you just keep breathing and deal with one minute at a time, that's usually enough." He poked her in the ribs. "You're not breathing."

She forced herself to exhale. "I don't actually have to breathe."

"Yes," he said. "You do. It's important. Only machines and the undead don't breathe, and look what happens to them."

"What happens to them?"

"Nobody asks them to parties," Zal said, lifting her up and helping her to turn back around on the saddle. He put his hands on her waist and saw the dress was looking at him with embroidered flower eyes. They were frowning, but they weren't mean. He stuck his tongue out at them and they unstitched themselves into ordinary pansies.

"Now are we going to look at some houses or not?"

She grabbed a portfolio of rentals off the local hub and displayed them on the upper back of her jacket so that he could see them.

As she pushed them off the stand and spun back onto the road, she wondered who was going to sign off real estate to her at six in the morning outside of town.

CHAPTER FIVE

As it turned out, Lila need not have worried about real estate agents. The process was handled entirely by the city network, without the need for human intervention. In spite of, or more likely because of, its reputation as the hub of otherworldly activities, Bay City and the surrounding country had a high transient population and properties that were empty and ready to let were few. Those fitting Lila's requirements were even fewer, so it didn't take them long to pick a couple from the fast-dwindling list and ride out into the forested hills of Lakewood.

Lakewood sat to the north of the island swarms and coastal inlets where the true grit of the continent finally got its act together and heaved itself out of the lagoons to form dry, regular hills. Rivers disciplined by broad swathes of emergent rock ran in wide beds and between them grassy glades and large patches of dense forest had sprung up. Needle and broadleaf trees mingled on the lower slopes, but it was higher up, where the land was rockier and the forest an older, pinewood type, that Lila preferred. Beyond the reach of the shopping malls and estate houses that circled like wagons around manmade lakes, in a region where the roads petered out into tracks, sat the house she had mentally ringed in red.

The bike crunched across the scattered gravel that made up the approach and halted. Before them sat a red wooden ranch house, single storeyed and set on pylons that supported it so that it didn't topple down the steep slope. A broad deck all around it was set with deep green canvas chairs and awnings, all furled closed and tied down against the weather. The whole thing backed onto a thick rise of dense evergreens and sheer rock. Above and beyond those was a scrappy grey-stoned cliff and beyond that the sullen, misty glower of the sky.

Lila sat and looked and listened to the forest sounds, waiting for Zal to speak.

Finally he said, "I can't see the moose head. There must be one somewhere." She felt him swing himself off the saddle and then his sigh as he stretched and turned. "But it is a long way from the beach."

She swung her leg over the handlebars and moved to his side. The clearing and the angles were as she had hoped. You could see across Lakewood's green clusters down all the way to the city's blue and grey clutter and then beyond that to the fog that hid the ocean. The smell of resin and damp mulch filled her nostrils. She liked the rock at her back. And beyond this house there were no paths into the forest for wandering hikers to stumble over her. The house was alone up here, half hiding, half poised to rush down and embrace the town.

She looked to Zal, waiting for his verdict on the energy, the subtleties of the location. She kept expecting to see him changed when she did this, as though Otopia would gradually erode his strangeness and make him the blond, tanned conformist elf of his earlier days. Now he was dipped in a sheen of permanent ink and he looked downright alarming. In the dull daylight his shadows were too intense, his colours unreal. When he looked at her, grinning, his eyes were so dark brown they looked black. Their enlarged pupils seemed to bleed darkness. Lila couldn't prevent a quick blink.

He saw it and that pleased him even more.

"I see I am too glamorous to be allowed any closer to the lure of cultured pursuits," he indicated the city with a glance, adding, "although I don't really feel like partying much myself." He dropped the pose and turned back to the building. "It's a good effort, Liles. Okay, if you want it."

"Don't you want to see inside?" She didn't. She couldn't have cared less if it was bare boards but it seemed the thing to say.

Zal shook his head. "It's a bolthole, a treehouse, a retreat. It's what you need."

She felt humbled by his understanding, shy in an odd way, as though she were overexposed. She turned and saw that even from their spot at the edge of the driveway you couldn't see directly into any of the windows. The angle was too steep. "It might be impossible in the winter," she said, in a token gesture at thinking things through.

"You wish," he said.

She wasn't sure how to say the next thing so she just said it. "Are you sure? I mean, that you want to be here all the time. With me?" The ease of Teazle's divorce and easy departure kept running through her mind.

One of his eyebrows quirked. "Is this a chink in the Iron Maiden's armour? Are you saying, Lila Black, that you want me to stay here all the time with you, hmm?" His eyes were fiendish. "Are you actually asking me for something that matters to your cold steel heart?"

For a moment she bristled but then she remembered two could play. "What poncery is this, elf? Games?" She looked around but there was no sign of the citrus fizz that signalled their old game was active. It had gone.

For some reason this chilled her. She couldn't remember either of them reaching a victory condition—a state of abject humiliation in which they were begging the other one for sex. It would have been sufficiently nauseating or alternatively so deliriously sweet it would have stuck in her mind. Other things stuck in her mind all too clearly: the dead bodies of Poppy and Viridia for two, rolling in the black, ice-clogged tide of Jack Giantkiller's lake. That had been their penalty for cheating a deal with the Hoodoo. The Hoodoo governed all magical games and forfeits. It never missed. It always collected. So where was it? Even a slight rise in baiting each other should have caused the old bargain to flicker into existence, but she felt nothing, smelled nothing. When had the surrender condition been validated? She looked at Zal, but he was apparently oblivious.

"Poncery," he repeated, wonderingly but not without pleasure. "Haven't heard that in a long time."

"Now you have," she said, deciding not to speak of the game. It felt like it would be a terrible mistake, calling it to account almost. She stuck to the facts. "It's two thousand standard dollars a month."

"Poncery," Zal said, flicking his ears like a horse dislodging a fly. "I probably should mention that I have a strange feeling about this place though, despite the crusty, rustic urban cowboy styling."

Lila looked over the building again, then back at Zal. She reread the lease notes: there was no mention of anything strange, although the place had been let three times in six months. "What sort of feeling?" she asked, ignoring the sensation of sinking that was going on in her shinbones.

"The sort of feeling that suggests inhabitants."

She tried not to be disappointed and almost managed it. She offered her last signal-flag of defiance to fate. "It's billed as empty. You mean squatters?"

"I mean her," he pointed up to the windows of the woods-facing side. Their angle and the sun meant she couldn't see anything at first, but then she thought she might have noticed a movement.

"Her? You saw someone?"

Lila reprocessed her image memory but was unable to find more than a movement of shadow, which no amount of fiddling could resolve into a meaningful shape.

"I *felt* her," he said. "We shadow elves have a built-in detector for living things, you know. Something to do with our unliving ancestors and their hunger for vital energy. Quite good at shorter ranges. Specially if things are powerful."

"Not human then," Lila frowned. She felt cross, her discovery spoiled, the house almost as good as lost.

By unliving ancestors she knew Zal meant the spirits of the dead planes, things about which the human race knew very little and had even less language for. "Spirit" wasn't a good term, but it was the only one they had. Even the grimoires of the demon necromancers had few facts amid their screed of speculations and graphic accounts of the results of encounters with these beings.

An image of her parents' house flared into her mind's eye, a shape like a sister behind the screen door, opening it up. . . . She pushed it aside.

"Or not exactly human?"

"Not entirely, that's for sure," Zal replied. He wasn't perturbed, only mildly interested, and he looked to her for a cue. "Want me to take a closer look?"

His heavy blond hair, slicked with its jet sheen, framed his face and large eyes like a ghoul mane. The eyes themselves slanted more than they used to, she noticed, as they glittered with vague amusement.

She wiggled her fingers. "Want me to pick the locks?"

He smiled and held out his arm, gentleman-style. "Sure."

They moved around to where a set of steps led onto the verandah and climbed them side by side. The sun was shining weakly through the low cloud and lit up the security lock—a touch pad.

"If I were alone, this would be a window job," Zal said, looking at the metal with disapproval. His elven skills were actively earthed out or repulsed by iron and its alloys.

"You're not alone," Lila grinned. "Although," she added, as she accessed the system via the estate agent's portal, masking herself as a routine tax-office audit, "this means that whoever is in there isn't using the door either."

"Back door," Zal said.

"Don't think so, they're both active and unopened." She smiled, the job done, and gave the touchpad a brief press of her fingers.

They heard the locks clicking back and the door slid open. A smell of furniture wax and deodorisers met them. The interior was dim, but a few of the storm shutters had been loosened and pried up from the windows, so not as dim as it might have been.

They stepped inside.

"Hello?" Lila called.

"Genius," Zal murmured.

"Well, it's not like they don't know we're here."

"And now they know we know they're here," he sighed, but in spite of his light tone of reproach his attention was elsewhere.

Lila could see his aura, strong with the room's shadows, flitting out and away from him like a cloud of black dust until it thinned into the general atmosphere. She let him work while she reviewed the furnishings. The hunting-lodge theme was firmly established—heavy wooden sofas and chairs surrounded a log table, which in turn was set before one side of a double open fireplace, the stone chimney acting to support the roof in this room and the next one, which looked to have some kind of dining set up.

She wandered towards the kitchen, alert but more interested in seeing appliances than squatters. She'd never really lived away from home, if you excused a month at an anonymous apartment block, and it was kind of exciting, in a small way, to consider that she could have her own stuff again, even if someone else with a taste for white with gingham-and-red-roses accessories had chosen it.

She was just nosing inside a cupboard, looking at a nice set of red-stemmed wineglasses and a clearly never-used fondue set, when she heard Zal's hiss and then the almost inaudible patter of his run across the boards. She was out of the door in an instant, following his back as he ran around the chimney's heavy shape.

There was a brief scuffle and then Zal fell into the light coming from the window that he'd pointed out from below. He landed on his feet, catlike, his hands held out in a protective stance in front of him. His shadow aura was completely reabsorbed and in the sunlight he looked remarkably solid, almost human in tone.

He had flushed out a small girl, who was in the corner. She was screened by a big tartan beanbag—one of several that made up an obvious nest in this, the least overlooked part of the house. She was possibly nine, or even twelve, Lila thought, coming to a slow halt behind Zal. Her hair was tied up in a scarf and from beneath its azure line her large eyes stared at both of them, wide and unblinking. Her skin was as dark as the old oak floor, and there was a faint sheen on it that Lila recognised as faery bloom, a touch of pearly lilac that showed only in the light.

"I'm not gonna hurt you," Zal said, lowering his hands and backing up into Lila's shins.

"No, I know," the girl replied. The beanbag muffled her tone a bit but not the resentful contempt it contained. "It's obvious. You don't need to shout about it." Her eyes narrowed and she briefly scrubbed her face with the beanbag cover as though she was rubbing away tears or exhaustion. "Are you an elf?"

"Yes."

"Well you look like a demon and you smell like a vampire."

Lila had to admit that, in spite of the cornering and the bag, the girl didn't seem terribly frightened. She saw Zal's right ear twitch, which was a sign he was suppressing a laugh. "It's a long story," he said.

The girl's gaze flicked to Lila and she pressed back against the two walls. "You're iron. Sort of. Living. Kind of. Elemental. Freaky." She sniffed and her eyes rolled up briefly into her head in a disconcerting manner, a flash of white.

"I'm human," Lila said.

"Hell you are!" the girl replied. She really did have a talent for vocally flipping the V sign, Lila thought.

"She's just a cyborg kind of thing," Zal said casually. "She's harmless. We only came to look at the house. She wants to rent it."

Lila kneed him in the back for the harmless remark and said, "Speaking of which, why are you here?"

"Is that a faery dress?" the girl said, staring at Lila with frank and open disbelief.

"What, this old thing?" Lila plucked at a ruffle of her over-the-leathers miniskirt and felt the cloth twitch of its own accord.

The girl stared at her, at the dress, at Zal. Finally she shook her head and said with feeling, "I never seen anything like you two." She frowned. "Never thought anyone'd catch me so easy." She was completely disgusted with herself. Then, "Are you going to send me away?"

"Where to?" Lila asked. "Why are you here?"

"'Cos I can leave fine on my own," the girl added firmly. "Got here by myself, can leave by myself, find another place, no worries. I don't hurt anyone. I don't do nothing."

Lila reviewed the details on the house's previous occupants. Both listed an early departure because they "just didn't like it as much as we thought" and "too rustic, rather be closer to town." Their personal logs mentioned other things, however; bad feelings, sudden chills, a sense of being watched, a presence . . .

"You haunt people," Lila said. "You made them go."

The scowl came back, full force. "I didn't hurt them. I just wanted them to go. That's all. I didn't do anything to them. I swear. I didn't take their stuff."

. . . I bought enough for sandwiches but then it was gone and . . .

"You ate their food."

The girl's mouth dropped open, revealing perfectly straight white teeth. "What are you, like, some kind of detective?"

"Some kind," Zal said amiably. "But that doesn't matter. We want to live here, so we want to know if you're going to haunt us too."

She was skinny, Lila thought, starving maybe. "How did you survive since the last people left?"

A glare fixed on her in reply. "They left their food." She grinned to herself, "They left in a rush. I hid it before the cleaner came. Under the floor."

"It must have run out by now."

The glare didn't falter. "You got any?"

Zal shook his head.

"I can get some," Lila said almost at the same time.

"I forget she has a constant link to everything she wants," Zal apologised. "Delivery take-out. There must be one round here."

"Pizza," Lila confirmed. "And pasta. With desserts."

The glare continued, rather more thoughtfully. "They were loud," she said at last, with grudging resignation. "Their heads were full of crap and it went on all the time, man, I mean they like never shut up unless they were asleep. It's the same down there," her eyes flicked briefly in the direction of the city and she shook her head, finished, not just with what she was saying but with everyone.

Lila nodded. "Okay. And what about us?"

The girl sighed through her nose. "I want a family-size veggie pizza with extra cheese and hot peppers and a large vanilla milkshake and a spinach lasagna with hot sauce and a large portion of angel cake with the faery flumsie on the side and a filter coffee, decaf, extra sugar."

Zal sat down and looped his arms around his raised knees. He sighed with resignation. "She's going to be expensive. Elephant-sized orders. Private schooling . . . ponies . . ."

Lila frowned her own frown in return. "Jalapenos or the kind you shake on?"

"Both," the girl said. She looked at Zal with an almost comical high flip of her eyebrows. "Ain't nothing going on in his head."

Then she fixed her gaze on Lila and it was back to scowling. "You're like a town on Friday night, though. But it's distant, and it's fast. So fast. Sounds like the wind."

"How many bedrooms are there?" Zal asked her.

"Two," the girl said, not moving an inch. "A king size and a twin. Just one bathroom though."

Lila sighed. She felt like she was doing the right thing, even though she had no idea what she was doing except tagging after Zal. "Okay. Go and stick your hand on the door and it'll log you as a keyholder. The pizza'll be here in ten minutes. I tipped them so you don't need to. They'll leave it on the porch and go. And the biggest bed is mine."

"Ours," Zal objected.

"Eww," the eyes rolled again.

"What shall we call you?" Lila asked. "Beanbag Girl?"

"Emmy."

"Is that your name?" She couldn't resist it.

"It's what you're getting."

"Sassy," Lila said. "Definitely a Sassy. Well, so long, Sassy. While you're up here, you could open up the windows and sweep the leaves off the deck. We'll be back later tonight. Don't stay up past ten."

"You're not my mom."

Zal glanced at Lila for the first time since they'd started talking and got to his feet. "We should go find Mr. Head."

Lila nodded and gave a last look at the beanbag and its fierce eyes. "Windows," she said firmly. "Deck."

CHAPTER SIX

"What just happened?" Lila asked, of herself as much as Zal. She kicked her leg over the front of the bike and sat down in a familiar gesture that mirrored Zal's mount-up action over the back. They sat down at the same moment and the engine vibrated briefly into its warm-up sequence until there was no sound left but a feathery whisper that was the opposite of the noise Lila thought bikes should make. Internally she edited that part of the world's soundtrack and replaced it with a properly throaty snarl. On the plus side, it meant they could actually talk to each other at low speeds without having to scream.

Zal just shook his head. "If you have to ask . . ."

"All I need," Lila said, backing them up with dainty pushes of her toes into the rough gravel. She was grateful Zal was so light. In spite of the fact that she felt the girl was in control of everything that had just happened, she found that she didn't mind. That in itself rang warning bells, but they fell on ears that had become strangely deaf. She suspected magic, and then the suspicion ran out of her mind and into the same place where unwanted appointments and obligations usually drained away. No matter how she tried she couldn't grip the notion.

"You protest too much," Zal said mildly, next to her ear, another short form. "Don't you feel better?"

"Maybe." She let the bike drift forward and put her feet on the pegs, feeling the minidress start to ripple in the wind. She did feel better. And that was odd too.

"Blood," Zal said. "Stone."

"Fiddlededee," Lila replied. She wasn't like him, taking happiness where it could be found as if it were pennies on the street. But now that she thought of it, that wasn't a good trait. She did what she always did in moments of self-doubt and accelerated.

You could do a ton on these little backwoods roads, leaning over, a split inch from losing your knees, sliding out on the corners towards the drop-offs into the dark woods with the slow drift of a surfer on the face of a massive wave. It was fun, when the numbers about survival went uncertain and the red flashed and the elf was sufficiently exhilarated so that he didn't speak, just squeezed her tight and laughed. She felt like she was flying, like she was free. It was how they were meant to be.

Unfortunately a ton brought the slowed-up, crunched-down flatness of normality back that much faster. There was a limit to the number of speeding tickets she could avoid and not appear to be taking the piss, so she was forced to slow down as they reached the suburban expressway and began the long wind south to Solomon's Folly on the other side of the city. The bike ought to fly, she was convinced of it. Something she had to work on. For now though it was weaving through the lanes and finding the best, cleanest, most beautiful path through the traffic that had to satisfy her will.

"Cyborg thing?" she said as they slid, fishlike, between cars on the avenue at the heart of the fashion district—a place she'd never set foot to pavement. "Harmless?"

"Yeah," Zal said, ignoring all the attention he was attracting from the promenading Pretty People who adorned the streets and the drifting two-storey-high show cars. They didn't know who he was, but he still made a sight in the human world. There was a noticeable lack of genuine fey and hundreds of human wannabes. Lila counted.

Among the ranks of the more ordinary mortals, demons walked in perfect guises. She knew them only because of the way they stared at her, fixated. They knew already about Teazle, she thought. They knew she was deposed, and Zal too. If they hadn't been together, she would have expected an attack. Perhaps her reputation as a killer would be enough to stop a bloodbath on the streets. She'd have to hope so.

"Do you think I look harmless to them?" she spoke Demonic, so that Zal would know what she meant.

Her own outfit was getting noted. Not for any good reasons. She was gratified to find she couldn't care less. A flashboy weaving on a floatboard, camera welded to his face, shifted close, taking pictures. She cut her face out of them all even as they arrived on his hard drive and felt a slight unease at her own virtuosity. There'd been a time when even she hadn't had the connection speed and ability to hack like that. Maybe technology had improved. Maybe she had, when she wasn't looking.

"I don't think," he said. "That's the road to hell."

"We're already on that," Lila said, seeing the lights change, the cars and floats piling up into stacks on all sides, grateful passengers ogling and preening as they stopped to check each other out at the halfway point of the promenade.

"It's all twaddle," Zal said, referring to the road and its sights with only a trace of envy. "But it impresses people."

"Got that right." Lila was forced to slow even more. She squeezed them between a limousine transporting several hot tubs filled with bathing-suited models and a long, low-deck car featuring various celebrities surrounded by posing dancers. There were a few real fey among those, looking as vainly glamorous as ever, although carefully toned so as not to draw too much attention from their paying hosts.

She passed and they were nearly clear when a small, fishlike sports car with an open top and an outrageously impractical spoiler cut in front of her with centimetres to spare as it moved to a more prestigious lane. A few kilometres per hour over fifty and the spoiler's downforce would probably glue the chassis to the road. At these speeds, however, it was merely architectural. Its glassine panels ejected a mist of softly scented water vapour, and into this projected what she assumed from the renaissance painting style to be the tastefully arty end of holoporn. The sight was so sudden and arresting that she almost crashed. As it was, she missed by fractions of a millimetre, taking the outside, her blood boiling. They drew alongside each other at the red light.

Lila's swear words were cut off as well by the passenger, who dangled her hand out of the car, showing off diamonds. She shrieked like a hysteric as Lila opened her mouth and then the driver's voice, rough from too many late nights, said, "Hey, isn't that an elf?"

Zal turned to the driver. "I'm not an elf. There are no elves in Otopia."

"You look familiar," the man said as the light changed. He kept up even as Lila began to accelerate past another limo and its one-car carnival. "Are you one of those fey that can be other things, or a Makeover? Yeah, I know, you're a Makeover, sure, one of those retro ones that looks like that rock guy, what was his name? You know . . ." He turned to his companion, who was sulkily examining the car in front—a large tank filled with mermen and mermaids and enough tropical fish for a minor reef. "Whatsisname?"

Lila eased off the speed, curiosity getting the better of her.

The passenger turned her lovely head with its perfect skin. She had diamond-enhanced eyes—every gem twinkling in the iris, bent flashes of light to the tips of her long elegant eyebrows where they stuck out in an unreal sweep of multicoloured fibreoptic feathers. "Get a mempack, cupcake. Zal. Zal of The No Shows. They were like, regal." She inspected Zal thoroughly, with a professional impersonality, used to assessing every tiny angle and relation of a body's parts and calculating its net beauty in dollars per minute. "Super-good copy too. Who's your surgeon, honey?"

"There's a copy of me?" Zal asked, incredulous for a second.

"Seriously," said the woman, although she drawled it out so that it sounded more like see-ree-uss-lee. "Still rare though. I only ever saw one other. Nice choice. Great value. Tell me, were you tall to start with or was it a whole body stretch? Those are so goddamn painful." She shifted her legs—bare except for a fine silvery net—and unconsciously pressed them together.

"I was just like this to start with," Zal assured her. Lila heard his tone change and pushed through the lines, taking them across the junction on the cusp of a red light and pushing forward to saner streets.

"Hey, call me! I can get work for you!" the woman screeched. "Or blip me that doctor's name!"

Lila pretended she didn't hear the protests and surprise that followed them as the woman discovered Zal was not connected to the Otopia Tree public internet and didn't show up on any registry. She routed the messages people were trying to send him into a junkyard address that would shortly return the kind of spamblurts that would take a day to purge. As she did so, she felt him lean close again. It occurred to her that her reaction was needless and territorial. She was actually threatened by those vapid, pointless people. She accelerated.

"There's a copy of me," he said proudly.

"At least she knew who you were." Lila wasn't sure if he were pleased or appalled; she thought both.

"Her memory pack knew. It probably even knows who Michael Jackson was."

"Who?" she looked it up quickly, turning them away from the rows of opening restaurants and clubs, the glossy frontages of the hotelinos stretching all the way crosstown, and smoothed them up the ramp to the expressway and the glorious illusion of freedom in the fast lane.

"Ha ha. You know I was thinking about making a comeback. Maybe."

"Hasn't the world moved on some?" She had no idea about the

state of the music industry, she only knew the population statistics for the undead, the Hunter's children, and the groups who had risen up to hate or champion them. She knew about crime, struggle, and two-faced, lying elf scum that she was so angry with she could have burned them to toast. This whole subject change put her off balance. Her snippiness made her even more annoyed.

There was a copy of Zal. Who? What for?

"Lila," he said. "What rattled you?"

"Nothing." They rose onto the elevated sections that overshot the city's oldest quarter and tiled roofs flickered past, beneath the wheels. But she didn't want to lie to him. They'd been far enough apart already. "Everything." She searched around in the uncomfortable feeling. It was like she was grubbing around a trash sack in the dark, trying to tell what was in there. "Everything changed. I want something to stay where it is."

"Me?" He was gentle, enquiring. It didn't justify the outburst that suddenly ripped free of her.

"Do you know that since I met you there hasn't been a day I haven't been fighting to save you from—whatever? I mean, I got that job, a temporary assignment, and then it's just one damn thing after another. When is it going to end? And you want to get out there again? With those—morons? Did you know there are people who specialise in killing outworlders to the tune of eight or twelve a week in this city alone? The morgue is filled to bursting with corpses awaiting repatriation. And you want to get up in lights and shout out that you're here again? When a dozen conspiracy sites even name you as a *primary cause* of the Hunter's Reign because you vanish and, hey presto, he appears and ruins the whole human world for them in one little year. And what, after fifty years of trouble, could possibly top that? I'll tell you what. The returning dead. And you. Returning. Dead or not dead. Who cares?" Only the fact that she was able to run a counter-vibration stopped the fact that she was shaking from disrupting the bike's effortless float. "Oh, what the hell, I don't know what I'm talking about. Do what you like."

After that, to top everything, she felt ashamed of herself. Rather than cause any more damage, she shut her mouth firmly and kept her gaze on the road, marking the miles, checking the route, watching the map rotate and move their position closer and closer to that bloody awful house. Zal didn't say anything in response, but he didn't hug her any less. After they had crossed the river and most of the tributaries between the city and the coastal parks he said, "It's not that I don't feel afraid of things. But if I give in, then I lose, they win, and I get to die in the other way, the worse way. A demon can't be otherwise."

"It isn't the demon," she said, sorry and resigned. "It's just you. And me. Don't quit, don't give up, don't give in, don't give a shit. Die on your feet and take 'em all with you if they don't like it. I guess I thought that after all that there'd be an end to it. We'd go home and there'd be this peace. It'd be over."

"The fat lady would sing songs from the shows."

"Yeah, and then we'd go crazy with boredom and chew our own legs off."

They had reached the turn. Silently they drifted into the deep shadows of the lane where the overhanging trees blotted out most of the sky. The brief lift of spirits Lila had felt a moment before vanished as she looked into the overgrown woodlands. An air of neglect and forgetting that had been there previously had matured into sullen hostility and a deep stillness she didn't remember. The last time she'd been on this road was in Malachi's car, and they'd burnt rubber to escape the incomprehensible, malevolent intentions of the elemental creatures that had filled the woodland. She looked now for the stag, for signs of a huge body made of mud and branches, but there was no sign of any kind of life, even the wrong kind. Only the bike tires whispered and hummed on the cracked asphalt, spitting gravel.

"Stop," Zal said. He was whispering but she heard him. As she pulled the brake levers she saw a film of darkness cover her hands—Zal's *andalune* body, spreading out. He was including her to enhance her pitiful aetheric senses. They slowed and came to a halt. She put her feet down and waited, wishing the damn bike had a sound again, so that it could at least feel alive and that they were not suddenly abandoned.

"What?" she prompted, hoping this stop would be short.

She didn't like to think about how spooked the place made her. Compared to human normal she was almost invulnerable, but here she felt very vulnerable, out of her depth. She looked up at the sky for reassurance, but between the heavy foliage the little chinks of blue and white were coated with a brownish green taint. Much as she attempted to formulate a proof of the phenomenon in physical terms, she failed. The forest was cutting down the light, increasing the shadows under its branches. Now that she looked more closely she saw that what plants remained on the ground were dying or dead. The only place they flourished was beside the road where there was still a channel of sunlight. There was a profound sensation of being utterly adrift from civilisation, even though the expressway wasn't even a mile distant, and the city itself just beyond. They could have been in the wilderness. Also, her signalling systems were having major connection problems reaching outside links and she knew for certain there was a support mast on the hill behind them relaying traffic at maximum width for the southern half of the city. Part of it was due to Zal—whereas he used to be dampened by metals, aetherically neutered, now he had the power to seriously dampen their effects in return—but mostly, she knew, it was the damn woods.

Zal leaned back away from her and turned, looking all around them. "That's so strange," he said, quietly, his words swallowed instantly by the swamp of silence. They sounded deadened even as they came out of his mouth. "When I was here before I felt the earth element, though it always had this tinge of something unusual about it. I didn't really care at the time. Now that's much stronger, and the secondary elements are here in force: wood, a lot of wood, and that's tainted too, with the same thing."

"I don't see the ghosts." She scanned on maximum detection levels, all frequencies. Ghosts could sometimes register on extreme electromagnetic spectra and occasionally traces of their passing could be perceived as absence of information, gaps in the signals. But unless you were almost inside one or happened to catch it against a background of some strong radiation, you'd be lucky to notice a thing.

"They weren't ordinary ghosts," he said. "This isn't an ordinary wood, not even an ordinary energy sink. I kinda knew it was weird when I could go out and find ways into Zoomenon. The gap between the worlds was so thin in places, you could nearly step across without meaning to. But just between Zoo and here. Not to anywhere else." He hesitated, sniffing. "It's gathering. Did something happen here in Otopia or old Earth?"

Lila filed "gathering" away under "ask later" although she thought she'd guessed what he meant already—the site had formed enough focus by the natural processes of being a sink to move from passive collection to active—and flipped through the historical records. Accessing the city databases was difficult. "I'm getting a lot of signal failure," she admitted finally. "And the long-term data on this site is in the slow archives. It could take hours to pull it all out." She sent a message to Bentley, asking for the data to be readied, not confident it would get through.

"Okay." He moved back into riding position. "Let's roll."

She eased the throttle and was almost surprised when they moved into a quick glide. With every turn their passage began to feel more and more like an unwelcome intrusion. Boulders that had not been there previously had moved close to the corners of the road, blocking sightlines. Trees near the edges leaned out precipitously, their largest branches stretching towards each other across the gaps. In places the canopy cut out nearly all light and this effect increased as they neared the lowest point of the hollow where the house lay in wait. Lila could hardly believe it was only weeks since she had been there with Malachi. Then it had been spooky and unpleasant. Now it was as though another hundred years had gone by. Once she would never have believed in the literal truth of such an observation.

She pinged the south-city transmitter and noted, with dismay, that there was a significant delay on the line. The reply was late, weak, and decayed, as if it were passing across light-years and around gravity wells, not just a few miles. She requested a time check. There was a ten-minute discrepancy to her internal clock.

"Time's accelerated in here," she said, to herself as much as to Zal, and then they came to the final curve and she hit the brakes. They slid to a halt on the rough surface. Before them the vast, agglutinated mass of the house slumped in blackened ruin.

Spars of old timbers jutted from it at all angles. Fitful smokes wreathed the air, oozing from crevices all over the crumpled wreckage and rising up towards the open sky only to be shredded by minute gusts of a wind that moved erratically, unpredictably. Lila suspected air elementals and then saw their angular, weightless shapes form and vanish in the darker gouts as they played with the rising billows.

Now she noticed heat, faint at this distance, but certain, radiating onto her skin. And she saw the fire. It was hard not to see it. It was every-where, blazing in sheeted infernos, jetting sideways from the mouths of the ground-floor windows as if fuelled by pressured gas. But it was not there. Transparent, nebulous, it stormed unceasingly over the dead house whilst the tiny smokes rose through it unheeding; the ghost of fire.

"What the hell is that?"

She felt Zal get off the bike and release her waist. At the same time a sudden slithering pressure ran over her, making her hiss with horror before she realised it was the dress—forgotten Tatterdemalion—changing shape.

From the flimsy straps of the sundress a torrent of heavy cotton jacquard and linen went tumbling to the ground. It swathed her arms and draped her to the floor in panels of perfectly pressed white fabric. Beneath them cream and gold robes came pouring in a flood. They were so heavy she felt herself adjusting to take the weight. Peaks of stiff, stitched cloth constructed themselves into a mantle with curious pagoda-like edging over each shoulder and drew in a close-fitted high collar to the base of her jaw. Undersleeves tautened, oversleeves billowed and edged themselves with silver and gold. Stitching ran like water into the signs and sigils of magical texts Lila had never read and never would understand. She only identified them courtesy of Sarasilien's vast database. The marks predated his knowledge.

There was sudden pressure on her forehead and around her cheeks and nose. She found herself wearing a headdress, with a mask and a veil and a kind of bandit facecloth that hung down in a point to her chest, where it was finished off with a silvered-charm tassel, heavy with miniaturised icons. From the inside the entire effect was stifling but she knew better than to argue with the thing. It must have its reasons, and for once they didn't entirely seem mocking, although she wasn't sure about that. She looked like High Priest meets Samurai inside a wedding cake. It wasn't what she'd have chosen, given a choice. There was no choice, however; there was only Tatters, a faery so ancient that even old faeries had forgotten her.

Through the winsome muslin of the veil and the mesh-covered eyes of the mask underneath, it was hard to see much of anything that Lila had seen two seconds ago. In its place what she saw made her wish she hadn't come at all.

She got off the bike, with some difficulty, and faced the intense, confusing maelstrom in front of them with blank incomprehension. She felt that too soon this would turn into horror and distress, but for the time being she could settle for incomprehension. In the distance she could hear Zal say, "Nice frock, Tripitaka." He was looking at the house, however, and she wondered if he saw what she was seeing with the faery's help.

The building was burning. The flames were furious, yellow and orange. They roared and snapped. The building was drowning. Streams of black light poured from its windows and doors, through the holes in its roofs. They twisted around, consuming smoke. The building was exploding. Every solid piece of it was bursting into motes of colour and light. All of this took place inside the eye of a tornado, focused on the house. Spinning walls of energy sucked the debris— flame, smoke, darkness, colour—towards themselves. They tore them apart and threw them together. The house was imploding. This destruction turned in on itself, as if invisible fists were punching dough down into smaller and smaller rounds. It collapsed, became transdimensional, inverted itself. From this pinprick at the heart of the storm, small as a hydrogen atom, something came leaking, came sneaking, came winding like a thread of smoke. So insubstantial. So almost nothing. It was less than visible to the naked eye, less than a dot. It was not light, not dark. The only reason she knew it was there was because something must be there and yet nothing was. Her AI mapped it and made up something so that there was something to see.

"I say again, what the hell is that?" Her voice bounced back at her, hot, damp, small, scratchy. She snatched up the veil and the mask and looked with her own eyes. The ghostly fire, the ruin was still there, smoking. No sign of any of the other things, just the air elementals gyring slowly, speeded, she now saw, if they touched the places where the tornado whirled. If you removed the complication of so much elemental confusion, of the layers and the temporal abnormalities and the rest, the thing she couldn't see directly looked a lot like a very, very small black hole.

Zal didn't reply for a long time. When she assumed he had nothing to say, he said, "Who was living here? Were there people in there?"

"Azevedo, a worldwalker, and Jones, the same."

"Calliope Jones, Malachi's contact," Zal said, filling in for himself. "Two strandlopers."

"Azevedo was time-lapsed," Lila said. Reluctantly she replaced the veil and mask and stared at the churning energy forms, trying and failing to deduce a cause.

"Before she came here, or after?"

"I don't know." It had all happened in the gap of fifty. She trawled the fire-service records, patching the files as they came. Her suspicion was rewarded in part. There had been a real fire here. "There was no callout. The fire service came only after someone reported seeing smoke from the beach. Maybe it was empty when this happened." She called Azevedo's number, yanking it from Malachi's database. It returned the disconnected tone.

"No, I don't think so."

She didn't ask why. She couldn't see anything that looked remotely like a human survivor, although the ruin was extensive and they hadn't even begun a search. A few weeks ago she'd been here and it was overgrown, but the house was fine. In part because she wanted to know and in part to stop herself from having to look at the maelstrom anymore, or deal with it, she walked down the path away from the house towards the hillside where the terraced gardens and pool area dropped steadily to the beach.

The vegetation—it couldn't be called a garden anymore—had increased dramatically in the time between her visits. Years of growth bulged and draped on all sides. Kudzu and other vines were consuming the abandoned furniture on the poolside and creeping down into the empty pool itself. Green lines of algae followed a trickle of water where the fountains and bubbling stream used to play. The path was choked with grass, and on the poor ground where stone walls shored up the hillside to stop it falling into the sea, huge glades of knotweed spread their diamond leaves. It made her nervous. She pinged the tower using a tangled quantum signal to get around the local temporal eddies.

The tower said it was three in the afternoon. Six hours in about six minutes, she reckoned. One day every twenty-four minutes. Almost three per hour. Given the growth rates and placing the start time back to her last visit just for theory, that indicated that whatever the time-slip problem was, it was something that had started out slowly and accelerated, was possibly still accelerating. Maintaining a constant signal measure, she began to run. The heavy robes caught on every-thing. She heard the odd rip but didn't slow down. At least the skirts were more like a fighter's tunic at the bottom and left enough room to move. A few moments later she pushed free of the last knotweed stems and emerged onto the rock-strewn sand of the small cove that stretched to the limits of the Folly's land.

The ghost ship *Matilda* belonging to Jones was still there. What was left of it had been dragged up above the high-water mark and left to decay. As a structure that wasn't truly material, it ought to have evaporated by now, if ghost research was to be believed. But the frame and remaining platework, though rusted and warped, looked all too material to Lila. However, the liminal blue were-light of ghostly things that had clung to its every edge was no more.

"Ghost leaves a body," she said to herself. She went closer. The metal was iron but it was very thin and broke up when she touched it, crumbling onto the sand where a large reddish stain of similar particles already marked the spot. "Blood of ships." Aside from that the cove was unmarked—nobody had been here. She took some measurements and left hurriedly, running to start with and then adding power so that her strides almost flew her up the steps and over the pool terrace. The conflagration burned on, half real, half done with, yet to come.

"Zal?" she shouted, though the fire wasn't a loud one, barely a hiss. A sinking feeling accompanied the notion that once again they had become separated, once again . . .

"I'm here."

She turned and saw him emerge from the thick foliage just behind her.

"I was checking the woods for elementals."

"I thought you'd gone inside." She couldn't conceal the relief in her voice.

"No," he stared at the house with dislike. "I don't think I can go in there."

"What about Friday?" She didn't relish the idea of trying to go any closer herself, but she wasn't convinced it was impossible.

"What about him? If he was in there he probably isn't anymore." He stood and stared at the conflagration, resigned.

"I hate to leave without trying." But the time slip preyed on her mind. The veil sucked against her mouth as she took a breath. "And what about Azevedo, and Jones?" But she didn't leap forward with enthusiasm. She walked, slowly, inching her way forward and felt a sharp increase in radioactivity as she neared the rubble where the door used to be. Aetheric charges became more powerful. She began to experience the strangest feeling of bursts of deadness in her limbs. At the same time the faery clothes became heavier, the linen a set of leaden plates, the delicate mask a helm. It cut down the trouble but it didn't cut it out. She reckoned she could last maybe two minutes inside the house. Maybe less. And then she didn't know what would happen but she was reasonably certain she wouldn't be coming out.

Reluctantly she backed away. "If they were in there, they'll have to stay. I don't like the look of this. Let's get the hell out of here."

"We should put a ward around the perimeter of the property." Zal retreated to the bike. "Stop any accidental trespass."

She nodded her assent. "So, nothing in the forest?" The bike started on the fourth try. She had to supply extra charge. The battery had run flat.

"Au contraire," Zal said, helping her to stuff the robes under both of them and out of the way of the wheels. "The forest is nothing but one big ecosystem of elemental power. The only difference is that it isn't manifesting higher forms anymore."

"And in human-speak?"

"In human-speak, there aren't any more creatures. There's just wood, earth, water, metal, fire, and the rest of it, sitting around in a huge weatherlike arrangement, gathering power. Around conscious beings, the elements behave a bit like ghosts, and accrue features like living beings."

"Meaning there are no minds around here?"

"Surely not for a long time."

Implying that very shortly, there would be again.

She couldn't get out of there fast enough but she made herself stop at the turn onto the road. Long afternoon shadows streaked across the hardtop. "Does it stop here? At the property line?"

"Not exactly," he said. "It's back from the road. And what's with the sun, were we asleep?"

She explained the temporal shift to him, or rather, she stated it, because an explanation was far from her capacity. All she could think about were the two women and Friday—who counted as a couple of hundred in his own right. Had they been in there? What had happened?

"It's bad, isn't it?" she said, feeling the press at her back, the urge to move forward inexorable as she let the brake levers slip.

"Pretty bad," he said, only the emptiness of tone in his voice giving away the impact it had had on him. "But you still owe me dinner and dancing, and I think we should focus on that, while there still is dinner and dancing."

"When in danger or in doubt, return to flip-mode and tune out," Lila said, scornful and envious.

Zal didn't answer.

Her stomach burned. She appeased her need to do the right thing by transmitting everything to Bentley and having a fast, data-only conversation about who should know and what to do. By the time they were on the road the Agency was already mustering its response and she felt she had bought herself a window of redress. If Zal had known what she was doing—but she thought perhaps he did, because he was sharp and knew her—he would be angry, so to deflect that she said, "It might be hard getting a table dressed as Our Lady of the Violent Gateaux."

He laughed and finally his hands found a way through the layers and rested on her waist. He gave her a squeeze that let her know he did indeed understand that she was already trying to put together a one-woman posse against the problems of the world and that she shouldn't, but since she had, he could only squeeze her warningly in an effort to retransmit his feelings on the subject. He spat a mouthful of veil out. "In this town? You must be kidding."

Privately she prayed to the dress for mercy. She hated to be noticed, or at least, hated to be noticed for looking like a twinky bishop of the latter-day morons, but as was its habit the faery had assumed a position on the day's events and showed no sign of a change. Today was Apocalypse Lite and Lila was the catwalk model.

CHAPTER SEVEN

The bathrooms at Pete's Grill were big, which was good because getting out of the robes was a space- and time-consuming exercise. Also, they refused to be got out of in the way Lila had hoped. The waistbands and shirts tightened up on her, the cuffs closed, and the collar threatened to choke. When she tried to pull the masks and veil off, they tangled on her hands. After a few minutes of this pointless fight she gave up with a furious roar and sat on the can in a stoney silence, acres of unsuitable ancient material, richly tapestried, bunched around her waist. The glyphs and inscriptions glinted cheaply in the economy lighting. An ancient ward against unseen evils rested against a graffitied tile bearing instructions that Angela would fuck for free, and a badly drawn illustration of the same.

"I can't believe you're doing this to me!" Lila hissed to Tatter-demalion, although she could believe it only too well and there was nothing left to do but roll her eyes and grit her teeth. She heard the door open and ordinary women in ordinary clothing come in, talking and starting to fix their makeup in the mirror.

At least Pete's Grill was unpretentious. Celebrities didn't go there, it wasn't noted in Best of Bay City. It existed halfway between the interstate and the suburbs in a part of town that was mostly made up of strip malls and light industrial units in the middle of a district known as Moths—the last bastion of otherworld-friendly locales. It served old-style Otopian cookery and outworld specials, had no menus other than what the waitresses could remember at any given moment, and was run by Pete himself, a ruggedly handsome cowboy type of man, rail-thin and unshaven, who couldn't have looked more out of place anywhere other than in an apron in front of a pristine barbecue range.

Lila and Zal liked it because Pete hated everyone with simple unmitigated contempt for all beings. He relished his hate as he lavished it verbally upon them through the kitchen screens. He hated them so much and loathed them so dearly that he loved them all in a deep, philanthropic, unshakeable manner, primal in its absolute nature, and they felt welcomed. Because of this it didn't attract many people who couldn't at least grasp this basic fact of grill existence, but even among the enlightened Lila didn't fancy being stared at and talked about. Not that this wouldn't happen because of Zal anyway. In fact, the case was hopeless. She was just thinking she had to give up even trying to have anything resembling a normal life, even for five minutes, when the chatter outside the cubicle caught her attention.

". . . being dead isn't all it's cracked up to be."

"Tell me about it. First they're happy to see you, then they're scared shitless of you, and after that pretty much everyone doesn't know what to do with you."

"Yeah, I can tell they kind of wish I was dead again, you know? And I can't help it that bits of their stuff goes missing. I mean, it's not like I'm taking it, you know? But as soon as anything happens it's like—oh, let's search Alice, she's probably evil."

"I know. And they're always watching you, like they think you're gonna freak out or something and nobody knows what to say. It's the shits. And they're always asking—"

"Yeah, like, what's it like, being dead, and you say you don't know because you're not and you don't remember, there's this gap and they're so pissed because you can't tell them anything. I mean. They totally got this priest out the other day to exorcise me. And they're all like—no offence, Alice, it's just that we heard a lot of stuff about you dead people not really being you and all. Can you believe that? I mean, we can't be dead can we, because we're like—here."

"Did it work?"

"Hell, no. Nothing happened. He made them all guilty like it was their fault I was here and went off with six hundred bucks on his card. The fucker."

"Totally." There was a pause and then the sound of the emergency door being pushed open and leant on as the two of them went outside for a smoke. Faery weed and 'bacco.

"D'you know what's the worst?" Alice said after they'd been quiet a minute. "I feel like a total disappointment. I can't work, can't do anything, have to carry this stupid tag around everywhere to show I'm supposed to be dead. Sometimes I wonder if I *am* evil. I mean, you wouldn't know, you'd just carry it, like a disease, like a cloud. Nothing's good since I came back whether it's true or not. I'd kinda like to die just so I could fix things, but I'm too angry and . . . I don't know how."

"Yeah," sighed the friend. "Tell me about it."

"When we get to the interstate we can get a ride. They won't know."

"Yeah, you think north?"

"Yeah, north or wherever. You know?"

"Mmn hmm."

Lila stood up and flushed, shook out the robes, and exited the stall. The room wasn't big enough for them not to turn and see her. Against the brilliant light of the late-afternoon sun they were just slightly transparent at the edges. They stood and stared at her, two teenagers in dated clothes with too much blusher on so that their faces looked like dolls' faces. They recoiled slightly, but when she did nothing they turned back to their smokey huddle.

Lila washed her hands and checked herself in the mirror as if she looked like this every day. Then she learned that her hat was nunlike, a kind of gothic wimple with drapes. The mask was warriorish around the eyes, fierce, with gold flecks for exaggerated lashes. For all she said about it being ridiculous it looked imposing. If you were going to invigilate the end of the world, it's what you'd probably hope to wear.

She dried her hands in the airblaster and watched her sleeves billow. Then, unable to prevent herself, she turned around and saw the dead girls again. There was an intensity, a focus to them that was unnerving. They held the cheap smoke as if it was precious oxygen and watched her, bold and strangely submissive at the same time, waiting for her to make her move. Since she'd already earwigged their conversation and intruded more than anyone had a right to, she felt bad, and because of Max she felt double bad, and the nun outfit, which was another lie felt worse yet, but as the seconds passed she found nothing to say other than a choked, "Bless you."

And with that pathetic line she made her getaway.

Zal had ordered for both of them by the time she reached the table and for once she didn't care. She slid into the booth next to him, so shocked by the banality and horror of the conversation she'd just witnessed that she didn't know what to say.

For the first time she really considered the question—why were they here at all? They hadn't appeared until Xaviendra's intervention. Xaviendra had made and resurrected the dead as a temporary army in Otopia. Certainly she was involved. But Lila's written message to Max was equally powerful, she thought. All her thoughts about causes led her consistently to one place: Under. But she dared not speak openly about Under, or even covertly, not anywhere where there might be people capable of overhearing.

"It isn't your fault, Lila," Zal said as the waitress arrived with water and a jug of Faery Lite. She placed frozen mugs in front of them, a plate of beernuts, a plate of some elf things Lila didn't know the name of but which looked not unlike a fruit salad, and a bowl of potato chips. She didn't give Lila a second glance.

Lila looked at each of the dishes, reached out, and filled her mug with clear golden ale from the pitcher, gave the pitcher to Zal, and said, "Why does it feel like it is, then?"

He paused and took a long drink. "You know what's interesting? I don't need to name anything specific and you just assume it's your fault. I don't even need to question that there will be something that fits the concept of 'your fault,' whether it's the crap that passes for motorbikes these days or the change in the weather or the existence of some weird-ass wormhole where my old house used to be. Or all of those."

"Still feels like it is though," she said quietly and defiantly.

Zal shrugged. "There are a billion people out there, of one kind and another, and about a million of them reckon themselves players in whatever's going down. Most of them are wrong. Everyone is a player, but few players ever have the trick hand, and when they do have it, most likely they don't know and never will know they had it."

He paused and she noted that he wasn't able to name Xaviendra, or was unwilling. "I got all this from Mal by the way. And what happened to you makes it seem like you're the middle of things, and you are. You're the middle of your things, your life, your stuff. But you're not The Middle. There are about a million other fuckers out there fucking up everything regardless of what you do. So relax." He was frowning as he pushed the plates away, pulling the beer and the pitcher towards himself with slow reluctance.

"Are you okay?" She pushed the dishes to the other side of the table, trying to look into his face to calm a sudden feeling of alarm. His hair hanging down made it hard.

"Can't eat," he muttered, anger a bad note in his voice. "I feel like I want to but . . ." he tried again, picked up the fork, brought it close, sniffed the fruit, opened his mouth. He threw it down suddenly with a clatter that turned the faces of the closest diners towards them for a brief moment.

Lila realised she hadn't seen him eat anything since their reunion. Drink yes. And she'd assumed he'd been feeding himself—their schedules hadn't exactly crossed much. "Can't eat because you're ill or—"

"No," he bit out, filling his glass to the brim and watching a few faery suds roll over and down the side of the mug, their iridescent bubbles showing tiny images of clouds that blew into the shape of dragons and then away. "Fucking dragons," he muttered. "But it's not their fault. Jack's doing. Curse him to the seven hells." He picked up the mug and took a long draught, but she could see it was a struggle to swallow it, as though it were mud and not beer, solid and not liquid, ten times heavier than its weight. When he was done, he was snarling and his hand on the mug handle was a fist.

She put her hand out to his, to touch his skin and make deeper contact. His fingers felt as they always had—bony and strong, but now that she realised it, too light. Zal was solid enough. He had flesh, he was as real as the waitress or the table or the food, but there was an insubstantial quality to him that couldn't be measured in kilograms or density. It was like he was made of something different altogether, something that was pretending to be a solid body very successfully, but wasn't good on the details. As there was no obvious data to confirm this notion with what she could consider factual evidence, it had gone straight under the mental rug where she swept everything she couldn't confirm. There was a lot under that rug.

She folded his hand into hers and felt him squeeze her gently, even though he kept staring straight ahead at the fascinating pink naugahyde of the seat on the other side of the booth.

She tried prompting, "When we left the void ships you had to go back with Tath, through Under. This is why?"

His face was grim, a rare expression for him, and his voice was barely controlled, though quiet. "When the second sister lifted me from Under, she didn't take my body with her. It's gone now, buried in Winter. Then the sisters made me a body out of cloth, but when Glinda took me to the Fleet, I lost that too. If I went to Demonia with you and Teazle directly I'd have been a ghost or a shadow. Any bloody necromancer could have eaten me for lunch. But Glinda told me there was a way for me to get a new body that would survive here. A dragon told me the same thing. I sat at Ilya's fireside and the longer I stayed in his firelight, the more solid I became. The element filled me up. But it's not the same as the old one. It wears away."

"It's too light," she said.

"Yes. It's made of light. I'm not what I used to be. I'm more like an illusion or a faery glamour. Good enough to drink certain things, if they're magical enough. Good enough to fight and fuck. But not good enough to eat it seems. I can't even put it in my mouth. It's like I'm blocked."

Lila felt the distance between them increase. "Who's Glinda?"

At that moment the waitress reappeared with the rest of their order and Lila had to lean back as the table was filled with steak, ribs, potato salad, and bread. Dishes of hot pie and ice cream filled the gaps. The smell rising from it all was thick and sweet.

Nostrils wide, inhaling deeply, Zal said, "Glinda is my death. Atropos, the last Valkyr, necessity, destiny, What Must and Shall Be—whatever you like to call her. Sister Number Three. Doesn't matter. I'm still hungry." He drained the mug on the second draught and gave a short, unhappy sigh.

Now that food was present and glorious, Lila found that she was starving. It seemed wrong to eat when he couldn't. She stared at the food. "Destiny. And you're not moved by her personal interference in your life? That doesn't make you important?"

Zal picked up a rib and licked it forlornly. "It makes me important to her for reasons best known to herself. That's all. I didn't ask her about it. Seemed—what's that word you humans like to use—

inappropriate. You had a dragon hanging around your bra for weeks. Did you ask it questions? No. Quite rightly. Because you know damn well that whatever you want to believe about yourself it wasn't your instrument, you were just some legs and arms it wanted to use for a while. Now eat for fucksakes."

"Playthings of the gods?" Lila said. She picked up a rib dripping in barbecue sauce and a cold, unkind pleasure rolled over her as she imagined what that was going to do to the faery dress.

"Not gods. Just bigger and badder than you in the scheme of things." Zal dropped the rib onto his plate and picked up the steak in both hands, running his tongue over the dripping, peppered edge. He licked his lips then tossed the whole thing onto her plate and wiped his hands meticulously on her immaculate sleeve. "Fuck 'em all to hell."

After that most of her hunger deserted her. She picked at everything and then asked for it to be bagged up. "We can take it back for Sassy. If she's still there."

"Yeah," Zal said, although now his voice was quite different. Wondering anger marked it so strongly it made her look up with a jolt. "If we make it out of here alive."

Lila followed his gaze. He was looking across the diner and out of the misted, greasy windows into the parking lot where a cluster of semis screened off most of the highway. She didn't see the trouble until a few seconds later, which was still earlier than most.

A large group of cars and trucks had pulled up on the outer edge of the lot and now the passengers were getting out. They shared a slow, deliberate style of action, which confirmed in Lila's mind and heart that they were bad news. They were wearing shirts and armbands with the same logo, a skull and crossbones in red. She counted thirty, until a group of bikers rode up bearing the same sign on their jackets—hastily applied in most cases, over older colours. Her data lookup was working perfectly. She heard Bentley replying in her mind's ear before she was even aware of asking the question, "That's Deadkill. They're one of the vigilante groups I told you about. They kill Returners and anyone who tries to stop them. Very organised. They will wait until they find undead before they start shooting, but after that I'd say all bets are off."

Lila replied silently, digitally. "There are demons with them, I see two. And maybe a kind of fae." Guns had begun to appear, methodically pulled from vehicles and handed out. Ammunition was loaded, checked. It hadn't occurred to her before that the Returners were as killable as any other human being, but it must be so. She didn't see any special weapons.

"Yes. The demons are part of a set that hunt around looking for violent crime most likely. There are a few in the City area. And Dead-kill have Hunter Children as members according to the last seized records but they organise by blip at the last minute and keep their plans off the networks. This must have been cued in the last twenty minutes—yeah, uh-huh, I see the phone nets passed out a list bleep forty-two minutes ago so that will be the signal, not that you can tell what it is until it breaks. Just unlucky you're there. Or lucky. Depending."

Lila took a bigger scan of the area and the net. "I don't see any cops."

Bentley hummed. "Ah, the emergency call record . . . they've been scammed. All the ones in your area have been pulled on fake calls, at least, I bet they're fakes. Just far enough to be away."

"Can you get backup?"

"Not sooner than fifteen minutes. On their way but . . ."

Now the other people in the diner had noticed what was going on outside. Disbelief and uncertainty meant they were still seated for the most part and apart from a few raised voices there was still nothing amiss inside.

Lila turned to Zal. "Demons, one fae, lots of guns. Fifty. At least. Maybe more on the way." She turned back, alert, systems running, lifting, speeding. Her blood seemed to freeze though it was accelerating. "Gasoline cans. Flame throwers. Shock prods." And there were other things in the arsenals that didn't fit with the story of simple killing either; ropes and shackles, and chains.

The waitress came to their table, her attention on the windows. She dumped a large brown paper sack full of food containers in front of them and said, mostly to herself, "Now what the heck is that? Some kinda convention?"

Lila stood up and pushed out beside her—no easy feat in the mass of the robes. The woman looked at Lila's hands on her arms and opened her pink-lipsticked mouth to object.

"Exit," Lila said, firmly but quietly. "Is there a back way out?" She had no faith that the lynch mob wouldn't have thought of this first but she had to know.

"Through the kitchen but—"

"Do you have a cold store?"

"Yeah but—"

"You need to get everyone and move inside it, lock yourselves in. Right now." Cold stores had at least some reinforcements in their structures, mostly, she thought. Better than being in the open anyway. Anything would be better than that.

She ran her eyes over the customers. They were moving now, standing, grabbing their stuff, dropping their cutlery . . . There were kids, teenagers, all kinds of people. She couldn't tell just by looking at them if any of them were Returners but there were certainly fae there in their "slob" glamour forms, disguised as ordinary people, so unspecial your eye would slide over them twice without noticing. And Zal. And her.

The outside mob showed no signs of hurrying their marshalling. They were forming up facing the door and windows, weapons hefted openly. They didn't shout too much. Another bad sign, she thought, pushing at the waitress's slack response. "Move! For your life! Get into the store room!" People heard her now and reacted to the voice of authority she'd pulled from her repertoire, but they were still slow and then the sluggish, dumb air and its steady flub of old country music was pierced by a howling scream from the dim corner where the sign for the ladies' blinked in broken neon.

Then everyone ran as Lila stood still, knowing what it meant, momentarily paralysed by the horror she felt, the surge of dry, deathly fear. The girls on the fire-exit steps had taken too long over their last smoke. They were caught.

She felt Zal push past her as he jumped over the table, from there over the heads of the panicking customers, onto another counter, onto the bar, over to the windows. Shadow flooded out from him, a cloud of unnatural, impenetrable darkness. His speed and the recognition that he could buy them a few seconds by hiding them and confusing the enemy galvanised her.

A staccato burst of fire from a machine gun broke through the screams that filled the room now, driving the panic. She registered its meaning—it came from the back—as if it were old news. The dead girls were dead again.

Now she had to struggle to fight through the bodies rushing past her. She heard glass break at the front and registered the presence of petrol in the air. Too heavy to properly ignite it coated a table in weak yellow flame. Fury and loathing filled her. She reached the door, crossing the zone of black that Zal had trailed. Beside her she felt his presence, stronger, brighter, and realised he ate the light—he ate the light—it was so important in its impossibility, but it wasn't important now, there was no time for it. Instead her hand was opening the door and her foot was kicking it aside on its pathetic hinges that gave just like the calculations told her they would so the whole thing burst free and went flying, low and whirling, a missile, into the front lines of the band standing below the steps. They scattered like bowling pins.

She held up the palm of her hand, displaying the lit Agency emblem, and amplified her voice, almost to the point of pain.

"Your gathering and assault is illegal and you will disperse or be arrested. Lay down your arms. Surrender the shooters. They are under arrest. Any obstruction to my authority will be considered an act of assault." Which covered her, not that she expected it to work.

The faces looking at her were a real picture with their comic mixture of disbelief, bloodthirst, hate, and incredulity. They really weren't in any shape for thinking straight. She longed to kill them.

Around her the robes shifted, tightening, drawing in, threads moving of their own accord, making new designs, new words. Across her chest a red cross appeared, tangled in a spiral of red like a spider's web, a white flower at its apex as the faery declared its colours.

And is this what it had come to at last, she thought as she surveyed the crowd, wondering which one was going to shoot first, or if they'd shout first and gather their nerves, wait for the ones at the back to signal they were in position. For surely they didn't look uncertain, no, they had decided there would be no prisoners, no innocents here. Lila against the humans, not human anymore, a monster worthy of hate? She despised her own drama even as she felt it catch and flame inside. But she stood and stared at them, judging their willing greed for blood and suffering, their righteous, ugly determination. She saw the promise of being crushed in the narrow vices of their eyes, she heard once more the burst of the machine guns in her mind and heard the silence of the despairing undead who had got what they wanted here on this luckless, lucky day, and she hated them more still.

Then a slow drawl interrupted her moment. "Well now, who the fuck are you dressed as?"

Their leader, a worked-out man, handsome, in construction-worker overalls and holding a shotgun, gestured at her with the double finger of the barrels. It was a contemptuous, lingering kind of move, the sort that men make in sleazy nightclubs when they're sizing up the girls on the poles. It gave the crowd confidence and their stunned moment of immobility departed in a ripple of sneers and laughter. They moved forward until his languid arm movement stopped them. The fact that she'd kicked an entire door into their front line seemed to have slipped their notice as they slid together into a pack.

Lila's attention sharpened to a point. She heard the group around the back talking, saying something about sending news round to the front, there was a brief argument, then a messenger came running around the side. The people in front of her stopped for a gawk when they saw the situation, then trotted forward to whisper in the leader's ear. Meanwhile Lila could see Zal inside the diner, clear on infrared despite his cloak of shadow. He was shepherding people into the kitchen area. They were almost all inside. She waited until the messenger had delivered his news, a whisper she heard clearly, and then said, "You're all under arrest. Put down your weapons."

In reply the construction guy primed his shotgun with the flashy one-arm style of a movie star and pointed the business end at her. "People who get in our way get killed. We came for the undead abominations. Stand aside."

"What's the petrol for then?" Lila asked, making her final calculations as she mapped the location of all the people and weapons.

"Tainted ground," he said, grinning. "Has to be cleansed. And places like this that harbour the filth, have to be razed."

"There are innocent people and kids in there," Lila said, stalling, though she sensed a fresh urgency as some of the mob checked the time and realised they were going to run into police trouble soon. She read them the full records, her conviction absolute. "And I don't take assurances from people who already made three similar raids in the last month all over the southern-states area. Fifty-six casualties. Twenty-one dead. Fifteen of them ordinary human citizens, four teenagers, one child of seven. You are under arrest for murder, attempted murder, conspiracy to murder, conspiracy to cause civil disturbance, riot, incitement to hate, incitement to riot, causing a disturbance of the peace, destruction of property, arson, illegal possession of weapons, membership of an illegal organisation, resisting arrest, and obstructing the path of justice."

Her litany had the desired mesmerising effect on the front rows even as some members were cautiously peeling themselves off the back of the crowd and sidling away. She wasn't done with the last word before she was already moving.

She saw the leader's finger on the trigger pulling steadily, but she was on him before they'd moved more than a few millimetres. Even his blink of surprise was a slow, clumsy piece of shutterwork to her as she took the gun away from him, popped out the shells, and manacled his wrists together with the twisted barrels. It was a tight fit. She broke a bone in his wrist doing it and then she broke a few more as she pressed the figure eight all the way closed. They snapped like twigs and she felt every pop as a bubble of cold glee. As she stepped back, moving into human time, the plastic shell cases fell at her feet. Most of the bystanders were too surprised by her speed to do anything but stand and stare, but some, the hardcore who had come wired and been frothing during the conversation period, were liberated by the burst of action. Their minds weren't on realism and whatever odd danger Lila represented, they were focused on violence.

Their liberation was hers too. She picked up the closest agitator, crushing his hand around the grip of his stun gun where it was trying to shock her into jelly, and lifted him off his feet. With a short spin and a burst of energy robbed from the gun that was meant to incapacitate her, she flung him across ten heads into the chest of a middle-aged grizzler brandishing a minigun. The stun gun, clamped by broken fingers, was still fizzing at maximum battery power. It connected with the other man as they both went down onto the tarmac, scattering several others and pushing their part of the crowd back. As they jolted around together, Lila was already airborne in a leap that took her in the other direction to where a woman was lighting up the pilot on her flamethrower—a homemade but serious object that reeked of leaking kerosene and was almost as much danger to the holder as anyone else.

With her fingers edging into blades, Lila cut the tank off its old rucksack-strap moorings on the woman's denimed shoulders and swung it around hard. The woman, still holding the gun end firmly, was yanked off balance as the hoses dragged on her arms, then she let go in surprise and got a spray of paraffin into her eyes as the loose end of the hose whipped around, sprinkling everyone in range. Tatterdemalion took her share, Lila could smell it, but she wasn't bothered by such small irritations as fire. She twisted and crushed the crude metal kerosene tank and flung it in a low arc across the thin strip of ground between the diner and the crowd, then directed her own burst of intense narrow-band microwave heat from the palm of her hand at the flying metal.

Liquid sprayed wildly out through the splits in the tank as it expanded, dousing the ground. The steel tank itself sparked violently, contorting as it tumbled to a halt. Mobmen scattered instinctively around it, most backing off. The pilot light, dying but still going, finally landed near enough to ignite the vapour and with a burst of hot yellow and a wave of fresh heat the entire left side of the building had been cut off from the assault by a low wall of flame. It wouldn't deter maniacs but it was bad enough that anyone with doubts wasn't going that way.

However, in spite of her quick thinking the diner door was open now and attackers were shouldering their way inside, ignoring the bellowing of those who had been downed, and spurred on by a sense of thwarted righteousness. Torches had been flung onto the roof. This above all convinced Lila that Deadkill were a bunch of amateur hate-suckers. The roof was tiled and, like all city buildings, it would take a lot more than a piece of burning wood to set it alight. She wasn't justified in killing even one of them on grounds of stupidity alone.

She blasted the outside crowd with a burst of infrasound that sent most of them grabbing for their pants as their bowels dropped everything without warning and then ran for the door.

She didn't trust herself to punch anyone without dealing a killing blow so she kept the violence down to some light slaps that cannoned skulls together in pairs with enough force to yield temporary unconsciousness and mild concussion. As they slumped in the gangways she bent to collect their weapons and destroyed them with a few casual wrenches of her hands before dropping them on the bodies. She sniffed the air. Something was burning.

In the kitchen a couple of meat patties and a bacon strip had become char. Lila turned off the burners and looked through to the store-room door. It was shut. A terrified silence like a held breath made the room feel as though it might burst. She wondered where Zal had gone, but her answer was soon discovered as she steeled herself and walked out through the emergency exit.

A pall of intense gloom hung over the open door and its steps. It didn't block out the sight of the dead girls. Pooling blood from their fallen bodies dripped down the open iron slats of the stairs onto the hardtop. Zal was crouched on the handrail above them like a great black crow.

Behind him, in the walls, a string of bullet holes peppered an uninterrupted line telling her that they'd already shot him. Beyond the darkness that he was maintaining she heard confused talk, complaints, and angry voices as people blundered around. It became clear to her that they weren't only lost in the murk he'd created, they were weak and sleepy too. She heard them fall over each other, mumbling as though drugged.

On the rail Zal was utterly still with concentration. She recognised the vampiric embrace of a shadowkin at work very late, with surprise at her own horror. The golden boy she'd first met had shown no sign of this. Zal the vampire was something that just didn't want to compute and she couldn't help drawing back. It was a microscopic movement, halted before it got under way, but it was still there.

Her dress didn't feel the same way about his activity however. It swirled richly, panels lifting through the twilight miasma, their threads unravelling to reach the air that sweltered with the energy that Zal was drawing out of the living bodies. They also, she was disgusted to see, eagerly reached down into the coagulating mass of blood from the slaughtered girls.

Her hem reddened, darkened. Confused embarrassment at her own moment of flinching from Zal and now from this fresh minor horror caught her off guard. Words died in her throat. She turned away and went back through the building. Tables and chairs got in her way. She threw them aside, hearing them smash and break against the walls, halting only once she reached the open door.

The forecourt was a mess of furious, humiliated people but their focus was gone, their purpose lost. At the sound of distant police sirens gravel kicked and dust rose in clouds as vehicles swerved onto the road and away.

Lila crossed to where Deadkill's local leader lay, conscious and moaning with pain, in a heap of his own feces. The bloody hems of the skirt panels around her ankles tapped him like the fingers of naughty children trying to annoy. She looked down at his spit-flecked face and saw pure hatred staring back at her. She knew she looked the same.

"They're not different to you," she said. "They came back and they didn't even want to. It's not up to you to destroy them." She didn't know if she believed her own line.

"Fuck you," he growled. "Dead stays dead. What fuckin' human thinks otherwise? Even the demons want them gone. Bible says—"

But she put her bloody, gravel-crusted boot on his mouth. "You aren't fit to say the words. You aren't the law."

With an effort that must have cost a lot of pain he wrenched free, twisting to the side, and spat. His mouth and cheek were smeared with red. "You ain't either."

She glanced down at her crusader's garb and its new crimson hem. "I'm *a* law," she said. "And if I see you again, you're a dead man."

Police cars wheeled into the lot with silent grace, their blue and starred sides sliding back to allow armoured officers to jump out. She went forward to complete formalities with them. A strange coldness, a kind of emptiness filled her with only one thing standing in its vast space: Max. She felt the pain of that loss again, sharp and cruel, and then on top of it the longing and the fear, the hope and the hopelessness engendered by the messages she could not bring herself to delete: *come see me, I'm here, I'm home again . . .*

The officers' amusement at her roundup washed over her in a tide that felt completely out of synch with the day. She cross-referenced with their networks, was discharged, picked up the ton of summonses from Greer, her boss, that she'd also been avoiding, and slowly made her way back to the diner's emergency exit on autopilot.

Zal was standing in the shade at the end of the building, almost invisible. He ignored and was ignored by the bustle of the diner's staff and customers as they restored themselves after the scare and emerged to watch the last of their assailants cuffed and driven away in blindsided vans. Some of them were already talking into their lapel phones as the trial lawyers got under way. By the time the vans reached the courthouses there would be a case waiting and a judge to hear it. This burst of efficiency soothed Lila a little, though the sight of Zal, standing so still as he leaned on the diner wall, arms crossed, slouched and withdrawn, did not.

She made her way up to him and pulled off her crusader's mask, tucking it under her arm. The cool air felt like water as it washed through her sweaty hair and over her face. "You okay?"

His gaze slid from whatever infinite it had been contemplating and focused on her face. "Not so much," he said finally, his ears flicking with irritated discomfort. As he stood straight he rolled his shoulders and eased his neck. She saw that his hair, so muddy recently, was bright silver and gold. The black aura of his *andalune* body lingered here and there, but as he became more alert it submerged into the suddenly photoreal colour of his physical body. She realised that he was heavier. He had more mass. They shared a look for a few moments.

"Not hungry anymore?" she asked, as if she were a woman asking a man if he'd had enough dinner and nothing more.

He shook his head slowly. His expression was grim, making him look dangerous. The tan of his skin shone in the sun, sheened with health. She wanted to touch him but she didn't even dare reach out with the ultrasound.

"Think you can ride it back home?" She jerked her head in the direction of the bike.

He gave her a filthy look.

"I have something I have to do," she informed him. "I'll see you there later."

His gaze flickered down over her clothes to the hem and his face contorted slightly. Finally he just smiled, a tired smile, and leaned down and kissed the top of her head. "Don't be late."

"Okay," she nodded and smiled in return with a reassurance she didn't feel, then made herself go back to where the bodies of the two girls were being zipped into plastic bags by the medical team.

They delayed for her to take a look, holding the bags open so she could see the bullet holes. The bodies were quite normal, utterly human, the killing wounds exactly what you would expect from close-range, high-power firearms. They were also quite dead. Lila looked up at the paramedic across the gurney from her. "They were Returners."

The woman nodded and slowly closed the bag up over the blonde girl's unmarked head. "Yeah, we see a lot of these lately. Don't worry, they won't be back again. Corpse is what you see. That's what you got." Unhappiness made her frown lines deepen and she looked back up at Lila when Lila didn't go. "Something else?"

But there was no data Lila needed she couldn't get just by reading the records. What she wanted to ask was impossible for this woman to answer.

"No." DNA samples, research papers, tests rushed through her mind in a second. There was nothing abnormal about a Returner, except for the fact that they reappeared fully formed, between one moment and the next. Otherwise they were the same as everyone else. She let them wheel the bodies away and watched as their small white vehicle slowly purred across the road and turned for downtown. Its onboard instructional log rerouted it towards the Agency's morgue. She wondered if there would be funerals this time but then all her delays were used up. With a gritting of her teeth, she turned around and began to walk. It was at least six miles home and she needed time to think, to clear her head, to keep on waiting and not arriving. . . .

Beyond the lines of hills and rooftops in front of her she could see the faint glitter and wispy blue colour of the sea.

CHAPTER EIGHT

Walking, admiring the built-up scenery and whispering traffic, was a pleasure that lasted only a few minutes. Then Lila found herself on the phone to Malachi, hoping he'd gotten back. Bentley answered and explained that Sarasilien had made himself known to everyone, but the tone of her voice didn't give away a lot. Lila shelved that problem into the official back-burner zone of her mind, and as soon as Malachi had been located and connected—faeries didn't carry all the human technogubbins as routine—she blurted what had been simmering away all day.

"I need to see Tath. Talk to Tath. Whatever. But I don't want to have to get flatlined to do it. What's another way?"

There was a brief silence on the other end of the line, then Malachi said, "I'm not sure there is a way," in a tone that promised it was carrying a lot more information than he was prepared to part with over a long-distance connection. That or he was being overheard by someone. "Why don't we meet up? There's a lot to talk about."

"You mean Sarasilien?"

"And the rest of it. Plus I've been gone longer than you think and I have quite a lot of downloading for you."

He spoke gently, as if he hadn't a care in the world; he was curiosity's favourite cat and the cat had the cream. She knew it for an old trick, mastered early on during the development of his human glamour. He could pass for a smooth-talking, laid-back cool guy as easily as crossing the street, and it wasn't exactly a lie, but she knew he wouldn't practise it on her unless he was telling her that he was covering something significant.

"Meet me at the old house," she said and speeded up her march.

The afternoon turned balmy as she made the middle two miles, and they took her right through everything she never wanted to know about the Otopian methods of dealing with things they didn't like, top of that list being the Returners.

Although they didn't exist in sufficient numbers to be any kind of minority, they cropped up with disarming irregularity. It took serious processing power to compute their statistics, but a few notable features had dropped out, features that were not so far in general knowledge. The first was that they always appeared when either the grave or the home of the Returner was very close to a place where there was a dimensional weakness; from natural causes or the interference generated by more conscious activities. The second feature was the one that chilled her, however. All the Returners had living relatives or friends who said, in some form or other, that they could not bear to say goodbye, that there was a connection they didn't want to break and couldn't accept was broken.

To top it off there was the nonhuman undead rubbish that Xaviendra had left behind when she decided to hold Lila to ransom, and for which crime she was now sleeping soundly in the Agency jail. They kept her to hunt down and tidy the mess she'd made, or such was the excuse. Vampires and other necrosprites had become a little statistic on the bottom of the crime pages all over the Bay Area. Xavi was on special privileges (allowed out with Lila) to track and contain these things, when there was time. They should have been on it today, but today had gone awry. In any case, although Lila had taken her twice on "missions," neither time had given her confidence in the activity. For one thing, she had to trust Xaviendra's choice of victims, and for a second, she knew that every second spent outside Sarasilien's magic-proofed cell was a second in which Xavi could be performing any number of magical activities that Lila had no hope of detecting. She used any excuse herself to keep Xavi incarcerated, even conducting what briefings they had within its walls. The fact was that because the Otopian authorities felt unable to execute or repatriate her, she was better off dumped where she was. At first, Lila had felt sorry for her. Later, however, that sympathy had waned as she realised the extent of Xavi's prior treachery to her own kin. This niggled at her. She felt there was more to uncover, and if only she had Friday she would have been able to see what it was. But Friday was not to be had.

Finally, among her extensive inbox, there were the urgent-flags of a detective in the Serious Crimes Unit operating out of Bay Central. They were all hunter cases—fae gone bad and half fae even badder—a string of murders awaited her perusal in gut-churning detail. All over town and beyond people wanted to be rid of the supernatural. It was a million miles away from the heady, optimistic times she remembered, before she even heard of the Agency, when elves and demons were rare, their worlds exciting new frontiers, their explanations of matter and energy fresh and exotic, rich with promise.

Lila must be behind the times because she still felt that way about them, even knowing the worst of their nature, but it seemed like nobody else in Otopia did. Aside from a few romances and soap operas featuring hot humans dressed up to thrill, there wasn't much positive media about the other worlds. But negative stuff, especially at the con-spiracy-theory end, of that there was enough to choke on. Deadkill were only the pitiful tip of a big, ugly iceberg. It didn't take genius to understand the pressure that Temple Greer and the Agency were under to get it out of sight.

With a final turn Lila reached the familiar streets of her home accompanied by a sense of déjà vu, not for the place, but for the fact she was always coming back only to run away again at the first opportunity. She didn't like the run away element, though it wasn't because she wanted to stay. She wished she could walk out with the feeling of a clean break and things made even, concluded, debts paid. Instead here she was looking at the changes in the neighbourhood and feeling guilt and shame grow inside her, twin poisons that sapped her will so that it was difficult not to march right past the end of the driveway.

Instead she didn't even pause. The drive was cracked. Weeds choked its edges. The grass was long and turning brown. The trees, small when she was a child, had either been cut to stumps or were huge, covering the small front yard in late-afternoon shade. To either side the houses were much neater. She could just imagine the kind of thoughts the people there must harbour about her old home, but she couldn't imagine and didn't want to know what they thought about the person inside it. She didn't know herself.

Without pause for thought she knocked at the door. Standing on the step was an odd feeling. She knew the place, and didn't know it. So much time had gone by here without her, she wasn't even sure it recognised her as one of its own. She was glad about it.

Footsteps sounded in the hall. The door opened onto a gloomy interior, and in the instant before she saw the person standing there she smelled the warm waft of cinnamon and pastry and the sharper bite of lemon. Then her eyes adjusted perfectly and she had to force herself to be still and maintain the mask of pleasant enquiry that she had made of her face.

Max looked back at her with the same instant of incomprehension turning to recognition. Lila's shock was the greater, she guessed.

Max wasn't an old woman, nor even particularly mature looking. This was Max as Lila always remembered her, young, late twenties, her short hair in a raffish pixie cut, her more-like-dad-than-mine face rosy-cheeked from bending over hot stoves or running along the beach. Her greenish-grey eyes sparkled and the left one quirked slightly, because they'd once fallen in love with the superior eyebrow of a film star and spent weeks practising the look. Ever after Max couldn't stop doing it and the quirk had become part of her stand-back-and-let-'em-have-it attitude.

Lila expected to see a ghost, a lost person, a desperate person, someone she didn't want her sister to have become, not just . . . Max. And certainly not the real thing. This should have been a pale shadow, a mockery, a monster.

"Lila!" Max stood back with a huge theatrical stride and swung the old door open wide. "Come on in! I thought you'd never make it!"

There was genuine delight in her voice. Lila almost ran.

She stepped forward into the dark hall, always inconveniently narrow, and as she passed Max said, "Jesus, what are you wearing? Is it costume-party day at work or have you converted to one of those weird kinds of catholic? I know your job must be intense, but I thought you'd turn drunk before religious."

There was no odour of death or decay, nothing to show that Max was anything but real and normal even though she had been twenty-five already once, long ago. Lila found it impossible to keep her mind from jumping with joy. Max was here! Something if not everything was going to be all right.

Lila walked on to the kitchen, the idea of being trapped in the hallway, perhaps in a hug, making her move forward in an awkward kind of dance that nearly stumbled as she crossed the threshold.

For a moment it was like she'd stepped back in time. She saw the kitchen of her early years, the old paint, the cupboards, the loose-handled drawer, the pinboard with its festoons of abandoned to-do lists and cat cards, the toppling slippery piles of special-offer mail that never got thrown out in case it held the winning ticket to some far-away dream. In her mind she heard her mother's voice objecting, "But you have to keep it in case they come with your number. What if you hadn't got it? You could miss out on the best win of your life."

The faeries had my number all along, Lila thought, but she was moving on already.

On the wall over the little dining table there was the picture of the poker-playing dogs seated at their green casino table. Chips and drinks and cards covered it. And one dog, a happy hound with an almost berserk smile, had won an enormous pile of cash and thrown all his cards in the air where they turned in the smoke and gloom of the dark bar—four aces, two kings. *Aces High!* said the caption in small italics above the cheap gold frame. It wasn't until college Lila had learned that "aces high" was a phrase about fighter pilots and not about cards.

Now for the first time ever she noticed the picture hanging on the bar wall behind the losing Chihuahua with his paws over his head—two spitfires, guns blazing against a cloudless blue sky. Seeing it now made a special pain turn in her heart, and tears suddenly blotted out the vision entirely, making her dash her wrist across her eyes before Max could see her. She'd spent all her young life hating the cheap, nasty tackiness of that picture with its low-rent glorification of drinking and gambling and the stupid ambition of hopeless people with their contemptible crass humour and their short-sighted focus on pleasure. The feelings engendered by this image had instantly and always shamed her, baring as it did her own embarrassment and as-pirations, her contempt of her family's failure to exert any real effort to pull themselves out of the mire. Her own secret treachery was thrown in her face every day by this damned picture.

She'd tried once to throw it out by stuffing it down the side of the bins in the backyard and in doing so cracked the frame, only to find her mother later that day restoring it lovingly but ineptly with craft glue that left an ugly line across it. The line was still there, the glue yellowed and ancient. Remembering her own arrogance and spite hurt like knives in her chest now. She closed her eyes to block it out and there in her mind's eye saw her mother's smile. She heard her mother's voice that would never say anything again, saying lovingly to her, to Lila, the daughter who couldn't save her, "Aces high!" Well wishing her. At the time it had made her feel sick. And she'd known about the picture and who'd broken it and never said anything.

Two spitfires, four aces. It meant love. It meant luck. It meant the good times were and always had been right here, in this kitchen. If she had seen them.

Suddenly Lila was bent almost double. A howling noise was coming from her mouth, though it seemed not to be her making it. The caving hole inside her chest was making it, trying to breathe, trying to hold together when she could feel herself literally breaking up, falling apart. Her body went rigid, attempting to survive by any means, frozen in terror of extinction and feeling it was already too late.

She felt hands and arms on her shoulders, moving her to sit down, patting her, hugging her. The faint thought that she should brush them off and get away was too faint to survive. Her own arms were clutched around herself, holding her guts in.

From a great distance she heard Max say, "Li!" and then, "Oh Lila," with such sympathy and this made her howl all the more. Her system cued up the procedures and drugs that could return her to normal, but she offlined them ruthlessly.

All she wanted was what had been before the machine, before the job, before the college, before growing up. She wanted to be lost in an ancient time when in her innocence and naivety the picture amused her, delighted her, when she had no idea about the way things really were in the world, when it felt like everything was safe and going right.

"What is it?" she heard Max say, when she got too tired to continue and was paused, eyes closed, rocking on her seat.

"I want to go home," she said, sniffing. As she said it she felt tired, a million years tired, and found the table in front of her. She put her arms down on it and her head on her arms. The soft sleeves of her shirt soaked up the wetness from her cheeks. She hated to be weak, but weakness had overtaken her. Everything she had shored up behind the dam of being competent and strong had found this crack in the frame and spilled out and she couldn't get it back. Her heart hurt with a cold, aching, unrequited longing so intense she couldn't breathe unless she focused all her attention on that and nothing else.

Max sat down beside her and kept a hand on her back between her shoulders. "Is that why you called me?"

The words processed slowly through Lila's mind, empty now that its efforts had failed. "Yes." She felt Max's hand rubbing her gently through the tough faery cloth with a warm and steady beat.

"It's all right," Max said quietly.

It was a while before Lila trusted herself to speak, longer before she trusted what she had to say. "Where were you?"

"When I heard you? I can't say. Far. Very far." Max let her hand be still but it remained steady.

"Was it hard? To come back I mean."

"Yes," there was real grit in the word. "Very hard. I was almost . . ." But then a noise of frustration, breath puffed out between the teeth. "Oh every time I think about it I lose it! I was sort of going somewhere new but that's all I can think of. And if you're going to ask me how I came back, I just don't know. I heard you and there was something to grab onto and it pulled, or I pulled, and then . . ." She puffed, giving up on an effort to explain it. "I woke up here, in bed. The house was full of faeries and a right mess it was. Still is. You can see they don't have much time for housekeeping or gardening."

Lila focused on breathing, on not being distracted. "Did it hurt?"

"Yes. No. I felt . . . dislocated. That I'm really not supposed to be here, like I'm out of place. I really do." She sighed, a sad sound.

"Do you remember?"

"Yes. My life. I remember. Or do you mean dying?"

Lila didn't know what she meant. "Do you remember that?"

"Yes. I remember all my life up to the end. But describing the end is hard. I saw light. There was some kind of movement. Everything that had been was falling. But I was still there, only not me anymore, the stuff of the memories didn't matter. Shit, I can't explain it and god knows I've wasted enough journals trying. There's a Returner blogfest out there bigger than the sea and I don't think one of 'em has ever managed to say it."

Lila breathed, counted, rested. She felt stupid and heartless but also wary, and guilty for that, but she couldn't help it. Now she was needy as well, but even that was partly calculated to discover if this was the real Max as she asked, "Are you angry with me? Do you think . . . were you the first? Did I make all of these people return? Do you wish you were still . . . dead?" She kept her eyes shut. It was better that way. She felt the air moving over the wet linen. That was good too.

"Yes, I damn well *am* angry," Max said in the mildest of tones as she leaned on the table and pushed back into her chair, making the legs creak. She cracked her knuckles methodically, knowing Lila hated it, and took her time over every pop. "Fifty years and not even a fucking phone call. And here you are looking barely a day older. Are you back as well?"

"I wasn't dead," Lila said, feeling the tabletop, the wood grain, focusing on it so that she didn't have to feel all of the reactions that were bubbling up inside her too strongly. "It really was only a couple of days for me. I just . . . skipped it. Faery—"

"Those little fuckers," Max said with quiet venom. She paused. "You're not going to leap in and correct me? Tell me not to abuse them in case they get all scary-wary?" On the last two words she let her voice fall into a nursery singsong.

Lila felt the kitchen move slightly, as though a tiny earthquake had happened underneath them. "I don't—"

"Yes, you always do and you always did. Leap in to defend, make sure nobody says boo. You were the peacekeeper." Max flicked a hand through her hair and stuck out her jaw unconsciously.

Lila snapped. "Well you were the griefer. No boot so big you couldn't stick it in your mouth at any opportunity."

"Yeah, because things needed to be said and nobody would say 'em."

"Nobody needed to say them with you around to do the job for them."

"People should wake up and face reality. They're weak, cowards, hiding behind all that booze and junk and card crap and special secretarial skills and nine to five."

Lila bit her tongue for a second, trying to find a different response to her usual. They could have run through it all again, but it felt very after the fact now, too late. If this wasn't really Max, it was doing a fine impression. Her blood pressure was sky high. She was surprised she could still feel riled. "Why unleash everything when it can't do anything but destroy? Why not wait for a better moment?"

As Lila had known she would, Max immediately understood it was the criticism of their parents that Lila referred to, and the criticism of herself.

"Because it's poison," Max said. "There'll never be a good time to let it out, never a better time than now; get rid of it once and for all."

Lila felt calmer, quieter; the storm course had been diverted for a time. "Do you believe in once and for all then?"

Max's chair's front legs thumped down onto the floor with a bang. "Yeah," she said. "One shot, one chance, one life, one go. If you don't do what you have to, then nobody will. You can feel as sorry and as mad about it as you like, won't make a blind bit of difference. I didn't live waiting for you. I lived with what I'd got. I didn't waste my time dreaming and pretending."

Lila let these cuts pass without comment. "Did you see them on the other side? Mom and Dad?" This time her quiet question created a pause of intense silence. She could feel Max beside her, fixed in place, not even breathing.

"No," she said finally. "I didn't see anything. I felt that they'd gone before, ahead, long gone. That's all. So if you were hoping for angels and white wings and heaven and bells and everybody waiting with a chorus of harpers, then no. Just some feelings. Nothing else. Or I don't remember. And then I was back. And I called you and I waited and waited and waited and finally here you are, asking all the questions like usual, doing the interrogations, making sure who's been naughty and nice."

"You're pissed at me." Lila couldn't but feel this was justified.

"Yeah. Calling and making me wait. That's bad manners. Not for the rest if that's what you're thinking. The little fuckers told me you'd been swindled and I couldn't expect you to come back. I tried to hang around but . . ." She thumped the table. "Anyway, I had a life. It was okay. I enjoyed a lot of it. The only part that I didn't like so much was keeping this place on."

Lila's curiosity raised its head. "How come?"

Max paused and Lila felt her weighing her words. "Well, how can I put it? If you give a faery an inch they'll take a mile, and then another mile when you're not looking. The place was like a dosshouse. I got sick of it and kicked them out. They didn't like that too much. I was going to sell up and move away, start again. Strangely, however, no matter how long the house was on the market, it never found a buyer. Then they came back offering riches."

"Riches?"

"Gold, to be exact. Spanish doubloons to be completely precise. They didn't want to buy, they wanted to rent with no questions asked. I could stay on, they'd look after everything. How nice is that?"

"It's faery nice," Lila said knowingly, pronouncing faery to rhyme with very.

"Yeah, like—fuck you, Max, after your kindness, now you're our creature. Fuck you faery much." She sighed. "I took the money, obviously. It's not like cooking for a living round here makes top buck and anyway I'd met someone by then." She paused. "God, it was a long time ago. I thought the money would make life easier, even if I did have to stay here waiting for you. And you know what? It really did."

Lila slowly sat up, feeling like she had to drag her too-heavy head from its rightful resting place on the table. She stared groggily around, at the room that was basically unchanged since the day she left, give or take a few items, and that looked every one of its sixty faded years. She didn't need to make a tour of the rest of the house to guess it was in much the same condition. So much for faery housekeeping, she thought, and then wondered if that had been their plan all along, to keep it unchanged until time destroyed it or it was forgotten. "They're gone."

"They had to quit when I died." Max followed Lila's gaze around. "I left it to Carolyn. She didn't have an agreement with them."

"Carolyn?" It was so weird, thinking of Max having partners she never met, never knew, a whole lifetime.

"Carolyn Cochado. We didn't get married, but I left her plenty of money and the house. Yeah, partly to spite the little fuckers, but mostly so she'd have somewhere after I was gone. But I guess she decided to leave. She must have remembered you though, or known something in the last few years. She let Mother Hubs back in to look after the place when she left."

Lila remembered the housewifely faery who had greeted her on the day of her return to Otopia, proud to show her the unchanged mausoleum of a house in all its ratty filth. It was almost too much to take in, but the trail wasn't ended.

"Where did she go? Is she still alive?"

"I guess so. She was Hunter Chosen and they live a long time. Probably still looks early forties; she didn't age much."

Lila looked out of the grimy window into the overrun shrubs of the back yard, the silent kennel. "Didn't you call her?"

"No, and you won't either, so forget it."

There was a conviction and a kind of desperation behind the words that made Lila decide to drop the subject for another time. She looked around, more carefully this time, but she didn't see any pictures or glyphs of new people. The place was virtually a museum. It was giving her the creeps. She didn't know how Max had stood it for ten seconds, let alone the weeks she'd been here.

"Can you leave?" It wasn't a simple question and they both knew it.

"I don't think so," Max said slowly and added, by way of explanation, "Faery gold."

"How far can you get?"

Max laughed with her dry, rasping half cough. "I can get anywhere, but I get to come back after a day or two."

Lila didn't question the last part. If the faeries wanted you somewhere, you got to come back whether you intended to or not. She knew how it was.

"How do you get away with calling them . . . what you call them?"

"Same deal," Max said with the weariness of ages. "I guess. Or maybe Carolyn killed a few too many of them. They've got long memories for little fuckers."

But now Lila was convinced that this was her sister, and not something else. Faery gold and a deal made on Hoodoo terms was binding beyond the grave, in realities humans didn't ever see. To take the Hoodoo's name in vain was to ask for a much shorter existence, or to never have been born at all. This thought flickered and then something clicked in Lila's mind like a small light going on in a large, dark room. There, in the Hoodoo, was a power to alter fate, the past, to undo the done, to make the impossible. It was deadly. It was not of any realm they knew.

She felt that even to think on it this much was to inexorably draw its attention to her and she dimmed that light, dimmed it almost to nothing and let her mind turn from it.

They sat beside one another for a minute or two.

Max broke the silence. "Why are you dressed like a mad nun?"

"Faery," Lila said, shaking out a sleeve to indicate Tatterdemalion's status.

"Weird. I didn't know they came like that," Max said, fingering the sleeve rather roughly as if she didn't think much of it and cared less. "God, now I have to look at every object and start wondering about it. Just great. I suppose you don't ever take it off, send it to the cleaners?"

"It comes off," Lila said. "Self-cleaning."

"Yeah, so all this dirt and staining is smuggery. Figures. Never thought I'd see one of them get your ass over a barrel though, ha!" Suddenly Max was laughing. "It kinda suits you."

"I'll remember that." For the first time Lila felt only a weary acceptance at Max's statements. "I thought I smelled cooking."

Max glanced around the room at the clean but deserted surfaces, cooker, and oven. "Last of the glamour," she said with a sigh. "There's sliced cheese in the fridge if you want it." When Lila's silence went on she added, "I don't feel like it these days. Ennui of the undead. Go figure."

Lila sniffed the last snot from her crying spree. "That should be a superhero. Ennui of the Undead."

"Yeah," Max gave a dry huff. "Special power: depression. Fills enemies with a sense of futility until they kill themselves."

Lila felt her face smile as if it was doing it without her. "Nothing bothered me about the other worlds. Until this. I thought I would be happy if you were back, but I didn't think you'd be housebound and—"

"What? Lost and purposeless, out of my time?" Max growled and sighed, her angers fading fast into disappointments and helplessness. "I guess nobody ever thinks about that. Never had to, since it wasn't real."

"But there is an upside." Lila said it more in hope than conviction.

"Yes. Another bite of the same old cherry." But Max still sounded weary. "Why did you call? How did you?"

"It was an accident," Lila admitted. "Kind of. I felt it was time to move on. I should, you know, get over everything that had happened and get on with things because it's not like I didn't deserve to be tricked into that fifty-year penalty. I knew the rules, or lack of them. I knew how it goes and I was careless, and that's why the Hunter was here so long and why I got my delay. I bought it, really, with my stupidity."

She felt Max's hand fall on hers, ready to interrupt, but overruled it. "And I had this pen, sort of, which wrote things that came true and I used it to write to you to say goodbye. Only, at the time I wasn't able to mean it. I was wishing things were back the way they used to be. It didn't matter what word I wrote, it took my meaning, not the letters. It was a mistake. The pen had so much power I didn't know about. I think it . . . warped something very important, just because I wished you back. And I don't know if I can undo it. I don't know if I want to, or ought to."

She faltered and stopped, unable to continue.

Max, on the other hand, sounded interested for once. "So where is this pen right now?"

"It went back to its rightful place," Lila said. "I think. Not here, that's for sure. Doubt I'll see it again and I don't want to." She remembered its other form, the sword, swallowing Sandra Lane whole. "It wasn't what it seemed to be."

"Too bad." Max paused. "And how is Zal? Is he . . . ?"

"He's fine. Sort of." Lila didn't know where to begin with that story.

Max wasn't so hesitant. "What did the faeries do to him?"

"They kept him. Fifty years. As a kind of Raggedy Andy doll, a pincushion. And now he's a vampire. Of a kind. No blood, just energy. Same effect though."

Max snorted and sat back, putting her hands behind her head. She whistled a long, extended wolf whistle of amazement. "And I thought *I* got a rough deal. And your other fella, Teazle?"

"He's okay. We got divorced. He went to Demonia. Anything could have happened to him."

"And you're back at work already, just like that?" Max was incredulous and disapproving, to say the least. She tipped her chair back again, balancing on the back legs. "What a good girl."

Lila scowled. "You make it sound so . . ."

"Crazy? There's not enough therapy in this universe to sort it out."

"I'm just trying to undo . . . to sort out everything I've made a mess of, I . . ."

"Yeah, you're going to sort out the faeries, undo the deals, make the undead into acceptable alternative citizens, correct the demons, civilise those goddamned elves, and make the human world into a beautiful utopian example of how to live and everyone will cry in delight and follow your oh-so-correct model. Why can't you find a worthwhile ambition for once, like gutting this goddamned room and putting in a decent range? Or taking your still-alive vampire man and settling down out of the way before one more fall of the dice takes him away forever? Something you could actually have a hope in hell of doing? You always thought you were so much better than Mom and Dad, but the fact is you're exactly the damn same. You place a bad bet and then you chuck your whole life after it trying to make it pay."

Lila felt the words cut deep and knew their truth. She stood up, straight, tall, purposeful.

Max thumped the chair down warily. "What are you doing? You've got that look . . ."

"You know," Lila said, gently putting her own chair aside and standing back to take a good inventory of the room. "You're so right." She moved to the first cupboard, opened it, and began to remove stacks of plates and dishes. "This is just cheap old stuff, right?"

"Yes but—"

"Good so . . ." The cupboard was now empty, except for the shelves, which Lila took out. Then she tore the cupboard itself off the wall, snapped it into smaller pieces, and carried them out into the yard, where she dumped them. "I guess nobody round here is interested in our old junk, so we can either call up Yard Sale and ask them to come get it or we can have it hauled to the recycling plant. What do you think?"

Max looked at her from the door for a minute. "Are we going to smash up all of the past like this?"

She sounded quavery, so that Lila stalled, her conviction wavering. She knew what she wanted to do, but this wasn't her place anymore, wasn't her house, or her home. But it was her sister standing there, wondering if she was going to be next on the list of things to clear up.

"I can't stand it," Lila said, feeling thwarted, dangerous, defeated.

She stood with the broken cupboard and told Max the story of the diner, and the two dead girls trying to throw themselves away, their unwelcome second chances stolen. There was something about it that she couldn't understand, couldn't get a grip on, some important, necessary meaning that slipped endlessly away, like water over rocks.

"It was so pointless, all of it," she ended, tears blurring the vision of Max in the doorframe, pain in her throat making it hard to speak though she wouldn't let it stop her. "There was nothing in it but one sad thing after another. And I want to burn the house down. I want it gone. I don't want to know about these things anymore. I don't know what to do. And every time I get some kind of hold on myself and move, do something that seems right, I turn back and find I'm here again and again. I want to destroy this place and never return but I can't. I'm stuck and I can't be stuck. I'm not the one that gets stuck. I'm the one that fixes things and gets on with what everyone else can't do. Because I've been given all this power. I have to act or what is it for? But I'm failing. I don't understand. Why would it all come to me just to bring me here again? Why has all this effort made nothing but the same old pain? You've lived. You're older now. You must know why. Tell me."

Max came slowly forward, taking the steps cautiously as if her legs might betray her—the stride of an old woman who's learned not to be bold. She looked at her sister Lila's face, contorted into an ugly mask with the effort of resisting everything, her hunched shoulders and crushed posture, chest sinking inwards, arms hanging lifelessly. Max put her arms around her gently, so as not to disturb her and leaned her head on Lila's shoulder.

"All I know is that when you can't go on, you gotta quit." She waited a little longer and added, "And I don't mind the past. I mind the present. I want a new kitchen, with one of those old-fashioned china hutches, and a dresser, but the biggest, most smartass range and gear that money can buy. What happened happened, leave it alone now. Doesn't matter anymore."

"But it does! It all matters! If it didn't matter, then what's the reason for anything, what's the point?"

"You're the reason. You get to choose. Blue and white or gold edged with Grecian motifs. Steel all around or hand-fired tiles. World domination or sitting at home reading a book. That's all there is. Saying there's a point is like missing the point. You get stuff, you make stuff, it gets eaten, and then it gets forgotten."

At last Lila said, "It's better with you being the oldest."

"Meh, I went through this shit years ago," Max said offhandedly. "But I got over it. The trouble now is I don't have any money. If you rip out the kitchen, who's gonna build a new one?"

"I'll sort that out," Lila said, sniffing and wiping her eyes on her sleeves. "Zal has money and I think I get paid."

"Malachi still around?"

"Yeah."

"Hm." But Max wouldn't be drawn any more on the subject. At least she didn't call him a fucker. "Are you staying for dinner?"

"I have to get back to Zal and . . . we've kind of got a lodger."

"Bring them over," Max ordered. "I'll do barbecue. We can burn up this old wood."

They separated rather awkwardly.

Lila cleared her throat and took a deep breath.

"Steel or tiles?" Max preempted her, leading the way back up the creaking porch steps and into the kitchen. She looked around, hands on her hips, ready to get stuck in.

"Tiles," Lila said.

"But steel is so easy to clean," Max objected, leaning back to stare at the light fitting, a plain cone shade so old and dusty that Lila was glad she'd never really noticed it before.

"But tiles can be so beautiful," Lila said, staring at their plain white tile, each one an island of greasy emptiness edged with crumbling grey grout.

"Steel can be beautiful too," Max said though her voice made it clear she was in two minds about it and was in the mood for a lot of catalogue browsing before she made any moves. She glanced at Lila then, and Lila knew she had not been talking about kitchen surfaces.

Lila conceded with a nod. "I'd better be going."

"Yeah, clear off," Max said, waving in the direction of the front door. "I've a lot to do suddenly. I mean, the kitchen isn't the only room that needs a makeover. The whole house has serious issues."

"See you later." Lila walked down the dark hallway, feeling strangely light, and tired.

"Alligator."

Max said it comfortably, not the way she used to leap in with it when they were children, so that Lila got to be the alligator and the crocodile as well.

When she got to her bike, she sat down on the saddle and rocked it off its stand, then sat and stared at the house. She felt a long-stretched cord snap inside her and release its elastic grip on her stomach and lungs. She saw the peeling paint, the old-fashioned round doors, the warped porch rails and felt nothing special at all.

She pushed with her feet and backed the bike around and then, as she started the engine, she noticed a faery sitting under the massive overgrowth of the hedge that bordered the road. It was child-sized, green and brown and almost perfectly camouflaged, which was important since it resembled a goblin much more than a human, but it had moved to attract her attention. Now it sidled forward and she moved until they met at the driveway's end, the faery still well hidden by the foliage.

"Friendslayer," it said quietly, as though they were familiar with each other. "I helps ya with this. Ye must send the dead home. Cloaked in shadows is they path, see? And path is open. Shadows comin." While ye still can, stop them, aye?"

Lila narrowed her eyes, "I'll take your words under advisement, Hob."

"Ah." The faery looked confused, because she'd agreed in a way and left no opening. "Whose advisement?"

"The Necrolord," Lila said, extemporising a title for Tath.

"Ah," said the faery, nonplussed again.

"But why do you ask?" she demanded, while it folded its large, gnarled hands together. They looked more and more like twigs as the seconds passed. "Faery has no troubles."

"When the walls are too thin, everything's heard, then they all falling down, see?" it said, as though this was obvious. "Hurry. Worldsend." Its words were fading, and by the time it finished the last one it had changed by imperceptible but rapid degrees into a mossy old tree stump, concluding the conversation most successfully in its own favour.

Lila considered this and then leaned down to the stump, her hands tightening on the handlebars as she revved the power and selected first gear. "Get off my land." She stayed there, watching as the stump slid with the same motionless ease along the hedge line and finally through the hedge itself until it was on the pavement side. Then, with a backwards glance at the house and a hollowing of her cheeks as she thought of Max's safety, she sped away.

CHAPTER NINE

Lila planned to go directly home, but the screamers attached to half the messages coming out of her office were so insistent that guilt, or possibly rage masquerading briefly as guilt, took her over and turned her wheels that way. She persuaded herself the detour would be nothing more than a necessary pitstop, although she only partly fooled herself. She was spoiling for a fight and it was better that impulse got some outlet here than at home. What was between her and Zal felt precarious; too much had happened too fast. But it was also precious— exactly how precious she didn't like to admit because it caused a fluttery, desperate feeling to rise in her chest—so she wasn't about to have a fight with him.

Inside the place was like a press room. For all the speed and ease of the communications technology that everyone had, there was nothing like really getting in someone's face to get yourself some attention, and everyone wanted attention, immediately. The corridors and rooms thrummed with activity and energy. Even her costume couldn't command much more than a second glance as Lila eased her way through gaggles of suited agents and their hundreds of milling contacts en route to Greer's office.

Bentley was at the door waiting for her by the time she made it, her smooth grey hand flat to the glass pane through which Lila could see Temple Greer hunched in his ergonomic chair in a cramped, troll-like pose. One arm was braced across his midriff to support his other elbow as that hand rubbed the stubble on his chin in a vexed manner. A uniformed police officer and a civilian agent were standing with him, both talking earnestly at great speed.

"Best wait," Bentley said, easing back now that her mission was accomplished.

Lila made a disappointed noise. "Do you think they'll be long?"

"How long is a piece of string?" Bentley replied, making a tiny gesture with her chin at the open-plan areas behind Lila's back. "It's been like this all afternoon."

Lila turned back from her second viewing of the chaos, a frown on her face, and saw Bentley's mildly amused smile. "The diner."

"The diner. You may assume nobody is bothering you because they have been ordered not to." She pointed over her shoulder through the glass door, indicating that Greer had been the author of that command. "I don't think he threatened them with death, but something about pay cuts was mentioned. On a similar note you can guarantee that all conversation out here is being severely earwigged."

Lila switched into machine-only mode, their spoken words translated directly into coded digits. "What's Xavi been doing all day?"

"Sleeping mostly. She was piqued when she couldn't go out but she's gone back to poring over those ancient tomes you gave her, drawing, making notes, pacing up and down, attempting the odd bit of strangeness I can only take for spell-casting though nothing happens."

"Sure?"

"If her face is anything to go by, I'm sure."

"And she doesn't know about Sarasilien?"

"If she does, she hasn't heard it here. I don't like to vouch for supernaturals though. Haven't got access to the same methods so I can't say for certain. You know."

Lila did know, and signalled as much. She expected that Xavi would try to break containment, and that she would succeed. The only uncertainty was when that would happen. She'd have given a lot to know the exact time on that particular clock. It made it all the more important to resolve her outstanding issues with Sarasilien right away, even if that meant dealing with the Lane clone.

Lila found herself grinding her teeth and had to work for a few moments to stop.

"You can AI-govern your chemistry so you don't get all that," Bentley said, appending a vast and extensive catalogue of human responses to illustrate what she meant by "all that." "You can have this instead." She showed Lila a handsome bar chart featuring the entire rainbow, every emotion and response calibrated and displayed to twenty decimal places.

Lila, who had switched that feature off so many times she couldn't count it, nodded her thanks. "I like my inadequate human reactions the hard way. Keeps it real."

"'To become a spectator of one's own life is to escape the suffering of life.'" Bentley said.

Lila mused on it a moment. "I love Oscar Wilde. But I was never sure if he meant you should become a spectator, so you don't suffer, or you shouldn't, because then you've missed out on something vital to the human experience."

"I am certain it is the former."

"And I'm sure it's not," Lila sighed and leaned against the low divider full of plants that screened the main office from all the negative chi streaming its way across the open zone. "Though better for him if it were. Isn't that the enlightened position, to treat your life from the distance of an eternal perspective?"

Bentley laughed in silent zeroes. "I guess it is. The machine makes it much easier than I remember it being before though."

Lila stared through the glass, watching Greer argue forcefully in his own special silent movie. "Will we get old and die?"

The grey android shrugged slowly. "The machine has kept me in perfect restoration. So far."

Lila spent a moment or two deliberately listening to the susurrus of the machine whispers that continued eternally throughout her body, the soft promises of forever from the Signal. She didn't feel convinced that it was a personal promise. She might not last forever, though it would. It might not be conscious except through beings like herself and Bentley, but that didn't mean much, although she took some comfort in the fact that her screw-ups weren't going to be global mishaps, just like Zal said. (Oh, Zal, how neglected he was! A burst of guilt and longing flared hot across her skin.) And yet her entire existence felt like it had been engineered to be pivotal. Why else bother? Super agents were rare. All-powerful ones, much more rare. Which left only the question—would she jump or would she be pushed? Greer suddenly caught sight of her in the middle of his rant and paused for a full second, halfway through the word "and," causing the two policemen to turn and look as well. He finished his line as he stood up and they gave way before him as he shouldered past them to wave at the door. It opened and, with misgiving and curious looks, the officers reluctantly let themselves be waved out as she was ushered in. The glass walls turned themselves an opaque white at their backs so nobody could see inside anymore.

"Black," he grated. "Nice of you to show up." The sarcasm was made all the more effective by his overused voice growling like a bear's. His eyes raked across her, taking in Tatters's display of gory justice with frowning disapproval. "I can see the headlines already . . . because here they bloody well are." He flicked out his hand and the walls obediently filled with the text news as delivered on the Otopia Tree's fastnet.

It was pure hallmark drama to which Lila didn't respond, having already dismissed the hysteria as uninteresting the second it came zipping along into her AI's inbox, and thence into the junk file and instant deletion. To humour him she looked across the largest typefaces where they stamped themselves across his potted palms and sofas and read them aloud.

"'Red-headed Knight Templar Saves Diners from Fate Worse Than Undeath.'"

Greer was glaring at her. "And yes, I did see the Hot Nun one, before you ask."

"'Cuffs leader with own gun,'" Lila said and then turned to face him. "See, no killing. Superman-clean action."

"And this one?"

The lettering changed and she obediently turned to read, managing not to hesitate.

"'Inhuman droid agent chops up dead-butchers; twenty-eight arrested.'" I hope you penalise inaccuracy," Lila said, surprised by the jolt she felt at reading it. A hot burn of injustice boiled quickly up from her belly into her face so that it was hard work to maintain the lightness of step that dancing with Greer required. She knew what the problem was from his perspective—it was the D word. Otopia had never revealed the existence of its few cyborg creations to the public: it was a subject relegated to the pages of conspiracy blogs. This headline had come from one of the most prominent of these.

Temple Greer, dishevelled even in an expensive, pressed suit, black hair flopping on his forehead, moustache bold, went through ten kinds of calculating behind his fixed stare. Lila supposed it would have unnerved her if she were younger.

"What I don't like about right now is that it's a god-awful untidy mess," he said. "Agencies leaking all over each other. Strangers treading my carpets, whining. Boss on my back, stamping feet. Dangerous creatures everywhere, and most of them in this goddamned building where I have to hide them, protecting them from execution whilst I wait for them to break my security, escape, and cause even more hell. Meanwhile you, pageant queen, are out eating burgers and getting involved in publicity stunts from which you dash off like Cinderella leaving nary a shoe behind."

Lila's chin had gone down several notches during this mini lecture and now she regarded him steadily. "And how you love it," she folded her arms.

His gaze became gelid for an instant. "If you had killed them, you would have looked like a normal agent at least."

"Pathetic," she said. "If that's the best you can do, I've got betraying bastards coming out of my ears back in my own office, not to mention their back-chatting, grudge-holding, bitch-clone sidekicks and a monster in the vault pretending to be a cute little goth girl who never done no wrong 'cept to ease the pain in her sweet, tiny emo heart. Do you think some headlines from a few humans is going to make a dent in that?"

Greer broke his righteous stance with a sigh and raked a hand through his hair as he walked restlessly across the few paces between himself and the sofa. He threw himself down into it and lay there, as if poleaxed. "You think Xavi is a fraud too?"

"I don't know what I think about her," Lila said honestly. "Mostly I don't think about her."

"She gives me the creeps."

"Zal gives you the creeps."

"Yes, but in a wholesome, rock and roll kind of way. I'm making her Malachi's special responsibility, not yours. I think you should stay away from her."

Lila was so used to his non sequiturs that they made sense to her now. She let this pass without comment. "What about dead duty?"

"They can patrol together."

"Did you have a feeling about this or something?"

"No," he said with a rising groan of reluctance that let her know he was about to admit something that he hated to tell. "A hexxing doll we seized during a raid on a demon nest down in Palm Beach said you had to stay away from her."

"Say what?" Lila frowned.

Greer flung an arm across his eyes, playing even more the fainting dandy although she wasn't sure the exhaustion part was much of a joke. "A doll. One of those voodoo things the faeries and demons make. They had one. When we broke in, they were busy destroying it—it had finished whatever work it was supposed to be doing."

"And what was that?"

"Faery dust, smuggling information, nothing to worry about. Not my point. Point is: we get in, they get arrested, the doll's on the table sitting on the drugs, falling to bits and we're in the middle of leaving when—"

"Why are *you* there?" she said.

He sighed. "Have to personally oversee all supernatural arrests. Black, stop interrupting me with stupid questions. Point is, doll sits up and speaks to me. Tells me some blessed rubbish about a thing called an assemblage point in the future at which you, a shadow, and the angel of death make a very unfortunate combination promising untimely demise for all if you deviate from something it called the path of the heart. I don't have such a good memory for these things but that did rather burn into the synapses. A message. From . . . I don't know who it was from." His look at her said he knew only too well and they were not going to mention the name, ever, because pulling its attention was the last thing anyone wanted. The Hoodoo.

Greer sniffed and rubbed his moustache violently. "I thought only the maker of the doll could order it to do anything. Demon that made the doll didn't like it much either. Freaked out. Broke the arresting officer's arm, ripped its own hand off making an escape. And now there we are, stuck with this hand: should we keep it on ice in case it returns for it or should we just burn it? You're the expert, so what's the etiquette on this kind of thing?"

"Serve it with a side salad," Lila said, all her attention on reprocessing the important part of his speech. "Angel of death?" she wanted to be sure.

"Xaviendra, it said. I was extemporising."

For a doll to be speaking without a making was indeed unheard of, but the cause seemed reasonably clear to her. Beings like the Hoodoo needed a vehicle. She remembered the ugly faery at her garden gate, devoting some time to delivering the same message, although with different details. No mention of Xavi in that one but still a vague promise of end-times, and her love of horror stories was long gone.

She set the information to the back of her mind to compile itself into sense. "Is Malachi in?"

"As in as he ever is," Greer said, feigning a state somewhere close to his last breath. "You kids, you'll be the death of me."

Lila smiled in spite of herself. She couldn't help thinking of Zal at times like this, because Greer's humour was just like his, and Greer had learned it off Zal's albums and escapades in the way-back-when, six months or sixty years ago. "What did Sarasilien say to you?"

"Well he didn't mention anything about a time machine or a dimensional polarity shift if that's what you mean."

"No explanations of his lost years?"

"Nothing. Just wants to see you. Prepared to wait apparently, although it's only been a few hours. I think you could easily let him stew for several weeks, see what pops out of him in the meantime. Unless the end of the world is tomorrow. But no. I'm sure he would've mentioned it. Actually, he seemed very sad to me, down about something, like his dog died."

"And you didn't mention Xavi."

"Hello? Head of the Secret Service here, not eager-beaver placement student." He huffed and put both hands to his face to rub his eyes in a gesture that looked as though he might rub them out entirely. It looked painful. "He isn't really an elf is he?"

"I don't think so," Lila said. Her prospects for getting out of the place anytime soon were beginning to look dangerously slim. Queue notifications, red alarms, message streams were popping up in her AI like fireworks on Chinese New Year. She knew that Greer had an implant not unlike hers and that his inbox could only be much worse. "Seriously, are you okay?"

There was a pause. She thought he'd fallen asleep. Then he said glumly, "The ex-Mrs. Greer has a gentleman caller. He didn't take too kindly to my serenading her at four o'clock in the morning with a rousing march on the bagpipes."

"Don't you ever sleep?"

"Only at Christmas and birthdays." He lifted his ragged, lengthening hair and showed her his ear, which had a narrow cut across it and a medium-sized bruise beside it on his cheek, mostly hidden by his sideburns. "Cat's dish. He throws like a girl."

Lila nodded, as ever unsure what to say to this. "I'm sorry."

"So am I, Blackie, so am I. You won't forget to phone me and tell me what's going on if you find out, will you? I know how distracting black ops elves in spandex can be to you young girls."

"No, sir."

He turned at this and looked at her, a pained expression on his large, rugged features, making him look like an alarmed basset hound. "Sir? What's this? Has that Bentley woman been talking to you? Sir. I'm not a goddamned policeman. Sir. Sir!"

"Sorry."

He made a grumbling sound and slowly, painfully, sat up, resting his elbows on his knees. "Get lost, would you. Oh, and congratulations on the new house. Etcetera."

"Thanks."

This time his grumbled response was more of a grunt, accompanied by a vigorous attempt at a soapless shampoo. Lila fought an inclination to go and kiss him as if he were some lovely grumpy uncle, because even though that was the effect he was going for she wasn't buying it, and this last ordinary step of their defensive dance took her breath away as its turns revealed their common pain.

She took a few steps backwards before turning on her heels and leaving via the already open door. Her throat hurt her and she shook her head crossly, almost hitting Bentley, who was standing, rock steady and rock patient, just where she'd left her.

They flashed machine messages at each other, verifying and exchanging news not important enough to put into words. A burst of rapport strings finished the moment, one misplaced digit in a key position sounding their common bum note about Sandra Lane.

Anxiety ticked in Lila's mind, repeating the suspicion that Lane had gone and evolved when nobody was looking, and now had a capacity they couldn't detect that was going to get them. She knew things like that were possible. It was in the Signal's whisper.

She had to fight the paranoia that wanted to gallop away with her. Now was not the moment. Now was so not the moment.

She passed the queues of people outside doors, the huddles at corners, the quickly sidestepping aides with nods of recognition, watching the surprise on their faces as their AIs and links updated each one of them personally with her replies to their enquiries. She created links and groupfeeds on the run, forming new collaboration teams, which she couldn't personally oversee, designating chairpeople and delegating her authority, notifying them that her AI would be acting for her, a subself, never sleeping, never tiring as it passed only the important news to her waking mind.

The AI whispered to her as she walked, digging out its little secrets from the hoards, assembling its bombshells from scattered debris: all magical and supernatural activity in Otopia was accelerating in frequency and magnitude; fracture lines in the Otopian spacetime fabric were opening in proportion to their proximity with Returner origin points; Hunter children and the humans made psionic by moth exposure were falling in number, but gaining in their particular aptitudes.

Someone had posted images of Zal behind her on the bike in that traffic jam downtown. He looked dark, surrounded in private shadow. She was only partly visible, just the line of her back and the edge of Tatters's embroidery crusade tattoos. It was different to the way the dress had become when they had fought later, at the diner, but it was too close a resemblance to go entirely missed. As she finished her polite circulation among the agents, she turned into her own corridor, finding a pocket of calm and a moment in which her heart hammered and her breath tried to choke her.

They found Zal. They saw us together. The diner. What will it mean?

Fear for him flooded her. Without thinking she infiltrated the network and erased the pixels that showed her hair, the shape of her head, the colours and patterns of the faery on her back. She got out undetected. Priority protocols helped a lot. It wouldn't last, she knew. Eyes had already seen it. Copies were out there. She must assume that her anonymity was finite. Zal's celebrity, faded as it was, would be enough to expose her as the diner knight. Eventually someone would wonder how it was that some Returner rockstar's girlfriend had bent a shotgun into bracelets. And after that it would be open season.

By the time she reached her own door, she had resigned and Greer had deleted the resignation and filled the reply space with expletives.

"It's too late," he said, his voice left of centre in her head as the AI relayed it. "Ops will fudge the information as much as they can. We might get a few more months before we have to come clean-ish in the public eye. That's a long time."

Lila said nothing to this but sent a sad face emote and closed the line. She remembered how much she'd wanted to kill everyone in the parking lot, the pulse of blood in her veins loading the magazines in her arms, changing her hands into guns. Then she opened the door to her offices.

The anterooms were full of Bentley's exquisitely packed and filed boxes where she had been collating evidence from old cases and clearing magical items that were too dangerous or outdated to be left around. Their monumental order rebuked her silently. The lab was spotless, surfaces gleaming. Lila moved quietly between the stacks of items, following the path to the last room, where the door was ajar and lights glowed in soft, moving colours through the gap.

Sarasilien, as elven as any creature she'd ever seen, was standing watching the wall where a display of the solar system was slowly revolving. Besides the nine planets, sun, and moons, a host of other objects were drawn in, some small and distinct, others streaks and strips. She recognised none of them. Behind his tall figure, the broadcaster of these images, Lane's clone, stood impassively, her hand held palm forward. Light shone out of it.

Lila knew that there was no need to speak as they were both well aware of her entry into their company, but she wasn't the girl who would once have waited patiently for them to give her their attention. A feeling like Greer's world weariness—a rumpled, tired feeling—spread over her as she kept her composure. She crossed to the couch where Sarsilien had once laid in splendour with Sorcha the Scorcher's foot in his hands and sat down, crossing her own booted feet up onto its elegant cushions.

"Spill it."

"We are here because of a crisis in Alfheim," Sarasilien said, turning to face her with that little polite bow of his coming automatically, though he didn't duck his eyes. They sought her gaze and held it steadily. There was real force in his look. She matched it, pushing back strongly across the gap between them.

"Not just Alfheim." Lila quirked an eyebrow in the Lane clone's direction—she wouldn't be here for something like that.

"Its effects will most likely be felt everywhere," he said. His face was compassionate again. It made her angry and she didn't appreciate the suspense.

"What do you want me to do?"

"Not you," Lane said, closing her fingers into a gentle fist and letting her arm fall to her side so that the projected cosmos swept across the room and vanished.

Lila turned up the lights, brilliant. *No softness for you*, she thought, and saw the elf blink and squint for a second.

"We need Zal," Sarasilien said in his most gentle voice, the one that had calmed and soothed her through hundreds of pain-filled nights in the first days of her machine life.

"Oh?" Lila tipped her head to the side and folded her arms across her chest. She noticed the Lane clone adopt the same posture as Sarasilien, hands folded gently in front of her black and grey shining form, chin down, like children obediently ready for the lesson. Her teeth closed against themselves.

"A great tragedy has befallen . . ." Sarasilien began, but Lane interrupted him with her more precise articulation.

"Alfheim has gone dark." She didn't need to append details of the meaning of this phrase. Lila knew what dark meant: out of contact. The humans wouldn't have noticed it; Alfheim had gone dark for them decades ago. Only the elves who stayed in Otopia and Faery remained to act as reminders that the place existed, and there were few of them.

She glanced at Sarasilien. "You know why."

He gave that slight nod again and this time his eyelids followed suit. "For every action an equal and opposite reaction. An age ago when the shadowkin were created—that was an action of great aetheric force, a collective action using techniques that were fraught with dangers. In an effort to mitigate the effects—"

Lane broke in again. "They used dampening systems that absorbed the backlash of the worst mistakes that they made during their research, but these only had the effect of deferring the results, perhaps altering their nature."

Lila narrowed her eyes, "Deferred to the future?"

"Yes," Sarasilien said. "It was thought at the time that this delay period could be extended—"

"Oh wait!" Lila held up her hand. "I'm ahead of you. The Lady of the Lake, Arie, that's why she wanted Zal isn't it? She said it was to separate Alfheim . . ."

". . . from the other dimensions, yes," Sarasilien finished for her. "That was not exactly honest, however. She was intending to divide Alfheim from the rest in order to protect it from her real intent, should it fail, which was to continue deferring the backlash of that earlier act indefinitely into the future. And when you took Zal back, then she had no way to maintain the disjuncture and her efforts failed indeed. So it was left to others to isolate Alfheim as best they could, once it was certain that the reaction could not be put off. She was the only one with the resource to even attempt such a thing."

Lila raised her eyebrows, "Except you, I take it." She was unable to conceal her bitter disappointment or continue the cool act in the face of it.

"Except me," he bowed again in agreement, unbending in every other way.

"And this . . . whatever you want to do . . ."

"Will be the final attempt, that is correct. The last attempt to prevent a catastrophe."

"And you want Zal's blood for your evil little spell?"

"No," Lane said. "That method cannot work any longer. Circumstances have changed. We want Zal to go into Alfheim as our operative. We think that he will be immune to what has happened there because of his demon nature."

Lila's mind worked fast. "And I guess it doesn't hurt that he got reprocessed by Jack and the Fates, does it? Or were you behind that?"

Sarasilien was shaking his head.

"Never mind," Lila cut off what he was about to say with a slice of her hand through the air. "I think it's time you took me back to the beginning and told me the whole sorry story. And then we can see if there's a shred of evidence in any of it that would prompt me to believe a word you're saying."

Lane took a half step forward. "There is no benefit to bringing your personal grievances into this matter, sad or difficult as they may be."

Lila leaned back on the chaise and looked at the cyborg. She could see herself in the polished reflectiveness of its vinyl body. She looked stretched and deformed in different ways depending on the part. Lane herself was smooth and perfect as a doll. "Were you this much of a bitch when you were human?"

"Coming from you I take that as a compliment," and for the first time there was an edge in the voice that sounded comprehensively pissed off.

"Finally we have liftoff," Lila said, rolling her eyes. "And before he starts, just fill me in on your part of this beautiful diorama."

"Sandra is my scientific advisor," Sarasilien said, impeccably gentle. "In your absence she has been invaluable in relating my aetheric knowledge to the laws that govern the strictly physical."

But Lila was still paused on the words "in your absence." She held them, filed them, considered them and their potential meanings very carefully, and then said, "I'm mad as hell at you." She pointed at him. "And I am about as likely to warm to you as liquid nitrogen," she pointed at Lane. "But I'll shove it where the sun doesn't shine if you can make the next twenty minutes I'm spending away from what I want worth the wait."

"Your petty personal grievances!" began Lane with spite but she was cut off by the elf putting a hand onto her shiny arm.

"Are long overdue for attention is what you mean," Lila said into his restrained silence. She stared at Lane, all her outlets closed, all systems shut, with real dislike. Sarasilien paused and she knew it for carte blanche to continue. Very well then, let it be done.

"You," Lila turned fully to the cyborg. "You are the voice of the machine. That's why I don't like you and why I don't trust you. I see vested interest whether or not I understand it. I see a devil's pact."

Lane's nonfunctional nostrils flared. "I went where you fear to go."

"True. But I'm still not going there and no cheap shot about my courage is going to make me. Scientifically speaking you're excellent. I don't doubt that. But you're not on my side and killing you can't have made you any more likely to move there, so unless you have a reason I don't know about to make you attach yourself to him and me, then we're done."

The android figure made a very human micromovement of frustration, weight jerking back and forth slightly. "And what exactly *is* your side, Black?"

"Lila Black is my side," Lila said, and for once her conviction was faultless. "What's yours?"

"I go where the interest is," Lane said. "Where things aren't certain and don't add up."

"And this elf story doesn't add up."

"The energy transferences between aether and matter, between the nonbaryonic and baryonic, as we understand them, do not accommodate the claims made concerning what is passing in Alfheim," Lane replied crisply. "Nonetheless, what is occurring is causing the structure of our information to undergo an unforeseen entropy acceleration, which, if it continues, shall begin to compromise the organisation of our fundamental materials. If you were attuned to the machine instead of shutting it out all the time, you would already know this."

Lila considered it. "None of the other cyborgs seem bothered. Just you."

"They do not have my levels of synchronisation," Lane said pointedly, but Sarasilien stepped forward at the same time, holding his hand out to the side a little so that it came in front of her, warning her off and protecting her at the same time.

Lila's heart seethed with jealousy.

"Lila, she is telling the truth, but what she is saying is only a machine interpretation of what I am trying to say also, from a different perspective. The aether backlash is affecting all of the realities at the most fundamental level, that of energy. However, there has been a result in Alfheim that was not foreseen in any way, and this is what I require your help with. And Zal's."

Lila finally managed to swallow the worst of her resentment. Maybe it was the pleading attitude he had, the way he looked like a picture-book Jesus with both his palms held towards her, though he was looking down at her face and not up to empty blue heaven. Maybe. "Go on."

"I cannot risk an entry into Alfheim myself," he said slowly. "In case what has happened there affects me too. However, after some reconnaissance taken by Sandra here, I believe that Zal may be immune."

"May be. Hmm. Why can't she do this work you have to have done there?"

"I'm not an elf," Lane said. "I can't perceive their psychic reality. And neither can you."

"And what did you find?" She directed her gaze at Lane.

"Nobody," Lane said. "And nothing." She meant the entire population.

"Where are they?"

"We think they have gone into the forest," Sarasilien said.

Alfheim was made of forest. Aside from its few civil centres, which barely registered on the scale of cities, they were a scattered lot. Into the forest meant only that the cities must have been abandoned. But his tone now was pressing and she got the feeling he was willing her to go along with him, not to ask Lane for more, though the reason why he wanted this was something she couldn't even guess at. That the two of them were slightly divided was enough to satisfy Lila for now.

"And there are no other elves you can ask?" she said, but she knew the answer. No elf was like Zal. There was no other elf to ask. "Teazle could go." If she knew where he was. If he came back. If. Thinking of him made a pang of concern knot her brows.

"I think, given the pressing nature of this matter, that it would be a good idea if you all went," Sarasilien said.

She decided to omit telling him about the divorce. "And you'll babysit the undead while we're gone? Safe and sound in the bunker? Because I sense more than a hand of yours in all this."

Apparently her mercilessness wasn't satisfied yet. She was still interested in all the things he so delicately didn't want to say. She gave in to the delicious desire to nail him.

"You were in at the start, weren't you? You were one of those who made the mess. And now you have to clean up, but you don't want to get dirty." She looked him in the eye and then she got up in one, clean, fluid rise that wasn't entirely human in either its speed or its elegance so that they were face to face. "Level with me. All those machine parts magically appearing here, at the right time, in the right place, pushed on people with so many good reasons—that was your hand, right?"

She felt Lane's entire electrical signature change as she said this and saw the pupils of his fox-brown eyes dilate fractionally, darkness increasing inside their perfect rings.

Grim satisfaction ran through her even as the confirmation of betrayal bit deep.

"What else have you made over the years? What for? Come on, spit it out, don't be shy." She made an expansive gesture with her hands and smiled to show her teeth, the smile as hard as iron. Inside its metal prison a little girl screamed and beat her fists against the walls. But the time for crying was over and that, more than anything, fuelled her rage and hardened it into ice. "We're all friends here." *And we all know what happens to my friends, don't we?* In her mind's eye she saw Dar before her, friend and lover. She saw the resignation and sadness, the shock and disbelief in his face as she pushed the dagger into his heart. In Sarasilien's arms she'd cried her misery, thinking he was safe and solid when all along it was his hand on her strings.

And she was still here, wanting so much to hear how she was

wrong, that it was a mistake, a comedy of errors that just looked bad, that it all had explanations that didn't add up the way it seemed. She could see the window for this explanation as if it were a progress bar in front of her, the rising colour slowly eating up the time, counting down to the moment when there couldn't be any more room for credulity. She willed him to say the magic words, the perfect line that would undo all that disappointment and set her free. She looked at the soft brown colour of his hair that had meant comfort.

"Yes," he said. "Yes, I did it. I made you to go where I couldn't go."

Beside her she was vaguely aware of Lane stiffening for a microsecond. Lila wondered if it would change things between them that the cyborg hadn't known this extra truth behind her own genesis in the bowels of this miserable building, but at the same time as she thought this she dismissed it.

She felt her shoulder push him aside as she walked between them and out of the room. The laboratory was dark, silent. She closed the door behind herself firmly and stood for a moment with it at her back.

In the corridor a line of hopefuls was waiting to see her, and a cleaner was there, quietly and wearily pushing a vacuum cleaner around their stepping feet, head bent low, looking for dust. Lila walked past them, avoided the vacuum, ignored their voices, went up along the familiar route to the garden, and bent down to fling open the door of the yurt there, ducking straight under.

Malachi was there, sitting in his chair, feet on his desk, asleep. The place was a mess, like they'd left it that morning.

Lila slapped his foot with her hand. "Did you know?"

"What?" he shook his head slightly, groggy. He peered at her in the room's natural twilight, slowly putting his feet down as he leaned forward to turn on the lamp. He rubbed his face, looking around him for the little moondial that told him the time wherever he wanted to be. "Know what?"

"Did you know who made me?"

The tone of her voice made him stop and be still. His orange-red eyes blinked and his wings briefly manifested around him in shimmering clouds of anthracite dust. His skin darkened to the true black of his faery form and around her the dress became lissom and floaty, rising in waves of bloodstained white fabric. The strips coiled slowly, taking on the movement of snakes.

"I was sent—" he began.

"I said—did you know?"

His face was a mass of changing emotional reactions but she held his gaze as he struggled, although that delay in itself was almost good enough for an answer.

"Yes, but . . ."

Lila took a step back, straightening up, and flicked out the fingers of her right hand, changing them into blades. His slit pupils widened and he jerked back. The chair bumped the yurt's back wall.

Lila stuck her fingers into Tatterdemalion's high collar cut straight through from top to bottom. Her edges were so sharp they made only a whispering sound as the cloth parted. She didn't know if the dress was surprised or not, but it wasn't important. She tore it off her shoulders and legs and bundled it up into a ball before flinging it at him. It was heavy and it sent him toppling backwards off his seat, although she didn't stay long enough to see what happened next. "Lila!" he shouted after her, sounding hurt and angry. She ignited the jets in her boots.

CHAPTER TEN

The rented house on the hill was glowing from all of its windows. Lila could see it from miles away after she turned to follow the line of the upstate highway—a few bright spots in a huge wall of dusk. She landed short, in the woods, and took off her armour and boots the old-fashioned way, leaving herself naked except for a vest and underwear. The air was cold and damp against her skin. It felt refreshing and she stood and bathed in it for a minute or two until the last of the heat had ebbed from her. She lifted her face to the sky, listening to the woodland sounds, the cicadas, the breeze. She would have given a lot to be able to sit there and do nothing but enjoy the night, but there wasn't time for that.

Instead she sat down on a rock and picked up the shoulderguards of her bike leathers and looked at them with machine eyes. In the days of her cyborg youth these had been her issued clothing, but lately she had come to spontaneously create and absorb the armour and even cloth items. Her surface could be remade in any material, her insides too. She knew that on the inside, although she felt as human as she ever had, there was little that resembled human biology now. She looked and sounded like the real thing, but it was like the faeries' glamour and the demons' generosity—an illusion. But she hadn't examined this process in action before. Probably she would never have, since it made her extremely uneasy to the point where she would rather do almost anything than continue.

And then Lane had turned up. A clone. A life-size, real, updated to the last living second clone. One of potentially many. But at least one that was an exact copy of the original at some point. Instantly Lila had wondered how Lane had done it and instantly her answer had come—in the same way that Lila made her armour.

Until this moment she hadn't considered removing her self-made armour the same way she'd take off ordinary clothes. Sure, she'd once stripped off some of her synthesised skin to make a point, but that was strictly to make the most of the moment. It hadn't occurred to her that she could remove pieces as a matter of habit, and then, after that thought did cross her mind, she felt like it would be removing a part of herself and she was repulsed and a little frightened. Now she sat and held the pieces and they felt and acted exactly like the human-made artefacts she had copied so faithfully. In fact, they were comically accurate when seen from a machine angle.

Lila had copied leather, Kevlar, and metal, picking the engineering plans out of the machine whisper as easily as breathing. She could have done what the machine had done to her and simply given the appearance of those materials whilst creating something entirely other beneath the surface, something much more effective, but she didn't feel ready for that.

More to the point, having removed the items, she could hold them now and in no way did they feel like holding her own severed arms. They felt quite detached, because they were, in every way except one, just leather biker armour. The difference existed in the extra information they contained at the quantum level, one step up from raw energy. This code was like a watermark. Their pattern was her pattern, a holographic exactitude of sameness at a fundamental plane. Lane and Bentley's choice of form was more than a political statement, it was a kind of ironic art. The evolved cyborgs were truly, exceptionally plastic. Having thought of that Lila still didn't get what was so great about being Boring or Evil Barbie without the hair or the little shoes.

She did wonder where all the material came from. Where did the sheer mass come from out of which these things appeared? She didn't feel smaller now. In fact, weight for weight, she was the same. So when she absorbed it, where did it go? Was she creating her own miniature inequality that would tear space and time apart when she left the two sides of the equation unfulfilled? Is that what the elves had done in their own way? Did it start like this?

She put one of her gauntlets back on and this time watched closely as her body assimilated it. Sure enough, the weight of the gauntlet vanished as it vanished into her skin and left her, freckles and fingernails, exactly the same as a moment before. The machine part of her mind revealed with impeccable observation that the gauntlet was simply unmade into pure energy again. But that begged another and even more curious question: Where did the energy come from, and where did it go to? The gauntlet itself contained enough pure energy to run Otopia for a week, if converted into electricity, say, but she didn't feel a thing as these processes—their speed and nature incomprehensibly rapid and accurate to her human mind—flowed effortlessly to the guidance of her will alone. She realised she could make anything.

Anything.

Surely there must be some price? So where was her debt?

A similarity struck her then. Lane could make anything, including copies of herself. She could make any object and fill it up with her own awareness. What then was Tatterdemalion? Did it make sense to think of the faeries the same way, as aspects of an awareness that existed in forms that weren't tied to living things, or places, or times?

She didn't know the answers, guessed it wasn't so simple, and picked up the rest of the armour from the ground where it had become cool and damp with condensation. She was about to carry it up to the house when she hesitated and put it down again. What happened if she left it there?

This time a spooked feeling did run up her arms and down her back. Magic operated to energy signatures; she knew it was a big mistake to leave it where it could fall into unkind hands. She bent and picked it up again and absorbed the pieces by putting them on and unmaking them. By this time she had started to shiver—her body was programmed to react exactly like a human one—but she saw no point in feeling extra pain so she toughened the soles of her feet as she made her way up to the house and heated herself. It was genuinely strange to be without the faery dress, but she didn't regret abandoning it. The relief was much greater. She hadn't known until now that half her constant discomfort was the unwanted presence of Tatterdemalion and its unfathomable motives. Without Tatters she felt vulnerable, especially when she realised how much she'd relied on the faery to do her magical defending. She was like a snail without a shell, but she didn't feel abused or overlooked or spied upon anymore and that was better.

Quietly she crossed the open expanse of the driveway and padded up the steps to the porch. The lights were all on inside, glowing low on standby. The door opened to her hand silently and she closed it behind her, listening. She could hear rock music playing very quietly. In the living area she looked past the central fire where logs were slumping down into embers and saw Zal's blond head resting on the back of the sofa. A reproachful smell of cold Chinese food came from the kitchen.

She walked around the cosy scene and saw that the screen was on showing a live Hyper Metal Angels concert from the other side of Otopia. It was in Marentz, she realised, as her AI matched city shots and ran TV guides. The show's gaudy colours shone on Zal, slouched in the corner in an uncomfortable position, eyes slitted as he watched. Sassy was lying full length on the rest of the sofa, her head resting awkwardly against Zal's shoulder where she'd fallen asleep.

Zal moved his eyes to look at Lila as she came into view although he showed no surprise. She felt a feathery touch and a slight sparkle and the room dimmed as he reached up to embrace her with his aetheric body. He glanced pointedly at the sleeping girl to indicate why he wasn't leaping up and slowly extricated himself. He pulled one of the back cushions down to act as a pillow for her and straightened up gently as if he'd been lying there for a long time. Lila started to apologise, but he put his fingers against her lips and pulled her into his arms.

Lila pulled back just enough to look up into his face. In the penumbral gloom of his *andalune* body it looked like it was made of rock. Then she smelled lime spritzers and recognised the smell of wild aether that gathered in sudden rushes around the blooming potentials of any major aetheric lightning bolt preparing to ground itself and discharge—suddenly her nose was full of citrus.

Zal's eyes narrowed. "I do so hate it when that gives me away."

"Me too," Lila said, meaning that she had been in the same state, would have done anything just then to fall into bed with him, and couldn't care less about the game and its consequences one way or another. "But I missed it when it wasn't here. Where did it go?"

"I wondered about that," he said. "I had a headache maybe?"

They hesitated even longer, enjoying the feeling of each other's bodies so close, the anticipation of the night, the fact that they weren't accompanied by anyone—at least nobody awake. Lila was especially happy. Everything was simpler around Zal.

Lila glanced down at the sleeping girl. Her breath was long and even, and she didn't stir. Zal's fingers against her jaw gently turned her head back to face him.

"Will you run away?" His whisper was soft but full of wolf promises.

She moved her lips closer to his, so that as she spoke they touched. "I never run."

They sprang together with mutual hunger. She was stripping off his clothes, feeling stitches rip. His hands cupped her buttocks, lifting her, and she felt his moment of surprise as he succeeded easily in getting her off the floor. She wrapped her legs around his hips as she pulled his shirt free. His mouth was hot on her neck as she flung the remains to the floor. Across his back the demon flare was burning deep orange and red, the shape of the wings looking like a clear window into his body—an interior of living flame. It shone its flickering, weaving light on her fingers as she raked her nails along the powerful muscles, feeling the delicious resistance of smooth skin over the hard contours of flesh and bone.

He growled in appreciation and opened his mouth wide to bite hard into her shoulder, easing a need to use his teeth where it would do the least harm, and she thrust a hand into his thick hair, pulling his head closer. The heavy fall of his hair slid over her forearms and tickled her. She kissed along the thick upper ridge line of his long exposed ear, feeling the gradual thinning with her tongue as she moved along to the tip and took the cool point in her mouth. She nipped it and he broke his hold to gasp in a deep breath.

On the sofa the girl stirred and muttered.

Zal carried Lila into the bedroom, ducking so that both their heads would fit under the lintel. He used the same movement with a well-timed burst of energy to fling her down on the bed and kicked the door shut behind them. Once it was closed, the darkness was nearly absolute. His demon wings lit the room as if it was on fire. Yellow-orange light bled out across his skin as he undid his belt and kicked off his trousers. He paused, a half-grin on his face, one knee on the bed, and she wondered what he was doing when she felt his fingertips brushing her face. She could see perfectly well that it wasn't his actual hands but nonetheless it was there and sure, very light but as tangible as real flesh. It was his *andalune* body, so strong in the dark that he was able to make it solid, she realised. She looked down and saw her own tanned skin lit by his golden light. Uncast shadows moved across her where his touch slid down her collarbones and across her breasts.

She saw the same dark patterns move across his body—forming shapes that looked like hands for brief moments before they dissolved into cloudlike, nebulous forms and remade themselves again. They crisscrossed the iron-shirt ridged muscle of his torso and surrounded the base of his erection, moving languidly there. At the same moment, she felt a touch much more like a tongue than fingers trail across the inside of each thigh. Her attention was all on Zal's face, however. She looked at him more closely than she had looked at anything in her life. In his expression she read beneath the desire and passion nakedly displayed and saw his abiding nature. Zal danced at the edges of all things, lightly. Beneath his apparent commitment to nothing was a complete commitment to his own nature. And there was love in his gaze, playfulness and deadly serious intent in equal measure as he came forward, prowling over the top of her, his breath hot. She lay completely relaxed and open beneath him. She had never wanted anything more than she wanted him. His presence was like medicine to her battered spirit. She reached up and drew him down. His hair fell around their faces like a veil, closing them off from everything.

"It's been too long," he said, not pausing as he entered her.

The feeling was so purely ecstatic she lost her mind for a moment, and when she came round she found herself saying, "Never leave me."

His reply was in elvish and muffled against her neck so that she didn't hear the actual words, but it didn't matter.

They made love for a long time, at first fiercely and later lazily until the light in Zal receded beneath his skin and Lila couldn't keep her eyes open any longer. They slept until dawn.

When she awoke, the first thing Lila saw was the strange girl, standing in the open doorway eating a popsicle. The headscarf was back in place, oddly adult and formal on her young head—reluctantly tamed dreadlocks peeked from its skirt at her shoulders. The pearly sheen on her black skin was distinctive, outlining her in a peculiar whiteness at shoulder and hands where the daylight streaming through the kitchen windows crossed the hall and caught her.

Sassy removed her popsicle with a smacking noise. "You're in trouble." She said this with certain grimness and licked her lips in an interested kind of way. Her gaze was flat and direct. Lila noticed for the first time that her clothing was ragged and unwashed and too small for her.

"Dial the news desk," Lila said, closing one eye. Zal's legs were over hers and he was heavy and warm. She didn't want to move.

The girl replaced the popsicle for a minute and continued to stare thoughtfully. Then she removed it to say, "I wish I could see into the spirit world, but I can't."

"I wish I could stay in my own room without being woken up by staring people," Lila said. She noted the angle of the light and considered the time and day. "Aren't you supposed to be in school?"

The girl rolled her eyes as if this was the most stupid question ever asked of a being. Lila closed hers in response.

"You know they're not human, right?"

This question made Lila open her eyes again, and now she was properly awake and resenting every instant of it. "Oh?"

"The dead. Undead. Whatever you want to call them." Sassy leaned on the doorframe at an exaggerated angle of insouciance. "But you probably want to think they are." She shifted her weight, unable to keep her attitude stable.

"Can this possibly wait until you go out and I get up and get dressed?" Lila asked hopefully.

"Most people don't want to know," the girl said with a shrug. "I guess you're the same."

"She's not the same," Zal's voice rose from behind Lila's head, hoarse but distinct.

Sassy rolled her eyes again, suddenly choosing this moment to feel embarrassment, and pushed off from the doorframe and away. Lila heard the sounds of cupboards being opened and the rustle of a bag. She forgot it for a while, kissing Zal, then as they were lying with their heads close he said, "I don't know all her story but she's from one of those downtown slums that have become no-go areas for the average human."

"I don't find any missing person report," Lila said. "But she's under age. Interesting demographic down there. No wonder she wanted to leave."

The place he mentioned was Cedars, a parkland development of social housing that had once been the height of the city's civic pride, but that was back in Lila's heyday. Now it was like the Diner, a gathering hotspot for outsiders and anyone who wanted to retreat to gangland safety from the twitchy arm of the law. Bay City's murder capital, it was covered in the red dots of assaults and the black dots of deceased victims on the cop map. They suspected at least one Hunter killer to live in the dens there, but nobody short of a swat team was going to go find out, and there were no swat teams not occupied elsewhere in the country with the combination of Returners and the Hunter's other rogue children. Cedars was one of the items high on the list of triple exclamation-point alert notes that the police commander had wanted to talk to her about. With the AI dealing with everything it could, the only items left in her Inbox were those that couldn't be dealt with except through her personal intervention and this wasn't one of those. If Sassy was on the run from Cedars, Lila wasn't about to rush to hand her over to the police or the gangs. It took a special kind of guts and guile to get out of a place like that, and maybe a special kind of reason.

"I hate that she always knows what's on my mind."

Zal didn't budge and kept his eyes closed. "I don't. Just wish I knew what was bothering her."

Lila sat up and rubbed sleep out of her face. "How many elves you know of here?"

"None," he said. "Teazle mentioned they'd caught a few in Demonia, but I haven't seen him since you have. Then again, I'm going on what you told me from memory and I haven't been anywhere without you so it's not worth asking."

She unpicked the sense of his statement after a minute. "There are some on the immigration and city tracking nets, thirteen to be exact, including Arie. Plus the mad one in the Agency basement. And you."

He stretched and resettled himself, waking up like she was, slowly and with reluctance. "Just cut to the chase; I don't need to verify your reasoning and the longer you take, the more sure I get that the news is bad."

"Alfheim's gone dark," she said, aware that the sounds of teenage exploration in the kitchen had stopped. "Sarasilien says that only an elf would be able to go back and find out what's happening, although he's lying-by-omission-his-ass-off and knows perfectly well what's going down if you ask me, and he's playing for time."

Zal opened his eyes and looked at the ceiling for a few moments. "I thought you were assigned to undead duty." His tone was disapproving and she felt the bite of his disappointment. He thought she'd enough for the humans, and with the Diner incident no doubt more than enough.

"Triage," Lila said. "Sarasilien and his droid think this is global-catastrophe duty, and that outweighs undead issues since they aren't world threatening. The worst part about it is, I kinda agree, while at the same time the desire to smash his face in with the nearest blunt object is almost overwhelming. And I feel like I'm towing you for the ride. And then he springs this and says he wants you to go. And I just got you back. I totally fucking hate the idea. I hate it all. But if the only way it'll go away and leave us in peace is to deal with it, then I'm going to deal."

She was able to place Sassy just around the corner from the open door quite easily. On his back beside her, Zal continued his stare at the ceiling. "Zal?"

"Why me?"

"Good question, I—"

"No, I mean, why doesn't he go? Why does he ask for me?"

"Because you're demon in part and he thinks that will make you immune to whatever it is that he apparently doesn't know anything about."

"So he's probably right about that."

"I guess there's a good chance." Lila hesitated; the girl was a wild card in her mind, allegiances unknown.

"You could come with me."

"I don't trust him," she said, almost at the same moment so they spoke over each other. She was the one to continue. "If I go with you, then there won't be any contact with him here, and I wouldn't be here to keep Xavi under wraps. He could do anything."

"There is the whole of the Otopian Agency—"

"Not capable of dealing. Malachi is their only powerful aetheric operative still on active duty and I wouldn't give him ten seconds against Sar. Besides which, he has his own problems and crossing Sar wouldn't be on his list. Plus I pissed him off yesterday and we aren't talking. Bentley's good and the other cyborgs are fine, but they're all human mechanoid, not an ounce of aether between them. And I don't like the idea of leaving Xavi off radar either, even if she is doing a fault-less line in helpful repentance. She's got to be nearly as old as Sar is, and executing her revenger's tragedy took several hundred lifetimes' worth of hard intent. Giving it up on the turn of one little psycholog-ical screw doesn't strike me as all that plausible."

"So, what were you going to do?" Zal was amused. He rolled onto his side and propped his head on one hand, putting the other one on her knee.

"I'm going to see Ilya. I was going to anyway, but Malachi said something about him having changed. Plus, now that we're not talking I don't know how I'm going to see him."

"Ah, so I go to Alfheim and single-handedly save it, and you go across the threshold of the spirit world and figure out the dead problem and then we're home free?"

She frowned and aimed a play punch at his arm. "Why d'you put it like that? Makes it sound like I'm an idiot."

"I know the way your mind works, is all," he said, making his index and middle fingers work out a few tango steps on the inside of her knee. "Mine used to work like that."

"You're saying it doesn't now?"

"Now it doesn't work at all, which is a merciful release."

Lila began to reply but then a fresh awareness of Sassy sneaking around outside the door broke in on her again and she hesitated. Part of her wanted to damn the situation and to hell with any consequences; she was sick and tired of sharing every moment with Zal with some other person as well, no matter how passively. Another part of her said that they had no idea what Sassy's agenda was, if she had one, and it would be wiser to keep her mouth shut. And then, having turned this way, her thoughts trotted down the path that suggested Sassy might have run here lost and lonely and was in need of help herself. She felt some empathy, but then again, she felt like screaming too.

Zal grinned and picked his fingers up, tracing circles around on the inside of her knee like a lazy ice dancer. "But . . ." His white teeth shone clearly against the dark of his skin, taken down many shades by both the low light and his aetherial body's emergence.

"But . . ." she said and let it hang there. "If I don't do this, who will? I'm the only cyborg with a hotline to the dead."

Zal's hand slid all the way up her leg. Lila rolled her eyes vividly in the direction of the door. He grabbed hold of the sheet and cover and pulled them up over both their heads. "We can hide in here." He moved in close, warm and delicious, and kissed her. She slid next to him until they were pressed against each other as closely as they could be. The strength of his aetheric body around her made her nerves tingle with a faint, just detectable resonance that spread comfort and pleasure through every part of her. She bathed in him and felt him hum with delight. She traced his face and the long lines and narrow, ragged edge of his ears.

"Contrary to popular belief, the ears are not the best erotic organ on an elf," he murmured.

"Really?" she altered the structure of her palms and fingertips and began to emit ultrasound, tuning the frequencies by his reactions. She travelled over pressure points and along energy channels. When, a moment later, she touched the two points of his ears with an exact vibration and depth, he was wordless.

It was an old technique, one she learned by accident when she'd been forced into performing emergency surgery on Dar and accidentally triggered an energetic total body response in him that had swept both of them into an intimate melding that was as much pleasure as surprise. There was also the enormous gratification of using sound to play Zal, rock star, elf, and demon, like a musical instrument.

Their relationship had been stupidly brief but the honeymoon long enough to experiment with sonics a great deal and she knew what she was doing now. She understood exactly why Zal had got such an enormous kick out of rock music—it hit him on a mental, emotional, aetheric, and physical level. By tuning her own body and creating points of transmission, she could create ecstasy in him. It delighted her, more than any other toy she'd ever known, and it made her shy and careful with him because it was so powerful and he was putty in her hands when she used it.

When she woke up for the second time, her mind snapped to attention. She looked around and found that Zal was already gone, the bedsheets tangled in his wake and the sun shining in at a late-morning slant through a crack in the shutters. The door was closed and beyond it she heard his voice and the girl's talking in the kitchen. Music radio played in the background.

Lila stretched her legs and toes out. The novelty of this, the novelty of making love with a full body again, was not lost for a second, and she wanted to stretch them out, aware that her chances of feeling so good again soon were very short. Surely, surely now she ought to glory in her abilities, but in spite of all the positives in the changes her feelings were slow to catch up. Before she even reached the shower she was already engaged in a fantasy of seizing Zal, leaving town, finding a place outside Otopia, away from Alfheim, far from Demonia's mad cities. It was a bland and impossible dream, safe to indulge because it wouldn't happen.

Lila turned her soaped face up into the streaming water. What did that song Zal wrote years ago say? *End of the line and no way out. Run in circles, scream and shout.* Other poets had put it better, but none of them had his basslines.

Because she was used to it and didn't know what else to do, she armed herself with her black leathers, boots to vest, and tried not to watch the change. It felt warm and comfortable, nothing more.

Zal was standing in the kitchen, half dancing to the radio and eating from a bowl. Small packets of opened cereal were scattered everywhere around on the worktops, mostly full, showing they had been tried and found wanting.

Sassy was crouched on a high stool at one end of the breakfast bar, a cup of tea in her hands. They made quite an odd sight against the kitchen's clean lines and design. Zal's clothes were still bloodstained and dusty and Sassy looked as though she'd dragged herself out of a dumpster, wadded in several layers of ill-fitting clothes that bore the marks of sleeping rough in the forest. She hunched over her mug as if it was the last tea on earth and gave Lila a cautious once-over, flicking her eyebrow as if she was the one in the odd costume. Lila was pretty used to this, so she ignored it and started peering to see if Zal had left any of his cereal.

"Your habit of mixing everything hasn't been lost then," she remarked.

"I pride myself that only the worst of me made it through," he said, moving with faultless rhythm as he sidled out of her way. "Couldn't find the cocaine though. Do they still have cocaine?"

"At the store?" Sassy said with a rising tone at the end that suggested he was being wantonly stupid. "But everyone does Voraxin these days."

"Is that at the store?" Zal asked between spoonfuls, eyes half closed as he paid most of his attention to the music.

"No," she sighed and put her head to one side before spelling it out. "It's street only. Why do you think Cedars is so rich? Got their own police force."

"You're not on it though," Lila said, finding a box of Rice Pops and starting to hunt down a bowl.

"I'm not stupid," the girl said with contempt, implying that this was true of only one person in the room.

"No," Lila agreed, opening drawers. "So why are you here?"

"Like I said, found it," came the reply. "You want me to go?"

"You said I was in trouble and left it hanging." She located the spoons after Zal tapped the right place with his hand, still lost in his tunes, only half there.

"You were the one didn't want to talk."

Lila had to concede that one. "This is all getting off on the wrong foot," she said, opening a thing she presumed was a refrigerator but seeing only an empty boxlike thing and a control panel beaming full of coloured pictograms instead. "Can we start again?"

She stared at the machine blankly, peering at the images, which seemed to be an entire market's worth of items, some of them flashing, some of them blued out. Zal's hand reached over her shoulder and touched a milk carton, tapped a red circle twice that registered the fat content, and ran his finger up the image of a jug that appeared until it was a quarter full.

"Open the cover," he said, flicking his thumb in the direction of the box front. She opened it and took out her milk.

When she turned around, Sassy was giving her a long, wide-eyed stare of disbelief.

"I've been away," Lila said, frowning as she poured.

"She's a bit slow," Zal added to Sassy as he went back to his position at the sink.

That got the ghost of a smile so Lila didn't say anything for a moment or two. She didn't need to eat the cereal but she wanted to. It tasted better than she expected. As she looked up from her bowl, she saw that Zal was also looking expectantly at Sassy and guessed they'd done some talking the night before.

Sassy made a giving-in face and looked into her tea. "I ran away," she said. "Like you didn't know that."

"No record of it," Lila said.

Sassy narrowed her eyes. "How do you know?"

"I'm the girl who is plugged in," Lila said. "My job to know."

"That explains something." Suddenly she wasn't an awkward teenager confessing something she'd rather not. The confidence of a much older person took command of her, and Lila found herself looking into eyes that were more than capable of dealing with whatever they saw.

"You're a machine. The ones looking for you must be the same. I have trouble hearing them. I thought it was a block but it must just be the speed."

"I'm easy to find," Lila said, but as she said it she knew there was one category of people that wouldn't find her easy to locate—machines. Thanks to her rogue-jacking habits, she was sufficiently able to mask herself on the networks and she wasn't plugged in to anything that was capable of hacking her. This meant she was closed to the other cyborgs. The only place she could be aware of them was inside the Signal, and that was too fast and complex even for her to track through it.

Sassy shrugged. "I just know what I hear and see." She stared into her tea mug, swirling the contents. Her face was tense. Then she sighed and set the mug aside. As she looked up all traces of the teenage attitude were gone. Without it she looked even younger although it had also taken all her vulnerability with it.

Zal lowered his bowl and glanced at Lila.

"It's easier when I pretend," the girl said. "Sort of. I mean, it's easier for everyone else and it distracts them." She straightened her back. "It's not an accident that I'm here, you're right. I came before you, to clear the way and make sure the house was safe for the time being. But you got here a bit soon. I'd have been gone myself only you caught me in the act . . ." She glanced at Zal meaningfully. "I didn't think you'd be so quick or so sharp. When you cornered me, I realised I'd never outrun you and I panicked and did what I do best. Afterwards it seemed like a good idea. I could keep up the old act and watch over you at the same time."

"Watch over us?" Lila frowned. "Who for?"

"For myself," the girl said. "You were looking for the one who made you, to whom you were important. You were trying to figure out why anything that has happened to you has happened—was it part of a grand scheme or only a series of incidents without a greater meaning? What you have found seems to point at the mage, Sarasilien, though you wonder if he too is only a lesser player in some even bigger plot, yeah?" She nodded, seeing Lila's silent agreement. "You see, I didn't know this until I got here. I was supposed to find the house and clean it, that's all. But when you got here, I realised who you were." Her glance included them both. "I couldn't help it. I overheard."

"You have a bit of a habit there," Lila murmured although she didn't want to interrupt.

"They're looking for me, and you," the girl said, without taking visible offence. "You don't have any guard. You know nothing about the spirit plane, or you'd be much more careful. I was doing containment. And anyway, even if you were half a mile away in a lead box, I'd still hear you. I can't not. Another reason I like it here. Quiet. Like I said."

"Who are they?" Zal asked, placing his bowl quietly down in the sink, his gaze never leaving the girl's face.

"The people who sent me to prep the house or the ones looking out for you now?"

"All of them," he said.

"The faery Malachi and Temple Greer sent me to do the house. Malachi and me have history in Cedars; he rescued me from some nasty business twenty-two years ago out in Cooper Bay, and we've been trading favours ever since. Greer I don't know personally, though I see you do," she took in Lila's expression. "He wanted me to check you out, see you were levelling with him."

"Because now they can't tap me directly for information?"

"I guess. I didn't ask why; that's not how business works for me."

"And the rest?" Zal asked.

The girl looked suddenly unhappy. "You've been gone fifty years, yeah? Well, a lot changed in that time. A real lot. Not on the surface—people still live in houses, still drive around in cars, still watch screens, play games, eat food, piss each other off like usual, yeah? Sure the fashions and some tech has changed, so it seems, there's a new space program and they're on Mars and they're on the Moon and they're doing this and all that, but on the big scales we haven't come anywhere since before the pyramids, you see what I'm sayin'?"

Lila nodded.

"Well, in the last few generations born since the Moths, there's been a population explosion in people with powers—psychics, seers . . . you can stick a bundle of names onto all the combinations of psionics out there right now. On the surface, if you're in the big social centres of the world, it looks like everyone's okay with it, yeah? And you haven't had time to get this, but everywhere else it's war by another name, not open war, kinda a cold war, a tepid war that keeps the surface okay, keeps the economy okay, keeps everyone more or less in a home and a job, but there's no real peace for anyone. It's so widespread now they say that the humans will be extinct in another hundred years. The only reason it isn't a slaughter is that everyone has someone close who's a changeling, though ninety percent of them are barely any different. It's not like you can pick them out by race or colour or creed. They come everywhere. But the camel's back broke with the Returners. Like you saw across town, the war's getting open now. Meantime the rogue cyborgs have been dealing in body parts. Their own. Criminal markets are full of upgraders. There are six chop-shops in Cedars will make you over into a machine in two days, for the right price. 'Course they have trouble getting plutonium and such, so they have to use batteries old style, but they aren't so bad these days. And other people have done other things. Your tech is in a lot of gear, Lila. A lot. The chatarazzi call it the Slag Pot—everyone melting down into psionic metal gloop. Some say harmony, but you know people. What do ordinary humans have to offer against those with special abilities, special powers? It's war. Anyway, the rogues were looking for you. Have been ever since Lane found you and lost you again. For all the talk, you're the only one with metal and aether in working order and none of their experiments at fusing those things have worked. Guess they found you." She gave Lila a curious look.

Lila admitted their execution and assimilation with a nod. "They paid you too?"

She shook her head. "I heard them, that's all."

"You must have a good memory," Zal said, wistfully.

"I learned to remember what's important," she replied. "We don't commit anything to a record. It's unprofessional."

"We?"

"Readers," she said and grinned, talking as if what she said was entirely old hat. "Readers don't write stuff down where anyone can see it. Bad for business."

"You're not just a reader."

"I am, far as business is concerned," the girl said firmly and there was a clear note of warning in her voice. "That's all I am."

"So how did we get to be your business?" Lila asked, leaning on the counter, still trying to figure out how Malachi and Greer had steered her to what she thought was her choice of where to live.

"Because I'm not just a reader," she said, and then she added awkwardly, "and because nobody ever offered to buy me a pony before, which probably seems like dick to you, but mostly people fear me or want rid of me even when they think I'm only a reader, even when they think I'm only a changeling, or just a street kid."

She took a deep breath. "I'm not any of those things either, except the street kid part is kind of right. I lost a lot of my abilities a time ago. Deal went bad, I got burned. . . ." She shrugged her tough little shrug. "Since I've been in Cedars, I've been hanging with one of their gangs. Didn't want to. Mostly I had to. They don't let you go easy. Mal got me out. I don't want to go back. They do nasty stuff to people, including their own. I'm sure you don't need a list."

Lila had been paying attention acutely, but she got no sense that the girl was lying. She glanced at Zal, who seemed more bemused than concerned although he was frowning and his shadow body had extended, diffusing to a fine haze around him. It didn't try to touch the girl, although he easily could have. He looked back at Lila and she was reminded of how much she hated the thought of separating from him again so soon. She turned back.

"I don't like being watched," Lila said.

"I don't mean any harm," the girl replied quickly. "Never have."

"But you're short of a name and a backstory," Zal said, "and we're too old to fool around."

"I can't give you my name," she said equally quickly. "It's too much of a risk."

"Oh, so we're supposed to trust you with knowing everything about us but you won't extend even half the favour?" Lila shook her head. "I don't think so."

"You're not the only one who doesn't like being supervised," came the retort, then, feeling clear anxiety she shook her hands in front of herself to erase the attacking force of her statement—a faery gesture if ever there was one. "Look, the fact is, I already know everything about you whether I like to know it or not. I know a lot about other people too. I can tell you whatever you like, if you just let me stay here. I can hide you from the spirits, if they come here. They'll never see you here as long as I stay."

Zal folded his arms thoughtfully and lowered his chin. "But the catch is that you're on someone's wanted list."

Anguished eyes flicked towards him and remained looking at him firmly. "Yes. But we're all on one of those."

"Might we know who's buying your ticket?" Lila asked.

The girl turned towards her and considered for a moment. "Sarasilien," she said very quietly. "I saw something, you see, in someone, and he knows I saw it. It must be very important. Those rogues I mentioned looking for you, they were looking for me too. He sent them, through Sandra Lane."

"The clone, right?"

"Not at the time. It was twenty-two years ago. There were no clones then."

"How many does she have now?" Lila was really wondering aloud and was surprised when the girl said promptly, "At least three I have seen. There are other cyborgs with clones too, of various kinds. Most of the old ones have at least one. Rogues habitually scatter clones over big areas—across continents. They're the reason I stayed so long in Cedars. There's a lot of old fey there, some demons in the gangmasters. They have enough strength to hold the rogues off. Nobody else does. And they can't do it off their own turf. I managed to get myself disappeared from the networks so they can't track me. It won't be long before they know I've gone though. My gangmaster has no reason to help me once he realises I'm not coming back."

"Was Malachi the one to get you out of trouble with Sarasilien?"

"Yes," she nodded solemnly. "It was a big risk for him."

"Why?"

"Because it interferes in a Long Game. The older forces, the long-lived ones, operate at timescales measured in centuries, perhaps ages. Malachi is the middle kind—centuries, millennia maybe. But these others are older ones. They are fewer. At least, they are now. In the past many more existed, but they got killed as the games went on. Sarasilien is one of the older sort, and what I saw is something concerning a Long Game that he has in progress. He is easily able to kill Malachi if he knew. I am only telling you because I know you don't wish him harm, even though you are angry with him at the moment."

Lila stared down at the countertop, considering. She looked at the motes of quartz, stuck fast in the resin of the fake stone, at the way their many different angles caught the light, or blocked it. She read between the lines and came up with an answer that surprised her.

"I suppose that locking someone away in Under for a few thousand years might be a move in such a game?" Lila glanced up as she finished, watching the girl's reaction closely. She didn't expect much. She'd already concluded that whoever and whatever the girl was, she was an expert at showing only what she wished someone to see. From the side of her vision, she kept Zal in close check—he had senses that could bypass lying and concealment even better than her ability to read the microresponses in other people's skin that unerringly betrayed the depth of their concern about what they said or did.

"Yes, of course," the girl said, shrugging it off in a way that neither confirmed nor denied Lila's suspicion about her identity. "Listen, I know that the more I say the less you want to trust me, yeah? And not without reason. I know what happened to you, both of you. But every game has its pieces and you must realise that you are those pieces, as I am. The players are not the gods, cold and on high, as you might imagine. Nor the Fates. They're just ones who live long and have power and like to play."

Zal's eyes narrowed, and the misty shadow of his aetheric body condensed and withdrew beneath his skin. He was solid as Lila and the girl, and waited for their replies. When they were both silent, Sassy moved uneasily on her barstool and drew her lips into her mouth, biting both of them between her teeth until a white line appeared at their joining.

"I always hated the idea of being a puppet," he said, with slow and exacting conviction. "But I have been one and it was every bit as awful as I imagined. But in the scheme of the universe, however, it stands, however weak it looks like it might be becoming. I don't buy what you're selling."

"No. You're a demon. You wouldn't," she said. "And I am not saying that your every move is pushed by unseen hands from on high. I'm not saying that! I'm saying there are those who like to play and they have liked to play with you. No more. Their age and their powers is all that makes them different. It makes them see things differently. They pick people up, see what happens; they don't take your will, they don't take your life away. They push a little bit here, pull a little bit there, see what happens. They lose some, they win some, they play short, and they play long."

"They're gamblers," Lila said, feeling the solid click of pieces falling into place inside her. They made a shape that was certain, a definite form, something she knew all about.

"Yes," the girl nodded. "That's it."

"So what's your part?" Zal said, glancing back and forth between her and Lila.

The girl looked each of them in the eye, first Zal, then Lila. "Everyone's got their price." She waited until both of them nodded to show they understood her, and agreed, in principle. "For some it's money, a little or a lot. For some it's honour, shame, vengeance—all the currencies of pride. You," she pinned Lila with a direct gaze of impossible clarity, "you played for pride. That's a deadly mortal game. I've never understood why anyone would want it, but that was your game, wasn't it?"

Lila lowered her eyelids, unable to nod but unable to say no. She had thought, early on when Sorcha had showed her the nature of her game with Zal, that it was a love game, perhaps even a sex game. But this girl, whoever she was, had it right. It was a pride game. And so was the one she'd played with her family. "I wouldn't play it that way again."

"That is why it lost its power. You changed," the girl said. "Games themselves can change in time, make new rules, lose old ones. Ah, you didn't know that, well, they can. Haven't you ever watched faeries play cards?"

Lila had. It was completely baffling, apparently random. She'd never figured out what was going on or how they knew who had won.

Sassy nodded. "Now your game has become only that—a lovers' game, a toy. If either of you decided to end it now by meeting its victory condition, that would be voluntary, a choice, and so you cannot meet the condition. A condition that can't be met is unplayable, so the rule changes. In this case it has become the spice to a foregone conclusion. It is worn out. You knew this."

Lila blinked; the girl had put her finger on feelings she hadn't been able to articulate herself. She glanced at Zal and found him looking at her with a glowing warmth she hadn't expected, his eyes amused, his expression a little knowing, a little bit sad. But before she could react the girl was talking again, her intensity begging and getting their attention.

"Zal, you played for your soul time and again. You always bet everything on it, and it always came up. That's a pirate's game, a free man's game, the stakes of angels."

Zal grinned, and his nostrils flared for a moment as he bowed his head.

"I've been instrumental in all kinds of games," the girl said, knotting her hands together around her knees, balancing on her narrow bottom on the high chair. Her feet pointed elegantly at the floor as she darted teasing looks at them now. "Win or lose, it was never my hand that mattered, I had nothing to play for, and freedom was impossible. When you've got my gifts, you can't breathe before someone grabs you round the throat. But I've seen a lot, heard a lot." She let go of her knees and unfolded with grace, sliding off the seat to stand on her feet. On contact with the ground she suddenly gained a strength that both of them could feel as if it were a force pushing at them. Energy surged up through her small frame and gathered in her gaze.

Lila felt her skin suddenly react, surging with a chill over her back. She saw Zal move unconsciously into a defensive stance, poised on the balls of his feet.

The girl nodded in acknowledgement. "You're like me. Sure you played some small-time business for yourselves, but in terms of the Long Game you're in over your heads because you don't see the big picture. Well, I see it—the players, the moves, the stakes, and I'm tired of watching. On my own I've got nothing. I can't get in by myself. But you two—you three, four, five whatever: you've got serious leverage, know what I'm sayin'?"

Lila nodded slowly. She knew that look from her mother's face. "You want in."

"Damn right!"

"I'm curious," Zal said, though Lila could tell he was interested just by the way his body was moving. "What's your price?"

"Power," the girl said simply. "The power to play, that's all."

"What if we say no?" Lila asked.

The girl looked her in the eye. "Yeah, you could do that. Run away from what you want. People do. But whatever you do, wherever you go, whatever happens, you know the game's on, like it or not, and your only choice is play or be played. Take it to heart or don't give a shit, doesn't matter. You'll live and die, that's for sure, only got a few details to work out here an' there. You keep trying not to play, eventually your offers are gonna dry up. But the thing about being someone else's powerful toy is that you got options. Your position is way better than mine right now, otherwise we wouldn't be talking. Trust me, no options gets old faster than you can believe, makes you ready to slip away, die maybe."

Lila rubbed her face. "And I thought people just lived the best they could and got on with what they could and suffered with what they couldn't until it was over."

"Mostly they do, live and die, never played a move, didn't notice or didn't care. Pity them. Or not," the girl said. "I don't care for all that. I made my move. It's your turn now."

CHAPTER ELEUEN

Lila gave Zal the nod, saying to the girl, "We need to talk, in private."

The girl bowed her head a fraction. "Then you'd better go at least two miles out."

Zal went back for his coat and then joined Lila on the deck where they both paused to look out over the forest down to the first houses and then, much farther away, the city. The air was cool and crisp even though down by the shore and in midtown it would already be warming up to humid.

Lila let her gaze rove across the skyscrapers and distinctive shapes of the skyline that was so new, noticing without caring when some important place went under her scan—the International Bank of Otopia, the Art Museum, the Magisterium, the University—and then she passed those and moved to the dull blocky shapes of apartments and low-rises that spanned the gap called Bonville before the last of the major roads vanished into a flurry of little bridges, walkways, and snakethrough passes that wound into the massed rises of Cedars like veins into a tumour. She didn't remember it like that. It had been so pretty.

But now Cedars wasn't ugly enough, considering what lay inside it, she thought. It had namesake trees in large numbers, breaking up the gaps and shading the goings on, smothering the worst of the neighbourhood in a yearround coverage of deceptively rich green. Cedars was a community park, made in what had been one of the more philanthropic moments of Bay City's history. It had been opened while she was still a teenager. The mayor had snipped the ribbons across the gaily painted Chinese gates and a hundred paper dragons had taken to the air, dropping an electronic shower of gift vouchers wherever the wind bore them across the city. She and Max had got on their bikes and ridden hell for leather chasing them down. Never got close enough to grab one though.

Her memory of Cedars itself was much hazier. It had been an enclosed place, meant to be self-sufficient, a place of respite and peace within the shambling heart of the city for families who couldn't have afforded the luxury in ordinary circumstances. It was close enough to midtown for work but far enough out that it wasn't competing with any substantially prime real estate. Max had an apartment there for a while when she first moved out of home, but soon left it for a place that went with her job at one of the north-end casinos. Even at this time in the morning the flashing lights of the strip by the shore were blazing. Bay City was a good-time paradise, thick with fey and demon interests from the cheapest motel on the strip right down Eighth Avenue to the International Bank. And in the middle of the line that joined those buildings Cedars festered, its aspiring young families long gone.

It reminded her of Solomon's Folly, an ugly junction of malicious forces.

"Where's the bike?" Zal asked.

"At the Agency," she said, realising how stupidly she'd behaved again thanks to her anger the day before.

"Come on then." He turned and walked down the steps to the dirt driveway. He didn't take the route towards the road but stepped off the property directly into the woods. Lila followed him, trusting his instincts on both directions and the forest implicitly. They walked for a few hundred metres, jumping a couple of shallow drainage ditches and crossing a forgotten access road that was overgrown with grass and young shrubs. Beyond this the woods became more dense and progressively wilder. It was clear to her that they were not in line for the Agency.

Zal hiked steadily for another kilometre, then two, then three. They came to a minor clearing where a few trees had keeled over in last winter's blowhard gales, and he sat down on the deadfall, waiting for her to join him. She sat beside him, carefully testing the logs before she let them take her weight. They had moved quite quickly, but neither of them was out of breath. It had been good to do nothing but walk and breathe the air.

"Lila," Zal said in the slow way that meant he was coming to say something important. "Where's Tatters?"

"We've parted company," Lila said, less confident of her decision now that he seemed to be questioning it. "Last night I had a bit of a session." He was quiet and she felt more anxious. "What's the matter?"

"I got the feeling you want to buy into this Long Game."

"I don't know that I entirely buy her story—"

"No, but all the same. But I'm sick of those things. I had enough before I left Alfheim—they were the reason that I left. I haven't been too good at leaving them behind. They follow me and pick me up it seems. But I'm not interested in being a player. I'm done. Even if the world is at stake. Particularly if that's the stake."

"God, you're such a liar," Lila said. "You primed entire Otopian generations—"

"I did," he said, cutting her off firmly but gently. "But it wasn't part of a master plan. It was me, doing what I do, which is pretty plotless and I intend for it to stay that way. I don't care if someone thinks I'd make a good whatever. I'll do what I like for my own reasons and screw the rest. But you, you're not like that."

"I'm getting more like it."

"Even so."

She frowned, not sure where this was going but sure she wasn't liking it. It smelled of separation, divided ways. It felt like a version of "it's not you, it's me." As the prospect of Zal going one way and her another grew more palpable, a jolt of anguish shot through her, and in its wake everything that had been occupying her for the last few days faded into a grey desolation.

"And then again," he said, looking at the wall of forest in front of them, "You're involved with the Agency and your own issues, and Teazle's fucked off without a word, which makes me assume he's got more interesting people to kill. Malachi, well, he's more your friend than anything to do with me. My friends are all dead or gone. I have nothing to do and nowhere to go. I feel the need to do something useful, worthwhile, of purpose since I've been back here. Never thought I'd say that, but I need to make their deaths worth something more than another few years of me living on."

"Zal, I—"

"Hear me out. I don't want a pity party. I want something to do so I don't have to think about what I lost twenty-four-seven forever because then I'll be a morose sonofabitch and drink, drug, or fuck myself into oblivion, which looks like a waste even from this end. Going into Alfheim is like a fucking godsend. But you going to find Ilya—I don't like that, and Sassy's story doesn't quite add up. You can throw in with her if you want to, but I'm out. I don't care if Sarasilien is playing the best hand in history across all of time and space and if I serve his purposes or not. Fuck him. I should probably thank him, because without him there'd be no you right now, but fuck him anyway." He sighed. "I guess you have to go satisfy yourself you know what's going on before you gut him."

Lila pulled at the rotting bark next to her leg, "Every time I think I know what I want to do I stop myself. Every time I do something, the consequences . . ." She shrugged. "You know what? If there are players in this Long Game, and everything that happened with me is part of some scheme, I think I get where Sassy's coming from. You get used enough, you want in. I want to dish out some of what I've been getting. And then I want out, and the way I see it, the only way out is to get rid of all the bastards in my way. There may be an endless supply of bastards, is the thing that worries me. In Demonia I can't move ten steps before I have to gun someone down."

"No," Zal said. "Of that I am sure. The stronger you get, the less you can be played. That's why I am the strongest thing that there is. I slipped up with Sorcha and paid Jack for it. I don't do that again."

She looked quizzically at him.

"I am," he said. "That's why I don't play."

She thought it over. "I'm so angry," she said, ripping bark free and throwing it down in the grass where their feet had crushed it flat.

"Yeah," he said and put his arm around her shoulders. "That's why I love you."

"So you're going to do what Sarasilien wants?"

"No. I'm going to Alfheim, take a look around, see what's happening. You can tell him it's what he wants if you like."

She thought it over. "I will."

"And you?"

"I'm going to find Ilya and talk to him. Don't know how I'll get to Ilya short of standing in front of a freight train and praying, but I'll find a way. I feel like I owe something to Greer, don't ask me why."

"It's the anecdotes," Zal said without hesitation.

She ripped another piece of bark free and scrutinised it, trying not to smile. It was covered in grey-green lichens, just a few of millions on that hillside. They took hundreds of years to grow, didn't go anywhere, didn't even look like anything special. "You'll need gear."

"I'll pick it up in Demonia."

"I'll come with you."

"Any excuse for a fight."

"You read my mind."

Neither of them moved to get up. Lila put out her hand and Zal took it. They interlaced their fingers and closed them.

"I liked our little house and our rebellious teenage daughter," Lila said. She didn't look at him; she looked at her feet and the crushed grass under them.

"Yes, me too. I was looking forward to the pony rides in the forest."

"Christmas, with everything."

"Throwing unsuitable boyfriends off the deck."

"Shopping for clothes."

"Being shunned at the school gate."

"Graduation day. Oh, the prom!"

"Walking through Alfheim, for the first time."

"Dinner at home."

"It would never work."

"No, not in a million years."

"Yesterday."

"Yes. Yesterday it did. Ten years in one minute."

"We aren't going back there."

"I will," Lila said. "Let her think I'm taking her offer."

"You're going to play?"

She took a deep breath and sighed it out through her nostrils. "You know, I never even played cards with Mom? Wouldn't. Not once."

"Why not? She must have known all the games."

"Sure. Every rule, every variation, every cheat. She couldn't lose."

"You didn't want to lose either."

"No no, it wasn't that. You forget that you're not a blackbelt in codependency, sensei. I was worried that one day I might win and break her stride. Poker's a confidence game. What if I beat her at something, anything, and she lost a bit of her faith? She got the stuffing kicked out of her three or four times a year anyway. I didn't want to be the person who did that. Not even a little bit. Even though if I had played with her at least we would have had one thing in common, 'stead of nothing."

"But you're going to play now?"

"Hardball," Lila said, closing her free hand into a fist until the black leather of her fingers creaked and it felt like a solid mace at the end of her arm. She turned it, admiring its flat knuckles, the gleam of the daylight cold and grey on the curving planes of her thumb.

Zal put up his own fist in response, larger and bonier than hers. He touched knuckles with her, and they pressed against each other for a moment. "This is where I'm supposed to warn you off the dark side of the force," he said, and opened his hand out then, shaking it as if he'd already punched someone and hit bone.

"Feel free."

"I would, but this way seems more fun."

Now they turned to face each other and touched foreheads, tilting slightly to the side so that their noses didn't clash and they could press the flat bones together like small bulls, staring wall-eyed.

"Don't get killed, Blackout," Zal said.

"Aces high, is what you're s'posed to say," she told him, grinning to match his grin.

"Why?"

"That's the code," she said. "That's what you say."

"Aces high, then."

"And to you."

It took only a slight movement to change the headbutt into a kiss.

Lila let it evolve of its own accord. To really kiss Zal was a pleasure she could afford and he never disappointed her. He put all of himself into it, and she could feel it and it made her dizzy and shy and gratified and strange with delight.

At last she murmured, "So, do you think she heard us?"

"Definitely," he said. "I guess she figures we're safe bets—I can't be arsed to lie and you . . . are you."

Lila frowned. She didn't like to be thought of as solid and predictable. "That's just my poker face."

He grinned at her, a fiendish, wolfish expression that agreed, but he wasn't going to say it aloud. This made her feel that what she had boldly said to lift her spirits might actually have potential as a truth. She kissed him again and stood up, brushing bark off her trousers.

"How about a little trip into Cedars? I'm pretty sure there'll be a portal there."

He cocked his head to the side, "And check a few small stories while we're there?"

"You see, telepathic again. I think you must be magical."

He made a slight kind of shrug, and for an instant she saw his shadow body emerge, flickering; black flames dancing across his skin. "Must be."

They walked a wide circle around the house, maintaining their nominal safe distance, until they reached Podunk Flats. The ground was low and swampy, being at the end of the mountains and at the edge of the vast, watery delta that ran over Bay City's rocky outcrops and along its faultlines to the sea. The sound of insects was loud, the grey morning muggy as they stepped out of the trees and onto the hardtop of the road. Lila had called a taxi, and it was waiting for them at her coordinates a few metres from their position, in hibernation, lights off, signalling systems offline.

One thing that had changed about Bay City in the last fifty years was something that had affected the entire human population. In Lila's earlier life citizens had been freer to move around. After the Hunter's Reign and the influx of new blood, the citizen registry had changed and now everyone was tracked, not only by their spending patterns and their phonecalls, but every device that contained an OS was enabled to collect data and match it to the national database, either online or merely as a precautionary memory of where someone had been and what they had done. It was possible to get around a lot of types of tracking device, but when almost every working machine could sniff your genome in seconds, it didn't do much good. Thus, although Lila had shut herself off from the other cyborgs, and from the network except for times of her choosing, she couldn't vanish entirely from the vast infopool that was the Bay City Memhub. At least she was more or less invisible thanks to her Agency markers, depending on the day. Zal had no entry at all, which made him an Unknown Entity, identifiable perhaps as an elf but nothing else. This would create a security alert that would instantly call attention and also prevent them from using the car, so to preempt that eventuality she signed herself on to one of the pending Cedars murder investigations and arrested him.

It was then a matter of a few easy seconds to wake up and direct the taxi, blotting it from the majority of the tracking subnets with regular police protocols. They sat inside, reclined on the two sofas, and watched the dreary smalltown stubble of buildings begin to roll past the windows as it slowly took over from the trees. Podunk Flats gave way imperceptibly to another, larger suburb with more crowded housing. Zal looked at it despondently. He wasn't happy in cities and suburban areas even less so. The filtered light showed lines on his face. Lila moved across to him, keying the windows to blank themselves, and pushed her way into his arms. They held one another, and in the still calm of his embrace she felt the seconds ticking away. She filled her nose with the smell of him and pressed her tongue to the exposed skin at the neck of his shirt, held him closely and listened to the steady beat of his heart, immersed until a note sounded and she felt the brakes bring them to a smooth halt.

The car had stopped short of its destination. Lila unpacked herself from Zal and stood up. She opened the door and stepped out into the sudden burn of sunlight as it cut between two high-rises. There was a roadblock ahead. To save herself trouble she started downloading hub-data, allowing her AI to surface sufficiently that she meshed with it in real time, her mind getting access to all its resources.

Between one step and the next she had armed herself in semi-plate under the leather harness and let her arms and legs revert to their machine mode, weapons forming and loads priming inside her fore-arms. She stood in line with Zal as he got out, shielding him from most of the unseen guns who were overlooking them from the shady balconies of the two closest high-rise blocks, and from the curious stare of the police officer looking their way from the city's side of a substantial barricade. On the gang side a cohort, including several demons and changelings, moved restlessly. It was a temporary stand-off, one of several each week. This one however was a lockdown from the inside, and the officers here were standing around bored as their leaders talked with gangmasters on private lines.

Lila let the taxi go, keeping Zal behind her shoulder. By the time she reached the barricade's gateway she'd burst enough comms lines to know that the gang known as Motley had called the freeze on migra-tion. Cedars obstructed the free flow of traffic from downtown to the strip—the major route in the city. Closing it caused a headache of big enough proportions that the city wanted to reopen desperately, but Motley were holding out for information and what they wanted to know was where one of their gang members had gone. The city would know, even if they'd left the limits and headed out towards another hub. The city didn't have the information—she found an Agency trace on the deletions—and Motley didn't believe them. The blockade was into its second day and tempers were short. It didn't take much to figure out that Sassy was the missing person in question.

Once the police had satisfied themselves that she was who she said she was, they let her through, eyeing Zal with a mixture of curiosity and distrust that was almost palpable, though Lila got the impression he was enjoying it. For someone who couldn't move without being mobbed, it must have been strange. For her part she could have done without the hostility—it felt so much worse than the past, when demons were still mostly features of lurid stories rather than actual beings on the street and when faeries were one-way tickets to the champagne lifestyles of the celebrities.

The police closed their side of the cordon, and the Motley gave her and Zal the long, assessing stares that she knew from gang members everywhere, including the one she'd run with in secondary school. She saw a savage-looking dog who was clearly a demon in his natural form, spiked all over with bony spars, teeth as big as knives, ears flat close to his red head. Beside him two other demons, one draconid, another a humanoid with natural bone armour and a scowl that could have curdled milk at a hundred miles, went through the lip-curling business of sensing and then having to double-take Zal's own demon nature as well as his elf body. Then they stared even harder at her, able to feel traces of aether but not able to pick the source. The human among them, a young man with a ferocious set of brightly coloured tattoos covering his face and hands, his hair bound in black rags, was the only one to break silence.

"Yeah?"

Lila showed her badge on the flat of her hand, letting it shine out of her skin and fade away as he recognised or at least acknowledged it.

"Feds?" he said uncertain and incorrect but cowed, his glance at Zal frankly disbelieving. "What you want?"

"Respect," said the bone demon angrily, glaring at his gangmate with contempt. "This not any cop. This Friendslayer and this with her is the rolling rock itself, ain't it? Ahrimani scum. We thought you dead and gone. You look like you returning but don't smell dead. Where you been all this time?"

His companions glanced at him. "Ahrimani?" the dog muttered, shaking its massive head as though at a mistake. Lila ignored it. Any demon running gangs in Bay City was either rolling for the fun of it or was too weak to claw a place of any power back home. Zal's old adoptive family had been a power to reckon with fifty years past in Demonia, second only to Teazle's rapacious broodclan, but their star had fallen when Zal was lost. He commanded a share of Teazle's recent reign of blood and terror, but only by marriage. Legally he was also dead in Demonia, which meant, should he do the prodigal thing, that he would have to start again to prove his worth. The Ahrimani name had been brutal enough to be legend in its own lifetime, however, and this couldn't be discounted. Here he was, elf, dead, alive, Ahrimani and standing cool, tall and elegant in their neglected gardens, a strange dark flower blooming out of season. He barely awarded them a glance.

"You must be older than you look," Lila said, shifting into the gap and taking up a relaxed stance, carefree as if she were at a party. "We want the answer to the fey murders taking place on your patch and then we want a portal to Bathshebat."

"Yeah, well I want a condo with a boat and a car and six chained naked chicks in every room," the human said, stepping into her path. "What you got?"

Lila made a laissez-faire gesture with one hand. "Life and death."

He blinked at her stupidly and groped around visibly in his head for her meaning. "Cops don't kill on sight."

"I'm not a cop. Now, do you know anything about . . ." She read the details, keeping her eyes in contact with his. She was going through the motions but if they worked she didn't care. ". . . the murder of Janie Six? Fullblood human."

"Shit no, but if she was one of those undead freaks, then who gives a fuck?"

"She was a dancer from the strip. Attack looks werewolf," Lila said.

The guy looked at her with uneasy distaste, picking up things from the demons' body language that kept him from outright attacking, but he was jittery. The dog growled.

"Well, I'm not here to interfere with the law-abiding ignorant," Lila said pleasantly. "I will take your silence as a no. Let's go." She saw Zal give the nod to the demons, meaning he wanted to talk to them alone, and without a word all four of them began to walk away. She turned to follow them, leaving the human gang member watching her with sudden misgiving.

"Police been here about that before," he hissed at her as she passed him. "Nobody's goddamn business what prying whores get their dues. Stay out of . . ."

Lila ignored him and what he wanted to say about territory although every word about the dead woman filed away in her mind, burning slow trails towards her gut. She could smell drugs on him, enough to convict, and perhaps something that might have been a doglike odour, but she didn't think he had enough fey blood to have a nightmare let alone be one. She heard him follow them a few metres later but just kept after Zal as they were led across a small open sandy area that had once been a kids' playground and was now the local cat toilet as far as she could make out.

The police called her, and she answered them with some platitudes until they shut up and let her alone. Meanwhile the demons led them across the tree-shaded gardens, cluttered with rubbish, and across the highway, full of gang cars and bikes circling and playing chicken with each other in the growing heat of the afternoon. It smelled of petrol; she heard old engines out there half a mile further up, and sniffed the air, trying to catch a trace more before they turned into a door and then a hall.

Lila expected the demons to try and jump them before they reached the stairwell, but when it happened she was disappointed. For Zal, because they weren't scared enough of him to do him the honour of running away and for herself for trusting them even for a split second not to be as stupid and petty ugly as they were. But as they launched themselves and revealed their blade weapons, claws, teeth, and guns, she felt delight in retaliation, a sudden cool, collected calm in her head in place of all the chatter.

The dog was first. It was nearly the size of a horse, but it barrelled in on Zal with dead weight, aiming to pin him to the filthy wall while the other two shot him. The draconid flung a flechette. The bone demon raised and took a shot with a handgun, which missed and ricocheted off the wall with a shrieking noise. It missed because Zal wasn't at the wall, he was in midair in a crouched position, feet tucked under him, chest to knees, arms wide as he jumped the dog's high back. The flechette blade jabbed into the concrete wall where his head might have been and exploded in a burst of purple poison that splattered the graffiti and began to smoke.

Lila put an explosive shell into the bone demon's chest that blasted it into a mist of bloody shrapnel. She felt splinters cut her cheeks and forehead and saw a larger bit jammed into the draconid's arm, making it look down for a second. Meanwhile Zal landed at the dog demon's side, shoving it against the wall where he was supposed to be with a violent jolt. He drove his fingers through the thick, greasy fur of its neck, and Lila saw darkness well out of the spot. The dog stopped moving and slid down the blockwork to its side where it lay still. Lila took off the draconid's long head with the flick of a chained blade from beneath her wrist and snapped it back into place inside her forearm. Her AI sampled and checked the residues as it cleaned up.

Meanwhile the human gangster hadn't expected the demons to attack. He was slower than they were to react, hesitant with a moment of troubled disbelief that they were about to murder an officer, not understanding enough demon politics to realise this was an internal affair as far as they were concerned, more important than any Otopian law. Lila had to wait with her hand behind her back for a good three seconds before he pulled his gun on her and she could finally shoot out his legs above the knee with ordinary rounds.

By the time she stood over him, listening to his whimpering

shrieks, the crime was already processed and the file closed. She bent down and injected him with a brief burst of painkillers, just enough so that he could get ahold of himself. "Who is looking for this gang member that's missing? Where is the Portal?"

In between inarticulate swearing, he managed to tell her that the missing girl was the property of one of the Motley's leaders, Shivaud. There was some challenge for top spot going on and the gang was dividing. Shivaud was the one with the issue and he had a portal too.

She left him lying there and went up to Zal, who was looking down at the dead demons, wiping blood, flesh, and bone off his face and out of his hair. "I forgot how welcoming they could be," he said, shaking off his hand with an audible splatter onto the wet tile floor. He spat to clear his lips of demon blood and sighed a short, shoulder-drop sigh of resignation. "Where now?"

"Up," Lila pointed at the row of elevator doors, their bronze panels glinting with crudely carved fey symbols. "Boss always lives at the top."

Zal glanced at the call panels. None of the lights were lit. "Looks like they didn't pay their bills."

Lila waved her hand. "I got it." She pulled off the panel face of the first set of doors, plugged into the system, and powered it up, accelerating her tokamak to provide enough juice to get the thing active and at speed. The blocks were high, and even if they had no idea how it was happening, someone would hear the lift moving and figure it out before they got to the top. The car was already in the basement, where the machinery had left it. She had some dread of the doors opening, but when they did there was nothing special to see except the mould on the old carpeting. She reached around to the car's own panel to switch her connection and Zal stepped in after her. There was a screeching creak of rusty cables and a juddering sensation as the winch took hold. She monitored the resistances but it was perfectly safe, just dry and rusted, so she piled on the power and they shot upwards. Zal groaned.

"Ugh, this is how heavy humans must feel all the time."

"Three point one g's," Lila informed him. "Only the very fat ones."

And they were there, the twenty-fourth floor, having moved from the selves that had come here, all talk, to the selves that stood here, sombre with action, in the space of a few breaths. Lila left the doors open, the car fixed, as she stepped out.

A panting, slightly wild-eyed greeting party had formed into a loose semicircle in the apartment's foyer. They were all male, young, human or human enough, and armed with a variety of automatic weapons and belts of the enchanted bullets known as "demon cutters." Lila could tell by the clean streaks on the handsome marquetry floor that nobody had walked in this way for a very long time. Other than the wear upon it, however, the apartment was a glorious vision of cleanliness and good taste, lit by solar feeds from the roof above them and powered, she assumed, by panels up there too. They wouldn't be enough to haul an elevator car, but enough to run any tech that was needed.

Behind the first row of ready regulars and the oddly angled one-eyed menaces of their black, stubby guns, a few handy-looking types of men and a couple of women had dashed in from other directions, darted glances to the elevators, and hurried deeper into the apartment's recesses through veils of door-hangings made out of plastic tape and beads. A smell of various half-cut drugs spiralled lazily in their wakes, the luxurious perfume of indulgence rather than addiction. Lila placed five illegal narcotics, amphetamines, and the curious taint of mescaline, and listened to the conversations going on across the rooms.

Meanwhile she held up her hands like a fainting southern belle waylaid by bandits. "I just want to talk to Shivaud." Trickles of blood ran down her arms and dripped off her elbows. "And if maybe one of you has a wet wipe, that would be nice."

Zal stood behind her at point position, face impassive under its pinto decoration of red from the dog and purplish blue from the bone demon. Neither of them looked armed. A couple of the men blinked and squinted, confused by the haze of darkness around Zal.

"Who the hell are you?" one in the middle said finally as they nerved themselves, waiting for someone with a clue to turn up and tell them what to do.

"I just want a portal and some conversation," Lila said, lowering her hands slowly and giving herself a little shake. Blood pattered onto the marquetry floor. "You really should look for the wipes. That's going to stain horribly if you leave it."

There was a briefly hissed but very audible passing of "what-the-fucks" along the line, but mercifully a woman in a tailored suit with fetish boots and immaculately waxed black hair appeared from the plastic veils and strode forward with businesslike predation in her expression, one hand tucking the tips of its fingers into the impossibly tiny pocket of her fitted tweed jacket. She moved like a catwalk model and was as tall and thin as a pole. The precise line of her lipstick left no room for compromises.

"Phitti, Dedalon," she addressed the semicircle of guards with easy authority. "Cover the back." And there she stood, waiting for them to slouch past her to their new, less interesting posts. None of them gave her a second look, which to Lila meant only one thing.

"Shivaud, I presume."

The barest flicker of a wintry smile crossed the woman's whitened face. She was beautiful at a short distance, the paint making her more so, a kind of geisha but with a sadist's mouth. "Most people assume I will be a man. I can usually put up my second in my place while I play hostess in the background. Then again, most agents are men." She flicked a glance at Zal and lingered on him for a moment. "And human." When her gaze came back to Lila, she put her head to one side and offered the merest of social smiles. "To what do I owe the pleasure?"

Lila showed her Agency credentials, and this time Shivaud paused long enough to read them before standing back.

"So?"

"We've come to clear the road," Lila said.

Shivaud's black lensed eyes narrowed slightly, but she inclined her head with the grace of a lady and gestured behind her. "Come in then, and we can talk."

On the other side of the bead curtains was a room filled with sofas and entertainment tech. They passed through it, trailed at a distance by first one and then another of the more handy types Lila had seen before. Then they came into a red and gold silk room with views over the strip towards the bay; clearly a demon's lair. If the opulence and grandeur of the furnishings hadn't given it away—piling style on style and packing in pirate chests full of concealed weapons—the people it contained would have.

It was a large room, separated into semicircular areas by lush waterfalls of satin in dark colours, offering multiple sightline issues. Within the outer zones waterpipes and incense bowls simmered with the mixtures Lila had identified earlier—everything from trip mixes to poisons. Bodies in various states of undress and consciousness lay around; the retinue of the favoured passing the boring daylight hours of afternoon in their comas of choice. Demons were among them, of several lesser kinds, but all this paled into insignificance as Lila and Zal were invited to the central area and its bordello of inflated pillows and pasha rugs, animal hides liberally strewn around.

In the midst of this lay a succubus wearing a leather harness of narrow straps and about a thousand buckles, a chain choke collar around her neck that was tied to a violet ribbon with a chewed end. Her face was uncommonly pretty and innocent looking, her hair blonde and fluffy, simmering with pale tawny fire that made Zal suck his breath in. Her skin was the colour of wholewheat toast and oiled to a lustrous shine that emphasised all of her humanly impossible curves and the scorpion tip of her tail. This was red with blood, and her victim lay in front of her—a naked man, not more than twenty-five, nearly as pretty as she was with his long brown hair scattered around. His waxed chest and abdomen were striped with whip marks turning purple and his neck was punctured in several places with the full stops of the scorpion stinger, though he still breathed and his glassy eyes were open.

The succubus was trimming a red apple with a tiny silver knife and had laid the peelings out around his half-erect penis in a kind of pattern. She looked up from this as Shivaud led Lila and Zal into the room and, in a matter of fact kind of way, stuck out her foot-long pointed tongue and licked the length of it. The man stirred and moaned—an ecstatic sound that contained a painful pitch in it.

Lila could pick up venom traces from the air. It was everywhere. She analysed it and discovered not only the enhancing factors for pushed nervous systems but magical coils whose purpose she could only guess at. The boy on the floor wasn't giving anything much away.

Shivaud strode to her place atop the only chair in the room—a straightbacked wooden Shaker style—and sat down primly, indicating that Zal and Lila could try pleasing themselves. The succubus turned her eyes to Zal and smouldered openly at him, her lips visibly swelling and reddening as she let them part in a pout and batted her eyelashes.

Shivaud all but ignored her entirely although she made introductions. "This is Roxa. Roxa get a grip, these aren't the usual pieces of shit." She dug one sharp stiletto heel into the succubus's perfectly circular buttock, and the demon lashed her tail, jetting a fine mist of venom in an arc away from them while she turned her attention to Lila and smiled sweetly with her corrupted schoolgirl's face.

Lila ignored her and said to Shivaud, "Your missing person is of interest to me."

"She's of interest to *me*," Shivaud said, and the succubus stiffened slightly at the words although she relaxed almost immediately after. "Give her back and you can drive free as the birds."

"Interesting choice of words," Lila said, and then carried on seamlessly as she dismissed all possible seating areas. "I want to know who and what she is to you that's worth incurring such enormous civil fines. By now you must be on your third mortgage." They both knew the city didn't have the balls to collect damages out of Cedars lest there be a retaliatory explosion of violence that would ruin the tourist trade on the shore, but equally the gang law knew that everything had a price. Shivaud was daring a great deal.

In the meantime Zal had come forward and was standing with the naked man's head at his feet, looking down on the succubus as she preened up at him from her belly-down position, lifting herself high to show off her breasts and arching her back. Her tail curled and quivered delicately, almost in his eyeline. He admired her with his expression and she gave a long, strange quiver that ran the length of her entire body like a belly dancer's shimmy. Lila watched with one eye while keeping the leader as her main focus. Demon standoffs were strange to see, especially when the demons concerned were so different in character.

She felt mildly threatened by Roxa, whose charms were blindingly obvious, but was also contemptuous because this upstart wasn't a patch on Sorcha, Zal's demon sister. Then again Sorcha had had class; the burning diva wouldn't stoop to seduction as a weapon, for her it had been a given and would have lacked sport. But at the same time Lila felt mildly aroused by the scene and knew it would be double if she looked at Zal, and that would confuse her as much as Shivaud no doubt intended. The humans of the Western world had developed a great deal, but their culture was medieval in its attitudes to sex, hence the mighty industry of the Bay coast and the success of this sort of tactic. Though it probably would have been successful regardless since the succy's venom was laced with pheromones strong enough to interest rocks. Lila had a hard time finding a way to get the stuff out of her system. She wondered what Shivaud used and then, on examining the woman's immaculate burlesque façade from cool stare to steel-boned corset, thought perhaps she had adapted to it. Zal must also be thinking of Sorcha, and it was hard to see how that might go. It didn't seem as though this Roxa recognised him at all, so that was one card in his favour.

Finally Shivaud said, "The Motley is not only a business, it is a refuge for many, adults and children. They are my flock. In return for their feeding and care, protection, I ask only loyalty and, if they are able to help me, for their favours."

"So the one who is missing was able to do big favours?"

"Society detests powerful changelings. I welcome all."

Lila looked down at the naked, semi-comatose man. The wounds in his neck had swollen shut and around them a network of purple stains had spread under the skin. "Interesting welcome."

Shivaud's icy smile appeared, her voice doelike with serenity. "This is a much-prized reward, not a punishment, though maybe it is a punishment that is its own reward."

Roxa pouted prettily and put out her tongue. It was really obscenely long, like a flattened snake, and towards the back Lila saw tiny barbs at its sides. The forepart was lusciously pink with a strawberry pattern of receptors shining as the demon gave another lick to her prize—a curiously loving and tender gesture that reminded Lila of the way she'd seen a leopard once adoringly lick the exposed bone of half an eviscerated antelope that it had dragged up into a tree. The succubus kept her hypnotising stare on Zal, and in return Zal folded his arms across his chest and looked down on her from his great height, stonefaced, although other parts of his body were responding quite differently. Roxa smiled with angelic slowness and a faint rosy blush spread over both sets of her cheeks. Her tail tip swayed slowly back and forth, the length of it making lazy S shapes above her. Zal's hair changed colour from muddy-blond to corn-yellow as all traces of his shadow body sank beneath his skin. Roxa blinked with pleasure. Lila could not tell if Zal had won or lost that point.

She decided to get to her own point without delay. "I spoke to your seer. She doesn't intend to come back. Nobody has any business forcing her where she doesn't want to go."

"She is not a citizen on the hub," Shivaud said. "I think that Otopia Security will be more than content to force her to be registered or else deported."

"If we do that, then it will be the last you'll see of her."

"Perhaps. You forget that people have families of blood or of kindness, and families must be looked after." The dark stare of her made-up eyes was arrow-straight now and speared Lila's slight flinch. "Is that all you came to say?"

"I want her name," Lila said. "And a portal to Demonia."

"She calls herself Oubliette," Shivaud said. "Of course it isn't her real name. I don't know what that is." Her mouth had gone tight with anger, creating sudden fine lines in her taut mask. Her gaze flickered over the blood on Lila and the gore on Zal as he slowly shed his coat behind him and began to unbutton his shirt. That got her full attention.

Zal pulled the shirttails out of his trousers and dropped the whole thing with two fluid moves. The tide line at his collar where the drying film of blood marked a perfect V against his skin was almost comical. Lila, Shivaud, and Roxa all let out exactly the same small sigh at the same moment, and Lila had to fight a quiver in her lips lest she start laughing.

There was a sound like dispersed gasoline catching fire, and Lila saw the demon flare brighten across Zal's back a moment before his shoulders erupted in seething yellow flame.

"Mind the drapery, darling," Shivaud murmured, lifting one hand to adjust the immaculate line of her fringe over her eyebrows.

The flames' initial surge towards winghood fell back and quickly spread along his exposed skin, including his face. Where the small tongues of fire licked, they burnt the filth off him, becoming green for a moment, then red, then bright, near white though he was clearly unharmed. They died back to a soft ripple of low light burn, but they did not go out. His hair lightened, bleached into sunshine and then into near whiteness beneath the flames' caress.

One of Roxa's eyebrows moved up a single notch.

"I suppose you will not tell me where you met her? And you want to use my portal for free," Shivaud asked, though it was more of a statement.

Lila didn't know if she were a better judge of a demon fight or not, but she felt that Shivaud was either conducting a plot for their massacre by invisible means—not unreasonable given the number of telepaths reported in Cedars—or else she figured herself outgunned.

At their feet Roxa slowly levered herself up to her hands and knees. With coy catlike moves she came forward to Zal, over the body of the lucky reward guy, until her face was inches from his thighs, at which point she sat back on her heels and gave him the full benefit of her frontal aspect, tilting her head back to bare her throat completely, head to one side, eyes half closed, hands softly relaxed and resting palm up on her thighs. Her tail swept across the body behind her, conforming to its shapes as it slid along. The man behind her made a soft moaning sound and a tear came from one eye, though otherwise he didn't or couldn't move.

"Unless you have anything to say about Janie Six." Lila felt left out of things. It was too bad, but she wasn't sure she wanted to see how this struggle was going to end if she left it unchecked.

"Finishing a little police business? How nice for you. But what would I get for my kindness?" Shivaud said, folding her hands on her lap and adjusting her posture so that she could tuck her feet under the chair.

Lila watched the succubus place her long fingers on either side of Zal's hips. At this range the beautifully painted nails were obviously claws, several studded along their central ridge with diamonds and tiny seed pearls. The claw tips grazed his skin above his waistband, testing it. When she didn't start burning, she purred. Zal, mesmerised, was reaching with one hand towards her face as if to caress it.

Lila turned back to Shivaud, her own hands folded in front of her, straight as a librarian. "You get to live and so does your associate here. That's generous of me, very generous indeed, considering that she is now on my territory and I am not known as a gentle punisher back at the Sikarza house."

The demon took a sudden inbreath, and her languor became the poised anxiety of a squirrel in a second. Shivaud's face fell with surprise and both of the women looked at Lila with fresh appraisal. Lila smiled at them both. "Isn't it interesting how everyone always thinks the man is in charge?"

"I am from Tantalor," the demon said quickly, recoiling from Zal with dancer's grace but lightning speed. "I did not recognise you. We are far from the capital and the great society. Forgive me." She bowed, her face pushed into the pillows and her bottom down, tail curling quickly around her legs until it wrapped her all around. When she came up, she kept her face down.

Zal sighed heavily and bent down to pick up his soggy clothing. The flames died back to their normal position in a wing-shape tattoo on his back as he straightened up and dressed. His disgust at his shirt and coat was only marginally less than Shivaud's expression as she kicked the demon with the toe of her shoe.

"Roxa!"

"It is no use," the succubus said, crawling back slowly to crouch over the unconscious body behind her. She seemed to gain some strength from it and sat up again. "Tell them and let them go."

Shivaud stared at her in disbelief. Lila could see that Roxa had always delivered in the past and was the undefeated champion of these parts. Suddenly Roxa hissed at Shivaud and came up into a pounce-ready crouch, her tail quivering.

"Do as they say and get them out of here!"

Shivaud's expression became stony. She turned to Lila. "Janie Six was killed by one of the Viperblood, from Cedars West, a guy called

Haddon, half demon. He's the Viperblood second. You touch him, you got a war with them. The portal is that way," she indicated her left with a wave. "Roxa will take you there."

The demon looked vengeful at this rebuke to her status, but she stood up obediently nonetheless.

Lila and Zal stepped over the prone man to follow her.

"You aren't going to demand I clear the roads?" Shivaud asked sweetly.

"I don't care about the road," Lila said and let that sink into the silence that followed as she trailed the succubus along a hall to a room at the far end of the building.

CHAPTER TWELVE

Roxa's stride was long and businesslike. She reached the door she was looking for, breathed onto her hand, pressed it to the cheap wood, and then flung back a couple of bolts. She went in before them and gestured for them to help themselves.

"All yours."

The room did not have any windows, only the light from the portal shimmer contained within the glowing marks on its bare floorboards.

"Where does it come out?" Zal asked.

"In a house on the Sangueste Canal, near Bladespark Bridge. There will be some liaison there but they won't bother you, I'm sure." She paused and then said with a teasing grin, "But in the stories that reached Tantalor they say you were a portal opener. I suppose that must not be true."

Zal's hand on her arm prevented Lila from moving forward. "It's true enough to recognise a rubbish chute from a gate. This is a dumping ground and it goes to Zoo, where everything gets taken care of." He pointed at the demonic runescript edging the broad ring. Blood and dust marked the boards, but that was only to be expected.

Roxa's moment of confidence vanished and she darkened, becoming a yellow-green colour. Her tail whipped around, almost invisible in the shadows, and a splatter of venom struck Zal's face as the tip of the tail point stabbed into his neck. The sound of Lila's gun was almost deafening in the tiny space, followed by the plaintive last sigh of the demon as she slid to the ground, almost severed in half through the waist. Zal slapped his hand to his neck, recoiling, and hit the door as he staggered.

"Zal!" Lila caught him by the shoulders. The gun had been and gone, a breath of violence and fear. It was an overreaction. She was shocked by that more than the result.

His eyes were rolling up in his head, but his teeth were gritted. "Just push her in the hole and let's get out of here," he hissed, breathing in gulps of air and snarling with the effort of resisting the poison. "You can shoot me with something, right?"

"Yeah," she said, feeling the strange surge of power as her body struggled to produce an antitoxin. "Not for the magical component though."

"That's okay," he said. "It will wear off. I can live with that." He reached out towards the door and caught hold of it this time, but the effort was too much and it brought him to his knees. By his feet the demon's twitching tail tip was still pumping out the dregs of its venom sacs, filling the air with the heavy, musky fragrance of roses and myrrh, romance and death. "Why," he gasped in between breaths, "do I always get it in the neck?"

"Just lucky, I guess," Lila said, bracing him with one arm as she injected close to the puncture wound with her other hand.

"Ah, that feels as bad as the first one," he protested, but his arms had gone limp and he was quickly losing his ability to hold himself up at all. He sounded drunk.

"Wait a minute, it'll work," she assured him, pulling him back so that she could prop him against a relatively clean bit of wall. "Got demon all over your face again though."

If something permanent happened to him she was happy to revise her verdict on overreacting. She walked back to the body and kicked it across into the portal where it vanished immediately in a fine haze of light and subatomic particles. "This thing has rotten containment. A couple of months chucking stuff in here and you'll be dying of radiation sickness," she said. "Short range though, mercifully for whoever lives downstairs." She went back and got Zal's arm around her neck and one shoulder under his to lift him. "Try to walk."

He mumbled something inarticulate, but he was light so she was able to carry him with her as she went back the way they had come. The second door she kicked in was the right one. At least, it had a portal and was in a room considerably nicer than the first one with a lot less in the way of x-ray bleed. The demon script was difficult to translate, but after a while she was convinced it wasn't a one-way ticket to the Void and stepped into it because she could hear running feet, voices in the hall, and the click of automatics being readied.

At the house on Sangueste there were six demons in attendance at the portal waiting for them, armed with a variety of interesting weapons and expectant faces. They attacked even before the portal had concluded transmission, which meant that one of them got fried straight off by a combination of the circle ward shield and the portal's outer rim microplasma, leaving five of them in motion, bullets in the air, blades singing, jet of flame mid-erupt as Lila arrived with Zal hanging onto her side, muttering gibberish.

She wished now that she hadn't been so hasty in getting rid of Tatterdemalion. But it was a bit late for that. She spun on the spot, turning her back on four of the incoming objects and at the same time spinning a shield of diamond filaments out of the back of her body. Because they were moving at high speeds and vibrating at frequencies that distorted local space and bent it almost double, they didn't need to be tightly packed to deflect the fast-moving bullets or the slower blades. A cloak of the stuff swept from her arm to cover Zal, hooding him in sheeting white strands of crystal. For him it happened so quickly it seemed no more than a white flash like a camera going off.

Meantime she drew her guns. By the time they were ready to fire, there were six barrels jutting from the outer edge of her forearm as she swung it around and they shot almost in sync and put six bolts through six foreheads. She used the recoil to help her drag Zal's deadweight around. It wasn't enough to finish the job, however. She caught the final shot in her hand, a half inch in front of Zal's face.

It was an armour-piercing round, and absorbing the impact was too much for her at close range. It punctured her hand right through, although she was moving it as much as she could so that when it exited it did so at an angle that nicked Zal's ear on its way past him and then went on to sail effortlessly through the plaster and stud wall behind them and, by the sound of it, into an innocent body on the far side—if a houseful of gangland demons could be considered innocent, and Lila doubted that.

The smell of demon brains and overheated, distressed metal was noxious and almost overpowering in its own right. For a second her eyes rolled with the stink. Zal wobbled on his feet.

"I see nothing's changed here," he rasped, clinging to her as he straightened up, forcing himself to regain full control of his body even though he was quivering with involuntary muscle tremors. "And sh-shame on you, you name dropper. Talking about Teazle to sc-core. That's a l-low blow."

She realised he was referring to Roxa's defeat and calling her dishonourable for rank pulling. "We didn't have time for the triple-X version of the knockdown fight. And anyway, I was jealous."

He blinked carefully at the room. "Didn't ruin your aim, I see." He had a slight grin on his face. His eyes were as dark as pits. She just managed to catch him as he fell.

"Zal don't faint on me, you big blouse!" His skin was hot and his eyes already flickering back and forth in venomous dreams. She cursed and lifted him up, over her shoulder. "This is MY position," she said to the empty room, as she stepped out of the circle. "MY position is the girl who faints and gets thrown over the hero's shoulder. Not yours. It's so unsexy."

Zal murmured something unrepeatable about positions and breasts, which made Lila think briefly of Xavi and her unconscious genius for talking while out cold, and that put her in an even worse mood. She couldn't face a houseful of demon wannabe mafiosi and their greedy, hopeful faces or their collapsing, bloodied corpses, so she shot out the ornate leaded-glass window, ignited her boot jets, and made a hasty exit upstage. They crossed the foul green waters of the canal, passed high over the masterwork of tiled roofs that decorated Greater Sangueste with mosaics of cathedral proportion, and made it to the relatively clear, if reeking, airs of the Sheban lagoon.

To forestall any ideas about pursuit, she paused to launch a rocket at the building and watched as it blasted three floors into a healthy, smoking inferno. The fire was more firework than bomb, only to make a point. It might be a mistake; it was hard to tell how the demons would react because she had no idea of her local standing in the ranks now that she wasn't Teazle's wife anymore—too small a blast insulted them, too large offended. Either way they might choose to follow her, as devoted servants if they were impressed, and as assassins if they weren't. She piled on the power and didn't look back.

Across the lagoon the colours of the aircars and balloons, dirigibles and flitters, were gaudy and merry lights twinkled from towers and palaces in the old town. She headed there. The streets were busy, the lagoon itself rather full of gondolas and cruisers cutting the water this way and that with their competing wakes, but she noticed changes that she hadn't had time to see on her previous visit.

There was less art and more smoke, less beauty and more savagery, a wildness to the place that hadn't been there before. Guilds and house banners with unrecognisable sigils crowded the markets, and these were full, not only of the magical items that the city was famed for, but with the wicker cages of slaves and the gleaming bottles and stone sarcophagi of imprisoned creatures whose nature was only guessable by the size and style of their pen. Whole districts had changed, boundaries shifted. But as she came down to the old flat shapes of the manse roofs that she recognised, she saw the Sikarza flags flying strongly in the onshore wind. Beneath them ran a host of smaller colours, advertising who was in and who was out. At the top was the blue-edged white bunting of Teazle's personal flare. The master was home, then, and still the master.

Relief filled her, and she landed on their flight diamond. The deck officer saluted her as if she'd never been away, even though he'd never met her and must have known about her change of status. Teazle himself hadn't taken against them, at least.

She almost ran through the halls, checking doors, and sent a sprite she found watering a large vase of flowers, to find Teazle. There were people living there she didn't know; names, shapes, faces all unfamiliar, but each one of them seemed quite familiar with her and with Zal. Some even bowed. Being Demonia nobody batted an eyelash at the state of them and she reached her own rooms without delay. Clean, immaculate, they were exactly as she hadn't left them.

She put Zal down on the bed and saw that the hanging cocoon in which Teazle normally slept had been recently used. Shredded bits of wool and fur hung out of it. There was a strange smell, of things that had been maintained but not used or lived in for a very long time, a museumish kind of odour of beeswax, incense, and neglect. She walked swiftly into the bathroom feeling as if she might throw up, which surprised her because she'd seen a lot worse and done worse than today's accumulated bloodshed. She found herself shaking, and though there was some reason for it with the chemical imbalance caused by the antivenom, she knew the real cause was that she'd promised herself—

dreamed, imagined, pretended—there would be an end to the slaughter after last time in this place. Now she saw that when demons were involved there would never be any other way and there would never be a stop unless she chose to die. It was the faces she couldn't stand. Roxa, whatever else she'd been, had been healthy, vibrant, interesting in the way of all living things, magical, fascinating, marvellous. And now she was disintegrating meat under a Zoomenon sun, being unpicked into the elements from which she'd spawned.

Sure, Roxa could have chosen not to take them to that doorway, to take them to the real portal instead, Lila reasoned. She just knew that to her it seemed an unforgiveable stupidity, such a waste. For that they deserved their fates and that alone, she thought, but even this view of justice was faked and it didn't console her. The truth was that there was no justice, no balance, no law, no will except her own, and theirs.

Her loathing of the Agency and her own position crystallised out then, as she hung over the bathtub, watching the water run into the huge stone basin. Her stomach calmed. She wanted justice, fairness, kindness, but it depended on the will of others and she couldn't touch that, not with any weapon in the world, nor any grace. Security there was not to be had either. Everything could change in an instant. She washed her face and cleaned her teeth, decided to forgo the old ritual of the betrayer's look into the mirror, and went back to see how Zal was doing.

The antivenom had done its work—the ugly purple swelling on his neck was down, the wound not much more than a pinprick. His eyes still rolled in his head, however, and his skin was hot. He babbled nonsense about pretty things, beauty and lust. She stripped off his foul clothing and threw it on the floor. Then she noticed the shadow body that it had been hiding. It rippled just over his own in smoky waves like a coat of oil. There was something about its movements that made her uneasy. It looked as if it had purpose, senses, and awareness of its own, separate from him now that he wasn't in a fit state to master it. It glided across him, as though searching something out. It flooded up his nostrils, from his ears and the surfaces of his eyes. And he had told her that this was all that was left of him for the fifty years of his exile in Under. She didn't know what to make of it.

A powerful instinct warned her not to touch it. Her immediate impulse was to do the opposite, challenge the fear and the cause of it, but this time she stayed her hands and threw a blanket on him instead. She had no idea what the magical potency of the venom was. If she became poisoned by it, that would make two of them who weren't up to anything. Seeing that he wasn't going anywhere soon, she went back for a bath.

The water was hot, and there was soap and a brush. She changed to human skin form and watched the disturbing slither of black leather and metal devolving to her old, pale tanned arms and legs. The blood and matter stayed where it was, coating her more thickly now that she had shrunk her surface, but in this form she didn't have a hundred angular planes, seams, and airvents, so it was easier to clean everything. She was struggling to get her hair to rinse clear when she felt a change in the air and looked up to find Teazle walking in the door. His near-silent tread was thanks to the combination of his grace, human-form feet, and the carpets, and he looked exasperated when all this effort wasn't enough to sneak up on her.

He stood, white and pure as the finest snow, his hair a fall of frost, eyes glowing and face alight with the abundant energy—enough for a thousand demons—that was barely contained by his six-and-a-half-foot form. A knee-length robe of white cloth was all he had on, with the hilts of his two swords rising above his shoulders at his back like the stubs of wings. There was a change in him from the creature who had slipped out of Malachi's tent days ago. Then he had been tired, introspective (for him), and in a rare moment of rest. Now there was a vibration in him so fine and strong it linked him to dreams and to other worlds. He came to stand at the side of the bath and then crouched down and rested his arms along the rim. He put his chin on his crossed wrists and watched her with his white eyes; god's tautly strung bow.

"You're losing your edge," he said, voice low and deceptively mellow. "Zal got suckied. Careless."

At this range she could hear the hum of the twin blades—a sound well beyond most hearing, a foreboding in the nerves. "I'm surprised we're not dead. We didn't leave on the best of terms with ninety percent of the population."

"Yes," he said. "In spite of your undoing all my efforts and giving away most of our fortune to create a false sense of equality, they retained a marvellous amount of resentment, enough to fuel more stupidity than I thought I would ever witness." He put a finger in the water and then into his mouth, sucking it thoughtfully for a second. She knew he was figuring out what she'd been doing. "It was hard work, but I have straightened things out."

She looked at him from her position higher up the tub. "You mean you killed them."

"Only those who resisted."

"So how many didn't resist?"

"A handful. They have seen fit to relocate to estates further afield. Let me run you some fresh water, see the taps work like this—fresh in, seven-demon residue out."

Lila moved her foot from its resting place to let him fiddle with the mechanics. "Is that why everything looks so different?"

"A couple of days can change a great deal," he said.

"So, the old families bail out and in come the slavers and . . . who are all those others?"

"They are merely temporary scum." He paused and gave her an exacting glance. "You're not going to ask me to kill all of them as well, are you?" He sounded wishful.

"It's up to you," she said, watching as filthy water began to drain out and jets of clear come in. "You can exterminate them all. Then what will you do?"

"I'm not old and mad yet," he said with some reproach. "Besides, you forget that 'shebat is not the only city. There is an entire world of demons, including those of the wilds who are far superior to the civilised kind. A few hundred off the register is nothing to be concerned about."

"A few hundred." It was so hard to accept demon reckonings. They were glorious. They were idiots. She didn't doubt they had all had opportunities to turn aside and stay alive. Their culture was their lifeblood. They were peacefully at one with it and all its consequences; it was only she, the outsider, who found it monstrous.

"I stopped counting after three hundred and forty-six," Teazle confessed. "There was this airship battery, lots of guns, plasma rockets . . . I got distracted."

"In, what is it . . . two days?"

"Three more like."

They might have been talking about fish prices, in another world and time. She decided to move on to something more practical. "What exactly does succubus venom do? I countered the physical properties, but it has some aetheric components."

"Usually it's some kind of love thing," Teazle said. "Love or lust. Could be focused on the sucky or could be more general. They like to incapacitate and enslave. Rarely fatal. Suckies aren't into killing; it spoils their fun. They die very easy."

"I noticed."

Teazle watched her body reappearing from the brown water as it was diluted and cleared. "Inkies are different. They don't have tails. They have a breath with a similar effect to sucky venom, and voices that charm, though not as well as siren suckies, like Sorcha. Also they can dematerialise into a vapour form for short periods."

She scanned her memories. "I never saw one of those."

"Nah, they're one in a thousand, mostly in the employ of the big families, often used as assassins. And now even rarer than they were before." He let his gaze slide over her and up to her eyes, and smiled.

"They're hard to grab, easy to kill." He briefly mimed wrenching something into two parts and throwing the parts aside.

"Is that the only way you classify anything?"

"Is there some other way?" he was candid. She had to look away from his eyes, and he blinked and toned down their gleam to firefly levels. "You summoned me." His smile was rakish.

"Not for that. Zal needs arming for a trip to Alfheim and I need to get to Ilya. Kinda burnt my boats with Mal, so I might need a few alternative transport routes. What happened to that mirror from Madame's house? I could try that."

"Still there," Teazle said, with a slight shiver. "The house is owned by someone else these days, so you'd have to break in through the warehouse. Nobody knows about that part of it, even now." Then he glanced towards the bedroom. "I suppose you'll stick with him now that he's back in some kind of body."

"Jealousy?" she asked, sliding down to her neck in the steaming water, although she remembered their days and nights of passionate engagements in perfect clarity. "Doesn't seem like you. You don't love me. You're my ex."

He frowned. It was nearly comical, as if he were puzzling over a difficult passage in a book. "I something you."

She smiled and stroked his hair with one wet hand. "Aww, I something you too, honey."

He growled slightly, quietly, and closed his eyes. "You smell of faeries."

She peered at him, but he hadn't moved. How he could smell anything over the powerful smell of the soap and the demon blood she didn't know. "Well, I was wearing one for a while."

"Ah yes, where did she go?"

"I dumped her."

Now his eyes flashed open, their beams going straight into her face, and, it felt, straight into her soul. "Why?"

She found herself pulling a shamed face; the truth seemed so petty now that it was time to speak of it. "I was mad at the time. I felt like everyone I had trusted was keeping secrets from me, and that they'd betrayed my trust. She didn't, but she was damn near the last one and, anyway, she's never said anything about why she was with me."

Teazle scowled and the room darkened. "That was very foolish. You should make amends. She was your ally."

"She was my ally *so far*," Lila corrected him. "Sarasilien, Malachi . . . hell, I don't know who else, but Sarasilien was responsible for introducing the Otopians to the cyborg programme in the first place and he kept damn quiet about that. Now he's back claiming some elf-Armageddon is about to hit, and surprise surprise, he expects me and Zal to go picking up pieces like we're his personal servants. Malachi knew it all along and said nothing, not a blind fucking word—he was more than happy to let me believe that I was a lucky survivor with a chance to help the world for as long as it played—and now he has the bare balls to sit there in a little bubble of beer and start pontificating about shitting tiger, hidden dragon, no, there's more, wait. Meantime Max is back, really, or as close to really as I can't tell, and there are faeries in the garden sitting waiting on toadstools to tell me that I need to get rid of her and the rest of the Returners because they're going to make the world fall apart at the seams. That's a message from all the faeries apparently, who can't seem to muster a soap bubble for themselves in spite of the fact there are several thousand of them living in the city and across the continent. No, they're occupied with covering up for various of their half kin who are deranged serial killers, or maybe just have some unfortunate life vectors, who knows? Greer expects me to do something about tidying up that. Even I think I should."

He nodded slowly. "But 'Demalion did you no harm."

Lila bared her teeth. "She enjoyed a lot of jokes at my expense."

"No real harm."

"No, no fucking real harm. Yet. You got off lightly with the faeries so far but I've seen their ways." She felt bitterly unjustified in making the statement, regardless of the fact it was true. She could have countered it with equally accurate pronouncements in the opposite direction.

"You think so?" He trailed a hand in the water, making idle patterns. His calm was determined and steady, but it had a sultry quality like a cloudy sky on a still day, waiting for the change of the weather that would mass it into a storm. "What's got you this paranoid?"

She glared at him. He had been there, he had seen it; what was he asking for?

"The faeries and these others, they kept secrets, they withheld information, they played some tricks, but have they done you such a bad service, really, considering?"

Fresh anger flared in her. "Apart from stealing my life and using up the remains for their own ends? Keeping Zal for fifty years as some kind of talking doorstop? No, I guess not."

"And if they had left you all alone, where would you be now? Six feet under, another ordinary human. Zal would have died along with Jack. You embraced the life offered, all of it. Else you wouldn't be here. Why do you keep returning to this as if it is the grave of your beloved?" The gaze he briefly awarded her was disappointed.

She folded her arms across her breasts and stared at him coldly. "Whose side are you on?"

He returned his eyes to the fascinating business of her bathwater and spoke his thoughts aloud as if they were a dot-to-dot puzzle he was slowly joining up. "Transitions are hard, but everyone must make them. You aren't always in a rage. I guess something else is bothering you."

With an effort, Lila thrust away the sense of righteous unfairness that was making her so useless. She felt that he was angry with her but there was more important business, so he was containing his emotions and she could at least match the favour. It was difficult, but after a second or so she let her hold on the need to win slip, "Yes. There's this

girl . . ." She told him the story of Sassy, leaving out no details, all the
way up to the present moment.

As he listened he continued to swirl the water lazily. The ripples
sparkled in the light of his eyes but they dimmed the more he brooded,
and finally, when she was done, all his effulgence was gone and he looked
at her from pale blue-grey irises, his hair and skin quite ordinary.

"That's an interesting story," he said. "And something of a conun-
drum. We can't go near her without revealing ourselves entirely, but
she can tell as many lies as she likes, and no doubt she will if it suits
her. You agreed to help her, you say."

At this distance that did seem rather foolish. She sighed. "I didn't
have my fingers crossed at the time, but I wouldn't say it was one of
my better promises. I thought it was the closest I could get to putting
her on hold. Are you going to tell me to go make nice to her, too?"

"If you *are* the product of a long engineering process put in place
by these players and the stakes are as high as they seem, then I
wouldn't go throwing away my allies so carelessly, is what I say," Teazle
murmured. "Especially if you fancy playing as more than the virtuoso
instrument of a greater hand. These childish fits of yours must stop,
charming as they are." He flashed her a look of amused indulgence that
made her instantly hot.

She bristled. "People are always saying that."

"Then they must be right."

Lila knew it was true. She felt a tension inside her shoulders and
upper back twist and turn—fish on a hook. The need to be belligerent,
to fight and deny, to kick away from any kind of interference, no
matter how well meant, was impossible for her to resist. It was a beast
in her throat, in her chest, spinning in circles of panic. Sure, his statement was true. But there were other true statements that flew against
it. She retaliated. "Is it childish to see the demon slaughter culture as
a stupidity?"

She saw he considered the arousal of her body a good reward for his ongoing efforts and in return he was conversational, rational, and emphatic though he didn't attempt to touch her except with his gaze.

"If all you see is unfairness and feel pity, then it is. If you see it as a comic tragedy of loss and accept its transient moments of beauty and its ultimately pointless glory, then it is not. One slip now, one mistake about the nature of reality, and you will lose. I guarantee it. You can't afford to be anything less than a perfect warrior if you want to win. Pitiless. Merciless. Without compassion. Without fault."

She was still in the grip of the beast within. "That's monstrous!"

He was unaffected. "It's the way of angels. All other ways are hell-bound." He looked at her once more with the kind of steady disappointment she'd hoped for but never found in her father. In spite of his hot and cold gambits, however, Teazle didn't mean to leave himself misunderstood and continued. "You've played around with hell a long time, especially in that part of it that is made of the dreams of kindness and mercy; the gold cloth of arrogance masquerading as the humble linen of the penitent. I think you must like it there. *That* is monstrous."

An awkward, horrible kind of pain, a rod between heart and gut, made her anger-beast spiral around it, moth on pin. She was silent, brooding, grim. Thoughts went through her head: Were the angels monsters? Did he mean it? Was she a monster as he said, not because of any physical feature but because of her behaviour? She didn't even understand why she was so angry. She thought she was over all the things that could have made her angry.

Meantime, surely this talk of angels was his way of irony. A demon and an angel could not be the same thing at all. Angels were Others, even as far as demons were concerned.

She struggled to find something that she believed in, to counter the onslaught. She must prove herself, redeem herself, justify. She scraped around, searching for her reasons, looking under them, and found a surprising lack from which only one or two bits and pieces stood out. Her mind was not the well-honed home of reason but more like the bargain basement of hand-me-down platitudes. This was a crushing disappointment but she grasped what she could and said, sure of its power and rightness in spite of the fact she didn't even know where it came from, "I have faith in kindness."

He dismissed this with the merest of head shakes. "Idiotic. Only the unassailable can afford to be kind."

"Like you?" she spat.

He considered her stomach, head on his arm, waving the water with his free hand in a vague manner. "My kindness towards you has been unending."

She assumed he meant that she was still alive. "Kindness and mercy build better worlds."

"Kindness and mercy don't build anything. They foster weakness, and that weakness grows to consume everything in its path." He let drips fall off his fingertips and made circle patterns. "Perhaps it would be sufficient, if *everyone* were kind and merciful, even if they were self-aware, but there is no population like that, though you won't find any who don't lie about it. Mercy is not a useful path to anything either, except your own death. It is a gate to corruption. Hell's royal road. I know you are thinking of the great priests of your culture when you bandy their terms about like banners, but let me assure you that only the immaculate can be kind and merciful without consequence. First be immaculate. Then you may be as cruel with your kindness and mercy as you wish. Let all manner of evils riot for your enjoyment and call it fair-mindedness."

"So what do we do, kill everyone who isn't a coldhearted bastard?"

"Kill your own weakness. Hunt it, stalk it, root it out. That will be enough. Others can do as they want; they have the same opportunity. Their choices are their own. Any of them might be the perfect warrior.

The least and worst of them could be. Nothing stops them. Everyone has the power."

As he said this her mind had churned with images of her own parents and their make-do lives, struggling. They had not done well, but they had tried hard to instill in her that kindness mattered, second chances mattered, there was always hope for a better future, and that things can be learned from mistakes. Where was the point of learning if one mistake was an execution offence? She burned with resentment, almost hatred for him, a protective fire inside her around the images of all the world's luckless victims. "Have you no empathy *at all*?"

Teazle considered and swirled the water. He watched the ripples he made reach the shores of her knees and then the far side of the stone basin.

"What *you* call empathy is merely the copying of suffering. You see someone in pain and you duplicate the feelings inside yourself and call that sympathy or empathy or somesuch. Then you wallow in it, and you feel pity and sorrow for the sufferer, first for them, and then for yourself. I know that you do this because it seems like a way you could lead them out. You go and join them, then you show the way out. But you can't lead from a weak position, and there you are, in the pit with them. You might change your state again, but they already chose their state. This braying about moral high grounds by thinking that your big heart is some kind of barometer of virtue is a junior alchemist's mistake." He glanced at her stony face and shook his head slightly.

"I expect some idiot told you that through the effort of pitying and commiserating you can make the world a place of love, embracing everything with endless forgiveness. But at the same time you can't stop suffering yourself, though that's where you must stop it. That's how it is done, not by crying along and forgiving the unforgivable. I hear that even your churches praise suffering as a road to redemption, but it is nothing and goes nowhere. Bleed your heart as much as you like, all it will do is kill you and everyone around you that much faster. Fine, if sacrifice amuses you, then at least it has had some positive purpose. But that was never the human way, with the exception of a few deluded fools who thought they could achieve demonhood through vice. Suffer and sacrifice. Redemption for the irredeemable. Devil's creeds. It is abomination. You are like the elves. Trying to save themselves from their own hate by turning it inward.

Excellent prey for the devils. Those bastards are grown to their billions in you. In ages past we have come to exterminate the hosts of such plagues, lest they cover the world." He sighed, and for a moment his shoulders sank down and he became briefly limp and gloomy with no prospect of a purifying slaughter in sight.

It didn't stop her blurting out, "Don't tell me that all the human kindnesses and mercies over the ages are meaningless nothing!" She was furious. "What about parents and children, kindness and love in relationships, or is that all crap and lies as well? You say this stuff like you have no feelings at all!"

"Love," Teazle said, shifting position, breathing in and regaining himself. "Love," he repeated slowly. "Is behind everything I say."

Now she was completely confused. "Teazle, you despise everyone and you kill everything and you don't care. What's loving about that?"

"I do that," he said, looking at her as if she had surprised him, baffled him in fact with a blatant mistake. "But I don't want to. It isn't my *geas*." He paused for another moment, searching her face, and she could see he was honest. "Is that what you thought about me all this time? That I am a demon of spite?"

The *geas* was a demon's primary calling. Zal's was music. Teazle's, she had thought, was killing. Now she didn't want to say yes and be wrong and even more shamed by her failure and the awful insult that it would be.

"What, then?" She felt small and worthless and that she must find an escape, of any kind, lest he find her out. Only a clear sense that he meant her no harm contained her disappointment and shamed her into biting her lips shut as she waited for the verdict on her own unkind judgements of him. So she was proven false or at least doubting, untrue where she claimed high ground, lacking. So what?

"Stop it," he snapped, flicking water into her eyes suddenly with a snap of his fingers. He did look angry now.

"Stop what?"

"Feeling sorry for yourself."

She wiped her eyes. "What's the answer, then?"

"I'm not going to tell you," he said. "You can answer it for yourself." He snaked his tail over the edge of the tub and around one of her ankles and gave her a swift tug.

She was jerked down into the water helplessly and could only watch it close over her face, screening his expression with a mass of bubbles. When she surfaced, he'd left the room. She got out and dried herself and then saw he had left her some clothes.

She remembered he'd done the same thing the day he and Malachi had moved her out of her old apartment. He'd laughed at her old clothes—even she marvelled at them—and thrown them down the garbage chute, every last piece. Then he'd made her new ones. Zal used to joke that Teazle had pulled them out of his ass because nobody saw him make them; they simply appeared. She'd realised since then that he teleported to get them, but he was so fast at it that nobody could see the joins.

She examined the one-piece after a moment of uncertainty. It was moss-green with some gold stitching, subtle, expensive, and soft. After a time she figured out how to put it on—it had many cutaways intended to expose various pieces of skin—and discovered it to be surprisingly tasteful and beautifully tailored. There was a kind of panelled jacket that went with it, and here she discovered a label showing Sorcha's personal symbol of a red flame. She and the demon had not been the same size, so she reasoned this was Sorcha's own brand. These things were antiques now. Collectible. She wished Sorcha were back again for one, fierce moment, and then put the jacket on and walked back to the bedroom in her bare feet.

Teazle was on the bed, reading something on a palmscreen and listening to Zal mutter in his fitful sleep. On the rug by the large windows lay a black sabretooth cat the size of a pony, idly licking the matte fur on the back of one gigantic paw. As it saw her from its orange eyes, it opened its claws and dug them deeply into the rug's ruby pattern.

"Mal," she said, as neutrally as possible. She saw Teazle shoot a glance at her as he paged through his document and then look back closely at the demonic text, reading as though engrossed.

". . . enormous . . ." Zal mumbled.

The huge cat stared at her, and the pupils of his eyes narrowed. "You are forgiven," he said. His voice was garbled by the shape of his mouth and his teeth, but it was clear enough. She noticed a bearlike quality to him that hadn't been apparent before.

"You've changed."

"I am changing," he said in his deep rumble. It had a slight break in it as though his purr box was broken. "All the old fey are experiencing the same. It is slow, but inevitable." He paused. "We are declining."

Teazle looked up now, and Lila said, "What do you mean, declining?"

"We revert towards our primal forms."

"Like you did in Under?"

"When you saw me there, we weren't in Under," Malachi said. "We were in Umeval, the Time of Winter. It was a very old place, one of the few changeless places that sit at the axis. After it come all the ages of the human races. Before it come the older aeons, millennia without mark, which in your reference is in time, but in Faery it is geography, or direction, if you like. They progress back to the time before demons, before elves, before there was anything except the Void and . . ." he paused and looked away, whiskers twitching, ". . . the machines."

CHAPTER THIRTEEN

"The machines?" Lila said into the pause that followed Malachi's statement. "The machines were before everything else?"

"The machines are not physical objects," the faery said. He hesitated, and she and Teazle saw him struggle with the change into his human form. For a second he was missing entirely from their world, and then he slowly appeared, trails of flickering colour at his edges as the threads of his being dragged themselves from their metamorphic cocoon. Lila wasn't used to seeing this because usually it took place so fast it was invisible. Her throat contracted with concern.

"Mal, are you all right?"

He was so tired that he didn't get up from his seat on the floor. His shirt was open at the collar, and rumpled. He fingered it as if he were going to close it and then turned to her without getting up and let his hands fall away. His voice was slow and deliberate as he remembered what he had to say.

"The machines are possibilities, the potential combinations of energy states that are permissible in this universe. The machines don't exist as we exist. They have no energy at all. And before you ask how I know all this, Sarasilien and the cyborg Sandra Lane told me. At the very first place, before even the Void opened up, there were the machines. The first actualised machine was the Void itself, the engine out of which all energy came. So when you were made, it wasn't through some secret spy operation of stolen plans and plotting from a higher machine power. Sarasilien did foist the blueprints upon the humans, because their technology was already so advanced in that direction. But he got them himself; he drew them by copying machine forms he was able to see through his dreams. They already existed. He simply found them and passed them on."

He glanced at Lila with heavy concentration and a frown. "He said you would know this, if you looked, but he expected that you wouldn't. I'd have to come and tell you. Like I have to tell you the rest. Before it's too late." He took a breath as if he was struggling for air, and his hand went to his throat and pushed his shirt away even further. He worked his jaw for a moment and swallowed, then made himself sit up correctly. He glanced at Zal with a scowl of annoyance and then up at Teazle with a more calculating stare and then began to micro-adjust his shirt buttons and smooth his sleeves as he continued.

"The trouble was always so little time. But even then it should have been all right, except for the unplanned business with Under." His tone was bitter. "*That* was my mistake, and it has cost everything. That fifty-year gap. We were counting on it."

Lila had forgotten her anger. "To do what?"

"For one of you to rise," Malachi said. "Yes, surely one of you would make it in that period. But you haven't. Because you were robbed. And the others have all fallen, or gone astray, or have no interest." Now that his cuffs satisfied him, he began to retuck his shirt with methodical exactitude, taking his belt out a notch in order to be more effective.

"Mal," Lila said firmly. "What the hell are you talking about?"

"You," the faery said, creating even pleating on his left and right, although the shirt was so well tailored it was hardly necessary. "I'm talking about you. And Zal. And others you never knew about. Many others. All of them some kind of mongrel."

He finished and tightened the belt and then moved to stand up so he could put the buckle at exact centre. He cleared his throat and began to adjust the lie of his pockets. "Sandra Lane. She was to be your successor, if you didn't come back. She had those years, every long damned day of them, and we tried everything to get her some magical power, but without success. All our alchemies have failed. Her clones have been most useful, as have the other cyborgs. Even the rogues, good in their way. But none of them stand a chance—"

"You're babbling," Teazle said sharply. His voice was like a dull whipcrack, and it made all of them start, even Zal, who rolled onto his side to face them, eyes half open.

"I have a right to babble!" Malachi snapped. His glare at the white demon was vicious for a moment, and his white fang teeth showed. Then abruptly he caught himself and closed his mouth. He slid his hands into the immaculate side pockets of his trousers and turned to the windows. Some savoire faire returned to his pose as he addressed them in their imperfect reflection. "By this time we had hoped there would be someone capable of dealing with the threat that the elves had created long ago when they made the Shadowkin. It's Sarasilien's story to tell really, but since he isn't here, I'll have to tell it."

The tall faery walked across to the bed and looked down at Zal critically. Zal blinked up at him, the pupils of his eyes huge dark centres inside paler rings, his mouth vaguely grinning as though Mal were a halfway decent standup act.

"Can you hear me?"

"Yeah," Zal's voice was dreamy and distant but it was clear. "We're all failures. You're disappointed. We're all going to die. Got it."

Teazle snickered. "Speak for yourself, tree hugger."

A brief, wintry smile flitted across Malachi's face, making his teeth suddenly shine out against the coal blackness. "Your mother was one of Sarasilien's students," he said. "Did you know?"

Zal peered up at Malachi and his grin faded. "No."

"But you know there was more to your birth than a simple affair."

Zal swallowed on a dry mouth and rolled his eyes. "Her ideas on genetics and the inheritance of aetheric power were more than enough to send me to sleep at nights." He put up one hand to shield his sight, squinting even though it was quite dim in the room. "But honestly, Mal, what were you expecting? A composite being with all the pluses and none of the faults of the ancestors? Some kind of . . . what were those things called in the stories . . . you know, we didn't have any fiction in the house . . . the creatures that were *summoned and born and moulded and forged and made and dressed and taught and trained to be the best of the best and then some?*" The last part of his speech had been sing-song, the form of an old poetic story.

"*Up to the test, fierce as beasts, hearts of cold iron and eyes of twin suns, like angels, like anger, the first breath of spring, the last stride of the race, faultless, matchless, the stars in their places, with strength of ages and minds of sages . . .*" Malachi continued for him in the same rhythm and tone. "Yes. The story of the Titans. Created to stand against chaos so that the worlds could be formed."

"Ah," Zal said slowly and he let his hand fall down to the mattress, limp. "Hubris has caught up with you. You tried to make a titan, but you got me and Lila instead. Yeah, well, I see your point. Carry on."

"He isn't serious," Lila said to Malachi. "He's mad with succubus venom."

"No, he's right," Mal said, thin-lipped. "Something like a titan was needed because something like a titan, or titans, was created. When it couldn't be contained and proved uncontrollable, it was imprisoned."

"In time," Lila said, remembering what Sarasilien had told her— the payback was to be deferred.

"Yes. By a trick, like the one you fell into with the Hunter," Malachi nodded and shrugged gently, some of his stern manner sloughing away from him. "And now that time is up."

"So Sarasilien created one mess by mixing things up that shouldn't have been, and now he's trying to clear it up with another mess the same?" Lila said.

"Oh, you're *nothing* like the first," Malachi waved his hand and snorted contemptuously. "After learning that lesson, everything else that was made was made on the strictest principles. This is why Sarasilien and a few allies worked alone on it. Only a few could be trusted not to fall into the old temptations. And even then . . . there are scattered hundreds of creatures, people and such, who were made to meet this test. Some will stand at the end I expect, but they will not be enough," he shook his head.

"Mal," Lila said, half concerned and half annoyed. "This is a bogeyman story. But where's the bogeyman?"

"Coming," the faery said with affected lightness. He turned on the spot suddenly with a ballroom dancer's swift and perfect spin and then sighed his way into a few twirling steps.

Lila glared at him, knowing all too well that if Malachi was dancing, then he was deeply uncomfortable. "How do you know? Why this year? Why not next year? I mean, in ages of time there's got to be some leeway, some give . . ."

"Yes," Malachi said. "They are early. Perhaps they discovered a way out of their trap or . . . well, who can say? But the harbingers are here, so surely they are coming."

Lila turned to Teazle. "If he keeps holding onto the information, you can beat it out of him." She turned to Malachi. "Spill it already! What harbingers?"

Malachi gave up his brief waltz across the floor, and with it all his exhaustion returned. He sat down on the end of the bed and put his head in his hands. "The harbingers are the Returners. New spirits in old forms. The fact that they are here means that the fundamental separation between the nebulous dimensions and the material ones is becoming thinner. The Titans were made to destroy the elves' ancient enemy, the Sleeper. They were imprisoned in such a place, beyond matter and time and the sway of the elements, so that they could not shape anything or kill anyone. But the charm that held them has been weakened and they are making their way back here. The Returners approach on their bow wave."

"How long?" Zal murmured. He was rubbing his face, trying to wake up, but the poison kept him logy.

"Weeks, maybe days now," the faery said dejectedly.

"What was the charm?" Lila asked.

Malachi turned to her with slow, sad resignation. "The Queen's magic," he said.

"The Queen's magic that was lost in Under," Lila said, for confirmation.

He nodded. "Although it would have broken anyway, once the time had run its course. That's what we couldn't understand. Why would the charm fail, unless the condition had been met?"

"And the condition was?"

"The rise of a new Titan, naturally," Malachi said. "So they couldn't come back before we had a chance."

"And that was supposed to be me, or Zal, or Sandra Lane or . . ."

"Or any of the others, yes."

"Well then they have to be somewhere," Zal said, and lifted the edge of his pillow to look for them there.

"*We have looked.* There are no Titans."

"I don't understand," Teazle said. "The return of these dark Titans or whatever they are . . . this will be the end of the worlds? Or the end of the worlds will pave the way for their return, in which case there'll be not much to return to?"

"What do they want?" Zal asked almost at the same time.

Malachi held his hands up. "It's not my story, like I say, but I'll tell it. Ages ago, before the human races, when the elves were already old, they had great magical power and a massive, enviable civilisation, greatly advanced for the most part, comparable to the best. But some of them had a great deal of aetheric ability and charm, so much that they were able to leave their bodies and travel in other planes, or see into other dimensions, and all sorts like that. They discovered Zoomenon, the place of the elements, and the Void that lies between and around and inside all things, and they discovered the places of the dead and the undead, and when they were around in there they disturbed something. A malevolent force that was very strong. It pursued them without rest and tried to use them as conduits to come into Alfheim. They were convinced that it would never stop until they were all dead and the world with them. And so after a lot of trouble and talk they made Titans to overcome the beast in its own lair. And you know the rest. The goal of the Titans was to destroy the Sleeper."

"And did they?" Teazle asked. He had begun to glow again with talk of destruction.

"Well," Malachi said uneasily. "Not exactly. The first thing that happened was that most of the mages who had created them came down with a wasting sickness and died. And so did many others. Not just mages. Ordinary people. That was when it was decided it had gone wrong and this was the result of all the evil done in creating the Titans and binding them by force to their task. More was out of the question. There was no way to recall them and so instead they chose to trick the Titans into a game—the only thing that could contain them. The faery Queen agreed to do it herself because she was the master of trickery. Her trick meant that she was lost in Under ever after that. This was the days before the fey republic of course; it was the cause of the republic really. Without her anyone could claim leadership and nobody could keep it. And it was to maintain the game that we had to lose the evidence of it and forget we knew about it."

"Until now," Zal said.

"It worked," Malachi insisted. "For ages."

Lila walked over to Zal's side and sat down by him. "So these Titans are going to carry on where they left off, you think?"

Malachi stared at the two of them with dulled orange eyes. "The Titans had only one purpose. To destroy the Sleeper. After that they . . ." he hesitated and glanced at Lila, ". . . they would have dissolved. Dangerous things, worldwalkers, you have to keep an eye on them always and when they have too much power you have to . . . well. Planned obsolescence, you see."

She returned his look steadily to let him know this information wasn't lost on her. "So the fact they're still around means they didn't succeed. The Sleeper is still there. It isn't them who are coming through to cause chaos, it's the Sleeper, and they'll come after. Or they didn't like your obsolescence idea too much and they're out for vengeance, or possibly just to exterminate any possibility that they could be . . . oh, let's call it *recalled*."

He blinked at the sharpness of her sarcasm and looked away. "We don't know. Look at Xavi. She didn't fulfill the purpose, but she was no Titan anyway. She was a near miss I guess. Maybe the real ones kept enough of themselves that they could break the *geas* set on them. Or they thought it would be better to stop short, so that it wouldn't be fulfilled. That would make them invincible and probably immortal. Unstoppable."

"But Alfheim is already dark. So how does that figure?"

"There's no knowing. We must find out. Dark doesn't mean dead."

"I know. Let's get drunk and wait for the end of the world," Zal said. "Easier that way. Also, if we haven't got a Titan or whatever, then no point worrying, is there?"

"Ah, now I see what kind of succubus has struck him. *Hedonic Nihila* is the heroin of the succubus world," Teazle said, cocking his head at Zal and looking at him with predatory interest. "It brings on a thoroughly enjoyable surrender. Although, he was always a bit that way."

Malachi gave Zal a disgusted look. "Titanically."

Lila had been thinking on other lines. "Does Sarasilien know about Xavi?"

"I didn't tell him because—the fact is I'm not sure what Xavi is," Malachi said. "Or how much she knows. Or how what you wrote in that book affects her. You put 'friends and lovers all.' Well, lovers. You know. Difficult wording to interpret, that, given all the possibles. You should have put something like 'faithful companions' instead."

Lila shrugged it off. "Well, she and Sarasilien have a lot of unfinished business. Does she know he's there?"

"No. I'm sure not. She'd have made more trouble if she did."

"Then we'll take her into Alfheim with us."

"We?"

"Me, Zal, and Teazle."

"Sarasilien said that Zal was to go alone."

"I bet Greer would be happy to see the back of me," Lila said. "I've been trying to make sure of it. But anyway, more to the point, Malachi. How long have you been in this plot? What's your interest?"

Malachi smoothed his hair and brushed invisible dust off his hands. "Since the Queen was involved. But you've gotta understand that when she went Under, and it was locked, I forgot most of it. I had to. We keep things safe by forgetting them. All I knew was that where Sarasilien went I was supposed to follow and see what happened and help. Nothing else. I never even thought about it until recently. I didn't remember all of what I just told you until a couple of days ago. Ever since then it's been coming back."

"Along with many things," Teazle said. "Even Zal was talking about a comeback."

"Not as myself," Zal said faintly from the pillows. "As a musician but not as a singer doing some sad retro act. Reinvention, not reiteration. You know."

Lila shook her head slowly. "Who plays games with Titans?"

Malachi lifted his head and looked at her with a slight revival of curiosity. "Games? You mean . . ."

"So this isn't part of some long game, then?"

His eyes, ochre with weariness, narrowed. "Who's been talking to you about long games?"

"Someone," she said. She would once have told him everything but it was time to keep her cards closer to her chest, she felt.

He measured her for a moment. "If it is a game, then it's one in very bad taste," he said finally. "Longer than most players have ever been alive. But these things can run amok in such ages. Could be I suppose. Doesn't matter if it is. The facts remain."

She switched tack. "What would happen if the harbingers were killed?"

He did a double take. "You have got some bees in your bonnet, haven't you? Kill them all you like, they'll keep coming as long as there's a way through."

"I had a message from some fey instructing me that killing them would stop the problem."

"They were misinformed then, or they've got things backwards. Happens a lot. We don't see time like you do. But don't blame them. They were right to want it stopped. The longer it continues, the more chances there are for serious problems." He yawned and got up. "Damn elves," he said. Once he was further from Zal, he brightened a little bit.

Zal chuckled, but it tailed off suddenly and Lila saw his face darken with some memory that made him close his eyes and go silent. Even the succubus charm wasn't enough to stall it.

"I should see Tath," she said. "You can take me there while Zal recovers, then we can get to Alfheim."

"Yeah, well, much as I like being your private taxi service, I told you, he's changed. I'm not sure it's a good idea."

She lost her temper. "Oh come on! I saw him days ago. He was okay. A little weird around the edges maybe but—"

"Lila." The black faery looked her in the eye with a gaze that was exacting and hard. "If you don't come back from wherever he is, then we have a thousand times less of a chance than we have right now. He took Jack's place. He was twice born, so that made him the Lord of the Dead, the good shepherd of the dark valleys. He's got more faery weird in him than anything else, even if he was once an elf, and he's been with the undead for a long time. Days here, but his time is now measureless, don't forget. Being in that kind of place doesn't sit well with minds that were made for finite lives in the material worlds. He's changed. You can't trust him anymore to be what he was, or who he was. Leave him."

She saw truth in his face. "You've seen him."

"And that's why I am telling you." Malachi turned aside, his face pinched and brows pulled together. "Went to play cards. We play once a . . . once upon a time. Cards night. We talk a little. We drink a little. I give him fruit. He gives me news. That's it. Cards. And the last time I went he wasn't there, so I went looking for him thinking it's strange, he never misses cards night. And I found him. And then I left him, way out there beyond the border, beyond Last Water. He used to be more like us, I guess, and now he's more like them. Don't go, Lila." His face was lined and heavy as he finished and all traces of dancing were gone. "But I should be grateful I guess. At least you want to do something. I thought you wouldn't even listen this long." He hesitated to say something else and kept it in.

Lila nodded. She didn't mention the dress. She felt she had no right to. "I'll do something. But not out of any faith in the future. I'll do it for Tath, or you, or Zal, or Teaz, maybe Greer. And I don't know what that something will be. Might not be what you and your craftsmen had in mind."

Malachi spread his hands out and gave another of his shrugs. "I was never that kind of player, you know that."

"I don't know what I know about you anymore," she replied honestly. She looked at Zal, at Teazle, at Malachi again. "Let's go." She stood up.

"There's a problem." Malachi held up his hand towards her chest.

"You can't go beyond Last Water. Not even with me. Not even astrally. If you do, you'll never come back. You can't see him that way."

"Then how?" She peered at him, but her mind was already searching for and finding the answer. "I'll summon him." "Not here!" Malachi's panic was sudden. Lila jumped, startled, before she could stop herself. "I know you don't want to believe me, but you can't bring him to a world of the living and expect it to be okay. Don't bring him if you can't send him back or where you can't afford a lot of people dying, and leakage."

Lila raised her eyebrows.

"He means that there will be some aetheric wake in such a summons," Teazle drawled, arms folded across his chest, head on one side. "We might expect anything from a change in the weather to an invasion of geists and ghouls. They might cluster around their lord and obey him or they might be free. It depends on what this friend of yours has become." He looked down at the bed again and over Zal's blissful expression. "This would concern me more. You can't send Zal anywhere with this on him. He could shoot himself just for the fun of it."

Zal waved a hand airily. "I'll be fine."

Teazle snorted. "You can't trust him."

"Nonsense!" Zal retorted. "I've taken hundreds of drugs that were way worse than this."

There was a strange ringing noise, and suddenly Teazle's blade, yellow and shining, was at Zal's throat. Lila was also up on her feet, arm poised to knock it away although she had held back at the last moment. "What are you doing?"

The blade, which looked more, like a strip of fire than a piece of metal, hummed with an audible sound that made her skin crawl as though it would very much like to run away, whether or not she was coming with it. It was the sword named Corruptor, she thought.

"These blades were both demons once," Teazle said. "After death their stone corpses were refined and the ore was beaten with dragon-bone ash until it made these blades. This one has an affinity for poisons and disease of any kind. She was a succubus. Watch." With a tiny movement of his arm, he nicked Zal's skin with the razor edge of the sword. A drop of blood ran out onto the blade, and the blade's fire suddenly intensified, the hum changed to a much more soft and mellow tone. Lila saw the blood vanish into the blade, and its light grew for a fraction of a second. She saw Teazle listening, his gaze empty as he concentrated, lips swelling and a half smile moving across his face.

"Happy with that, is she?" Malachi asked, also watching.

Teazle brought the sword back to him, its tasselled hilt gleaming in his hand through its bindings. "She is only delighted when she tastes venoms that match her own inclinations. In her lifetime she was an enslaver who ruled an army that was devoted enough to conquer the known world. Her venom charm enabled them to be fearless or hopeless, according to her will. They would do anything for her. Their love for her knew no limit. His sting hasn't got a living demon attached to it anymore, so its charm wanders. It isn't as strong as a *Nihila* strike from a major demon; it's weak, but it's there." His eyes were bright. Holding the sword was exciting him. With a strong, determined move he sheathed it again and let it go. "It could take months to wear off depending on the potency of the strike."

"She was only a second-rate pusher for godsake!" Lila snapped. "It can't be that bad."

"Well, on an ordinary person maybe not, but this is Zal," Teazle said. "He's like walking *Hedonia Nihila* anyway. Love, death, there's nothing he won't dice with. If there's time, then I should get him to a demon who can get rid of this."

Lila shrugged. "Meet me back here in two hours. I'll go alone."

Malachi heaved a long sigh. "If proof were needed we have no control over you, this is it."

"Whatever you say," she said. She checked Zal's neck where the sword had bitten, but the one drop was all that had come from the scratch and it was almost healed up already. Livid lines spread from the sting site. She glanced at Teazle and trusted him to pick up her intentions from what she was about to say. "I'm going to the place we found before. Look after him."

"I will," the demon promised. His eyes were very bright, but he blinked slowly, shutters on a furnace.

Malachi's expression darkened at being left out of the loop, though his tone was amused and slightly wondering. "The three of you are truly an unholy union."

"Three's the magic number," Zal said. "I want three baths. And three drinks. And three f—Never mind. Three shots of something good."

"Don't worry, we're going to just the place," Teazle assured him. "You're good as you are."

"I don't want to know, do I?" Lila asked.

"You look very beautiful in that dress," Teazle said.

She was taken aback. "I . . . have to go."

Malachi laughed. "Compliments. I should have known that was the weapon."

"Weapon?" Lila frowned at them both.

"Never mind," the faery growled. "Speed to your respective dooms. I must return to Otopia and find a way to spring Xaviendra from the gaol without anybody noticing. I'll bring her here as soon as I can."

Lila smiled. "Could you send a message to my house and say we won't be back for dinner?"

"I think you mean for days," he said with an air of weary resignation. "Very well. And to whom do I send this message?"

"To Sassy. You know, your cleaner?"

He nodded thoughtfully and gave her a glance that assured her he would be looking into this at length while she wasn't there to interfere. "As you wish."

"And please explain things to Temple."

"Oh I always give a good excuse," Malachi said. "Covering up is the name of my game." He paused, "I know it looks bad, Lila, what I've said and done, but think about the alternatives and I did—I do—like you. I wouldn't wait fifty years for just anyone. But I won't be your whipping boy over it either. We've played that game and we've both lost it."

"We're good," she said. "I won't ask another favour." She would have given him a hug or a kiss, but she was still too angry to make it. Instead she hoped her sincerity showed in her eyes. Her feelings would have to catch up in their own time.

"I won't give you one." From a faery this was a kindness. He gave her a brief smile and turned on his heels. In a whirl of black, glittering dust he vanished. The dust circled and fell. It darkened the floor for a few moments, winking as if it was a night sky, then it was gone.

"He must've been working on that," Teazle said, mildly impressed.

"Lila, are you naked under that dress?" Zal mused. She felt his hand slide over the fabric across her hip.

"I'm in full plate," she replied.

"It really feels naked to me," he said.

"Yes, it looked naked in the bath," Teazle agreed.

She lowered her chin and glared at him, "You didn't leave me any underwear."

"How thoughtless."

She saw Teazle's white-light stare intensify and felt it shine on her face, or it might have been her blushing. Then she glanced down, and Zal's darker eyes were looking at her with the same expression, as alert and predatory as he had been zonked five seconds earlier. She realised he'd been fooling around the whole time.

"I can't." She held up her hand. "Not now. Really."

"Why's that?" Teazle moved closer. Because he was standing, his height and his posture made him look down on her and his jaw lifted with arrogant confidence. There was much less playfulness in him than in Zal, although both of them could shift gears from nought to hot in less than a second. She loved that moment when all their teasing vanished into pure hunting conviction, and she saw it flickering close in the demon's white face.

He raised his hands and slowly unbuckled the bandoliers that held his swords in place.

Her own conviction wavered. "You heard what he said. You heard what I told you. Anyway, we're not married anymore."

"But we're here now," Zal said and his hand slid over her lower back. The thin fabric made the gesture extremely soft, although he had the most gentle hands she'd ever felt when he wanted them to be. His gaze was warm and sultry; he blinked as slowly as if he were underwater.

"No fighting," she said.

"No fighting," Teazle agreed, advancing.

"No," Zal said, pulling the drawstring that closed the back of her dress.

"Wait!" she slipped aside, pulling it with her. "You smell like you've been in the grave already. Get clean."

Teazle's nostrils flared in disapproval; he had a demon's typical taste for gore. The tip of his long, lilac tongue flickered briefly against his lips. He gave Zal a dismissive glance. "I suppose you can walk?"

Zal slithered off the bed, only his natural athleticism saving him from a bounce onto hands and knees. He gathered himself and walked reasonably well towards the bath. "Like I'd been doing it all my life." He bashed Teazle's shoulder with his own, slightly higher one, in passing, and left a smear of tacky coagulated blood on the pristine tunic. Their faces were close enough to have touched, but they angled away from one another, eyes downcast, snorting and growling with a soft tone that only Lila's exaggerated hearing could have caught. She saw them inhale one another's breath to take the measure of their condition, and then Zal had reeled lightly into the bathroom on his toes, dancing as he shed his clothes in piles on the floor, and she was left with Teazle brooding at her.

"I didn't know you two were cosy," she said, watching him so closely, but even so she didn't see the movement as he crossed the few metres between them. One second he was there, the next he was beside her, his hand sliding under the dress's deep scooped back onto her buttock.

"You are in great danger," he murmured softly, his breath warm on her ear. "I feel your instability. I can taste its slow changes. You are weakening. Your anger fades and with it your discipline is fading. Sadness eats your resolve. Grief wounds you. Your need for control saps your strength. You are bleeding into the water. I smell you everywhere. Zal knows—the part of him that's demon and the elf too. We have spoken. Our mark will protect you. Not for long though. Take it or leave it. Without it you will fall to the hungering darkness that surrounds you. Its claws are deep in you already. What elves call Sleeper. There it is. Lila, I would not see you fall, yet I would stop you and cannot. All I can do . . ." His fingers caressed her skin lightly at the edge of the high collar she wore, but he didn't finish the sentence.

She'd been naked with him before, a lot, but now she felt more so, even with the robe still on. It was intimate, and that was new for them.

"You exaggerate." She put her hand up, and it served to hold the dress in place at her chest although it caught his hand beneath. His skin was cool and soft. He leaned in towards her readily as her hand touched him with an eagerness that sent a jolt through her. She felt heat rising in him.

"All this talk," she said, in an effort to deflect him—a foolish effort because it wasn't entirely sincere. "As if you were my imp." Her attempts to become, in his words, immaculate, kept falling over their feet. An imp would keep score. They always knew who was strongest in magic, or in spirit, or where your energy was going, into what locked circles of the mind. She was prey to Teazle and his kind now, kill them as she did. She might slay them all, but she was on the back foot and they knew it. Teazle was trying to tell her how much worse this would be with Ilya, and she felt that he was honest, even though Teazle's method was seduction and his intent clear.

"What I am can't be helped," he replied, his lips brushing her forehead at the hairline. He slid his hand free at her neckline and cupped her breast in his hand. His breath deepened. "Nor who you are. I know this and still I return to you. Faith drives me. I am not free. The marriage was a legal device. The bond is a bigger game." She knew that she didn't appreciate the difficulty he had in saying this to her, and that is why he could say it, because she was no demon to spring into all the openings that it presented. He was a fighter, and this was the equivalent of him laying down all his weapons and declaring himself handicapped.

On her breast his fingers were supple as he stroked her. She loved his touch. It was like Zal's. They shared the same directness and self-command. They knew who they were and what they were doing. She envied that with a strange hunger that prevented her from saying no to this new binding between them. She would have eaten them both if their wholeness were something that could be got that way—and with a shiver of surprise she realised this was exactly what they were proposing. Their energy could lift her above self-doubt for a while.

It was a user's fix, a crutch. For demons to offer it to another demon would have been sufficient insult to start a war. But she didn't count herself demon. Shame flickered in her nonetheless. Her walks in the demon world had always had more front than a luxury department store, and about as much depth. She was a penitent here, and the priests were offering her a brief burst of respite through possession. The strangeness of this hit her, an exotic intoxication, a sudden jolt of vision switched through one hundred and eighty degrees so that she saw her usual comfort around them as a foolish illusion of a creature spellbound in the glamour. Vertigo made her falter on her feet.

Teazle's lips brushed her cheek close to her mouth. "It is good you react so readily to us. Already you begin to see."

She looked up into the pale lights of his eyes; doors open into heaven. She dared honesty, for a moment, feeling that she stepped into nowhere. "The more of you, the less of me. I'm afraid I will drown in you. In Zal. It's what I wanted."

"Nothing can touch you unless you agree," Teazle said, the movements of his lips kisses on her temple and across her forehead.

"But I want to agree," she said.

His gaze flicked back to meet hers, and she saw movement in the fire that lit it from the world behind them. His mouth was slightly open, lips full. The breath from his nostrils bathed her face with animal warmth. "Then you are indeed in the greatest danger from your old friend." His body was tensing up to contain something.

She looked into the light. "And you?"

He exhaled slowly. "It calls to me." He kissed her mouth very gently. "Through you and your abilities, think what I could become . . . But I am the master. And . . ." He kissed her again with a tenderness she couldn't reconcile with him at all. It disarmed her, confused her, and tripped her up so that when he did finish this line she finally understood the meaning of something he'd said to her often. "I'm your dog."

She'd thought he was joking.

He smiled, a cold expression directed at himself. "What a filthy secret for a demon, wouldn't you say?"

She put her hand to his face and felt the hard bone under the muscles and skin. She felt, with all of her senses, the beginnings of its shift in form from man to demon. It was constantly beginning, being suppressed. She opened her mouth to speak, but he was already shaking his head.

"Better I am a man for you now. You're too quick to rush into your sleeping darkness, Lila."

His forbearance touched her the most. She put her arms around his neck. The dress fell around her ankles, and she felt his long, soft hair tickle across her shoulders and neck.

Zal came through the door, naked and rubbing his head with a towel, transformed from fool to the rock star's sanguine cockiness, as though water and soap had been enough to wash off everything and return him to the figure she remembered when they first met. His tread was strong and sure, not a trace of poison in its conviction as he came to them. The dark flow of his shadow body was integrated into his skin, giving him the metal-in-oil look she was getting used to, but at the same time she saw it was necessary—a kind of fortification. His physical body was evanescent; it was beginning to fade, losing matter. Anxiety for him fought with her attraction and admiration and won. He was so damn slender.

He showed no concern for himself as he draped the towel on Teazle's shoulder, turning him away from Lila so that the two of them faced each other. "Take off the shades," he said. "Pump me up."

Lila's eyebrows were raised so far they were nearly in the roof. She was more surprised when Teazle actually pushed her behind him, saying, "Close your eyes."

She had an inkling of what was going to happen, but she was almost too slow. The light shock made her stagger backwards, body convulsing on itself in an effort to reduce exposure as Teazle let the searing radiance from his eyes pour onto Zal's naked skin. For a few seconds she was blinded in all her senses as systems shut down and then, as the cascade of failures built up, she lost contact altogether and found herself conscious but unable to perceive anything other than that she was still alive. There wasn't even darkness. There was nothing.

Slowly, painfully slowly, things came back. Out of a half-second blackout she discovered her body was still there, lying on the floor. Something like dust covered her. She wanted to brush it off long before she could move. Then she felt herself being lifted and the vibration of the men's voices like a report of distant weather. She was moved and brushed over, the dust gone. Then she felt how hot she was and knew that if she'd been an ordinary human she'd be burned.

Hearing returned with sudden, total clarity.

"It does qualify as fire, then," Teazle was saying nearby.

"Apparently so." Zal, much closer. "But next time there's no need to overdo it."

Teazle laughed. "You're *my* bitch now, elf."

"I don't think I swing that far," Zal replied.

Lila felt herself swaying, but that was replaced quickly as her orientation found gravity. Everything came together rapidly after that until only the emotional shock was left. She opened her eyes and saw that except for several shadowed spots in the shape of their bodies every surface in the room had been turned to ash. Flakes of it fell from her eyelashes and lips as she tried to say, "What happened?" and stopped before she started.

Zal was standing in front of her, holding her up by the shoulders. His grip was faultless, but this wasn't what silenced her. He had become as solid as the demon behind him, a fully fleshed and healthy creature, brimming with energy, as vital as the moment before Jack the Giantkiller had crushed all but the life out of him. His *andalune* moved around him, a confident ten centimetres above the surface of his skin, and extended into transparent black flames shot with yellow and orange lights that grew over his shoulders into two vaned wings that spanned the room from wall to wall. Their slightest movement caused whirls and eddies of white ash to rise.

He smiled into her speechlessness. At his throat the demon sting was no more than a fading mark the size of a small coin. "Lila? Are you all right?"

She was, though she had to take an inventory to feel confident about it. "What happened to you?" She looked around Zal to Teazle, who was glowing, his expression smug. "Did you . . . supercharge him? How?"

"I have fire affinity," Zal said. "Part of my aetheric nature, which Jack couldn't take away. Teazle has inner fire."

"Oh yeah," she said, nodding. "That explains it completely. I'll file it under Closed Cases."

"Aether can become matter, temporarily," Teazle said. "Unfortunately it isn't permanent. Any fire would do."

"Inner fire?"

"He's an angel," Zal said, as though this were obvious and uninteresting. "Their eyes are the windows onto the light of creation blah de blah etcetera."

"Yeah," she said again, with elaborate emphasis, "I knew that. Everyone knows *that*. Demons are angels. Primary school stuff." She glanced at Teazle. He looked amused.

"Oh he's still a demon," Zal said, slowly releasing his hold as though he were afraid she was going to fall over without his help. "Angel is the ascended form."

"I thought angels were bound to serve god, or whoever, without will of their own."

Teazle shrugged. "I wouldn't know. There is only one will, and it feels very much like mine."

"From a threesome to barfly theology in less than two minutes," Lila said, looking around to help herself acclimatise. "That's some going." She became aware of the distances between them—a metre to Zal, one between him and Teazle. The emotional gap had widened too, the intimacy of a moment before crisped to nothing. She searched their faces for signs and saw that they were waiting for her to settle into one response or another. For the first time since she'd known them she felt the balance between them shift into a position of equals, a triangle of even sides.

"Now I'm lost," she said and ran her hands through her hair. Ash flittered down. "But I don't want to be the one who's helped. I don't like it. That's the world on a wrong axis."

"Do you want to bet your life on it?" Zal asked.

She thought it through, said finally, uncertainly, "Ilya wouldn't really kill me."

They glanced at each other. None of them were what they had been.

"All right," she said. "Let's do it."

CHAPTER FOURTEEN

Lila thought of armour; knights in plate, infantrymen in mail, leather-strapped gladiators testing their range, textile flak jackets full of smart gel, being cheerful when you were sad all through, your smile deflecting every threatened sympathy like a shield of shiny happiness. As she thought, her hands worked, the tips of her fingers pulling and stretching, rubbing and smoothing as she spun strands of what appeared to be metallic cloth out of her skin.

She didn't do it in front of the demons. She sat in the bathroom on the toilet lid and worked silently. She could remember Zal's measures in perfect detail and enough elven manuscripts from the archives that she could copy a typical Jayon combat harness down to the last buckle and glyph. Her glyphs were not magical, however; they were forgeries without power. The power was in the harness itself. It was her clone.

When she was done, she held it up and looked it over. As an afterthought she fashioned a dagger for the belt. Then it seemed finished to her. She put it down and looked for the last time at her arms and hands before she got dressed. She couldn't stop looking ever since she'd got out of bed and noticed what her husbands had done for her.

The demon marks ran in her skin in networks of tiny fire, markings in an ancient script of simple dashes and crosses. They flowed in chaotic rushes, met, diverged, dissolved, blossomed, and died. She could feel their effect, a kind of precision constant tuning to frequencies and melodies that the machine could not reach on its own. The script talked her into calm. She was the eye of a strange storm.

The demon data networks were full of designs. She picked some out and reprocessed her usual black body armour and military fatigues through their ideas. Bigger boots and gloves were in, gleaming leather zipped up the neck in high collars, plate inserts made to look like they had been ripped off the bodies of monsters. She toned it down and resized it, checked her hair, got distracted when she realised she could put any colour she liked anywhere on her face, then settled on red lips, bigger blacker eyelashes, and pink cheek tints.

Then she took the harness back into the bedroom and stood for a moment watching Zal and Teazle sleep. Their efforts had exhausted them. She wasn't about to wake them while she was running on their donated powers. She left the harness lying on the end of the bed and glanced at the white demon's face.

He was chalky and ordinary looking, like a tired human man taking a nap at the end of a hard day's labour. She wanted to leave something for him, but she couldn't think of anything. In the end she bent over him and left a kiss on his cheek. He didn't stir.

On the way out she caught sight of herself in one of the many vanity mirrors and stopped. It wasn't beauty that snagged her. It was that, for an instant, she'd thought it was a painting moving because the figure seen from the corner of her eye had a resolute, confident stride, so determined and forceful that it had triggered her combat protocols before she realised it was herself. The lipstick and the red shock in her hair stood out lividly against the ash-white dust of the room.

She knew then that she could do anything. The notion filled her with a cautious sadness. Without limitation whatever borders she ran up against would be her own. Surely this is what Teazle had intended for her to understand and what Zal had ever understood. She wondered if she could die.

Out on the causeways around the house the demons of the canal traders and the mansion servants were entangled in the day's bargaining, waves of colour moving through them in ripples of emotion that she could read as easily as the day's papers. There was an undercurrent of tension in the city, a strip of violet blue, grey with the load of uncertainty it carried. She felt it everywhere, even on the main promenades where the Maha were gathered for the day's combat of beauty and wit, talent and chutzpah. The ones who still recognised her got out of her way and the others followed. She got attention, but no challenges. Instead, a resentful deference ensured that her way was clear. She was followed, until she turned and offered a fight. Then, miraculously, the streets were empty.

The way into Madame's old house was simple. Lila didn't have the keys, but she made them and opened the locks. Teazle had bought the property and left it empty, knowing what it protected. It was maintained as though it was occupied by a small group of servants he paid to watch over it, though nothing had changed since Madame Des Loupes had abandoned it decades before, perhaps through a vision of what would happen there. In one of the living rooms she found a large throw of woven silk, thick and heavy. She pulled it off the chaise it was adorning and threw it over her shoulder before following the way through the halls to the place where the secret door waited. In a moment she had opened it and gone down into the dark, dank tunnels of the labyrinth.

The mirror chamber was as they had left it too—crowded with the stone remains of demons who had stumbled here searching for treasure only to be unfortunate enough to find themselves looking into the chamber's sole and very particular treasure; the Mirror of Dreams. Even in total darkness the mirror had the power to suck the beholder out of their body and into the potentially endless mindscapes within. Lila knew it well, hence the throw.

She moved between the stone figures—unlike normal demon statues these were genuinely empty, having no spirits left to be imprisoned within for the ages of their deaths—and eased in reverse up to the mirror's majestic span. It took a few moments of careful work and jigging around, but she was finally able to cover its face completely with the cloth and secure it to her satisfaction so that it wouldn't fall by accident, but a good yank from either corner would get it off easily.

Then she pushed the statues out to the edges of the space. The largest weighed several tons and almost stuck fast on the uneven floor so that she had to grow spikes down from the soles of her boots into the stone to get any leverage on the damn thing. After the work she listened until she was satisfied that there were no curious or accidental tourists in the labyrinth—it had openings up into the city and down into various underwater lairs that were probably known to some criminal groups even now—but only the drip and trickle of water and the distant burr of engines up on the lagoon permeated through to her. She was alone.

Lila put her back to the mirror's position. The reason those with aetheric power didn't want to give their names away was because they could be commanded by them. But she knew this one because its bearer had lived close to her heart once.

"Ilyatath Voynassi Taliesetra, come to me."

She repeated it the standard three times, feeling that her voice was surely not enough. It barely carried beyond the confines of the room. At least it wasn't hesitant. After she'd finished, the deep quiet of the labyrinth returned and for the first time she became aware of its penetrating cold and damp qualities. Then air moved against her face and hands. It was cold too, but something about its steady push told her it was breath.

"Tath?" she said into the total, utter darkness and felt the sound of her voice immediately reflect back at her off something not more than six or seven inches from her face. An image of it did not resolve into anything resembling an elf. It didn't resemble anything. Inside her skin the demon runes grew agitated. She tried resolving the data on higher detail. It made no difference. The feedback was inconsistent, as if the sound were coming off moving mist.

"Tath," she said, with a confidence that was difficult to muster. "It's me, Lila. I need to talk to you."

She thought she heard something. It was so faint she wasn't sure. A kind of sigh or drawn breath. She retuned her hearing again, blotting out the ambient noise and amplifying. "Please say it again." Her own voice nearly blew out her ears before she remembered to nullify that as well.

A fine line of cool, damp air crossed her face, and a much deeper and more penetrating cold wound around her. It had the sinuous grace of a boa constrictor, but it didn't grip. A feeling of dread permeated her, from the skin inwards. It was such a strange, unmistakable sensation, a different kind of cold sinking inward towards her bones, her flesh wanting to recoil. The hum of the runescript became a buzz, and abruptly the cold spirals around her withdrew.

This time she heard the voice. It was so fragile, as if the lips and throat that spoke it were constructed from vapour. "So long," it said. "I . . ." and then it faded away, still speaking, the words lost.

All the time she was tuning and retuning, searching every wavelength, every frequency, every piece of information for something definite that she could detect and build on. Her mind's AI built her the image of the room and its forlorn objects and tried to place what it found within it so that she could see. Brief flickers of something like fine cloud came and went around her. She saw it manifesting almost randomly, but this was only because where it appeared it caused a sharp local temperature drop, which made the water in the air condense out for a moment. She was reminded of Zal and the way he threatened to fade out. She wondered if there was something that would enable Tath to manifest a body in the same way. "I must talk to you."

There was a slow, general shift of the motes of cold. They began to gather and clump, winking in and out like fireflies. She was completely taken by surprise when they snapped together in front of her, their cloudlike clusters bursting into white shocks of vapour that quickly froze into tiny ice crystals. These were attracted magnetically towards an invisible surface tension that began vibrating at a high frequency—in a few seconds they outlined the shape of a tall figure. The head and shoulders were clear, but the rest was vague and ragged as if it was drawn by someone who could only block in the most basic shape. It had arms and a robed body. There were no features in the face, only two empty spots in the place of eyes. Darkness cloaked it. The empty air acted as shadows, making it look like it wore a hood. At its back, as though at a distance, the shape of curved crescent blades was sketched in the air. These moved lightly, vanes on an unfelt and restless wind. A faint keening sound came from their direction—the impersonal whine of resonating metal.

Meanwhile Lila was experiencing the most acute sensation of mortal dread. It was so strong that it blotted out almost everything else she ever remembered feeling at any time. There was nothing concrete to cause it. She was in no danger; all systems reported good conditions. The thing in front of her was barely an illusion—a few crystals, nothing more.

It was all she could do not to fall on her knees. She had the clear feeling that there was a rod of something fine and heated that ran directly through the vertical centre of her body from pelvis to the crown of her head. It reached through her legs and anchored her upright, on the ground. It stretched through her arms and automatically closed her hands into fists. Immediately the dread lost some of its grip. "Ilya," she said in a warning tone. "Don't fuck around."

The voice sighed—it sounded as if the room were sighing because it came from all sides at once, as though she were surrounded by open mouths. "I have dreamed . . ." These words came from directly in front, but they were continued by a lesser whisper slightly to her left. ". . . of the golden meadows of the sun, the silver lakes of the moon." After that words came singly, from random directions. "I have been in the dark and I am dark. I know your name. But I do not remember you. There have been so many."

"So many what?" Around her the air was moving now in more normal fashion as denser regions massed and pushed through lesser ones in a restless prowling. She tingled with the anticipation of something awful, and her fingers clenched tighter on one another until she felt her nails begin to cut her palms.

Phrases came again from all sides. "Longing. Waiting. I see them turning. Falling."

She wanted to keep the conversation going. She was afraid of what would happen if this dissociation got itself organised. The rime-crusted face in front of her was deteriorating, its eye pits growing larger, more skull-like. "Who are turning? Where are they falling to?"

"Lost," said the face thing, forming a mouth like a puncture wound. "I followed them so far. I felt . . ."

The sudden snap of cold caught her off guard again. It was direct this time, more sure of itself. Ice motes flew past her, tearing her skin on the way to the looming ghostly figure. Its sabred wings rattled. They looked feeble, powdery, but the noise was harsh and absolutely clear, ringing as though they were standing in a grand cathedral and not a rough hole in the ground.

"I . . ." said the voice, this time from two places at once. Elsewhere its whispers had sunk to babblings of emotional words, must and ought, must and have to, need . . . it rambled. The whispers lowered until they were a faint, indecipherable bubbling of sound all around her. She got the impression that although they sounded the same, they were not. They rose from a mass and subsided into it, and she couldn't know if that mass was even able to differentiate itself again.

"Ilya," she said firmly. "Listen to me. You must find a way through."

"Ilya," repeated the ghost face as though the syllables were new. "Ilya," it said again, more cannily this time and the bubbling subsided and vanished.

She felt a presence growing in the room. It wasn't just in front of her. It was everywhere. Weightlessly it weighed on her. Breathlessly it

breathed. It coated everything in a purplish, sticky nothing that did
not exist and reminded her of tar, feathers, burning flesh, and dust. Her
nostrils and eyes became so thick with it she couldn't see, or breathe.
She convinced herself this was an illusion. Her body and AI still
thought everything was fine, just a few minor temperature fluctua-
tions, nothing more. Nothing stopped her breathing, but she couldn't.
Nothing blocked her senses, but they were failing. At a subconscious
level she had been commanded to stop, and she was hypnotised and
obeying. Fortunately, she did not need to breathe, or to sense, in order
to survive.

The demon runes skittered, dancing, popping. She knew that
death was moments away, but she didn't know how it would come. She
felt unutterably stupid for not believing Malachi and taking his advice.
But this paled in the face of the last moments. She wasn't afraid because it was too certain for that. Instead a sharp awareness came to her,
so acute that time seemed to stretch itself thin, longer and longer, and
it occurred to her that if she were going to do anything it must be now,
no matter how pointless or idiotic it seemed.

"Remember the dog!" she shouted, waiting for the immaterial
blades to cut her off from the world forever. "Remember you were running with your dog in the forests! Ilya!"

A vast agitation made the air thrum with a deadly, rising whine.
Unstable to stable, it went in a moment. Lila couldn't see anything, but
she felt pressure rise. The image in her mind was the blades of a food
blender whirring up to maximum speed. The sense of threat peaked,
and without knowing why she screamed, "Dar! What about Dar?"

In the context of the world Dar was ancient history. Zal's ally, he
had led Lila to find Zal and she had been forced to kill him in re-
payment of this favour. Ilya's hand had, metaphorically, been on the
knife with hers. It was a raw wound to her still. Perhaps the most raw.
Any reminder was quick to flay the skin off it for her. She knew that it
had been the same for Ilya. It was their deepest bond; that moment of

horror and shame was a blade that could cut through anything. It was her only weapon.

The whining of the spirit blades became a scream. The pitch of it rose and rose unbearably and without warning reached a febrile height and then stopped. She felt whatever it was—she had no means of accurately describing it—shatter and the pieces, sharp and tiny, go flying everywhere in a storm of hurt confusion.

In a split second of silence the room was empty once more. She felt that she was alone. As her senses returned to themselves, she realised that the silk throw covering the mirror had been ripped to shreds.

"Lila?"

The voice scared her more than the huge show had done. She leapt a foot in the air, caught herself awkwardly in a panic, and felt herself flare hot with shock and fear. It came from behind her.

She could not turn to face the mirror, so she made herself stay where she was, in a half crouch. Her whole body burned to escape but she did not move. It cost her every bit of willpower that she had. She knew the voice, sort of. It sounded like Ilya, but it was odd, too high, too uncertain, and the elvish accent of its Otopian was very strong. It was young, she realised, that was it, and it was speaking to her from the mirror.

"It's me," she said.

There was a pause. "Where am I?" the voice said.

"Who are you?" She didn't mean to be so untrusting, but there it was.

"It's me," he said, shy. "Ilyatath. Where am I?" Now he sounded scared.

"I don't know," she said truthfully. "To me you're inside a mirror. Mirror of Dreams. Do you know it?"

"It's so dark," the boyish voice said and hesitated. Then, "Yes. One of the seven mirrors. I know it. Are you a dream, then?"

"No," she said. "I summoned you here. This is Demonia. The mirror is in Demonia."

Another pause, as this was digested. "Where was I, then?"

"I don't know," she said, honestly. "Some place beyond Last Water. Don't you remember?"

"Last Water," he repeated slowly. "Oh." This was sad, and final. "Am I dead?"

"I really don't know," Lila said. "You must remember something."

"Dar," the boy said. "I am old. But not here. I am dead, but not dead. Oh. Yes. I remember now. It was so long ago. Or yesterday. And it is there still." He sniffled, and she realised that he was crying and trying not to show it.

"Ilya, something bad is happening to Alfheim, to Otopia and the other planes."

"They are coming through," he said. "The walls are breached."

"Who are they?"

He coughed a little and cleared his throat. "Betrayed. That is who they are. Thirst, that is what they are. I followed them and ran beyond Last Water. I tried to see where they were going. They ran through my domain, and I was nothing to them, not king, not shepherd, they did not stop for me. I didn't know what they were, so I followed. They are spirits, like those of the beyond, but they have all that the spirits crave and do not have; will, integrity, focus, mind, power. They knew me, but they did not speak."

"You met them?"

"We hunted each other." He was smiling, then he stopped. "They were better than I was, and my hounds. We stood in the forest. They were old, so very old. Angry, so very angry. But there was a moment when we ran together, side by side, and they knew themselves to be elves again. I saw their faces. I talked, but they didn't answer. Their eyes . . ." He swallowed with effort. "Their eyes are terrible, Lila, don't look at them."

"Did you?"

A pause. "Yes. Don't you look at them. They do not live and they do not die. They are not of that form, but their gaze is death to the living. They consume souls and they possess what cannot be eaten until it weakens and falls apart. They took me beyond Last Water and left me there when I did not satisfy them anymore."

"Ilya," she said gently, trying to convey as much kindness in her tone as she was able. "The dead seem to be coming back. What is happening?"

"They are the host of the Betrayed," he said. "When people die, their spirits pass quickly through my domain. Once they have gone beyond it, they don't come back. But where I am king there are many spirits of many kinds, including those that fail to pass and those that are yet to move in the other direction and become elements. The Betrayed are massing enough impulse to break through into the material worlds and regain their forms there, otherwise they will have no effect on those planes. The spirits you see returning are riders of their storm. They copy the patterns and memories of those passing who have died in your reality, and remake themselves in their images on the other side."

She steeled herself. "So it isn't really . . . it's not really them?"

"In every aspect except for the spirit, it is probably an exact copy," Ilya said. "But there is almost no chance at all that it is the same in its numinous or aetheric form. Mind, personality—these are things not of spirit, so they will be identical."

She took the news with numb acceptance, moving on through the glum path of the facts. "They're young," she said. "Not like when they died."

"The spirit remembers itself in an archetype," he said. "Most people do not associate their true selves with their physical age. The body, the mind, and the personality are one intricate device, a vessel for the spirit, a journey, a love. They feed and are fed by it. Ultimately they part. One passes onward. One ends and is recycled."

"In Otopia it isn't fashionable to talk about spirits like that. It's like chatting about the existence of good and evil. People think you're nuts," Lila said, but she took his word for it.

"Humans are in love with the machine because it is perfect and seems to offer the cure for every ill. They are at an elemental stage of alchemical philosophy," Ilya said, and she could hear the dismissive shrug in the slight nuances of his emphasis. He couldn't care less. "I could hunt these stealing spirits down and bring them back to me. But I could not do anything with the Betrayed. They are beyond my reach because they are wavewalkers. Is that why you called me?" There was a hesitancy now, a tentative appeal that she felt as clearly as if he had reached out to touch her.

"It was one reason," she admitted. She was beyond lying to him, even to console him. Still, it was hard to tell the truth, and she didn't know why. "But Malachi said you'd been out too long and were changed. I thought maybe you were lost and that I'd like to find you. He made out that you were some kind of monster."

"Yes," he said. "I am. You saw it, before I got caught here."

She was tempted to deny this, but resisted. "What was that?"

"Beyond Last Water are the things of spirit that one would least like to encounter. Hungry, relentless, cold. They will consume anything. They will attach to anything. I resisted them a while. I thought I was their master. They beset me, and I fell. I was consumed. If you hadn't tricked them here, you would be theirs now because I would have killed you." He sucked his breath in on the last word and waited.

She wanted to turn around, but she didn't dare. "Why?"

"In the world of the spirit no memories remain. I was only the walker of the dark valleys. Even that meaning was failing. There was nothing except thirst and hunger and longing and shadow. I would have severed you from mortal things and taken your body for my own. Ironic, wouldn't it have been?"

"What happened?"

"When the mirror appeared, we were caught. Only I could stay, because you summoned me. And here I am as I was in my dreams— the dream you named."

"Can you get out?"

"In death there are no dreams," he said. "I don't think I want to. I have been so far, so long. I never thought to get back to this place and these ways. I may never have the chance again."

"I need you, to track the hunters for me," she said.

"They will kill you," he said. "They have no business with you. Leave them."

"I have business with them," she said. "What happens if they manifest in Otopia, and Alfheim, and Demonia? What then?"

"Then you will know what they want," he replied. "But you will not be able to stop them."

"We'll see about that," she said. "But if you want to . . . will you die there, in the mirror, Tath?"

"If I stay, I will be only a dream," he said. "And without a dreamer, then yes, I will be gone. I have no form to return to unless I return to Faerie to my haunt at the Soulfall where the snow and ice remember me."

She wanted to say he could ride with her, for old times' sake, but she didn't know how he would take it. She didn't know how she'd take it. "Come on," she said. "One last journey, one last hunt, one more time. We can always die later. Why hurry?"

She had to grate her teeth as she said it because suddenly she was in tears and she wanted to sob. There was a pain in her chest like a flat, crushing iron. The buzz in her skin spiralled inwards. She closed the fist of her will on the pain and extinguished it. She knew that the dream he was in was his heart's desire, no nightmare, but a heaven; a boy and his dog, in the forests, running. He could stay there.

She said, "For old times' sake. They're in Alfheim, I'm sure of it. For Dar's sake."

There was a long pause, very long, in which she was glad there was no light at all to see by. "Very well," he said at last, his voice small. "Call me, when you must."

Then she was alone in the labyrinth. She ran out as fast as she could, given the low roof height, the twists and turns, the yawning empty mouths of its pit traps. In the room above she stood and gulped the stinking lagoon air with gratitude.

When she arrived at the Sikarza house, Zal and Teazle were on the roof deck. A drake was parked there, ignoring them and looking over the city, its ugly head turned away. Its rider was arguing with Teazle. Drinks had been drunk and spilled by the look of it, and insults were being exchanged. Zal was a bystander, cup in hand, lounging back in a sun chair as he watched the proceedings. His air of insouciance almost blanketed his exhaustion. Food was being brought out and laid with the golden plates, so Lila guessed they were in for a long deal. She took a seat beside Zal and accepted a cup of wine from a server.

"What gives?"

"We're buying a drake for me to commit suicide on in Alfheim," Zal said. He leaned forward to a box of smokes and picked one, bit the end off it, and lit it with one of the candelabra. The flames danced lazily. It was one of those windless days where nothing seemed to move and the air sat over the lagoon like a toad on a rock. "Teazle wants to have an expedition to find a better one, but there isn't time for that so he's trying to find out if they have special stock they're not letting him see."

Lila looked at the drake on the deck. "What's wrong with that one?"

"It's the trader's own. They're loyal. You can't jump on and off like bicycles."

She saw he was wearing the silver harness. "You got your present."

"Yes," he grinned at her. "Kinky."

"More than you know," she said, taking a sip of wine and finding she was thirsty and starving. She got up to reach the table herself. Within moments she was stuffing her face with sliced roast meat. She picked up a beer jug by the neck and took it back to her place with her.

"You didn't find him," Zal said, as a question.

"I did." She met his iron-brown gaze and lost herself for a moment. "He will come when I call. I think."

Zal watched her with narrowed eyes. "He was as Mal said?"

"Yes. He was." She put emphasis on the final word and saw Zal take her meaning. "We will pursue this until we find out what it is that the dark Titans are after, and then we'll decide if it's worth being in Sarasilien's pay. So far it is all hints and coyness from every side, but having seen Ilya I think I'll take my chances as they turn. The whole game is like this place. It looks civilised and regulated, if you're standing at the top of the heap."

"That's how you see it now, as a game?"

"Players are crawling out of the woodwork," Lila said. "If it isn't a product of a game, then it's a sports field they want to be on. What do you think?"

He discarded his wine cup and frowned. "I wonder at what people will do to pass the time. Life is here, and they manage to be bored enough and cold enough to do all this. At such moments it is hard not to hate them." He'd fallen back into an elvish way of talking, no shortenings, no common phrases. She wondered if he'd noticed. "I think they come for him."

"Who?"

"For Sarasilien. And whoever else is still alive that was a part of their creation. That's what I'd be doing if they made me into a creature and sent me to hell to fight devils and left me to die." The throwback moment was gone, his everyday self returned. "Wouldn't you?"

She nodded. "I would."

Zal grinned at her, with the wolfish abandon that was both fierce and lighthearted. "And as a failed monster at least the pressure's off."

"It has been suggested to me I might collect an army of lame halts to make an heroic stand," Lila said, putting aside the empty beef plate onto the floor and taking a drink from the jug. "As if by banding together with a common goal of great goodness we will be lifted by valour into victory."

"Did you swallow an elf on your way here?"

"No," she said. "Sometimes I like to try it out and see how it feels. Well, it has. The thought popped into my head, much in the way they usually don't. Just now."

"You're hacked?"

"Possibly. Anyway, since it's the stupidest idea I've heard in a long time I won't be doing that."

"No," Zal said. "Though it has poetic and moral appeal. It could be an artistic feat."

"Not my style," Lila said.

Zal stroked the silky smoothness of the harness and felt her skin. When he looked at her, she saw his memories of their lovemaking in his eyes. "I wouldn't say that. Is this what I think it is?"

"Wait and see," she said, turning her attention back to Teazle's bickering. "I think he will resort to violence soon."

Everything waits to break through.

The words, the idea, formed in Lila's mind as clearly as a voice speaking, so much so that she looked around for the speaker before realising that it wasn't to be found in Demonia. She'd had a lot of this kind of thing with Tath, when he had lived in her heart, so she quickly got used to the idea, but now there was no physical connection to whatever or whoever had spoken. If spirits spoke, then they spoke this way. She waited.

In her mind's eye she saw the surface of reality splitting and breaking open like ice, smashing into shards, also unfolding like complex bundles of cloth, unravelling like twine and reknitting into other forms that broke through the fine, thin crust of the real and stretched it, pulled it. Everything tumbled under and boiled up again, places remade like personal memories of themselves. From these places unrecognisable creatures appeared and wrestled free of the grey goo that formed them, fishlike, ottery, and went dashing away.

It lasted an instant, and then it was gone. It was nothing like the idea of forming the halt army—something she felt was a tease rather than a genuine suggestion, a test perhaps. She glanced at Zal, but he was unperturbed, watching Teazle with an expression of tolerant wariness that surprised her. She had turned a blind eye to their rivalry, much as they did themselves because it suited them temporarily, but it had not vanished.

Since she couldn't detect or stop these two messages, nor discover their route or author, she decided not to worry about this new style of communication or speculate pointlessly on it. She drained the beer jug and wiped her mouth on the back of her hand.

Teazle gesticulated and dramatised and swore his way to a deal with the hardbitten figure of the drakewarden. At last, as the sun began to go down, they slapped each other's shoulders and turned away. The dragon behind them, which had gone to sleep, lifted its ugly eyeless head and sniffed the air before getting to its feet, claws grating on the stone roof tiles. For a moment it moved its attention to Lila and she felt as if it were looking at her, then it hefted itself into the windless air and was out over the lagoon leaving her wondering if it had been her secret speaker.

Around the city the lights were coming on. A cruiser balloon floated past, thrumming with engines and music. Somewhere in the twilight street below demons screamed and squabbled. Teazle said, "I'm going to watch. I don't trust them." His wings opened as he took his natural form and then sprang into the air. Where the drake had flown so swiftly he arrowed even faster, gliding on nonexistent air currents. She was left alone with Zal on the roof.

"When you go out to Alfheim, I'm heading back into Otopia. You can talk to me anytime. I can be there instantly." She hesitated, not wanting to ask the next question. "Did you get your cure?"

"No," he said. "There isn't one. Teazle thought if he leaned hard enough on some of the mages up at the Eternal Light they'd be able to fix it, but they all said that because she's dead they can't do anything."

"So stupid," she said. "Why did she do it?" She tapped her fingers restlessly on her thigh.

"Demon," he said, as if that was the answer to everything. "Forget it. I'll be fine."

She looked at him and shook her head. "Don't get yourself killed."

"I don't know what you're so worried about," he said. "You didn't get yourself killed. Why would I?"

"Because you gave a lot of your energy to me. Worked too."

"No it didn't," he said and smiled, brilliantly. "That was just one of Teazle's cheap tricks."

She peered at him. "What do you mean?"

"Well I *am* knackered, but it wasn't from any aetherical donations. That was a placebo. We fooled you."

Lila felt the beer making her heavy but not heavy enough to stop her blood rising. "But it reacted to the . . . things . . ."

"Of course it did. But that's all it did."

She sat, mouldering on her anger a little, settling into it, trying it on for size, and finding it didn't quite fit. "You tosser," she said finally.

"Yes, well." He lay back in the recliner as if bathing in the murky streetlight. "True to form, and that's what counts. Now you know how the world of the spirit works."

"Trickery?"

"Trickiness," he corrected. "If you believe it, they will come, and if you don't, then they won't. Or if they do, then you can be rid of them, as long as you keep your wits and don't fear them."

Lila didn't remember fear. Dread wasn't the same. Fear had some kind of hope in it, but she had expected death so completely there was no point in that emotion. "Ilya said that the three Titans were migrating from beyond Last Water into the other worlds. Seems it'd be a lot easier to say no to them before that happened."

"I guess he tried it and they ignored him."

"Yes. Which makes your previous statement less persuasive."

"Poor old Ilya, too much time with the undead and not enough with Tinkerbell. Always his trouble." Zal turned the full force of his attention on her, and she felt his strength of will like a physical force breaking against her so that for a minute she was convinced that it alone had the power to remake her. His smile cracked the spell. "Never my trouble."

"My trouble is that I don't know that it's my business to stop them," she said. "These Titans may be special, but I doubt their motives are anything to write home about. Maybe all they want is Sarasilien's soul and maybe they should have it."

"Yes, could be," Zal said. "I'm curious to find out."

This statement pleased her and soothed her more than she understood. "So am I."

CHAPTER FIFTEEN

The drake they finally obtained was as promised, a large, ominous-looking creature with green fire burning behind the sealed skin of its eyesockets and a strange, mottled hide of cadaverous purple, which was lit from within as though by glowing globes rising to its surface and falling back. It touched down on the Manse roof with barely a whisper of claws on the stone and immediately angled its ugly saurian head towards Zal.

"It speaks," Zal said faintly, so that only Lila could hear. "This is the one they call Unloyal and it knows and keeps the name."

Sikarza servants fussed around, fixing the drake's harnesses and rigging Zal's seat between the shoulder blades. An image appeared in the centre of Lila's mind, a thought without words of someone who would not throw their lot in with anybody, for any price. It was the drake's introduction, she realised. She knew how to speak that way in return; it was like forming composite patterns for another cyborg.

She asked it what it was doing as the servant of a drake trader and its reply was an inscrutable smooth blank. At the same time, she saw Zal frowning and guessed he was talking to it as well. How the signal passed from one to another she couldn't detect. Her wondering about this became a question, and the answers returned as fast as deflected shots—Unloyal had been getting fatter at the trader's expense while he waited for an interesting opportunity to appear and was content for the demon to act as his agent. The thought sharing was transmitted because Unloyal was a telepath, not because she was.

And what was telepathy? Lila wanted to know a scientific explanation.

Two-way aetheric radio, Unloyal returned. In her case the drake was powering both sides of the operation, since she had no aetheric body of note. The transmission medium was the aether itself, clearly, and the packet rate was unimpeded by physical constraints and virtually instantaneous and as wide as the world.

Lila told it she would stick with her clone and the old quantum transmission she understood, and the drake glanced at Zal's harness, made an equalisation, and said they were the same thing.

She objected—surely aether and matter were not the same? Yes, it said, they were the same, but they were not simultaneously expanded in the most material types of universe. Then its interest wandered and she felt it turning to Zal, leaving her sitting in her sun lounger in the dark, looking at the gaudy pulsing lights of the dirigibles as her mind turned this new factlet over and over like prayer beads. She had begun to have an inkling of who might play games with Titans.

Meanwhile Teazle returned, appearing like a white genie out of nowhere. He assumed his natural form and prowled across the roof to the two of them.

"This is where we part ways again," he said. "There is news of strange events in the Uathtan Wilderness and a sudden silence from the City-States of Zrae, which lie on its borders. Rumours fly of a demon horde from the wastes, and in the Elusive Sanctum mages pack their bags and flee. They have sealed all portals into and out of Bathshebat."

Lila frowned. "Same thing as Alfheim?"

"I am sure," Teazle said with great, pleased confidence. He was sparkling with anticipation. She could see she only warranted a part of his attention. "Zal, can you ride?"

Zal got up and reeled slightly though he kept his feet. With a steady motion he eased the joints in his neck and shook out his arms. "I'll survive it." He bent and picked up a light elvish pack that had been brought and laid at the side of his chair, went through it quickly, and then slung it over his shoulder. "Don't forget if they come to sack the place that you need to save the instruments from the Opera House. Put them away in one of your vaults or something. You'll never be able to replace them."

Teazle's bright gaze flicked briefly over Zal. "I intend to defend the city," he said, almost hurt. "It might be the last bastion of demon culture."

Zal nodded. "If I don't hear from you, I won't come back here."

"I'll find you," Lila said to Teazle.

"The elf is right," Teazle replied. "You should consider Demonia closed from now on. Much as we may feast and party, it is no time to let loose our wild brothers on foreign soils. All entry points shall be sealed as my first duty. I will do any finding that must be done."

"You're really enjoying this, aren't you?" She got up herself and finally conceded that the beery happiness must go. Within moments it was reconfigured to sugar and water in her system.

"Why not?" Teazle said. "It is interesting." With that he sprang up into the air on his own, white wings. Beside the looming bulk of the drake he was small, a lithe figure of beaming brilliance that flicked itself quickly up and over the observatory tower and then stooped with the speed of a falling dagger and was lost to sight somewhere in the night streets below.

"Right," Zal said, blinking as if with a mighty mental effort. "One final thing. It seems to me there's a slight chance of possession by unstoppable phantoms circling about. I didn't want to burst his bubble, but as from now on, all things being equal, we have no way of verifying anybody's identity. I seem to remember something from my days as a spy that in this kind of situation we can't trust one another at all. If you, for instance, got taken over by infernal evil able to copy your every move, how would I know this . . ." he touched the silver harness, ". . . was still okay?"

"I won't be in contact with it as long as you're in Alfheim," she said. "I did think of running it as a simultaneum, but one consciousness is really more than enough to deal with. If you need to contact me, you can instruct a part of it to return to Otopia. It will find a way. Of course, then I won't be able to believe a word of what it has to say, but . . . you know . . ." She smiled and put her hands on the front of his shoulders lightly.

"Thought that counts," he smiled back, and his long, pointed ears fanned out their ragged edges in the way that always made her laugh. He leaned down and kissed her. She stored the moment in full sensory maximum-width capture and smelled lime zest. He wobbled on his feet. "Typical for the bloody charm to work now," he said and straightened up. "I'll see you soon."

She watched him walk across the tiles to where the blotched, craggy form of Unloyal, who for some reason she couldn't stop thinking of as Unholy, waited in his own septic light.

Zal had the same easy stride and arrogant swagger he'd had when walking out onto a concert stage. If anything, he looked more convincing now and less like a set extra from a movie. His leap to the high saddle was an effortless bound of the elastic sort only elves could muster. He landed as though weightless and buckled the safety straps over his legs, ignoring the drake's sudden lurch as it got to its four feet and stretched itself out for a shake. He took hold of the saddle bow and then Unloyal turned to her.

Again she felt the sensation of a pause in conversation, but it said nothing. She did not attempt to conceal her conviction that if Unloyal did anything harmful or neglectful to Zal she would hunt it down. A faint amusement came to her that wasn't her own, and then with a swing of its head Unloyal crouched and burst up from the roof. A single flap of its wings sent all the tables and chairs and everything else loose scattering and tumbling across the tiles, servants falling down headlong to save themselves. Only Lila stood fast, her hand lifted to shield her eyes as she watched them take off into the humid murk of the demon night. She felt lonely as she followed their going until they were only a speck against the greater darkness out over the ocean. She tracked the burst of particles that showered their departure through the drake's own portal and then knew them to be as far away as the faint stars overhead.

Then Lila went back the way she had come, to the ruined gangster house and through the portal in the room with the broken window.

The Cedars apartment block was quiet as she came into it. She didn't know much about portal technology, but enough to know how to ruin one. Teazle had taught her. She found the locking crystals and smashed them, then watched the circular time-space distortion decay over a few seconds until its presence was only a piece of history visible to high-end forensics. There were better ways of disposing of the things, less dangerous ways with less risk of blowback, but she didn't care about the other end of the system, only that one more wormhole was shut.

She did the same to the Zoomenon garbage portal in the opposite room, noting that Roxa's blood was still sticky in places on the floor, and then walked back into the apartment proper. There was nobody about. The cushioned area with its two thrones was vacant, although incense still smouldered in a dish on the floor. She heard voices on the floor below. Something about their pitch, a feeling of anxiety, made her open a tentative spy channel into the Otopian networks.

Silence greeted her.

She closed the link and recrypted her operating frequencies, then crossed to the window, opened it, and stepped onto the sill. From there it was a quick leap up to the roof, which was high enough to give a reasonable view over the city and the bay.

From shoreline to hills every road was jammed with cars, every street full of people. Some rushed purposefully; others stood and gaped around them at the incomprehensibility of a world suddenly without its lifeblood of electronic chatter. She was glad she'd lived on the outside of it for so long, self-sufficient because she had the world of information in her head. There was a giddy unpleasant fretfulness to the movements she saw and heard everywhere, a panic not far away in spite of the fact that barkers were already out, moving through lines of stalled traffic to reassure everyone that this was a temporary and relatively unimportant setback. Fine, unless you wanted to buy, or sell, or travel, she thought, watching cars trying painfully to work their way across gridlocked junctions. Going by the activity, she figured the whole network was down, but she could feel local traces of electrochatter here and there, so individual machines were working and there was power.

Beneath her several gang-coloured cars were gathering, teams moving quickly, arming themselves. She knew a raid forming when she saw it and expected that a thousand other opportunists would be making ready to snatch and run while the systems failure inhibited the police response. Her anger at them was brief, useless. She could only stop them with death or violence close to it, and after them would be more and a billion other unstoppable things. She felt the Signal, its eternal hum of bee-busy knowledge, but whatever she did that hum never altered. It didn't approve or disapprove, it gave no sign that something was gained or lost, if she had won or if she was just another one of the features pushing the numbers of the dead up and up. There was no payback either way.

In the cracked concrete yard, the car doors were sliding shut. Bullets counted themselves into guns, voices swore, laughed, said obscene things with the emphasis of overconfident foolishness riding fear. So alive. So uncertain.

Everything waits to break through.

She ignited her jets and took to the air.

Temple Greer waited for her in the open courtyard—what he called his "ready room" at moments when he couldn't stand to be indoors. Malachi was with him outside the yurt's cream-coloured woollen dome. They were playing quoits. Greer was winning. Bentley sat to the side, a grey statue on the bench where the trees cast the most shade. Her hands were folded in her lap. She looked demure, quiet, an android from some period film of social manners. Her face was tilted towards the sky.

As Lila arrived, Bentley turned towards her and half lifted her hand in a wave. Lila waved back, coming in to land on the browned grass, worn almost to its roots by so many feet. Malachi was slow to notice her, because he was hidden behind a clump of shrubbery. As she moved around it, she saw another reason. His graceful figure had broadened so his shoulders split the seam of his coat. His arms protruded far below his cuffs, and they were furry with clawed hands that handled the rope rings of the quoits with a degree of clumsiness. His head was more square, more flat from the back, and when he turned she saw that his face had lengthened. Halfway between a worg and a tiger, he was a hunched aberration in his tailored camel coat—the only clothing he had left. But it was still Malachi. The orange eyes and a way of moving as if the air around him was silk would have given it away.

Greer tossed his final quoit at the post and missed. "Goddamn it."

She reached them. "They always said the old games were the best."

Malachi blinked at her. "They?" It was barely distinguishable as words. It was a growl that had a shape like a word, and that's all.

"Chess, shove ha'penny, billiards, dominoes, all that stuff that was good before computers," she said. "Quoits."

Malachi held out two rings to her, speared on the bulky, gnarled shape of his index finger. She unhooked one and stepped up to the line as Greer moved aside for her. She looked at the stumpy stick that was the mark and turned the ring in her hand for a moment before tossing it with a flick of her wrist. It spun down and snagged the mark, coming to rest so that it lay centred over it. She stood aside to let Malachi have his last throw. He sighed and made a cast, opening his hand with difficulty. The ring bumped and rolled on its edge, turning away into the rough.

"Quiet around here," she said as Greer went forward to collect the rings, shucking up his trousers to bend down and gather them all up. "When did all this happen?"

"Two hours ago," Malachi rumbled. "All systems at first. Then some things came back on. No communication though."

Greer came back, sorted out the rings marked with orange and the rings with green. "I guess it's the same everywhere."

"Demonia's out," she confirmed. "T stayed there. Zal's gone to Alfheim."

"Well, it's not like we were a big alliance," Greer said, handing the orange rings to Malachi again. "I mean, we're all cut off. So what? Most people here are over the moon about it."

"Don't I get any?" Lila asked.

"No," he said, edging her out of the way so that he could line up to throw again. "You're no fun at this."

She moved back and stood shoulder to shoulder with Malachi. "Nice coat," she said to him.

"You're playin' with fire, Black," he snarled, literally curling his lip to show the size of his big yellow teeth. They were oddly whiter and sharper than she remembered. His gums and tongue were black, with red edges. It was hard not to stare. He lined up his rings on his finger carefully.

"Do you know where Tatters is?" She tried to make the question sound casual.

He jerked his head in the direction of the yurt's open door flap. "On the rack."

"We didn't expect you to cut and run so fast," Greer said. "But thanks for tidying up that police job. I crossed off one entire line of my to-do list."

"Sir," Lila said. "How comprehensive is this isolation?"

He paused in his lengthy stance process and stood back to eye her. "What do you want to know?"

"Are any internal networks functional?"

"Nothing. Individuals and within individuals, yes. Everything else is as quiet as the . . . what's your point?"

"I think this is a by-product and not an attack. It's like a necessary prequel."

"It doesn't make sense," Greer said, recreating his position and leaning forward, ring balanced in his fingertips. "I had a guy up here to explain it and he couldn't."

"It's aether disruption," Lila said just as he made his move. The ring tumbled forward, hit wide of the post, and flopped in the dust. "And it does. But not to a pure-matter physicist. My point is that it doesn't look like we can evacuate the city without networks. But I think that at least we should evacuate this building and the surrounding area."

"The entire army and every officer able to walk is presently super-vising contraflows downtown," Greer said, easing a shoulder as he moved to let Malachi take his place. "Those that are able are dis-tributing themselves to keep order. Why do you want this building turned upside down as well?"

"I think this is all about Sarasilien. Where he is, that's where trouble is coming," she said.

"He is our only adept advisor, with the exception of Malachi here," Greer said watching Malachi flick a ring and just edge the post. "And he's the only one with significant powers. The only one, Black. One. In a world of trouble."

"He *is* your trouble," Lila said.

"You've got proof of course." Greer moved around Malachi and smoothed one side of his moustache with a finger before squinting at the post and adjusting the position of his toe to the scraped line in the dirt.

"There would be no silence without him, no crisis."

"No cyborgs," Malachi growled, making the word sound like a beast's curse.

"You see, Black," Greer fiddled with the shoulders of his jacket and took a deep breath, "Sarasilien is a royal pain in my ass but I have to be grateful, and the rest of us, because we've got you, and you are something that stands on the line between the humans and the rest of the aetherials and their goddamned business. Without you we'd go back to being the wildebeests on the savannah with a lion explosion in process. So while you may be right, I still have to protect his skinny elf butt."

"Everything you see is just the tip of a much nastier iceberg," Lila said. "And I believe it's going to try to shove itself right up that skinny elf butt. So the further away everyone else gets, the better."

Greer tossed his quoit. It thumped solidly over the post, the first one. "How far away?"

"I have no idea. For my money, about one country."

"I can probably manage a couple of miles. What else?" He walked behind Lila as Malachi moved in front of her to take aim. A smell of hot animal fur and baking minerals pushed out towards her from the folds of the camel coat. She watched him flex his pawlike hands, trying to straighten the knuckles, failing.

"Xavi's got to go," Lila said. "She's a wild card."

"Yeah well, that's not a problem. She's gone already. That was what I was going to give you as your next assignment, always assuming you survive this assignment."

"She's gone?"

"Completely gone. Mal came to sign her out, the comms went down, and she skipped town at the same moment. My guess is she cracked the aether part of the cell a while ago and was waiting for an opportunity."

Malachi made his turn and watched his quoit thud into the scrappy weeds next to the post. He grunted in disgust. "I picked up traces of her spells. She went to Alfheim."

"You sure?" Lila was taken aback and puzzled.

The huge cat-beast gave her a baleful orange stare and stepped wearily off the plate. "I'm sure."

"Who made that cell?" Lila asked. She dreaded the answer.

"Who do you think?"

"Then he knows," she said. "Crap." She'd been relying on the information as an ace up her sleeve; now she was back to nothing.

"Maybe not," Malachi said as they both stood back and watched Greer rerolling his sleeves. Faces came and went in the windows of the surrounding building, but nobody tried to come out and disturb them. "If she was correct about him, then he had no idea she was alive. He will be in shock. Shocked people are not at the top of their form."

"D'you think she's in touch with them—with the Betrayed?" Lila asked.

Greer picked up his remaining rings and skimmed one low, too low. It hit Malachi's previous throw and fell over, making a little Venn diagram of near misses. "From what she's told us, I doubt it, but then, she might be a good liar. Mal here thinks your diary charm made her unwittingly honest, so I'm gonna make a bet and go with him. Say she hasn't, but she still is more like them than not. She could be in touch. Who knows if they're in cahoots or not?"

"I have a taped interview." The voice was Bentley's, carrying clearly from her spot on the bench where she was beyond human hearing distance but obviously not beyond cyborg pickup. "Would you like to see it?"

"Yeah," Lila said, watching Malachi miss again. He groaned and rolled his heavy head, easing the massive neck muscles under their thick ruff of coal-black hair. She excused herself from the game with a slight bow and backed away from her position, going to join Bentley in the shade.

The grey woman greeted her with a smile and as Lila sat down reached out and took hold of her hand. With the contact established, passing across the files was as simple as usual. Lila unpacked the compressions and closed her eyes, keeping hold of Bentley's hand even though there was no need anymore as she watched the recording.

Bentley and Xaviendra were sitting in Xavi's holding cell. It was a single room with an adjoining bathroom, and in the weeks that she had been there Xavi had furnished and decorated it extensively—this at Lila's expense—creating a pretty, well-lit sitting room complete with a work area in which a huge array of painting materials lay ordered with two canvases up on easels, although they were turned from the camera. It was hard to say who looked more unreal in the situation, Bentley with her uniformly grey plastic exterior or Xavi's purple-and blue-toned elf skin with its mane of black hair hanging almost to her ankles and her blue, saurian tail coiled neatly around her hoofed feet. They sat with an ease that spoke of their familiarity with the situation. Lila knew there were dozens of recordings of Xavi. She had taken many of them herself, but by far the most had been patiently undertaken by Bentley.

This one was partway through. Bentley was speaking.

". . . did you ever know about any successes in the experiments?"

"Yes," Xavi said in her immaculate, accented Otopian. "There were three."

"But you weren't on the site anymore at that time."

"No, I had escaped, but I stayed close by—I didn't know where to go. I didn't want to go anywhere." She sighed. "I heard them, you might say. I felt them. They had a presence in that . . . place . . . where I was."

"Was this place physical?"

"No. It was shadows. The place of the undead. I don't know its name. I don't know if it has a name. Nobody speaks there. There are things without names, without bodies. I didn't understand how I could be there. I was very frightened. When they came, I knew them because they felt like me and not like the other things there. We could touch each other and I knew their thoughts."

"Who were they?"

Xaviendra's hooves flexed and her tail wound itself more tightly about her ankles. "It doesn't matter. Who they were didn't exist any more. Nor me. We chose new names there, so that we wouldn't get lost."

There was an expectant pause and then Xavi said, "I cannot use them here. It is not right for you to know them. Magical naming. I am sure you know of this."

Bentley nodded. They had never tried to coerce anything out of Xaviendra. She had been a broken creature and readily forthcoming with anything they asked, so it hadn't been necessary to push. Having her withhold something was new.

"You must understand I wouldn't ask for them unless we had a strong belief that we would need them," Bentley said.

"I would not give them to you unless I was certain it was necessary," Xaviendra countered. "You do not know the three."

"And do you?"

"We suffered the same fates. In that I know them. When it became clear that they were much more able than was I, and that they were bound in a way that I was not, then we had to separate. They went to their duty and I stayed in case any others came that way. But as time passed, I knew that I was losing myself there. If I stayed, I would decay and be as dead as I was supposed to be, as undone as the elements. In that place there is no time, nothing to see, it is dark, an eternity of darkness, a space without limit. The three suffered no loss there. But I had to return to one of the heavier planes. I tried to go to Alfheim, but I . . . was barred." She became straighter, taller, narrower in her chair with the effort of holding back her feelings. "My father's magic kept me out. I was dead to them all."

Bentley was the soul of compassion, her expression gentle as the turn of the subject. "Did you encounter the thing of which they were afraid?"

"The cause of the atrocity? No. After all I had been told, I expected to face a monster of perfect horrors, a hell of vileness beyond my imaginings. That is why I was lost for so long there. I thought it was a mistake. There was nothing there except the spirits, and they were neither kind nor useful. They were malignant, but nothing at the same time.

They were fond of my misery but they were . . . of no consequence. There was *nothing* there." She sounded puzzled now and spread out her hands on her knees. Bright paint covered her fingers, and she absently scratched some of it off.

"Where did the three go?"

"To search," she said.

"Did you meet them again?"

"No." She shook her head, and her curling, thick black hair moved like a waterfall, rippling its full length. "Never. They had to search until it was found. They went far beyond any place I came to. Mages tried to guide them from without, they said. I did look of course. I was lonely. But I hated it there. And I never found any trace of them. Nothing."

"You didn't call their names?"

Xavi shook her head. "When I understood that they might never find their quarry, I knew I couldn't wait. I decided I would be revenged for us all. That decision saved my sanity. And I pursued it. The rest you know."

Bentley nodded. "Do you think they may have come to the same decision?"

"I suppose you think that because the mages died," Xaviendra said, smoothing paint flakes off her skirt. "No. They were bound to the duty."

"Interesting that the attacks and the sickness stopped when the three were trapped Under," Bentley said.

Xaviendra frowned slightly. "I don't have an explanation for you. Perhaps the Sleeper was bound to the mages, and their attacks on it killed them instead. Such things are not uncommon among magekind and their creatures."

Bentley smiled. "What do you mean, creatures?"

"They can make mirrors of themselves, like clones, or creatures of other dimensional natures, which are linked by sharing spirit. A mage creature has most of the powers of the master mage. A mage always has control of their creations; they have the same will. The Sleeper consumed all."

"An anti-magic?"

"Something like that. A mage vampire perhaps, but without mind. Nothing they did could touch it. I believed their actions to be evil and unforgivable, but at the same time I witnessed their fear. It was overwhelming. They were provoked by terror of annihilation and guilt, because if they had not opened their way to this place, they would not have attracted the creature's attention. I did not see it myself. As I said. I saw them and what they did."

The recording ended. Lila opened her eyes and looked at Bentley. Quite aside from the obvious information was an implication it was impossible to ignore. Cyborgs weren't the only ones with clones. "She's been out the whole bloody time."

The android moved as if it sighed. "It is possible."

Lila ground her teeth. Just as it seemed there could be no more complication, one presented itself, fait accompli, right beneath her nose. "Where's Sarasilien?"

"I believe he is still here."

"Doing what, I wonder?"

Bentley made an equivocal face and shrugged.

"What bothers me the most about all of this is that I can't reconcile him with this monster that history paints him as," Lila said. "I don't know what to believe about him anymore and I don't trust him to tell the truth because he kept too much back."

Bentley nodded. "When I first decided to take this form on, I thought it would liberate me from the weaker parts of my humanity. It was a sign of the war, of my loss of so much of myself, I thought. I was a walking testament to the horror of a kind of murder. I thought I'd search the Signal and find the truth there—of who I was and would have been, of what was stolen and what could have been changed without harm. But the Signal is everything, all information that could be. Yeah, the world and everything that ever happened is in it, but among all the possibilities it's so hard to find. The past is there, and the present, and the future, and all the never-was too. I thought it would have all the answers. I'd mine them out. I'd mine myself out. I'd be . . ."

"Saved," Lila said, feeling the word as Bentley said it too.

"Yeah. Knowledge would have the answers. How could it be wrong?" Bentley laughed gently. "And you know what? I bet you do know . . ."

"Tell me," Lila said.

"The more I saw and looked at it from every angle, the more I saw that it was meaningless. I was trying to find the end of a story and I was looking at numbers. I was looking for the happy ending, but there's no ending except the terminal numbers and then after them an emptiness. There's no meaning, unless I make one by the path I follow through the numbers, my pattern. That's the sum total of everything. It is truth, but it has no meaning at all. How can that be? I wondered at it and I tried to make that into a meaning as well." She laughed harder this time and slapped her knee. "I think you are heading the same way."

Lila squeezed Bentley's hand for a moment and felt an answering squeeze before they let go. For a second or two they watched Malachi and Greer shuffling around each other and the faces in the windows, anxious, pressing, wondering.

"But," Lila said, seeing a quoit fly erratically from Malachi's claw and hit the mark nonetheless, "human beings do not exist in the context of the sum total of all possibilities. They are finite and extremely particular. The world of relevance to them is small, much smaller than they like to imagine. They have no aetheric skill. They have short lives. They are primates, social, with extremely limited perception of their environment, which is nonetheless more than good enough for them to live rich, full lives, if only they are able to live in tune with their own nature. But they don't want to recognise their nature, because it is so absolute, so definite, and so inescapable. So they pretend it is something else, that they can be and do everything, anything, and that they are fit to do it. They believe that science and technology has transformed them into masters of the universe, or that surely it will in time, and think they have changed somehow from their foolish, ignorant ancestors who had nothing but sticks and stones. They think I'm different. But I'm just a woman, human, with a lot of sticks and stones to her name. Even if the sticks and stones of my body mean I will not die easily, nothing will prevent it in the end. And nothing, no matter how marvellous, and I have been and seen some marvellous things, truly, nothing will change me from my self. I am human, and that is all. There can be no more for me. I know that you're right. In the lens of everything there is no meaning I could make that is of any use or significance except that I could maybe help someone else to live a more satisfying life, but that's a vain aspiration. The best I can do is live my own life as I feel it is best, as if it mattered more than anything because it's all there is, even though none of it is of the slightest importance."

Lila grimaced. "Suppose the three Betrayed do come, and can't be stopped, suppose they end the world as it is now, take their vengeance, destroy Sarasilien, break the order in which humans live and die? You know, I try to care, but I can only care for myself, and what matters to me. It really doesn't matter what happens at all. But I can only carry on living if I feel that it does. Action is purposeless, meaningless, but it is demanded of me, because I was made this way to act, not to sit around talking and watching dead people walk and talk while others die, innocent or damned, well or badly, deserving or not."

"Another go?" Greer looked over and held his rings out towards Lila. "You could play each other. Might be a bit of a long match—"

"I'll sit this one out," Lila called. Bentley gave him a friendly nod.

He nodded back, clearly wishing he knew what they were talking about but not insisting.

"There is much satisfaction in action," Bentley said quietly, keeping her voice low.

"It's the consolation of the weak," Lila said. "Look at Xavi. Look at Sarasilien."

"You're very angry with him."

"Yes I am. I prefer to believe that power is given to the strong and deserving. And he spits in the face of that belief. He treads it and smashes it flat and throws it at me. I want him to be worth all that he has spent."

"Because?"

"Because then there is justice and a happy ending to be found. There's fairness. And I don't have to pity him and destroy him."

"Destroy?" The whisper was so quiet nobody but Lila could have heard it.

"Surely," Lila said, gripping the bench with her hands, her feet tucked under it together, her face set like a little girl who has to endure being the outcast in the playground day after day. "But I will look very hard for any reason not to. Very hard. But it will have to be such a good reason I doubt it exists."

"Revenge?" ventured the android curiously.

"Necessity," Lila said.

"I don't understand. You're not the kind of person who does that."

"Yes I am," Lila said. "I am strong and I will not let evil run wild in weak creatures to spoil the world when I see it happening and have the ability to stop it."

"Evil?"

But Lila didn't answer Bentley this time. Her jaw was set. She watched Greer hustling through his game and Malachi grumpily keeping pace. They were waiting for her, not the other way around. Slowly she relaxed her hands and let go of the wooden slats. She sat back and rested, turning her face towards the sun and finding a patch of warm light. It shone through her eyelids red, glowing, blood red. When she was a little girl, she had found its colour and brightness so comforting, the heat and the light soothing and calming. It still had that power. In the garden the quoits thumped and the men's voices mumbled.

Lila leaned back and let the sun shine on her.

CHAPTER SIXTEEN

Zal watched the filthy black waters of Bathshebat lagoon pass under him and resisted the urge to turn and look over his shoulder, but he saw it anyway in his mind—the receding shape of Lila Black, growing smaller. The only thing he didn't see was the expression on her face. In his imagination he couldn't get the grim resoluteness to change, or the misgiving to soften into a smile.

The black water sparkled where it caught the nightlights of the Opera House—a building that still employed real flaming torches, enhanced to brilliant whiteness by magnesium and other elemental powders. The vast glass dome above the auditorium was glowing with colours and the rippling lights of a concert in performance, and he could just hear the higher notes and feel the driving thump of the bass as they angled overhead on their turn out towards the ocean. He wished he were there instead, lost in the music.

As it was the drake was listening in to him though it didn't make any observation. Its wings beat at the heavy, dead air, stirring the miasma of smoke and cooking oil and spice up with the stink of the water. It was in some reverie in which its emotions ran a similar line to his own. For reasons best known to itself, Unloyal had its own regrets about parting with Demonia. Years ago Zal would have solaced himself with a bottle of Jack or a hit of elemental fire, but now he hadn't even packed alcohol in his bag. He felt the strange tidal pull of the succubus charm in his blood. It beat at the walls of his heart and threatened to break it in bits, drumming love songs unrequited. The drake heard him, and its amusement showed in its skin, as demonic as any native creature; flaring blue and gold.

He touched the clone harness he wore with his fingertips, wondering how it worked and thinking he really should have asked that earlier. But at the time he had wanted to convince Lila that he was strong and fit, sure of himself, the old Zal, and he didn't want to confess that her talk of clone material made him uneasy and sad for reasons that he didn't fully understand and wasn't sure that he wanted to. He thought maybe it was that he was surpassed now, and worse, that he didn't mind.

As the drake pounded through the night, forcing great curtains of it aside, he saw the portal point opening far ahead of them. Drakes like this made their own transit gates from world to world, limited only by their foreknowledge. He knew nothing about them. He went on trust, on a whim, on the edge of a risk he couldn't have calculated even if he did understand it. He grabbed onto this moment with everything he was and felt the spark of an older and much more glorious feeling come to life in his chest.

To his surprise, the drake reacted to this and moved with fresh purpose towards the rapidly expanding veil. At the edges of the gap Zal felt the aetheric turbulence of a critical wave and pulled his *andalune* body as close to his core as he was able. Still the riptides of the edge dragged some of it away into their odd gravity, across other perpendicular planes, and he was flayed as they passed through. Another reason not to take too many of this kind of ride, he thought, wondering how many crossings it would take to pare him away to nothing and what would happen then.

The drake, by contrast, suffered no degradation, possibly an improvement if its shift of mood was anything to go by.

They burst into the cooler, fresher morning skies of his home world, and he looked around him for familiar landmarks eagerly and found none. The only feeling of recognition within him was the drake's presence. It knew the place very well.

A mountain range was spread beneath them from side to side, and to his left one of the lesser peaks bore the distinctive marks of geomantic carving. Black pits filled it like a hundred sightless eyes, and here and there regular lines showed where walkways cut across the jagged, impassable cliffs from point to point. Tattered banners of purple and red hung down from several openings, their symbols of gold thread too small to see at this distance. A bitter cold wind tore across the peaks, making Zal hunch close in to the saddle although this did nothing to protect him.

"Where is this?" he spoke aloud though the words were ripped away and the drake couldn't have heard him with its ears.

It told him the name of a place so old that he thought it was a legend. It occurred to him that the creature could easily have moved them in time, but the drake assured him this was a perfectly concurrent reality. He supposed it didn't matter. One place was as good as any other to start. He wished it weren't so cold though. Fire and shadow might be his elements now, but he was elf enough to freeze his ass off, that was clear. He stuffed his hands into his armpits and hunched even lower.

The drake banked them down, negotiating horrible shear off the cliffs with ease and took them towards the settlement, aiming for the largest of the black openings in the rock. Above them the sky was a fierce blue, the sun a dazzling glare. It felt so empty, and peculiar, a wild place—uninhabited, Zal thought, and only then realised it was because he felt no connection or answering *andalune*, as if everyone and everything had died.

He pressed his lips together, biting them and narrowing his nostrils, eyes closed as they slowed and came to alight on the ledge. A sudden darkness enveloped him, and the wind's force eased although now it sounded like a freight train all around him, booming and thundering enough to make his ears try to fold themselves closed. In the relative shelter of the hall he let his aether body reach out. He was strong and it reached far, and it found nothing to connect to.

Gasping and holding onto the freezing saddle, his eyes open to see the world reduced to a blue archway of shocking brilliance, Zal knew two things that made no sense to him. People were there and, in the most important way, they were not there. They were alive, but to him and to the world around them they were dead. He was a jack without a port to connect to, and there was no sound.

The drake heard him perfectly and agreed. It affirmed what he already knew. Alfheim was silent. In communications terminology, it was dark. Lila had said it, but he hadn't believed she meant this. He thought she meant the elves had sealed themselves away behind a diplomatic wall, not a literal thing. What he knew of as life, as people, as Alfheim, was dead air.

With numb hands he fumbled the saddle straps and released himself, taking more time and care climbing down from the seat than an old man descending steep stairs. When his boots touched the grooved stone, his eyes had at last adjusted to the light and he saw they were in a hall that was used to flying visitors and their mounts, though it wasn't expecting them now. Old snow had formed ice on the trash and debris of what had been awnings and furniture. Doors into the cliff were closed fast or hanging on their hinges. Nobody had been here in a long time.

Delatra, he remembered its name as he saw its sigil on one of the banners—a silver leaf backed by a black sun. His mother had told him about it because she was apprenticed there in her youth. It had been a seat of the highest learning, where everything most precious to the elves was taken and lovingly stored, where magic was learned, developed, and coveted. The legendary status came from the fact that in the more recent years of governance Delatra had been reduced, saved from extinction at the hands of the shadow uprising only with the sacrifice of many lives. Delatra had ended the worst of the conflict, because the shadowkin had turned aside from destruction and surrendered there, on the verge of victory. The story had never made sense to him. The offered reason for the change of heart was their awe at Delatra's grandeur and riches, its unparalleled value. Zal didn't buy it then, and he didn't buy it now. He was sure that there'd been a better reason, and no doubt it was one that was secret to save important heads from the block. With something like remorse, he felt his long-neglected Jayon Daga agent's wits flood back into his system full force.

The drake chuckled in his head, a soundless mirth that was knowing and watchful at the same time.

Zal shivered and slung his pack onto his shoulders. He instructed the drake to get out and look for other settlements or anything in the area. He would meet it here again by nightfall. As he stood staring with misgiving at the broken doorway ahead of him, he felt the creature's psychic presence increase and for the first time felt it as a predatory gaze between his shoulders, but he didn't turn around to see what it was doing. With a scrape of claw on stone he heard it move and then an airshock hit him and knocked him forward as it took off. His misery would have been deep then, but at that moment he felt the harness heating up and it was better, not by much, but better.

By the time he reached the door, he was his old self again, that watchful, careful, sneaky, angry, and frustrated being he thought he'd left behind for good. It was almost funny. And then the razor edge of his own spine's sense of self-preservation returned, waiting for blades, listening for lies and the breath of his doom. It spread its paranoid fingers out around him and in the astral silence found foreboding. It was good the wind howled like a banshee. It meant he didn't have to do it for himself.

The cliffs of Delatra's hostile exterior did nothing to prepare him for what he found inside. A city had been carved from the stone with vaults open in the high mountain above enough to light parks and gardens, farms and lakes. Zal stood, mite-tiny, on the interior balcony that looked across this magnificence and imagined how it must have been when it was whole. He couldn't, because it was smashed to bits.

Rubble, covered in snow powder, buried in ice, was all that was left, with a few walls here and there to suggest what might have been. The shadowkin had not left without starting their work, then. There looked to be nothing down there of any interest. The vast hills and banks of ruined shapes were pristine. It was only the conviction of his aetheric body that made him stay a second longer. It said there were living elves in these remains. Under normal conditions he would have been able to place them within a few metres of their location because under normal conditions they were all subliminally aware of each other, unless they were trained and in hiding. Here he could feel their presence, but there was no response and no intelligence of any kind in it, no sense of any awareness of the aether at all. They felt exactly like humans. Thus he set out to hunt them, his tread silent, dull, and already hopeless.

It had been some tale of his mother's that Delatra was a great city of the most talented aether-rich individuals, served and administered by the most dutiful and devoted servants, all of them united under the cause of progress and scholarship. She had said it with a scoff in her voice and, after drink, that scoff turned to poison. He'd never understood why. To Zal it had sounded boring. All his experience of the diurnal elves and their highly mannered, rigid society had rubbed him the wrong way. The shining idea of Delatra was one of the first great ideas he forgot, and he forgot it twice—once on the island of the abandoned children, shamed for their lack of magic, and once when he escaped that place and came into his father's instruction in the night forests of Lower Hajaf.

In between those forgettings he did remember it, when he was forced back on the last stock of stories he knew in order to survive the sea voyage to Hajaf with his sanity intact, but even then it had been hard work to speculate anything interesting about it. His mother's tales centred on her dormitory of female students and later on her dislike and then hatred of the ruling mage priests. Since those priests had been the descendants of Sarasilien's brood, he supposed there was probably a lot to dislike about them. They had supported apartheid and exiled his friends, so as far as he was concerned they were dismissible, worthy only of his utter contempt although he rarely mustered the energy on their behalf. Now he wondered if he was going to have to get this hate out of his soul's footlocker of neglected things, though what magery was left clearly didn't have the strength to set a single stone back in place.

Hate would have been more welcome than the leaden feeling he did have. He found a way through the wall's considerable architecture and discovered it was the administration centre, surely, with its endless meeting places, small burrowlike storage places, and modest little rooms. Ruined furniture and machineries of various kinds blocked his way, but it was all old. Here and there cupboards and chests showed signs of looting, but for the most part it was a deserted place and the only thing filling the passages was the boom and yowl of the wind. Even when you were used to it, he thought, it could drive you mad. Then he remembered something about a pipe organ, that the wind played. Great music. That surely was broken too.

The day passed slowly for him. Only the harness kept him warm enough to move as he slowly wound his way towards the faint sparks of energy moving about in the lowest tiers of the cliff. He knew, even with the urgency that drove him—Lila's words and the uknown fate of Alfheim—he was delaying, but he could only keep the pace resolute rather than eager. All the time the age of the ruin ate at his conviction. It was threadbare, iced, a coffin of a kind that was long past holding anything but bones. That meant it must have been destroyed just after his mother left it, although even that time seemed too short to account for the degradation. And then his foot caught on something and he fell forward, jerked out of this reverie and into the necessary moment of cold stone under his hands, and he looked back and there was nothing at his foot, nothing at all.

At this point he began to suspect an illusion. When he found the elves living there at last, his puzzlement deepened, because he was certain that any magic at work wasn't theirs.

He hid himself among the rubble of a fallen archway and watched them. They were living at ground level using the rooms in the cliff wall as caves. They looked like elves, wore elvish clothing, and used bows and small knife weapons. They didn't talk, but communicated by gestures alone, and few of those. They were, in every way, as un-elflike as could be, but they were thin and agile and fast. They moved in sudden darts and their eyes, brilliant, were empty and wary. They reminded him of crows, or monkeys. Their caves were littered with scavenged junk. They cooked something over a fire that was visibly constructed out of broken scroll woodwork and the ripped halves of large-size books.

He backed away very carefully, as he would from a pack of predatory wild animals, and dulled his brain yet further so that he wouldn't have to think about what else he saw—their public rutting, their vicious squabbling or the howling wind that had occupied their empty eyes. They did not notice his shadow body although one of them looked around as he touched her foot with it and promptly brought her hand down to scratch her ankle. In a second she was more interested by the activities of a fighting pair of men on the far side of the tiny fire.

Another troupe of them were detectable, at the far side of the ruin. He saw tribal kinds of markings scratched on stones, feces left at prominent points, tracks and old bloodstains showing the site of ambushes. This time he used his skill to avoid them and crept back upwards. The only other feature of Delatra he knew of was the library—a place containing a copy of all documents or artefacts of interest. He knew, from his mother's stories of girlish foolery, that it was located inside the peak of the mountain in something like a bunker, inaccessible except through a narrow corridor. They had used to joke about it being a fire hazard and the books in the fire had made him think of it again.

After an hour of searching had failed to find it, he decided to give up and head back to his rendezvous with Unloyal. At this point an arrow thudded into his back and knocked him off his feet. It had hit squarely between his shoulder blades, but the harness had stopped it, even though he was pretty sure there was no harness at that point. Even so the force was a blow that hurt and winded him. He spun as he fell, landing on his side and springing up again with a move he didn't know that he still had. It left him facing his attacker, who said as she put up her bow and gave him a flat glare, "You've lost your reflexes."

"Xavi." He stayed where he was, feeling the arrow slump down from where its point was stuck in the harness.

"And there I almost thought I knew what she saw in you," Xaviendra said, plucking the bowstring awkwardly. She held the weapon up into the weak light coming from a high window, and they both saw it was old and worn, the string frayed. "A good thing this isn't a real bow. But then, nothing much is real here."

Seeing that she didn't seem bent on more violence, he straightened up and relaxed his defensive stance. "What are you doing here?"

"My job," she said, primly. She tossed the bow aside to clatter on the stone floor and composed her hands in a parody of demureness, her head with its cascade of black hair on one side. "Librarian."

Zal decided he wasn't too interested in following her guidelines. "I thought you were in Otopia."

"Yes," she said. "I am, also there."

He took this at face value. "What happened here?"

"The city was—"

"I mean the people. I don't really buy the city."

"Oh." She seemed disappointed. "They are all that's left. My father's grand project. Excellent work."

"This is recent," Zal said, frowning. It was hard to discount the cold, but then Xavi waved her hand and although there was no change in temperature he was able to make out tables, chairs, shelving that was solid and held various items against the walls. There was no snow and no ice.

"I am protecting what's left," she said. "It took them a while to get used to it. They woke up one morning to discover the whole city devastated. Ran around screaming, fighting, fucking each other like crazy, but now they've accepted it. It keeps them out of most of it, especially the centre city. They're not very determined. They accept what they see. Within a day or two they retreated to the places that seemed most welcoming. It was really no trouble."

He digested this as he kept watching her closely. She seemed pleased with herself. "But the people," he said. "What happened to them?"

"As I said, my father's noble goals happened to them. Wrath has been here. I guess he must have come here first, looking for him of course. That would be several weeks, maybe a month ago."

Zal laughed at her, hollow and rasping. "They can't have come to this in a week or two."

"Of course they can," Xavi said. "Those you see here are the ones who survived. The bodies of the dead are in the crypts." She gave an odd kind of shiver, and for the first time he noticed her hands were stained with darkness and her clothing was ripped and bloody in places near the hem. "No mages survived. These are the servants you see."

"The ones without magical affinity," he said, feeling as if he were speaking the words of a curse.

Xavi nodded. "Just so. And now they have lost their minds and their memories, or perhaps it is only the memories, I am not sure. They have lost something very important, that's clear. Anyway, salvaging them is a project I can't afford. All my efforts are to preserve what is left. I'm sure you noticed that some of the materials from the library have already been destroyed. I don't even know how much we have lost. Whole areas are desecrated. It would be years of work simply to correct the catalogue."

Standing in the freezing room, aware of what was happening outside, watching her prattle on about books made something in Zal want to slap her very hard, but he was used to restraining these impulses in his Jayon guise and instead he felt the muscles around his face tighten up as he kept to the point and released any notions he had had of her being of some use. "Have you seen anywhere else?"

"I came directly here." She was actually surprised at this. Her tail twitched as she sensed his displeasure and she became impatient. "You must understand the importance of this place and what it represents now."

Zal, who had considered reaching out to her, recoiled his *andalune* body very carefully within his own skin. A wave of desire for her swept over him, making him hot but he ignored it. "Now?"

She frowned and he was reminded of her singular, fixated expression aboard the Temeraire, when she had been flanked by angels and determined to get her prize at any cost. For all their shared spirit, she seemed not to have noticed his lust or his curse and that in itself was interesting but she was already talking.

"Now that Wrath is in Alfheim. Nothing can stand against him. Or the others. If all of Alfheim, or even most of it, falls prey to this . . . plague of degeneration . . . then the only thing that remains of our whole culture and all its ages are the records of this library and others scattered across the world. Would you see them burned in order to toast rats?"

Zal considered it. "I'd rather see it wiping shit and rotting than re-creating this situation, yes I would."

Her eyes narrowed and she spat at him. "What an ignorant slut of a creature you are! How you can be her son I'll never know! You have no idea of the beauty and the wonder contained in these things."

"Nothing of any importance, I'm sure of that. Sure as I am you're your father's daughter," he said, as disgusted with her as she was with him.

She scowled with displeasure and glanced at the bow and then at him. Her voice would have stopped his heart if she'd only had enough demon blood to transform its tone of vicious hatred into a literal lance of spite. "How dare you mention my father. I wish I'd killed you. You're not fit to be here."

Zal bent down and picked up the bow. He was aware now of how powerful she was, and it was orders of magnitude beyond what he had expected. It confused him, and the swirling vaporous desire in his body filled his judgement up with silty, suffocating confusion. It took all of his focus just to unstring the bow, adjust the tension with a few twists, and restring it correctly before handing it to her. He let a little of his suffering flow into his own voice, so she'd understand he meant his next words as a threat. "Don't throw away the one useful thing you've got. There're no angels at your back now. It's only a matter of time before they find you."

She seethed at him. "*You* didn't find me."

"Lucky me." He turned on his heels and began walking away. His head pounded with agonising pressure that promised it would ease if he only went in the other direction, back to her side.

"Where are you going?" she snapped.

"To look for the living," he said without pausing or turning. The meeting with her and the demon's curse had wearied him so much he knew he didn't have long left before he'd be fawning over her feet. Only the burning heat of the harness kept him going; an embrace that was strong enough to hold him up when he felt that he was defeated. The succubus charm in his blood shrilled at him that he must stay, take care of her, love her, and he remembered Lila's writing in that book—"friends and lovers," she had written, in her misguided, rushed, too-kind way. He grit his teeth and kept walking one step after another, and finally he felt he was clear of Xavi or at least had no idea where she was. Ideas, concerns about her role here, her relation to her father, the meaning of her presence tried to rush him, but he battered those aside too. Then it was only a matter of half an hour to retrace his way to the landing platform.

Shrieks, almost but not quite torn away on the wind, found his ears as he turned through the shattered panels of the last door and saw the blank arch of the indigo sky before him, framed in black rock. Unloyal, he wasn't surprised to see, was not there.

His hands and feet were painful as he sat down in the lee of a rock to wait for true night and final confirmation of his abandonment. He folded his legs and wrapped his arms around them and put his forehead onto his knees, pack on his feet, and the thin cloak he had with him over all. The wind boomed and screamed around the cliff, but his aetheric body told him there was nobody there.

He began to murmur a tune to himself and then, to his surprise, he found he heard the original track and realised it was the harness. It hadn't occurred to him that it would respond to sound, but then he thought of course it would. If it was Lila's clone, then the way to communicate with it was to talk. Strange ideas began to come to him about what he might be able to do with it, and the pressure in his blood abated as he sang.

By the time Unloyal landed on the pitch-black platform, its own hide scoured and chilled beyond comfort, it was surprised to see its former partner dancing across the empty space. It was wearing a strange, flexible suit of plate armour that was radiating heat and trailed cloaks and streamers of shadow around it that acted as siphons on the darkness itself, drawing it in and making it denser. Unloyal knew an ifrit when he saw one, even if it was using shade and not flame. The whirling dance it did was also accompanied by wild music which Unloyal's own *andalune* body could pick up even when his sharp ears could not. He recognised some of the rhythms from the demon city. Then the elf noticed him and came waltzing up, a bizarre knight of darkness with a tattered flag of dirty blond hair.

"Thought you'd forgotten," it said, recriminating.

Unloyal felt peeved, but he put out his foot. The elf vaulted to the saddle without bothering to take it. Then Unloyal felt they were squared again and wondered for a second or two at the ease with which he had accepted an *andalune* link with such a lesser creature. "Turn up the volume," he ordered, taking them both to the edge of the wall. The wind slammed and sheared here, badly enough to rip off a wing if he were not careful or able to use more than aerodynamic means of support. The strange aetheric disruption of the atmosphere made life difficult, but not impossible.

Then Unloyal felt something even more unexpected. The elf was winding a metal wire firmly around one of his neck spines. "There," he said. "Now you can listen yourself. Just ask it to play."

There was a moment, poised on the edge of oblivion, where the drake was honestly lost for words, but then it found two. "Thank you."

Its muscles bunched and its aether body swirled beneath it, gathering power, then they bolted forward and upwards. Within seconds they were whisked far from Delatra, over the lower peaks of the mountain and down towards the continent below, Unloyal making for places he had scouted out himself, wondering how he was to speak to a wire, and Zal with his streaming eyes watching the familiar constellations glitter overhead.

CHAPTER SEVENTEEN

Lila considered Bentley's tape, Xavi's face, Greer's throwing arm, and what it had felt like to stand in the bottom of the seeping labyrinth with Ilya, hearing his boy's voice promise her to leave his heaven so that he, the failed Lord of Death, could track Sarasilien's hounds of hell. They didn't sit easily together.

Dusk was coming. In the offices the lights were on, showing people the way out. The evacuation processed silently. In the garden a few blackbirds chattered and some cicadas set up their louder hum. Malachi went into his yurt and lit his lamps. Through the open flap-way Lila could see Tatters, hanging on the coat rack just as he had said.

She was the spitting image of the green tailored clothing Teazle had given her, and Lila briefly put her hand to her sleeve, realizing she'd been tricked. Tatterdemalion was already on her back. "You two-faced sonofabitch," she said quietly. Bentley glanced at her but saw the remark was an interior moment briefly breaking the surface and ignored it. Lila wondered if cursing angels was some kind of sin. She got up.

"You're going?" Bentley asked, signalling Greer with a wave of her arm.

The quoits game was long finished. Greer had been sitting near the pitch on one of Malachi's deck chairs, taking the air. He eyed Lila gravely. "So? As you can see, we're all making tracks for the hills."

"Stay cool," Lila said. "I have to check something out. I won't take too long. When I get back, then we'll see." She saw Malachi looking out at them. He'd finally admitted defeat and taken off the camel coat. He had hung it, closed the buttons, and was brushing it down with a velvet pad. She went across to him, ignoring Greer's huff at her lack of detail.

Lila made a show of examining the green dress. "Were you in it with him?"

"I don't cross angels," Malachi said.

"Never mind," she sighed and looked up into his ugly beast's face. In the last few hours it had darkened further, becoming almost purplish in its shadows, the eyes dimming from their lava burn to a sulphurous yellow. Around him the little woolly cavern of the yurt was darker than it should have been given the prevailing light. There was a smell of pine forests and night-blooming jasmine.

"You should get out of here too," she said.

"So sayeth little red riding hood to the wolf? Get about your own business." His reply was one of those faery moment-turning charms that was meant to avert a misfortune by belittling its possibility. He adjusted the sleeve of the perfected coat, and in doing so his claw snagged on the cuff button and tore through the threads, ripping it loose so that it hung by a single strand. He growled at the ill omen and his own clumsiness. His massive shoulders slumped until his paws were nearly at the floor. The velvet buffing pad dropped soundlessly from his other hand.

"Yeah, so say she," Lila clapped him on the shoulder. "This isn't your fight. Faery will be safe. It didn't feature in the story so far."

His growl became nastier, and he turned on her although she felt his malice wasn't aimed at her.

"Faery worked so hard to contain all the horror that has been spared, and I have caused it to be freed. So long was it at bay that even you humans had come to think maybe there was no such thing as true evil, but now you will find otherwise. I set that in motion. I was the hand. It is my fight if it is anyone's, so don't you boss me about."

She lowered her voice. "Ilya was beaten. Even he didn't say how. I got the impression he couldn't. It's not worth all of us . . ." She couldn't finish the impossible sentence. "It isn't worth it."

"No. It isn't," he said firmly and flicked the button off its last thread with a lightning movement of his paw. It struck the wall and bounced down onto the floor. "So what?"

She sighed and took her hand from him. "Take care."

"I wait for you here," he said and turned away as if he was very busy. Then he added, "That girl at your house. Did she tell you her story?"

"She said you sent her, you and Greer. You sent her to clean up the house. And to clear out the previous tenants. Nice call, pussycat. You could always remodel yourself and become a real estate agent."

He made a low, swinging motion of his head that accepted his guilt and pushed it aside as necessary. He wasn't about to apologise. "I must check on her," he said, more slowly and calmly. "You go your way. Your business is short?"

"Short one way or another," Lila agreed, thinking of the Folly's inferno. She must find Friday. She had to know the truth. "I should be back in an hour. Two at the most. If I'm not, you can cancel my rent agreement."

"Mmnnn," he assented, a sound that was half a purr and half a growl. He was down on all fours then, and when he turned towards her he had become entirely catlike, a panther of gothic and prehistoric proportions. "Don't come back here. Go home when you're done. I'll see you there. Zal too. No more coming here. Understand?" He blinked once and then he flowed out of the door and vanished into the twilight so completely that she couldn't track him across the yard.

Lila took a bike out of the inventory, for old times' sake. The quartermaster saw her coming and rolled his eyes. "I'll order another one shall I?" he said as she passed him, smiling.

"Several," she said, thinking that this might be the last time she'd ride one. She could have gone a dozen ways under her own power but only the bike felt like the right way, and she knew enough of what they were doing by now to know that however dumb or pointless it seemed, it was most important to do things the right way. It was how you moved in the game.

The ride to Solomon's Folly was the ride of her life. She'd been along it many times, and every time had resulted in one turn of fate or another. This wasn't going to be different, even if she had to burn down the dusty edge of the highway to pass the standing traffic. From the first turn out of the garage to the last slide on the loose gravel of the private road she felt that she was running on a rail. The time shift separated her from the rest of the world again, but since she expected it, she felt no particular fear. It was only as she came to the depth of the woods surrounding the house and saw that the road had grown over completely, didn't exist anymore, that she was forced to stop.

She dismounted and the green elegant folds of Tatterdemalion sank slowly round her legs, wrenched out of shape.

The trees of the scrub woodland that had surrounded Zal's rented house had grown to full size, fallen, rotted, and given way to a new and more vital forest, which was itself mature. Undergrowth as thick as hedging barred her way and the enormous trees vaulted into a dark cathedral overhead. She thought that an hour was possibly too short a time to have allowed herself as she dismounted and put the bike onto its stand. It looked forlorn and helpless in the shadow of the trees. She checked the time shift and found that it had continued to accelerate. Tendrils of grass crept up the tires.

Because what faced her was a wall of impenetrable trees, twined with brambles as thick as a man's arm and tangled as a medusa's hair, she jetted up into the sky. Immediately wind buffeted her. Though nothing had stirred the branches a second before, suddenly she was caught in a powerful cross-stream that flung her sideways out of her path. As she corrected, more and more force gathered and then changed direction, sweeping her around the perimeter of the Folly's elemental sinkhole. She swore and rode it, ignoring the tornado's gathering mass as long as she was making headway towards her goal at its eye. The dress changed, coating her armour in a skintight sheen of lace. It formed a mask over her face, lace even covering the eyeslots although it was so open it didn't blot her sight.

The vortex picked at her, stripping off the superficial layers of her atoms. She remade them, watching for a place to set down. Foreboding filled her, but she wouldn't proceed against Sarasilien until she had all the evidence in her hands. She had to make one final attempt to locate Friday and his secrets.

Below her she saw that the land itself had begun to reform in pure elements; gold and copper littered a grey-pumice ground between massive trees and running streams of clear water. The house, covered in the ghost of ancient fire, burned here and there with real flames that licked on the final remnants of its timbers. The fire was weak, however, since there wasn't much left that hadn't been returned to clay or carbon. As long as clay was still good, however, she had hope.

Try as it could to dissuade her, the air elementals were only capable of increasing or lessening their force and changing direction so she was able to punch through the diversion without trouble. Landing was difficult, right at the edge of the frying zone where already she could feel herself responding to the radiation levels and the deep magnetic forces massing around the house's unknown core.

"Suit up," she said to the dress. She didn't know if it would respond to a command. It was as likely to fly off in a huff and make itself into a paper bag, but her rending of it seemed to have bought her a few moments of repentance. The lace unfolded rapidly into the full white and gold priest's outfit of before, complete with lead-plate shielding and a surface of woven symbols. It vibrated constantly at a frequency she felt was almost desperate in its struggle to maintain integrity against the entropic maelstrom before them. Even time was getting ripped apart in there.

"This'll just take a minute," Lila said, knowing that was true, regardless of the outcome. She pulled up the files on the house's morbidly confused floorplans and set off inwards.

The way was blocked by more than just debris, which she had to shove and kick aside. The entire structure flickered. Like its one-time inhabitant the worldwalker Azevedo, it was yanked in and out of existence, at one moment solid and threatening, at others insubstantial or even vanished entirely so that she could walk through the ghosts of walls or run through fallen beams. Tatterdemalion anchored her to the base reality of Otopian space-time, threads unravelling in all directions so that they walked like a strange anemone through a roaring ocean of fire. Walls powdered at her touch.

She crossed the last spot where she'd seen Jones, Malachi's friend. It was in the kitchen, with Azevedo flickering around them, the house itself steeped in what felt like a sentient brooding. Its death throes had the same quality now, in spite of the firestorm's lively digestion, and Lila was almost running as she reached the head of the steps that led down to the basement.

There was nothing but a hole in the ground left. The rim flickered with reflected light, but that was lost immediately in the billows of black smoke filling the cavity. Behind the facemask of the helm Lila gave up on human vision and went to infrared, ultraviolet, and radar. Microparticles and hostile frequencies beat relentlessly at her. She felt the dress, Tatterdemalion, tighten and smelled that they were themselves on fire. Her skin temperature began to rise quickly. She jumped down the hole before she could second-guess herself.

The basements of Solomon's Folly were large—carved out in days before refrigeration when ice blocks in straw kept things cool and because the owner had been a collector of wine. In Zal's day they'd drunk the wine collection, and everything that was unwanted from the house had been shoved down here either through the kitchen door or the coal-hole trap outside. There was nothing left of any of this except great piles of feathery ash, which billowed up around Lila in the sun-burst heat, thickening the air and bursting into radioactive bomblets of ultrafine dust. This clogged the robes entirely and stopped the burning, though it began to eat at them in a newer, more scientific way, as though it intended to render them fit for Zoomenon within the minute. She saw red warnings, heard alarms, knew that in spite of all the aetheric and metallic shielding, the reconfiguration of her surface, she was beginning to disintegrate.

Mostly blind she waded through the burning dust, feeling her way with her hands and Doppler. The time differential had increased too— she calculated an hour passing in Otopia as she crossed the first room in a dart of movement that would have been fast enough to blur. She discovered the cellar arches cracking under the load of the house rubble, because they were also being rendered to dust. And there in the second room lay a prone figure, humanoid in shape and about two metres tall, covered completely in radioactive ash.

Friday. Being an earth elemental, and a golem of great power, this vortex of earth-based energies had done as much to build him as to harm him. Victory gave her a final burst of conviction that he would still hold her answers.

As she approached him however the lintel behind her gave way and with a smashing billow of pumice and dust the forepart of the house crumbled into the cellar, letting out a wave of new heat as it did so. Only the absence of almost all oxygen saved her from burning like a torch. Above her head the ceiling groaned. She had no idea how much was up there, or what state it was in. Even with all her senses, the storm made everything into so much mud. Instinct told her she must get out. There was no time. The ground shook violently, and she was thrown off her feet onto her stomach into the smelting zone.

She reached out to touch the clay figure, and her hand closed on the smooth shape of his foot.

Once, years ago, Friday Head had been nothing but a small earth elemental in Zoomenon who had happened to be next to a dying elf. Then he had become a golem, occupied by the ghosts of Alfheim's dead. Now, after a hundred years inside the furnace of Solomon's Folly he was melting. Under the pressure of her hand the foot slumped into a pool, dragging the leg with it into a quickly forming puddle.

She'd imagined grabbing him and blasting her way out of there, but now it was clear that was never going to happen. Even if she could pick him up, the cooling change to the outside world would shatter him in pieces.

"Are you in there?" she screamed in Elvish to the collapsing form. "Is anybody in there?"

Since she'd never known whether or not Friday himself was a person, she didn't know to ask him separately, but she figured in the circumstances all bases had been covered. Friday had once had the means of independent motion. If he'd wanted to save himself, he could have.

"Please!" she shouted, unable to feel her face.

Then that possibility had passed forever. The body became a flat ooze. The holes of the eyes and mouth and nostrils gaped for the last time and exhaled a final burst of scalding air into the ash clouds—and something else went with it. She saw a bright shadow streak towards her. Cinders furled in its wake just as Friday's remains pooled around her hand, glowing cherry and orange.

At the same moment the precariously balanced mass of the ceiling surrendered to gravity and the entire weight of the dead house crashed down upon her head.

No, she thought. No, this was a mistake. She took a breath and the shadow zipped inside her mouth in a fleeting second. Her mouth melted and then there was nothing as the entropy storm took her.

The spirits of the long dead had inhabited Friday Head the golem for fifty years. This was nothing compared to the time they had been interred within their own dessicating bones in the deserts of Zoomenon, preserved by charm against the chance of their discovery and the possible telling of their miserable tale. The command that had preserved them against Zoomenon's special case of entropic decay had also preserved them for the duration of Friday's immolation, although the same couldn't be said of Friday himself.

An earth elemental who had grown to semi-sentience under Zal's babbling insistence, he had long since deserted his insignificant form to join the wellsink of primal forces gathered deep within the cavities that honeycombed the region beneath the house and surrounding low hills. Tiny calderas of pure forms had been accreting there since the detonation of the quantum bomb. Bomb faultlines riddled the area of Bay City and the entire western seaboard of the collated states of what had once been America, and was agreed, in general story and some histories, to be the site of that astronomically unlikely explosion. Thus that part of Otopia was like a piece of rotted wood, decomposing to some interesting elements and propositions whilst at the same time being woodwormed by concentrations of aether. It was as curiously porous and also strong as a bone.

The quantum inferno at its heart was the marrow of this bone, generating fresh chances, fresh possibilities, and scattering them into local potentials. It was a place that was as close to being a raw furnace of creation as anything that had ever existed. It was the kind of place that, if you were going to make something very, very impossible, you would go to.

Most makers capable of this sort of thing stayed well away, because the furnace itself was as likely to undo them as help them. It had no mind and didn't take kindly to the sort of linear organisation that most minds required. Only a fool or someone who felt extremely lucky would try to use the furnace to fire a new being into existence.

Or someone who had no choice because they were stuck and temporarily stunned by several tons of falling rubble and because the last moments of their only protection from annihilation had just melted into a puddle of treacly, golden goo. You could go there to die in the hope of rebirth.

Lila understood all this to be true and concurrent as she regained consciousness. She was glad, because otherwise the feeling of being inhabited by screaming, endless planescapes would have thrown her presence of mind and prevented her from blasting out of the inferno in the form of a ballistic missile, engines on full throttle, moving from subground to high atmosphere in something slightly under ten seconds.

As she ascended, soaring, cooling, the tale of the lost elves and the Three Betrayed unfolded in her head. The Three Betrayed were three of several thousand who were put through the soul forge that the mages had created in the heart of Delatra. All were volunteers.

Some emerged as the forerunners of the shadowkin, but others came back deformed beyond recognition as the Saaqaa—more beast than elf—and in noncorporeal forms, which could only be detected or communicated with in *andalune* form. The vast majority were of these three sorts. For the purpose of defeating the horror of the intangible Sleeper, they were useless. The void energies and spirits that had been forced by pressure into them had remoulded them, but it did not make the spirit warriors that the mages needed. Not that they didn't try it. Those that were able to make the transit to the spirit plane didn't return. The embodied ones, who travelled astrally, died in their beds.

They added other beings into the mix, first separating out their parts with elemental fragmentation, then recombining them. This killed most subjects outright. It would have been abandoned altogether if they had not raided Demonia and captured the eggform of an archdemon of the wilds. Within the shell a physical aspect had not yet been determined, and this embryonic creature was the first to emerge and live as a successful hybrid.

It destroyed a large part of Delatra in a bloody rampage before it was subdued and imprisoned in a psychic cell. It spoke by telepathy in an unstoppable flood of hate that drove almost everyone who survived away from the city, glad to have their sanity merely shredded instead of consumed. It whispered, it cajoled, it played with them. Its name was Hellblade.

Eventually they found a way of putting it to sleep. And it lay there, flickering like a malefic fire between worlds as they worked feverishly on the *geas* that would bind it to the single task of slaying the Sleeper. Needless to say work of this scale consumed most of Alfheim's wealth and all of its greater minds. It was a time of plunder and raiding, of open war with the Fey in the name of acquiring artefacts of power with which to gain mastery over the new creatures. Since that first trial, Demon crossbreeds were abandoned.

Void elements created the next phantom Titan, patterning themselves on the flayed frame of a girl whose own spirit was pulled from the brink and left as bait in the Void ocean for all the forces to consume. This one named itself Nemesis and had no physical form at all. By the time it came into being, the *geas* was in place and it was bound, unable to act until the command to seek the sleeper was issued.

It was rumoured that Nemesis was held prisoner in Delatra, but this was just conjecture—how could a place hold a noncorporeal being? Nemesis didn't speak or rage. Nemesis was silent, though those who came close to the point of contact with her on Alfheim's plane reported experiencing an unbearable terror that forced them away.

A shrine of forgiveness was constructed upon the site of its prison, attended fleetingly by priests. Flowers and little texts, food and milk were left abundantly in peace—at least in peace as long as peace could be felt by someone delivering a plea for mercy whilst experiencing an inchoate terror. Every offering withered to ash.

The necessary third party was created with spirits that were lured from the dark night of the valleys beyond Last Water. It was thought that this would be a leader of the three. So it was. Only the best of the remaining candidates for adaptation was chosen to host their combined forces. He emerged, an elf worldwalker with only a few visible signs of his change and the ability to dematerialise. He was sane, apparently, and accepting of the task at hand, though he had sacrificed all memory of his previous life. Like the others he gave himself a name. If this gave cause for concern, it was too late for anyone to care. So Wrath was born.

They woke Hellblade, summoned Nemesis, and gave them to his command. He took them and vanished from Alfheim, never to return.

A few days later most of the participating mages, the pinnacle of elvish civilisation, died slowly, withering like spring flowers in an unexpected winter snap. But no monster from the unknown planes descended though they waited, sure it had all been for nothing. Night became day, days became years, and in the absence of any further incidents Delatra was abandoned, records of what had happened searched out and destroyed for shame, and the activity moved elsewhere, culminating in the long, grinding cold war of loathing between the shadowkin survivors and the remaining light elves.

This was the story, neatened, tidied, ordered, made sensible by the ghosts of that long-ago experiment, some of whom died at the beginning and some after the end. It was the last and only memorial, the last and only weapon, the last and only blessing that they had. With its delivery they were free.

The tornado of primal destruction took them and unmade them in the moment of their glad ending, and then Lila was alone.

Lila was left gasping, standing on a superheated airstack six miles

above Bay City, abruptly enraged and bereft and frightened to such a
degree that she froze there in the bitter cold, thin air, and for a few
minutes dared not move.

Escape was so narrow for her. There had been none for her brief
guests. She flipped through the story again and again, but each time it
remained relentlessly stripped of most of its personality, all particulars
that could have made it anyone's.

All that for what? There were so many dead, and each of them like
her and they had not escaped. There was no happy ending and she
could not revise one from it.

She hated this so fiercely and so fully that she felt her heart would
explode. She stood in the sky, a useless metal angel filled with useless
tricks. Wrath, Nemesis, Hellblade. She could have chosen those names
for herself, feeling as she did, in the hope that so much pain could be
focused through the lensing of the names, and might galvanise an
angry energy that was enough to break any resistance and make a difference to the way things were. But she knew already that this would
not be so. The monster was immortal and would go unslain forever,
and still it must be faced.

She wished she hadn't let Zal go. She felt she wouldn't see him
again, or if she did it would be in another time and place, not her. She
was so sorry for herself that she couldn't stand it and, with a scream of
rage, tore downwards through the cloud and darkening twilight.

In all of that bloody story nobody had mentioned a name. She still
could not fit Sarasilien for the crime.

Around her heart a dark violet flame twisted and whispered, but
she was so used to the Signal and so full of cares that she didn't notice.

Teazle teleported in chunks towards his destination on the far side of
the world. He chose places carefully to observe the progressive effects

of the rise of this strange Titan. At each site he stayed only long enough to observe the locals or chat a few minutes about conditions before he took off again. In this way he was able to build up a picture of the influence of his enemy and also he was able to pass unrecognised and thus unmolested by either duel challenges or calls for him to champion the civilised demon world—a call he felt he'd already taken and would have been annoyed somehow to be further spurred towards. For once notoriety had lost its appeal. He must approach in stealth since it was likely that his best or only chance of success lay in a surprise assault.

As he closed slowly on his target, however, his speed lessened and he found himself pausing at uninhabited sites. He moved forward and came to a town called Kvetchin, one of those jokey names at someone else's expense that were popular in this region.

Few demons here had any real talent or power since anyone with these abilities gravitated instinctively towards the capital cities, but it was apparent at once that someone with great artistic vision was resident. There were piles of stones everywhere, and they were stacked in great abstract sweeping shapes like little paisley hills, decorated by colour in infinitely subtle shades. The effect was beautiful and it propagated all over, in fields and on roads, cutting around and through buildings and the other structures of arable life. It was decoration for its own sake on a massive scale. Teazle expected the perpetrator to be somewhere on the madness borderline, as obsessive as it was possible to be without falling prey to devil possession—though that was possible. Out here in the wilderness all kinds of depravity could occur. He landed from his flight position—it never paid to materialise suddenly in the middle of things unless for the purpose of killing—and stood at the outskirts of the village where the blackened pits of the firewatchers were ashy and cold.

It didn't take much to see that most people had moved on in the last few days, driven by news coming from the East of the horrors wiping the worldface. He didn't expect that this creator would have abandoned their life work, however, and he was proved right. After a short search of empty pitbeds and locked halls he found the centre of town—a circle marked by torch posts and the wide expanse of the duelling arena.

Sitting in the middle of this space was an old demon, humanoid, tall and covered in tough skin and thick bony spurs, with a beast's hairy mane, massive shoulders, drooping wings, and a lizardlike head fitted with less teeth than seemed probable. It was dark purple, and its flare was dulled, a slumberous crimson streaked with the whitish-grey flecks of depression. It sighed as it saw Teazle, apparently without surprise.

"You are headed East," it said, not so much a question as a statement that wanted confirmation.

"Yes." Teazle was in his natural form, the least angelic or human of his potentials, the most in tune with his fellow demons. On all four clawed feet he paced across the old stones and sat down at an oblique angle to the old one. At this distance he could see its massive fingers with their claws worn almost to stubs playing with a few small rocks. As he watched, it absently crushed one and sifted through the pebbly results, sorting by colour gradations so fine they were nearly imperceptible.

"That's what the stones said," the old one rumbled. Its tail lay along the ground like an abandoned rope. "I waited for you."

"Further west there are still caravans with food and spirit," Teazle suggested, for form's sake. "You could still reach them."

The old demon turned its yellow eyes on him coldly. "I am no bumpkin for you to play the fool with. I have waited for you to come and kill me. I deserve that much. Death at the hand of the Sikarzan, the champion of the mindful ones. My calling meant I could not go anywhere of any use or note. My life has been wasted. My death won't be. You will take my remains and crush them. Anoint yourself with the dust. It will double your resistance to certain spirit energies. You may live long enough to do something useful with all that wasted skill of your own." It sighed. "Are you waiting for something in particular?"

Teazle was taken aback. He thought of Zal and realised he had grown more like the elf, less focused and less attuned to the fine moments of demon feeling in which everything turned and fate fell on one side or another. "Can you tell me anything of the risen Titan?"

The demon took a rock up, turned it, crushed it, and looked at the powdery results. "It is a jumper, moving from body to body, searching for the strongest form. Sometimes it can hold several, or many. When it finds you, Sikarzan, then it will settle there, and you might become the annihilator of worlds. One will shall prevail: its, or your own."

"But there must be a way—"

"Must there?" the demon interrupted him, brushing the dust away with a few flicks of its hand and scattering all its pebbles. It stared at him with its flat gaze, and he saw the endless years of patient work in them—a lifetime focused on a single, simple task. It was a focus he didn't have and probably never would, and he believed that it was able to perceive things beyond his ability to detect, including within himself. "Because you want it there must be a way? This is your preparation for the fight of a lifetime? A childish wish?"

"My life is my preparation." Teazle felt stung.

"As was mine."

"For what?"

"For death. Must you wait much longer? I am hungry and tired."

Teazle blinked, confused. He had never considered his life preparation for anything but other people's deaths. "I guess I'm waiting for you to tell me something important, like the secret to defeating this thing and how not to destroy . . . what you said."

The demon stared incredulously at him. "And how would I know that?"

"Because you are a master," Teazle said. "And a master may know what any master would know."

"Recognition," the demon snorted and then coughed and scratched its snout with both hands. "To hell with your recognition. Do me the honour of the final silence and let's move on. I told you the facts. If you want to wish yourself to a fresh hell that's your business, but dreaming is not your mastery. Execution is. That is why I have stayed to ask the honour of you one final time. You are insulting me now."

"What of the effigy?" Teazle wanted to know about the stone remains the demon would leave. "Will you strike a pose?"

"Scatter the pieces as you will." It nodded. "That would be an unexpected kindness."

Teazle withdrew the yellow sword from the dead demon's spine a moment later just before it petrified completely. "My pleasure," he said sadly to the empty square.

The second death took only a little longer. The demon's power showed in the final stages of its stoneform—it hardly shrank at all. Teazle could find nothing that would break it, or really even scratch it, so eventually he re-formed himself in his largest potential shape, and heaved the statue skywards with aether-assisted beats of his massive wings. He went high, to be sure, and then let go.

The form plummeted towards the tiny town, struck true in the centre of the duelling ring, and smashed on impact, leaving a small crater. Bits flew everywhere. Teazle repeated the process with the larger chunks until nothing bigger than a fist was left. He took up a handful of the brightly coloured dust and tiny stones that rayed out from the centre of the ring in bursts of brilliance where chance had laid them, and rubbed it on his chest beneath his tunic. The rest he left where it lay. From high above it looked like strange flowers.

He felt better now that he had no hope of success anymore and that was a blessing. He said a prayer for the old demon and the gift of his death as he turned to the east and blinked out.

In the canopy of the night forest, ten metres above the ground, among shrouds of dense foliage, Zal lay on a mat of broken branches and looked up through the last high leaves at the sky. He was safe and he needed a rest.

The drake had flown off somewhere more convenient for its size and preferences to fool around with its new wired horns and figure out how to use the music library and the Otopia archive. Zal had figured that out already, and also that what he was wearing might look like a harness of elven filigreed leather complete with silver buckles and glowing runic marks, but it was actually Lila Black wrapped around him like a set of softly flexible iron arms, a Lila Black who was a complete technical masterpiece.

Zal liked contradictions of form and nature. He guessed she could be almost anything, but for now he was content for her to be his battle harness, maiden-holder of his weapons and general grip. They were being stalked and he wanted things to stay simple. Through the whispering *andalune* of the forest, still alive and well, he could feel the movement of blind, stupid things searching for his trail of tantalising order and coherence amidst their own chaos.

What had once been elves and were now something else tracked him with difficulty. They kept all the skills, all the sharpness they had had before, making them formidable opponents, but they were hindered by their inability to comprehend anything of the aetheric universe. He thought, judging by their behaviour, that they couldn't feel it except as a vague kind of hint here and there; they were blind. They were also stripped of everything that had bound them to an identity.

He suspected that their memories were gone. They reminded him of nothing more than the animated dead, but they weren't dead and never had been. They were relics, empty shells . . . he didn't know what the hell they were, but they would be glad to catch him and he'd seen what they did to those they caught all over the land in graphic, disgusting detail. They hadn't been quite reduced to beasts, unfortunately. They were organised, tribal, and if they didn't speak, they made up for it with signs. In their primal competitiveness they reminded him of demons, and in their bloody killings, their furious couplings, their frenzies of destructive rage in which their impulses could turn on a whim and rip one of their own to bloody pieces they were perfect examples of demonic ferocity—an impulse unrestrained by any hint of conscience.

The worst part was that they looked exactly the same as before, their faces serene and intelligent-seeming under their masks of green and brown mud and the splatters of drying gore. If he hadn't known better, he would have called it a demon vengeance on his kind.

He wasn't sure he did know better. He was sure that he wanted to find someone, anyone, to whom this had not happened, but he was a day out of Delatra and he hadn't found anything except more of the same. Even the Saaqaa had run feral and alone. He didn't believe that he was, but he felt like the only living elf on the entire surface of the world.

"There is no contaminant and no contagion present," Lila's voice whispered to him.

He stroked the belt under his fingers as a reply. Taking samples and having her analyse them had been something to do, in which he'd had hope. Now that there was no biological or poisonous culprit to search out and counter, he felt a chill run over him that he was unable to stop. It wasn't like he'd expected one. He hadn't. After the briefings he guessed this wasn't going to be something simple like a disease. Now he was left with sorcery and necromancy, neither of which he knew a great deal about.

"No spectral or aetheric residues present," Lila said.

"Sweet words of love," Zal murmured, flat of affect and exhausted. He didn't even know what he meant by it. "Map?"

"You didn't search enough to make a pattern confirmation of cases," she said.

He rolled his eyes and watched the stars spin overhead. Maybe he'd get really lucky and fall flat on his face right on top of the cause one instant before it fried him, he thought. Then at least Lila would know what happened although there wouldn't be much of him left to bother about it. He'd never had much confidence in the demon-immunity theory. Then again, he didn't believe the entire world could have fallen as fast and completely as it seemed. He knew next to nothing about this region—searching it only made him more anxious about his home turf. If he were there, where he knew all the hiding places, all the safe spots and everybody—if he were there maybe he'd stand a better chance than running around here.

The closed wound in his neck pulsed. He felt a wave of longing wash across him, as if he swam under it. It searched for something to latch on to, and for a perverse reason he couldn't understand he found himself thinking of Xavi. He'd been short with her. She'd been in the right too. Someone had to try and save something of what had been. She was vulnerable, and alone. He felt a need to go and protect her, to shelter her, that was nearly overpowering. Even reminding himself that she hardly needed protection did nothing to defuse the tension that now pulled his guts taut, all their bowstring energy focused on that single point: Delatra.

"Your heart rate's gone up," Lila's harness said.

"It's that charm," Zal said. "No trouble." But the images of Xavi didn't go away.

He thought of the elves in the ruins burning books and made himself remember the moment when a group of teenagers, playing apparently innocently by jumping through windows in remaining buildings, had suddenly turned on one of the girls and smashed a rock into her head over and over as she screamed. He hadn't even seen what had made them turn. Some signal, a feeling so like the one they'd lost maybe, a signal of togetherness or of hate or of simple ferocity; he had no idea.

He'd seen a lot of things like that in his life; things that must not be allowed inside. A lifetime's *andalune* sensitivity made sure most elves he'd known had been masters of boundaries, allowing only what they wished to affect them and keeping everything else safely out of reach of any tender feeling so they could not be hurt, or involved. And still the memory of the girl screaming, her erstwhile friends tearing the clothes off before she was dead, finding interest in her body as well as her head, finally silent, shed an inordinate scarlet into the filth of the doorway.

He moved himself far away from this recollection and watched from a cold distance, a black and white distance, like a master god. He made it shrink and cool until he felt nothing. He tried to push Xavi into this distance, but the succubus charm resisted him, locking his aether body to her vibration. Her colours gleamed at him and he felt her heart yearning, lonely, sad—she was an exile, a monster, like him. She was a living elf. Like him. They were the only ones left. He must go to her.

"Zal?"

"It's okay," he reassured the harness, stroking, but he wasn't sure. The urge to go and be sure nothing happened to petite, delicate, broken Xavi was almost intolerable. He remembered her *andalune* body with longing. He would have given a lot to feel the casual contact of his kind, the reassuring awareness of another who could understand what it was to be a part of the whole; apart, together. But here was no other and maybe, the thought came persistently—maybe there would be no other. He couldn't allow that notion to rise yet. It was too soon for that.

He gripped the harness and felt himself beginning to sweat. He pressed on, covering mile after mile until he was so tired that the only desire he felt was for rest.

CHAPTER EIGHTEEN

Malachi played cards with the girl in Lila's house. After a few hands he had a reasonably good idea of who they were dealing with here, but he wanted to be sure so, when it seemed polite enough, he excused himself with a plausible tale about Greer and the office and some downtown work he must do before nightfall when the vampires would make it too difficult.

The girl, who answered only to the name Lila had given her, Sassy, folded the last of her cards delicately and collected up the rest of the deck. Under her fingers their pictures changed although he didn't look too closely at this.

"Look, pussycat," she said, indicating the pile of empty takeaway cartons they had made, "that wasn't bad. What do I owe you?"

"It's paid for," he said, backing away and minding the furniture. He had grown in size although also in darkness, and gained, if that was the term, a certain insubstantiality that reminded him of Zal.

She nodded, matter of fact, and wiped her mouth and nose on the back of her sleeve. "I don't suppose you've got any of those peaches around, you know the ones?"

She meant Madrigal's peaches, the fruits of faery's Summerlong. "I could find one maybe," he said, which was as close to a promise as he was going to get between faeries.

Sassy grinned. "Can you check on my old folks in Cedars?"

"I can," he said, a policeman doing his duty. He knew she meant the people she'd stayed with before some change beyond his understanding had set her free. Human people. That she cared enough to remember them made him kind.

"Then tell them I'm okay. I think they'll understand."

He considered the address she'd scrawled on a ripped-off piece of cardboard carton. "This the name: Saija?"

"She was my pretend sister for a bit, when things weren't too bad. Saved me a lot of bother. Friend. That's all." Sassy looked a bit sad, although she defiantly faced it out and he thought he detected a quiver in her lip and what might be a tear forming. "Tell me they're okay, won't you?"

"Sure." He hesitated, considering the address and the precinct it was in; a magic shop under the thrall of a very pissed-off gangster community. Fortunately he didn't need a car because she'd just fleeced him of his last paypacket. He checked but Lila hadn't called. He knew it was late, very very late. He called Bentley, and she said there was no message. They were evacuating. Sarasilien refused to leave. Greer of course wouldn't go before everything sank. Nothing else to report.

Sassy watched him and then got up to see him out.

He felt quite wrong leaving her alone in the house and said so.

She smiled. "I'll be fine. All quiet. And if I hear anything, I'll run. No worries."

"Where will you run?" he asked as they reached the door, testing the locks with great distaste.

"Away of course," she said, her lips thinning and whitening. "Get lost."

He sighed and agreed, sure that everything was as bolted and shut as it could be though he was no electronics expert. He guessed Lila would have fixed everything well enough.

Sassy was looking at him with great interest. He shook his head, but the other thing he'd lost that night had been several of his names. There was no point in pretending he wasn't what he was. With a sigh of misgiving he put his heavy paw to the crack between door and frame and flowed through it, softly as air.

"Goodnight, Nightshade," she said, giggling.

"Goodnight," he said and then he felt very foolish and a little bit embarrassed on the other side of the door. It was easy and a relief to melt away into the pitch blackness of the woods and flow down into the heart of the city where there were no girls whose fingers could change the shapes of fate.

As he emerged from the shaded trees at the corner of ninth and Cedar, he found it hard to get his form. Magic struggled here in Otopia, but that wasn't the problem. The trouble was that he was losing the ability. Before he'd been a beast of any kind, he'd been the shadows of the darkest night, an ephemeral creature who might come anywhere that light was not and the darker the better. He was a thing of corners and alleys, caves and everywhere there was night. He gathered under beds and in closets, among forgotten and hidden things. He was curiosity, and a body was no use to him for his work was subtle, the essence of shady business. He struggled to remember how to make himself solid and encumbered and slow and particular. The beast was the best he could do, because that was the form that came after Nightshade—Nightbane.

He looked down at his hands and saw the massive claws, the brute shapes that were more wolf than cat, but with a special hideousness of their own because they so resembled human hands and were not one thing or another. His feet were similar, his heels off the ground now as he fought to stand straight and ended half bent in a permanent forward lunge. The legs of the beast were cloven footed, soft like a camel's but also toed and clawed. He knew that he was in every respect terrifying, but at least his thick pelt and mane made clothing unnecessary. The worst part was that in the yellow gleam of his eyes he could see his little Leaf card—a delicate and pretty link to Otopian tech-nology—lying in the palm of his massive paw, but he couldn't use it anymore. He didn't even have anywhere to carry it that wasn't in his hand. He debated smashing it but that seemed wrong, so he held it instead and turned towards the long parade of shops that led up to the apartment blocks of Cedars itself. He licked his lips and flexed them. He wasn't sure that he would be able even to speak and felt fresh humiliation pending.

In the last light of the afternoon he took one more look towards the south bay, hoping to see any trace or hear any sound of Lila. When there was nothing, he turned towards the storefronts and looked for the hanging sign of the pentagram and the violet roses that Sassy had described.

As they noticed him coming people fled, screaming. At the corner of Tenth and Cedars there was honking and shouting as car automatics narrowly avoided accidents caused by their drivers. Malachi prowled onwards, head down in an imaginary trench coat and fedora, pre-tending it wasn't happening. His little card kept signalling who he was, but he wasn't convinced it would be believed. Nevertheless responses were slow today, thanks to the surge of outworlder activity and the evacuations, so he didn't meet an armed response and made the shop door with everything except any sense of dignity intact.

He opened it on the third try and shouldered his way through, ducking and squeezing and turning around to be sure his tail didn't get trapped. It was a small, dark, cluttered place, full of shelves con-taining large numbers of fragile things. He barely dared breathe although he still sounded like a small steam train or a very, very large bull. Over this the tinkle of the door chime was barely audible. Fortu-nately there were no other customers.

Behind the counter a young man of about seventeen, coca brown with dreadlocks to his waist, was standing slack-jawed, eyes round. His mouth was working, but no sound was coming out.

Malachi held out his paw with the Leaf card in it so that the shop's master AI could verify him. The lad glanced at the counter screen to see this, but it didn't make any difference to his speaking ability. After a few moments he staggered backwards through a beaded curtain and into the back rooms leaving Malachi watching the swinging strips in silence, surrounded by scented candles, books, bells, and bones, plus posters advertising psychic readings, all genuine, good rates, forecasting available. Sassy's picture stared down at him from some of these, smiling. One of them winked at him now.

Malachi felt something touch his arm. He looked down and saw it was drool. He realised with absolute digust that he was slavering. His stomach growled suddenly as though it was reminded of meals past. He pretended to himself that he was not in any way thinking about eating the shop staff. Voices, rushed, high pitched, hysterical and slower, measured, calmer vied for positions in the unseen rooms beyond the curtain. Malachi swallowed firmly.

At last a human woman came out, cautiously but without obvious signs of mental disturbance. She was in one of those indiscriminate age zones that could be anything between twenty-five and forty given the dim lighting. She flicked a long hank of brown hair over her shoulder and fixed him with steady eye contact. He saw that she wore a name badge on the lapel of her beautifully tailored chinoiserie jacket: Saija.

"How can I help you?" she said.

He fixated on the precision handstitching of her collar for focus and presented the Leaf card. It was displaying an image of Sassy, just taken at Lila's house. Sassy had her thumbs up. Malachi let the leaf fall out of his paw onto the counter, and the woman picked it up carefully as the image came to life.

They both heard Sassy's short, definite message about her safety and apologies for absconding. The woman watched it twice and then expertly cued the card to Malachi's personal details. She studied these for a few moments and then looked back up at him.

"I think I have something you'll need," she said. She sniffed and he saw her reach into her pocket for a tissue as she went back through the curtain. When she returned, she had a small thermoplastic card case and a lariat with her. She put his card into the case and attached it to the clip of the looped cord and then handed it back to him.

Awkwardly he settled it around his head and neck, giving up when the thickness of his mane made it impossible to tug further. "Thank you."

The woman looked at him with misgiving. "Will she come back?"

Nightbane, who was Malachi in another, future life he could only just remember, considered the question as he tried to cling onto what remained of his civilised being by recollecting the feel of a cotton sock on his elegant foot, the slide of a perfectly polished shoe over the top of it, and the nimble thoughtlessness of tying laces. "I hope so," he said. The words were garbled by his jaws and inept tongue.

Saija looked at him sadly, her face setting into a stalwart mask over its mixture of relief and anxiety. "She always was a pain in the ass, you know. Never could tell her anything. Best reader we ever had though."

His long mouth cracked into a smile and split his self-pity in two. He grinned. "I can imagine."

"I miss her. You can tell her that." This was said with a defiant lift of the chin.

"You can tell her yourself when you see her," he growled, unintentionally sounding much more aggressive than he imagined he would. He huffed an apology, muttered about the situation, the times, and left, backing out in a storm of his own blarney before he made a mistake and said too much in his effort not to become the go-between.

The shop bell rang merrily at his back as he closed the street door and blinked in the sudden glut of light. The rosy sky signalled the end of the day. He listened to the card, but it made no noises. Lila was still not back. He was considering where the nearest alley was in which he could find some dark corner to dematerialise when a whoosh and a streak of heat went past him. Then he heard the close-knit roar of high-powered jet boots and the clump of feet landing on the pavement, just before his eyes made their final adjustments and beheld Lila herself standing in front of him, a black silhouette in a stance of grim determination edged in blown rags and the short, heavy streaks of her hair on the wind. A heavy reek of brimstone and carbon wafted towards him, and he felt tiny flakes of ash patter onto the wet tip of his nose and across his whiskers.

"Mal," she said. Her voice was hoarse. For a second he thought he saw right through her, but then she moved forward and he moved forward and they were both in the light. He almost recoiled in shock from the smell and the powerful aura that was coming off her in waves. Her black leather and tough-girl look were still there, but swathed in a mummy's worth of grave shroud wrappings of a dark grey fabric whose edges were burned and seared, some parts still smoking and winking where the ends were red embers. Elvish script swirled in the fabric, and the writing, unreadable to his eye, looked like the rise and ebb of silvery scum on a black tide.

Lila's face, pretty and human and unhurt, was frowning at him. The scarlet slash of the burn mark was brilliant red, and her eyes, normally silver, had become blue and grey with a deep ring of black around the iris that made him want to cross himself in front of her though he wasn't anything to do with Catholic and didn't believe in that sort of god. The aura, which he could more feel than see, was a miasmic thing, an aetherial spirit of a kind he'd never experienced before. It fairly boiled off her in waves that threatened to immolate him. He saw Lila, he knew her, but she was a dark revenant of a kind he didn't know at all, and in spite of himself he cowered back from her intense, angry stare.

"What happened to you?"

"I went to get Friday," she said, rasping like an old woman. He realised her throat was burned. "I can't prove it was him, Malachi. What shall I do? What's the matter?" She looked down at her arms as if only just noticing them. "It's just a bit of burning. Nothing to worry about."

He didn't know how to tell her that it wasn't. Apart from anything else, he didn't know the words. "How do you feel?" he asked, hopelessly. It came out as 'r'ow djoo 'ee-ul," a beast-snarl of defensiveness.

Her distracted eyes flicked around, dismissing the street and all it held as of no interest. "Fine. I have to get to the office, face him down. Should have done it ages ago." Her restless gaze lighted on him. "What is it? Did you see Sassy?"

"Yes," he said. He was concentrating on putting what he was feeling into a frame he understood. The black radiation was like an onslaught. It smelled of pure terror. He was amazed that she seemed to be completely unaware of it. Gouts of it leaked from gaps in the bandages that wrapped her limbs and body and all the way up her neck to her skull. It came out of her mouth and nostrils. He wanted to touch her to find out more, but he daren't touch that. Some instinct told him he wouldn't survive it. It was anathema for his kind. Maybe for every kind. *Looks like we won't be needing Tath anymore*, he thought to himself, and the notion made him give a half bark of humourless laughter.

"Mal." Her preoccupation was so focused it was letting her bypass all his signals that tried to warn her of danger. She didn't notice his discomfort or register it as more than his previous discomfort with his changed state. "Will you come with me?" In that question her voice sounded like the girl he'd first met years ago in her hospital bed, small, pale, deathly ill, and frightened of almost everything. In spite of himself and his own will to live, *in spite of it*, he knew that he would say yes, but suddenly he felt tears rising in his bear's eyes and to cover it he gruffly demanded, "Did you find nothing?"

"There are three of them pushing through from Not," she said. "Wrath, Hellblade, and Nemesis. They are coming."

Then he knew what was wrong and he had all the words for it but

no heart to say it. Her use of the old faery word for the planes of the
undead that lay beyond Last Water proved it. Not. A simple term for
a simple thing. A place of things that did not live, did not have form,
that weren't, in any sense, alive except that they existed and had
intent. He'd never really understood how this didn't qualify as alive,
but he did understand that they were inimical to what he usually
understood as life. They were an antiform of a sort. The theosophy of
it had always eluded him, even when he did have a much more scientific kind of brain. Now it wasn't important. The way to deal with
them was not scientific. He'd believed Tath could hold them there, but
even the elf had fallen to their bleak souls. He couldn't begin to
imagine the force of their annihilative despair and what Tath must
have gone through, and he didn't want to, though he smelled and saw
it on Lila now, hidden in plain sight. Not.

"They'll be here soon," Lila said urgently as Malachi dithered,
silently wrestling with what he should do now.

"Ah, that's good, that's good to know," he said, as if it was when
it was anything but. *Names to faces*, he thought in a faery rede—a
charm to pull hidden knowledge into the open—*bones in their places*;
yes, I see. He would do what he could do, which wasn't much. He
could play for time. "Yes, of course I'll come. Meet you there."

She nodded quickly and he heard the jets igniting. He felt the
rumble of them and the force of the airblast in his fur as she took off,
arrowing quickly away into the twilight; a slight figure lost soon
against the clouds.

"Nemesis," he said to himself, picking the name that fit, the bone
that he'd seen in its place. Nemesis it was that rode Lila now. "Yes, I
am coming."

It had never in a million years occurred to him that Lila was not
the opponent to a process, but the culmination of it. Even as this revelation had built to its climactic failure in the story of the Titans, he'd
thought she was a part of the resistance. But it looked as though heads

had turned tails and maybe she was the Titan in its intended form. Without knowing the players, he could not say which of these two, if either, were true.

Now Malachi wondered if Lila had just become the vessel of a being in the last moves of its own game—and whether that game was to fulfill the ancient *geas* or not. He racked his brains to remember *who* had told him the story. Was it a faery or an elf or a demon? Where had his information come from, and through how many mouths? How trickworthy was it, exactly? How credible was it?

He was still searching for this vital detail as he dropped to all fours, ran around the nearest alley corner into the yards where the bins were kept, and slid into the form of absolute shadow. There he was able to connect from one darkness to the next and leap with the instantaneous connectivity of darkness to his desired location just beneath the locked and spellbound door of Sarasilien's old/new offices in the heart of the abandoned Agency building. At least in this form there was no horrible trafficking with the Void in order to change form. He spread himself thinly in the millimetre-thin rectangle and considered.

He reckoned he had two minutes on Lila, but this remembering business was a struggle. Without flesh and bone memory swiftly unpicked itself. And then in the rooms beyond the door he heard the cyborg, Sandra Lane, uncharacteristically exultant.

"At last! I have it . . ."

And then the elf saying, "No need to give me all fifty years of it. Just the highlights."

Malachi figured that this meant Lane had cracked some or all of the Agency's security controls and was scanning archives.

There was a brief pause and then Lane said, "She was here. They held her in the aether cell. Xaviendra is the registry name. She left recently. To Alfheim."

"Alfheim?" spoken with incredulity. "But why?"

"She had no reason to think you were here."

"She would have known the moment she was out of the containment."

"Then it is a plan that does not immediately involve you."

"Rooks," the elf said wearily. There was a clinking sound of glass on glass, the neck of a carafe and the higher tone of a cup, then a gulp of something being drunk.

"Sorry?" The android had gone back to her flat affect.

"Come home to roost. It is a metaphor for curses."

"The phrase commonly uses chickens as its . . ."

"Not in Alfheim."

So, thought Malachi, he does know. They're coming for him. Then there won't be long to wait now.

Zal didn't sleep that night. He was used to the semi-lightness of Otopia, and before that the strange halflight that persisted eternally at the edge of Under where the first weird sister's house stood. Now it was so dark the sky looked like it was a black paper pricked with thousands of varying-sized holes through which a brilliant white light was shining. He could see his hand in front of his face only as a silhouette. Leaves splotched his vision with blank spaces. He drew strength from the dark as he'd drawn it from Tath's fire on his return from Under and later at the diner. It reminded him of his father, who had become twice as strong at night and ten times as fast.

To the true shadowkin Zal was a nocturnally challenged idiot. He wasn't sure that was still true. He hoped it wasn't, because he could hear a lot of activity near the ground and it wasn't all down to the night animals. A mindless shadowkin that was nothing but predatory wasn't something he wanted to tangle with. The continuing absence of their signatures from the greater world *andalune* also bothered him. Even hunting creatures of the lowest kind had a clear presence in it.

He could pinpoint elf activity because it had none, the worldly sounds not matched by patterns in the spiritform. Just as the leaves blotted the sky, they were blanks in the tapestry of the world. He should be grateful it made them so easy to avoid and himself so hard to detect, but he wasn't grateful at all. He shared some of his thoughts with Lila, and in response the harness spread and changed shape, flowing across the light shirt he wore and over his back, arms, and legs. At his wrists and neck she made contact with his skin. He felt discomfort on the point where he'd been stung, and then a flash of lemon scent made his nose twitch and he sneezed.

Fortunately nothing heard him. The clone was silent—he found it hard to think of it as Lila just because the shape was so wrong even though the sense of being held, even caressed, was so pleasing. She was also listening.

For a long time he lay on his mat of branches and didn't move. Then, as certain kinds of noises grew fewer and more distant, he got up to get down (smiling involuntarily at the notion of himself as some kind of night soul demon), and after a moment or two of consideration of the wind and directions, he set off through the forest alone. Wrapped around his torso and limbs in blackened, silent platemail, the grown-out Lila clone rode him as a second skin.

They were a long way from Delatra now. The cliffs were lost in the mountain range whose jagged teeth bit the sky at the horizon. Settlements in the boreal zone were more common but much smaller, threaded together by a variety of tiny paths. In such places hunters or gatherers might head out for weeks at a time on their rounds. The high tops were littered with the remains of their temporary bothies.

Zal hoped that somewhere among them he might find an escapee who had been away when this disease or whatever it was had struck. He jogged along the hidden paths, following them by their strong *andalune* signature, watching for anyone taking the same routes. The idea that this devastation of the people was a blanket effect persisted in biting him the entire time, saying he would find nothing, he should get back to Delatra and help do something useful, with struggling, lonely Xaviendra. There was nothing to find here but more abomination. Running through the woods in the dark was just that—running, and tempting fate, both top of the list of his class acts. Besides, there was something fun about hurtling on at speed when you could only reliably see a few centimetres in front of your face. The armour plates pushed and pulled gently on him, like horse's reins, adding their extra guidance.

His reverie had reached a zoned-out space of perfect bliss—quite lacking any sense of danger or purpose—when he felt something far out and ahead of him; a presence like a brief sniff of water in a seemingly endless desert. Panting heavily with disgust at his lack of fitness, he stopped and came back to his senses. Yes, certainly, somewhere in the eastern valleys he was sure that what he could detect was an elf presence. It was slight and it was alone, but it was unmistakable. It made no reaction as he reached across the distance—a vast distance, further than he'd ever noticed anything before—and he hoped that meant it was asleep and not near death or worse. The land between them was filled with gorges and thicker forest that would take hours to cross even at his best speeds, and he wasn't capable of those. He gave in to necessity over caution and summoned Unloyal by radio Lila.

A wave of longing swept over him, taking him by surprise. For a second all he could think of was Xaviendra. He cursed the charm of the poison and waited for it to ebb. Armour Lila kept him warm and said nothing, if she knew, for which he was grateful. As his breathing returned to normal, he heard the flap of giant wings overhead and felt the downwash of aether turbulence before the air made the foliage overhead rustle and shake. A couple of strong upward leaps, assisted by branches, and he was able to jump directly to the drake's side, clinging to the saddle like a monkey before swinging into it.

A faint, tinny sound of orchestral music filtered from the direction

of Unloyal's head as it bore upwards and made a turn. It turned it off
as it attuned itself to Zal's aetheric body and the distant note to which
he was listening. Within moments they were gliding away from the
mountains. The journey took a few minutes.

When they arrived, there was no place to land but the presence of
the elf was growing fainter all the time, so without much care Zal
dropped straight down into the trees, trusting that his natural agility
and some dumb luck would be enough to save him from serious injury.
The cracking pains he received as his back and legs hit the branches
were a shock, but he grabbed hold of a few of them with relative ease
and his light weight spared him from worse than bruises.

The sudden noise had made the immediate forest go silent, even
the insect burr, but it resumed again a moment or two later. By then
he was moving much more adeptly towards the other person. Some
climbing and jumping was required, but he found them within a
minute. They were hiding in a shelter fashioned out of leaves at the
highest point in the canopy that was reachable. Zal perched outside,
further down in the branches. He could tell by the agitation and terror
in the aura now confronting his that she had heard him, but in spite of
the link and his patient identification of himself she was too hysterical
to calm down. He could feel all her efforts to pull the *andalune* away
inside herself, but she hadn't got the strength or the skill to master
that trick. If she had, he'd never have found her.

He broadcast reassurances, but she was clearly able to at least
detect either his shadow or demon traces because this made no noticeable difference. She cowered in the tiny leaf tent, too exhausted to run
away, so he moved up there, making plenty of noise to show he wasn't
trying to attack. She was so tired that she didn't manage to throw herself out the other side of her makeshift hide before he grabbed her. A
half-scream of fear escaped her, loud against the hum of the insects, but
he put his hand over her mouth, gently.

"I am not here to hurt you. Be quiet. It is not safe." This was to convince her he was on her side as much as it was a warning. In fact, he didn't detect any of the absent blots that signalled danger, only the forest's usual life. He took his hand back.

The elf whose arms he had hold of above the elbow lay back and curled in on herself, shaking. "Who are you?" Her voice had an accent he didn't recognise and the words were archaic.

"Zal, once Suhanathir, though that was a long . . ."

"I know you," came the reply quickly. All the fear vanished and was replaced by relief and curiosity. "Ah, now I see. Yes. How very odd . . ." And with that she fainted.

It was so very dark that Zal couldn't see anything of her except what his spirit body could sense, and he recognised nothing about her at all. She had fainted from exhaustion and there was nothing he could do but wait for her to recover enough to wake up. The treetop was precarious. He decided to play safe and summoned Unholy for an evac.

By morning they were several hours' flight time from Delatra at an uninhabited region of lush boreal forest on an island just off the coast of some bit of Serinsey that Zal had maybe read about once in his boyhood and forgotten long since. He only knew the place because Lila had maps and showed them in rich detail on the surface of his arms as he looked down. Although the island was deserted, it did possess one feature worthy of note, and that was a dry cave, free of bears, in an outcropping large enough for Unholy to land on.

The elf he had found was rather young to be knowing about him, he thought as he watched her sleep. The morning sun warmed things up nicely and it woke her, streaming through the cave mouth in golden bars as though everything in the world was perfectly all right. She jolted, froze, sucked her breath in through her teeth as she realised things had changed while she was away, and then relaxed enough to close her eyes and breathe normally for a minute or two. At last she rolled onto her side and opened her eyes again. They were green and they stared at him with avid intensity, so much so that he found himself blinking for her. Once she glanced upwards, in the direction of the sleeping drake, and then back at him.

"From Demonia," she said, in a whisper.

"Yes," he confirmed.

"Real," she said.

"Yes." He could feel her tentatively expanding, trying to search the area for danger. "There's nobody close," he said. "You can rest."

"No," she said. "No time for that. We have to stop it." She tried to get up but it failed as an effort, and he held out his hand quickly.

"Rest there, at least a while. You must." He handed food across to her, and she grabbed it quickly without noticing or caring that it was from Otopia and not much like elven food.

In between mouthfuls she said, "It's why you came, isn't it?"

"Yes," he said.

"Where are the others?"

"There's only me."

She stopped eating midbite and lay prone and motionless for a moment, then spat the food out onto the sandy ground. "Only you?" All the animation went out of her and she lay like a doll, eyes closing and her mouth curving into a disbelieving half-smile. "Only you." She laughed silently with a couple of quick moves of her ribs. He counted more than ten serious bruises and scrapes on her exposed skin. She was wearing light clothes, something suited for indoor living, and they were mostly ripped and dirtied. Her braided bronze-coloured hair was a mess. He betted she'd been running for a while. Though they were well separated and she looked all given up, her *andalune* body clung fiercely to its contact with his, drinking in all she could about him. He guessed there was a lot to drink, given Lila's presence and all.

"And are you all that's left? Only you?" he asked.

"I don't know," she said after a while and coughed, so she had to roll back to her side. She pushed the spat food reluctantly away from her, and took another bite of the cereal trail mix bar from her hand. She chewed it slowly, deliciously, enjoying it in a way he wouldn't have thought possible. He hated the things himself. "Am I the last elf?" she asked rhetorically, taking another bite. "I asked myself that so many times I thought I would go mad."

"You're not. So do you know what happened?"

She swallowed, went for another bite, thought better of it, and licked around her teeth so that he could tell her gums were sore. "Meaning you're here I suppose. Did you find others?"

"You're the first," he admitted. "But I only got here yesterday."

"You saw the people here."

"Yes." He held his impatience in check.

"Yes," she said and her hands began shaking. "I . . . was . . . I am a librarian, at Delatra. All the others went . . . as you see, after the creature came. It asked for some records. Looked like an elf, of course it did or we, but anyway, I went to look for them because the Master Librarian was arguing with it. There was something strange about it you see and . . . I went looking and I was in the rooms when I felt them all disappear." Her green eyes were round, completely ringed with white. It was the only outward sign of the freezing horror that gripped her. He felt it and flinched, but he was still on guard and the despair and sadness that followed didn't infect him.

"But not you," he said quietly.

"Not me." She dropped the food bar and her hand went to a pocket on her beaten trousers and fished around quickly. "I had this." She held it in her fist and wouldn't let go, but he could see it, a pinkish stone object. The smile of slight hysteria played across her mouth again. "It's a soulcatcher. There can't be more than four in the world, and I was holding it because I was looking for those cursed records and it was with them in the box." She stared at it in disbelief.

"And what does that do?" He'd almost forgotten what it was like to be in the Jayon Daga but now he remembered. Questions, efficiency, action; it felt so comforting.

She caught the tail end of this emotion and smiled for a moment—a more genuine smile. "Yes. I thought it was a paperweight. The only reason I held onto it was because I was so frightened that I couldn't let it go." She regarded the object—not carved really, more like a smoothed rock polished lightly into a suitable shape for a hand. You could have thrown it down on a pebble beach and lost it forever on the instant. "Later I understood. I realised that there must be something important about the ledgers. I thought that it was a temporary attack on the library you see, not a full-scale war. I could not imagine what could do such a thing as wipe everyone out like they were chalk marks, forever. I still do not entirely . . ." She broke off. She was shuddering convulsively and couldn't keep speaking. Zal maintained his strong, compassionate energy, but he didn't move closer to her. Their *andalune* bodies twined like ivy meanwhile.

After a minute or two she was ready to continue, the stone held in her hands, over her heart. "So. I took the ledgers." She released her hold briefly to pat what he saw were large inside pockets on her soft jacket—book-sized pockets. "And I took the stone and I went through the rooms by the back ways until I was able to get out, thinking I'd hide until the worst was gone and come back when everyone woke up. I've been at the library for over fifty years, so I knew every inch of it back to front. It would be possible to find someone there hidden in any of its places, so I went down the mountain through one of the long tunnels that led to the forest. There's an energy sink not far from the mountain, at Orlinn, a water place. It felt right to go there. I went and hid there and when it passed over it didn't find me. I tried to pull everything in, but I do not have your skill with that. There was never any need to hide before." She paused. "I wonder why it did not see me. I think it was not really looking. It swept over and killed them all and it was gone. That was all. But it wanted these." She put the stone back in her pocket and slowly, one at a time, drew out two old and battered sheaves of manuscript.

"May I?" Zal asked.

She nodded and he moved forward and took them carefully. They were perfectly preserved and easily legible, but he couldn't read the ancient words. "What is this, Old Yashin?"

"Earlier actually. Shavic."

"What is it, can you read it?" He handed them back to her and watched her smooth the curled edges carefully.

"Yes, I have read it many times now," she whispered. "One is a ledger of names. The other is a mage's journal explaining exactly how to strip the spirit from a living person without killing them and to put something else in its place. And before you ask, yes, I do think this is the work of the Genomancers who made the shadowkin. It is not signed. There is no name attached to it. The ledger is, I think, the record of all those who were so used. But I cannot be sure of that. I do not recognise any of the names, except that they are commonly used."

Zal thought of Xaviendra, and a wave of heat and discomfort passed through him. He pushed it away, but the other elf had noticed.

"You are cursed," she said, startled.

"I've had worse," Zal insisted. "Tell me more about this stone."

"It anchors the spirit of the bearer in their flesh and bone. Lesser versions are used by necromancers in their studies, but this book," she tapped her right breast, "says there are a few master stones that have much greater powers. They are a kind of lightning rod, earthing the spirit, or chaining it, depending on your viewpoint I suppose. It was after I read about them that I understood what this must be and what had happened to the rest." She stopped and closed her eyes. Tears flowed out of them, and the shuddering returned.

"May I see the names?" he asked.

Without looking she fumbled the book back out and handed it across again. Zal addressed Lila quietly, "Can you read this?"

His left hand warmed. He lifted it on intuition and put it over the book, palm down where the soft skin of the black gauntlet could "see."

As she had shown the map she now showed him the words written in contemporary elvish characters. He was poring over them when suddenly he was crowded by the female elf, coughing and wiping her face as she stared at the back of his glove.

"Translation!" she said, astonished. "What is this? I thought you had some sort of barbarian armour with a demon inside it, but this is—"

"This is Lila Black, my wife," Zal said, pulling a face as he did so because it sounded like stupidity even when he knew it was true.

The elf recoiled but stayed where she was, drawn to and repulsed by all the notions rushing through her feverish mind.

"Alive," Zal supplied. "Human. Machine." And after a pause, "Harmless." He turned the page, hoping that Lila knew more than he did and would highlight something if it was important because, as the librarian said, to him it was a list of names that meant nothing and attached to nobody.

"I . . ." the elf began but was unable to articulate any more. She stared at him.

"We need to know who else is still surviving," Zal said calmly as his survey went on through sheet after sheet.

"And then?"

"And then . . ." Zal said but he didn't know what happened then. "I am supposed to report back to Otopia and figure it out from there."

"So they know. They are preparing an army."

Zal continued reading. "Did you see this creature, as you call it?"

"It looked like an elf," she repeated. "I was not paying attention. I was preparing some documents for . . . I am just saying that there was an elf who asked for these things, and she had a very strange aura now that I think about it. She was cold. Some people can be that way, you know, when they have had a shock so that was another reason I did not look at her, in case it was too much for her. I do not know that it was a she. I assumed . . ." She had started to babble, and the hysteria in her voice was rising.

"It seems a reasonable assumption," Zal broke in firmly. "I would agree with it. In any case, it is all we have to go on at the moment. Later you said people died and it came for them. How did you see it then?"

"I saw it," she used the word for seeing with the *andalune* body, rather than with her eyes, "as a wave of silence. And cold, but I think that the cold is only my feeling and there was no coldness as such. Silence came. But they were not dead. I heard them. They heard me. I had to run away. Very fast."

Zal watched the meaningless names scroll across his hand. "When I met you, you were afraid of me even though we heard each other well in advance. Why?"

"I thought it was how she would hear me. That she would find me and kill me for the books and the stone."

"How would she know that you even had them?"

"Because I was alive when I should be dead."

Zal thought that was reasonably screwed up, but it made sense enough. "She has no reason to search for someone she doesn't know is missing though."

"No," the elf sat back and then lay down again in the sunlight, curling up small. "I think of her in the room, looking for the books, seeing they are gone."

"I don't get it," Zal said in reply, thinking aloud to himself. "What does this gain anyone?" The names rolled on and on. There was no mark anywhere to show what had happened to them—if they survived as shadowkin or were killed in the process. Then a name flashed at him and made him blink.

His father.

He got up and stuffed the paper booklet down the front of his shirt. "I have to go. I'll be back soon as I can. Stay here. It's safe." He was already pressing the collar of the armour, signalling Unloyal so that the drake got up from its nap and came down to the sandy area in front of the cave ready.

Theelf . . .

"I don't know your name," he said as she backed away rapidly from the drake, staring at it with loathing and wonder in equal parts.

"Tellona," she said but had to say it twice because her voice was choked. "Will you be hunting us all down with that thing?"

Zal glanced at Unloyal's hideous mass, the eyeless head at an angle that suggested it didn't care for who said what about it. "If I have to." The thought of exterminating the "survivors" had passed through his mind—his demon part wanted to do it badly—but he'd let it go along with all his sense of connection to the victims. It had been surprisingly easy. Why that should make him, the arch defector, so sad, was another mystery. Then he restated firmly, "I will be back."

"What if it comes?" Tellona was suddenly holding out the other book. "You should have this."

"To preserve it," he said in a neutral tone, recalling Xaviendra again and her vivid insistence on the preservation of the library. He went back and took the paper.

Tellona watched him with thin lips. "The acid in your skin will hasten its destruction," she said reprovingly. "You should take it because you have a chance of defending it. Whatever it wants I am thinking it should not have if only because I am vengeful." Her look became a glare.

Zal stuffed the second book down the other side of his shirt and felt Lila press them close as her chestplate stiffened and moulded itself around the forms, sealing closed up to his jaw. He saluted Tellona. "You have the stone."

"Yes," she said, hand already around it, knuckles white.

"Keep it." He saw relief flood across her face.

"You are immune?"

"I have no idea," he said and went back out into the blazing sun, climbed to the saddle, and adjusted the leg harness so that he was held fast. "I am going to Halany. I hope not for long."

"That's halfway across the world!" Tellona sat up. "What's there?"

"I don't know." As an afterthought he took off the saddlebag that was loaded with most of the food and threw it down. "You'd better have that. There's nothing to eat here except what you can suck out of the aether." They shared a glance for a moment, and he saw the slight hesitation of the light elf when faced with the prospect of drawing out the life force of living things by the shadowkin method of feeding. It was only a twitch though, not the whole nine yards of horror, so he guessed she was one of the progressive ones. He nudged Unholy and the drake took off with a leap that sent showers of sand in all directions.

CHAPTER NINETEEN

It took Teazle a long time to understand what he was seeing. He watched from several vantage points high in the rocks of the wastelands as a huge humanoid demon, some ten metres tall, staggered its gigantic way across the vast red tundra of the desolation, which lay between the true wilds and the borders of civilisation.

A miasmic crimson cloud flowed over and around it periodically closing in on its body where it would modify some part—growing larger hands, bigger claws, or sprouting fans of razor edge bones from the processes of its spine. Meanwhile the figure was a drunken, leering monster who groaned and lashed its purple forked tongue as though it had been thoroughly poisoned. Sometimes it clawed at its face and opened large gashes. When the blood poured, the crimson aura speeded into a cloud of blood drops and grew darker and stronger.

Other demons came to meet this creature, hypnotised into complete submission from afar. When they got close enough, the giant would pick them up and rip them to pieces, gorging itself on blood and pain. The pain part interested Teazle the most. He would have bet that this demon of the wilds—a barbarian creature of sophisticated form but basic drives—would have gloried in slaughter and possibly had some skills at luring gamma-class demons into its clutches, but the aura it possessed immersed itself in the dying, tormented bodies with a lush devotion. Not that there weren't tracts of demon lore and life devoted to torture, but there was something about the crimson cloud that smacked to him of a fetish, which was absolutely not a demonic quality. No demon would be slaved to a desire.

After killing, the giant threw the bodies down with disgust—again, an undemonic kind of notion. It took time and some patience but after a while Teazle had found a name for what he was watching and it surprised him; he wasn't used to thinking about anything in terms of evil.

Legions of demons with a bent for philosophy had done all the thinking about evil that needed to be done long before Teazle came along, so he had only to apply what he learned in school. He watched this monster lurching into shape over the course of several miles. It changed en route, gathering up the talents and abilities of those it consumed and adding them to itself. This rarely required a physical alteration, which is why it took him some time to figure out what was going on. When it paused and looked around, scratching but clearly bothered by some intuition that made it turn his way, he knew he was running out of time in which to stay hidden. Intelligence, talent, and power were approaching a critical mass within it. If the old, dead demon he had met on the way was correct, Teazle could expect to be added to this collection, which is why he hadn't gone in with a direct attack, but as time went on he didn't perceive an alternative. And then he remembered that the cloud's behaviour looked a bit like Zal's shadow body when Zal was asleep and it remained wakeful.

Zal kept his shadow well away from Teazle at all times when he was conscious although Teazle had seen him envelop Lila in it completely. Great intimacy with Zal wasn't something he wanted, so he hadn't given it any thought. If Zal was still mostly like other elves, then it was an aetheric form that demons could fool around with destructively though they hadn't got any other influence on it. Demons with a taste for elf got some pleasure from the buzzing pain that the ordinary elf aether body could inflict on them, but the general loathing between the races meant there was no science of the interaction. They only used it to torment one another.

Faeries of course were rendered unconscious by the elf aether body, so there need be no science of that. Some speculated the aether body was the spirit of the elf, but this wasn't quite correct because it had mass of its own. All Teazle knew is that when Zal slept sometimes his aether body spilled out of him. He knew because the buzz of it touching him had woken him up and made him drag himself off to sleep elsewhere on several occasions. When this happened, he had briefly found himself dreaming Zal's dreams. He knew they were Zal's because they made no sense and were full of music.

Now he stared at the lurching hulk moving towards a distant town and considered what that might add up to, if the cloud were an elf body that had taken possession of a demon of the wilds, starting with stupid but powerful and ending up as a giant collective horror with the intellect of a master magus. He liked the notion, and he had no doubt that if he were included it would be a horror that could conquer worlds.

This, then, would be the legendary Hellblade moulding itself a body.

Teazle stayed back as the creature advanced. On his back the two swords hummed softly and he wondered, not for the first time, what they were. He knew they were only in the form of swords for a convenience, because the form suited their intent and that of their mistress whose instrument it seemed he was, and in that he was no different to the swords themselves. He knew he could expect no direct interventions from her. He *was* the intervention, as Hellblade was someone else's.

With delight approaching ecstasy, he stalked the beast and watched it grow. He delayed the precious moment of death or victory, savouring its approach. For him this was the perfect moment, predator and prey on the edge of forever. He let it go and teleported.

At his largest and in his deadliest form Teazle was only half the size of Hellblade, but he was more than big enough to blow its physical body to bits when he materialised in the centre of it, every scale a blade, vibrating on frequencies that shook apart what wasn't shredded and burst by his arrival. A rain of bloody ruin fell around him, splashing down into a pile of ruddy, steaming gore. The thick, awful stench of half-digested flesh and stomach fluids filled his nostrils for a second before the aether body, in which he was now fully contained, snapped tight and cut off the air.

At the same time an awareness of Hellblade's total existence filled him. He had expected frenzy, but instead there was a calm that almost matched his own. They permeated one another and knew each other in an intimacy far closer than anything Teazle knew before. The wholeness of Hellblade's story soaked into him with every nuance of retreading that the spirit had given it over the long years of its banishment, and he knew its purpose at last, even as he began to asphyxiate. It was a simple story.

The three had been told that they were to face a horror beyond comprehension at the gate of death itself, beyond which even spirit would be dissolved forever. The power they had taken on and the monstrous transformation they had endured meant that they could stand on this plane and give battle to the creature that was waiting there, slowly wearing away at the wormhole the mages had inadvertently created between Alfheim's reality and the peculiar no-place of the unliving things.

They were made according to what they had absorbed. Hellblade had been a guard at Delatra once, so long ago it boggled the mind, and he had been as demon-hating a son of the trees as the next pureblood light elf. Some insanity had leaked in when he found himself fused with a demon of blood and necromancy. They had fought within the confines of their joined minds as their bodies disintegrated under

Zoomenon's pitiless stare and neither had exactly won or lost. They had come to be a new thing that called itself Hellblade and which knew only the *geas* of the command to kill the sleeper.

They went, all three of them, Hellblade, Wrath, and Nemesis, incorporeal, transubstantial, into the lifeless no-space beyond Last Water where even the Void and its massive emptiness came to an end and there they found their quarry as promised—a darkness of exquisite malevolence and unbridled hatred. Because they weren't hampered by the corporeal world anymore and had what Hellblade laughingly recalled as The Sight, they recognised it immediately and realised the mages had got it all wrong. All of it.

The whole story was bullshit.

Yes, there was a place full of spirit forms. Yes, some of them had never lived in the material worlds. Lots of them didn't want to. Lots of them were beyond comprehension, and most were below it in that they had nothing like a mind or an identity. They were things without names that would never have names. There were certainly beings that corresponded closely to the unmentionables mentioned in the *geas*. But none of them were what the mages had seen in their vision quests. The mages had seen something living. It vibrated lower, it existed closer to their own plane, they could see it from where they were, and what Magus Xaviendra and the rest of them had spied was a very dark thing indeed. But it was not a separate thing. They had created the Mirror of Souls and thought it was a window.

They had seen themselves from the other side, from spirit, and not recognised what they were looking at. Immediately they had judged themselves monsters. Correctly as it happened, but that was another irony not lost on Hellblade or the others. Their ambition and their lust for power was manifest in spirit form, visible, tangible, all of its tendrils and might illustrated. It was the stuff of spirit and the aether itself, from which all ghosts and constructs flowed across the totality of the dimensions.

The three phantoms understood that their mighty fight, their sacrifice and heroism was a goose-chase of a spectacular proportion, fuelled by blindness and fear.

The *geas* was a bond, and now it was also, for Hellblade, a revenge.

Hellblade had reached across the fragile veil of the Mirror's flickering surface to rip away the closest souls, of those who'd sent him beyond life to this undead hell. His was the power of slaying, and he gloried in it like a true demon and abhorred it like a true elf and there was no reconciliation of these things; they existed in contradiction that was fierce and endless. He seized and rent. Then, true to her making, Nemesis judged, sundering the remains into pure spirit energies for Wrath to consume. They had other names then: Render, Judge, and Eater. Those were their names from the book in which their task had been written in the ink of blood and tears.

The mages they attacked from the spirit plane soon died, gibbering and mindless as babies but with a deal less charm. Time moved faster for the spirits. It left enough in Alfheim for the last remaining mages to rally and investigate.

Mage Xaviendra found the three and offered them a bargain: if they spared her life, she would ensure that the *geas* was lifted. Without this intervention as soon as the last mage died they would be sucked beyond the edge of everything into true death. She also offered them a second spirit mirror, the Mirror of Refraction, through which they were able to see into and partake of the material worlds, watch their loved ones, and remain connected to Alfheim and Demonia and Faery. They took this.

The mirror was a trick, however, and as soon as they looked into it, they were trapped. It was the mirror of the Faery Queen and although it did exactly what was promised it kept them in the thrall of the visions it offered, helpless to escape until a faery King or Queen should look into it.

What happened to the mirror itself the three didn't know, but there was a moment when someone did come and look into it—an elf boy with golden hair and a nondescript dog, white with black spots—and then the mustered strength of all the years was enough for them to break the trance, not least because the mirror was hoping to find its way home by then, since it was one of those objects that doesn't like to be lost.

Then they came to finish their task, but by this time their rage had cooled. What Teazle found in Hellblade was a cold determination to escape the hold of the *geas* by any means and so end his existence. The demon part of him didn't want to die, but the elf did.

Both of them had taken a hateful pleasure in enslaving and driving their erstwhile hosts here in Demonia, but they were changed now. The flesh had made them remember their mortal lives. What had been called Hellblade before was really only an intent to catch and slay with a few fleeting memories still attached to it like dried flesh to an old bone. But with the addition of blood, they were suddenly vibrant with the possibilities of life and the will to die was at war in them. Meantime Teazle had destroyed their lovely new body, that perfect essential vehicle of meat and blood. So they would have his.

Teazle recognised immediately that he had no defence against Render, Hellblade's purposive element. The soul-rip that Render could perform was the same method through which the beautiful Sorcha had been killed the last time Teazle fooled around with wild demons—and it was this kind of creature that had been involved in Render's making. However, Teazle wasn't quite what he used to be. The swords he carried began to vibrate at frequencies so high that they were imperceptible to ordinary beings, but they were quite perceptible to the phantom that screamed in agony as it felt itself beginning to shatter. At the same moment that Teazle was feeling terrible pains and the loss of his senses from lack of air, Hellblade felt an inexorable entropic force beginning to ruin all that was left of him including his final plans.

Both realised the solution, and offered and accepted the deal on that instant. Air returned, pain and loss abated.

Teazle and Hellblade stood in an uneasy silence in a pile of stinking meat, sharing one body. Because Hellblade was a phantom they were no longer exactly one or another but they were sure that in this state, however long it lasted, there was nothing earthly or much divine that was going to stand against them.

Teazle stepped out of the heap of guts puddled around his legs and smelt the blood in the air. Hellblade's necrotic *andalune* weaved around and through him in a strange revelry of lustful satiation with his excellent body. He felt violated and exultant but also he felt the compulsion of Hellblade's bonds and his will to execute the poetic justice therein decreed.

One of the escaped mages had come, it seemed, to Demonia, to find a necromancer able to sever the spirit so that it could be hidden, come the inevitable day of Hellblade's rise from damnation. The phantom had planned to scour Demonia to find this soul canister, leaving no bone unturned and no blood unshed but Teazle, after a moment of exquisitely pleasurable revulsion at the turn of events, deemed this unnecessarily dramatic and a waste of time. He knew necromancers and clairvoyants who had inexplicably gone missing whilst hiding a Mirror in their cellar. Madame Des Loupes had made her exit early, but she hadn't been wrong about who was coming to call on her and what was likely to happen on that day. He had a very good idea of where to start looking for that canister.

He spread his huge wings and took to the air, much as to feel the joy of being able to do it as for any practical need. Blood and matter that still clothed him exploded outwards, scattered, and fell around him as he thrashed higher, delighted by the physical struggle and the air's resistance. He beat slowly across the brittle rocks and then, when he was sated with the mastery of flight, winked out. With every second Hellblade soaked him and the distinction between them grew more and more blurred. He feared he would never be rid of the thing, but then he forgot to fear it, even as they appeared over the familiar greenish muck of the Lagoon in a sweltering Bathsheban afternoon and descended, a white dragon slicked in gore, to the centre of the city, at the square in the souk outside Madame Des Loupes's house.

Lila found herself face to face with Malachi in the corridor outside what had been her office. She smelled of jet fuel, and her scowl was as black as her armour. "The mountain's come to Mohammed," she said. "Let me pass."

"Wait," Malachi croaked. It was so difficult to speak now. He was forgetting words. "The phantom is with you. You carry Nemesis."

She froze in a nonhuman way, utterly still, for a split second, then slight movements returned and he saw her eyes flick as she considered this and all its ramifications.

"That explains a lot," she said tightly. "It's funny, I'm so used to silent knowledge I didn't even think it wasn't me. We've got the same wishes. I guess that makes me a Returner, doesn't it? Or does it make me Lila at all? Even so. The time's come." She made to move past him, but he blocked the way. She gave him a long, even stare. "Move or be moved."

"Lila, think . . ." But by the time he'd said this she had grabbed him and spun them around in a pirouette so that she was at the door and he was behind her. It was locked, but she unlocked it and pushed it open with a small kick of one boot toe. She walked through, slowly, letting the sound of her boots on the tile sound steady as she moved into the new silence beyond.

Malachi followed her, a beast shadow.

"Lila," Sarasilien's voice was loud and startled as Malachi heard it, then he saw around her shoulder and the elf's face was stricken—by the sight of Nemesis, he was sure, even though this was only the faintest sheen of spirit light around Lila's figure by now. He stood up from where he had been reclining on the chaise. At its foot Sandra Lane moved forward from where she'd been resting at attention, taking a flanking position. Lila ignored her.

"Time for our little chat," Lila said. Her tone could have frozen steel. The voice was a fusion of hers and that of another so that it sounded distorted. "Tell me about your daughter."

Malachi edged around so that he was just behind Lila and to the side. Lane faced him as he manoeuvred, but he stayed back.

"Lila," Sarasilien said, his hands held forward, slightly open, and a look of deepest concern on his features, "you are in a very dangerous position."

"No," she said evenly. "That would be your position. Time to convince me you don't deserve what I'm bringing. Your hell has been visited everywhere, and all I see is your running, lying back."

There was a presence about her that Malachi had never witnessed before and he wasn't entirely sure it was down to Nemesis. It was formidable and the room felt so still he could feel his own heart beating, and that seemed like too much.

"Either you talk," Lila said, "or I will take you apart to find out the truth."

That was and was not Lila, Malachi knew. The promise was hers, the backup truth behind it was the phantom's.

"Judge," he said, holding just one hand out now, palm forward, placating. He moved very cautiously, as Malachi wanted to. The sense of something about to spill over into violence was so acute that the air felt hard to breathe. Sarasilien spoke quickly and quietly, "Judgement will not be necessary. I have one daughter and she is here."

"She is not here," Lila said. "She left and went to Alfheim to do something. What was it?"

Sarasilien blinked, "Do you mean Xaviendra?"

"Is there another?"

He looked slightly blindsided and stumbled over the name. "Xaviendra is not my daughter."

Lila might have hesitated, she might have debated the points for some machine aeon, Malachi didn't know, but he saw her reach forward and grab Sarasilien by the front of his jacket and lift him up and shake him an inch from her face as if he were a rag doll. Finally she slammed him against the wall and moved in until her nose and his were a millimetre apart.

She spoke in a whisper that was soft and quiet, full of malice, "Say it ain't so one more time. I dare you."

Her anger was a crackle that ripped through Malachi's fur like static. At the same instant Sandra Lane was there holding Lila's arms, trying to wrestle her off Sarasilien, but she might as well not have been there for all the effect it had.

"Look at me," the elf said, although his lips had gone white and he was holding her gauntleted wrists with yellowing knuckles. "With Lila's sight, Nemesis, you can see the truth."

With a bellow of rage Lila flung him down to sprawl at her feet. In a continuation of the same gesture, blasting off her feet with power, she knocked back Lane, sending her flying into the far wall with a force that smashed plaster and made the entire room vibrate. An inch crack shot up and down from floor to ceiling as Lane crashed to the floor and the walls and floor shuddered, but Lila's attention was only for the elf as she spat, "What? How can this be? It was written in that book, *that book I wrote in*, it was all in there, her diary, the journal of Xaviendra Sarasilien, your name, the history, the experiment . . . it was all in there! I read it. I see it now. Every line. Every word!"

Sarasilien made no effort to pick himself up. "I have only one daughter, and she is not the Mage Princess of Delatra, which Xaviendra surely is."

"Then who is she? And what about that book? I wrote in it. Because . . ." Lila stopped.

Malachi could see Sarasilien's face. He expected avoidance, because a faery would twirl away through the gaps and elves preferred to keep secrets, but there was an odd light in Sarasilien's eyes.

"It's you, Lila," he said, using the Otopian shortening of the words.

"The second time you were born, I made you. I have no other offspring. I never have had. There is only one person I had a hand in making. It's you."

Malachi thought he saw Lane flinch a little as she stood up, plaster dust falling off her.

Lila drew herself up and back like a recoiling snake. There was a moment of complete stillness.

"The book you had," Sarasilien said, still slumped like an old blanket on the floor. "Who gave it to you? Where did it come from?"

"Zal," Lila said, poised. "It was in his pocket. He got it from the Three Sisters."

"A faery book, Fate's book," Sarasilien said in the same even tone. He didn't need to glance at Malachi for the implication of this to be understood—faery books of great importance almost certainly were able to write themselves as occasion demanded. "What did you write in it?"

"I wrote . . ." Lila said and hesitated. ". . . friends and lovers all . . ."

The slightest smile flitted through the elf's face, a wry expression. "Xavi must have loved that," he said, almost to himself. "A perfect disarm. So written in such a book with Night's blood, it became true as you wrote it, and she who was your clever adversary was suddenly your ally."

"She?" Lila repeated, almost in a kind of trance although her posture remained balanced at a point of absolute threat over him. "Who the hell *is* she, then?"

"Xaviendra of Delatra is the greatest of the ancestral mages of Alfheim," he said. "She is the last surviving member of the Final Council, except myself and the Lady of Aparastil. The opening of the phantom plane was her doing. She created the shadowkin and the phantom Titans. The original mistake was hers, and she has sought to avoid the consequences ever since."

Lila frowned, unmoving. "She said she was a consequence of the experiment. A victim. She is . . . shadow. Some kind of shadowkin."

"Yes," Sarasilien said. "She is, but at her own hand."

"Why?"

"I'm afraid that's a lesson in obsession with power that must wait," he said. "She has gone to Alfheim to finish what she started before the phantom Titans find her. She knows they are coming, perhaps closer than she thinks."

Now Sandra Lane's black vinyl head jerked like a bird's. "Finish?"

"Godhead, dragonhood, one or the other, only that will do. She made her ambition everything, or it made her."

Lila finally stood down from her stance and crouched to take his hand and pull him back up to his feet.

"You did not mention a further motive," Lane said to him resentfully.

"You never know what someone will do until they do it," he replied. "You can only guess and hope you are wrong. I thought she might only try to save herself from Hellblade, but I believe her actions at the time, in betraying the Titans and their purpose, pointed at a new opportunity she—"

"Cut to the chase, in Otopian," Lila butted in, still unforgiving. "Some of us aren't immortal."

He grimaced, standing stiffly. "If she can gain enough aetheric mass potential in her present form, she would be able to consume the phantoms. With their power and her own, she would be in a position to make another try for ascendancy and I think it is reasonable to assume that this time nothing would stand in her way successfully."

He sighed with exasperation as they all stared at him blankly, not seeing what he was trying to say. "She intents to transcend her present semi-material state for the plasticity of a true dragon, able to move in any dimension, in any manner, without losing cohesion as an individual, all consciousness and memory preserved without the need for any material anchor. It is extremely rare, but it can happen."

"Yeah, but what is she doing in Alfheim that's so important?" Lila said. "And we still haven't come to your part in her rise either."

"I was the one who opposed her," Sarasilien said. "Perhaps it is why the three came for me last. I was against the entire project. Later would be a better time to discuss these details."

"Sure," Lila said sarcastically. "Like there's gonna be a later at this rate."

"She is correct," the Lane android said. "The instability of the fissures in the aether-time expansion are becoming critical. There is a possibility of a quantum implosion event."

"I . . ." Sarasilien began but Lila overrode him.

"It's all me me me with some people," she said, glaring at him, anger radiating off her in waves. "I hate that. Make me a portal to wherever we have to be and let's get this over with." She half turned to Malachi. "Come with me. I need you."

"I will come too," Sandra Lane said.

"Not you," Lila commanded, looking at Sarasilien as he concentrated. "You stay right here."

For once in his life, Malachi couldn't see the way it was going to fall. He wasn't sure who was speaking now, Lila or Nemesis. Burnt rags clung to her, edges alight with ember fire that flared in breezes he couldn't feel. Her skin was white as snow, the red of her hair, the magical scar and her lips bloodred, the armour black as the void. Her eyes were perfect mirrors. The portal opened and they passed through into a darkness so absolute that for a moment he wondered if the last joke was on them and Sarasilien had routed them directly into the Endless that lay beyond all things.

But then he heard a dog bark.

Teazle found the mirror room in the labyrinth beneath Madame's house by memory, his eyes closed fast all the way. Some superstition had made him take the slow route inside. Now he patted his way around the rubble-strewn room like a blind man, only much more ineptly. Relics of the dead were everywhere. Behind him he could feel the weight of the mirror's stare all the time, like a force on his back drawing him towards it, but he almost jumped out of his skin when he heard a voice from it say, "The object you are looking for is to the left. You will have to dig. It's in the corner." It was elvish and fussy, and it spoke Demonic as if it was being forced to eat excrement, but it got the words right.

The weaving presence in his blood that was Hellblade reached out to seize the speaker, and Teazle had to scream, "No!" even as it recoiled in response to his reaction. He didn't know if Hellblade were capable of seeing in any sense that the mirror needed but he didn't want to get sucked in again.

The elf voice laughed, a merry and unrestrained sound that really rubbed Teazle the wrong way.

"Who are you?" he snarled even as he began to grope his way left, finding a large pile of dead-demon stone and bits of fallen ceiling lying there. The rocks were damp and slimy. They slipped and clattered as he started to excavate. "And how come you get to look out of that thing?"

"My name is Ilyatath," said the voice. "And because I am who I am. I see you've changed, Teazle. The pure one is ridden by the polluted. And there I was thinking you'd escape change and be yourself forever. I wish I'd known it was you they were looking for. Then I wouldn't have tried to stop them, and I would have escaped myself."

Teazle paused, and Hellblade recognised who was speaking at the same moment. It was surprised. It thought it had killed him, and then it was afraid and awed and this almost blew Teazle's mind because he hadn't thought it capable of anything approaching fear. Awe was more like it. He was more shocked when with his voice Hellblade said, "You're still alive."

"I am neither alive nor dead," the elf said. "I am just a dream. I thought you had finished me too. But it seems you cannot, Render. You cut me apart and the lash of Judgement laid me bare, it's true. That was agony. But Wrath did not consume me. I thought it was to be my final torment, to be left in pieces forever in the dark. I might have deserved it. But it was a favour in the end. Now I am clean and everything is equal with me."

Teazle absorbed some understanding of this through Hellblade's comprehension though usually he was the last person to buy stories of cathartic enlightenment. Lords of Death probably had a lot of baggage though, and so it wasn't impossible. He was further astonished when he heard Hellblade say, "I will find her before you do. She shall not escape us and you will not spare her."

"It is your business," Tath said. "But there are some you will not take. Teazle, dig faster, it's right underneath, at the corner."

"Since you know so much," Teazle said between breaths as he threw rubble aside and hauled at slippery boulder-sized chunks of ex-demon, "what are you doing hiding in there?"

"Waiting for someone to come looking for the phylactery and the other mirror," Tath said as if this were patently obvious to any numbskull. "Hurry up. It is a plastic food container, about the size of your fist, inside a bundle of rags."

"What is?"

"What you are looking for. The mage's soul bottle. Faster!"

"What's the rush?" he asked, wondering why Xaviendra would have chosen to store her soul in something as crassly ubiquitous and modern as a plastic box and then thinking it wasn't such a stupid idea if you were going to hide it under rubble in a labyrinth under a lagoon, and then he felt Lila die.

There was a moment in which he disbelieved it, because it was Hellblade's senses not his own, but he heard the elf's sharp intake of breath and at the same time he felt a drag on his heart as though it suddenly weighed a ton. "What the hell?!"

"Keep digging," the elf said hoarsely. "The rockfall is considerable. Keep going."

"If I don't see her again, you will all die," Teazle promised, feeling it hollow in his mouth. He flung a man-sized chunk of rock aside. It broke on impact with the floor, and splinters tinkled on the surface of the crystal pane behind him. For a second he felt the most unfamiliar feeling in the world: impotence. "Mirrors as well."

"Just dig," Tath insisted. "That's your business. The rest is mine."

He dug, and Hellblade wove through him, crimson thread on a razor sharp needle, piercing and binding, sewing itself into him for life or death. That didn't matter. He knew that if Lila wasn't there anymore then everything could come to an end, himself most of all.

He dug, and suddenly the box was in his hands. There was nothing else with it, just a cheap takeout carton sealed with duct tape and wrapped in an oilcloth.

Now all he had to do was find the others, and Xaviendra. That probably boiled down to finding Zal, he thought, and teleported to Alfheim.

Lila, Malachi, and Sandra Lane stood in the absolute darkness and heard the dog bark again.

"This way," said a boy's voice from the same direction. "About thirty steps. Careful."

There was no floor, no up, no down, nothing to walk on, but they did walk, thirty steps that way.

"At your feet, Lila, just feel and you'll find it," said the voice, and suddenly Malachi knew it.

"Ilya?" he said, hearing the word although there was no sound here, he realised. But it wouldn't do to realise too much of the truth, or he would fall to bits. He felt it clearly, so he decided he'd heard it, like usual.

"Mal," Ilya's voice was fond, he thought. "Don't worry. You aren't staying."

"Good because I thought . . ."

"This is the end," Sandra Lane said and there was a tinge of wonder in her.

"Got it," Lila said at the same time, sounding sure.

"Back you go now," the elf said, and his tone was so forceful that Malachi felt himself obeying without trying to, retracing the unseen steps. At his back and all around him he felt eyes watching from the darkness, closing in; heard their stare screaming like gulls, closing in, closer and closer, beaks open.

"Impossible," Lane said.

"But I . . ." he began as Ilya's power forced them back across the threshold.

"*Now*," Lila said.

There was light, there was rain, there was ground and mud and sky and more trees than Malachi had ever known existed. It was blinding.

There was a high-pitched sound like a bee and something hit him in the shoulder, spun him around, and knocked him down.

CHAPTER TWENTY

Zal found his father at twilight. He and Unloyal had searched the region for hours, sweeping back and forth across endless hills of billowing green foliage like clouds of life. They didn't fill Zal's senses as they once had, not now that he was attuned to the darkness and searching there, in the permanent penumbral gloom of the forest floor amid the swirling clouds of wild magic. Still, they filled it enough to make looking hard work, particularly when you were strap-hanging off the side of a grumpy drake who kept insisting that he could see perfectly well and there were people down there all right, why couldn't Zal identify them?

Zal could identify them, he replied, equally grumpily, they just weren't the right people. Mercifully they were at least people and he was infinitely grateful for that. His nightmare that the atrocity of Delatra had been visited on the entire world was proven to be just a daydream.

Just as he could see them, however, they could also see him and Unloyal swooping around above them. They were frequently mistaken at first for a demon hunter, and Unloyal's wing was holed by one of the many potshots that had been directed their way until those on the ground tuned in a little more sharply and found the oddness of Zal in their neighbourhood; weird, tainted, and heavily influenced by a soul dub that made him pulse like a throbbing wound in their consciousness, but still, for all that, elf and not, one bent on destruction.

Small parties tracked him, trying to keep pace, but even their leaping speed in the canopy was no match for Unloyal's aerial glissandos. Zal at least finally had the notion of trying to communicate more than his peacenik attitude and reveal who he was searching for. He wasn't helped by the fact that Unloyal had decided he liked to sing along. Like a mournful klaxon, he incompetently blared occasional phrases across the birdsong skies. It took a lot of swearing from Zal to shut him up long enough for them to lose their little audience and finish the hunt in silence once they'd received a tip-off. They were also pelted with fruit, which Unloyal said was helpful, but Zal insisted was for the crime of Unloyal's vocal murder of fine songs.

"I don't hear you singing," the drake muttered as they soared far and high in a turn that would take them out of reach of the interested ground pursuit.

Zal gave him another mix to listen to to shut him up. He didn't say that he didn't feel like singing. He wasn't sure when he would again. They crossed a river, came to the fork they had been told of, and followed the line of water down a valley into isolated canyons that grew narrower until it was hard for the drake to fly in them without clipping his wings on the sides. Here Zal got out of the harness and hung down underneath the drake as it started to get dark and the river became a stream of golden fire in the sunset. He picked up the trace he was looking for and asked Unloyal to stoop lower. He didn't fancy another smash through the canopy, so he aimed for the water this time and prayed it was deep enough. When they came to a falls with a small pool he took his chance and let go.

For a second or two he was free in the air. He felt the Lila armour pulse around him and seal at his wrists, waist, and neck to protect the books that he hadn't even considered, and he thought that he slowed down, but it was hard to tell. Then he hit the water feet first and its cool enveloped him.

Unloyal was a receding mote in the distance by the time he surfaced and swam to the side where he pulled himself out onto the flat rocks and waited for most of the water to drain out of his clothes. The armour squeezed hard and pushed it out. It gave, he thought, a whole new meaning to the notion of being wrung out, and that made him almost laugh. Then he felt the presence of his father grow stronger and turned to face the tall, dark gaps beneath the nearest trees, tossing his head back to fling his wet hair out of his eyes.

The old Saaqaa companion of his came first, a saurian shape, still bigger than grown-up Zal as it paced over the marshy grass and stopped on three-toed feet a few metres from him. Its head, blind as Unloyal's, wove from side to side constantly, an axe shape with a mute savage mouth underneath. Feathers and beads covered its arms, and it rested the ends of its spears on the bank as it came to a halt, leaning on them a little bit. It smelled of the citrus zing of wild magic and greeted Zal with a cautious extension of its *andalune* body. This was articulate, though very quiet—serene in fact—it verified Zal and withdrew. Afterwards his father came out of the darkness and stood where the shade dappled the grass. Zal realised that he was avoiding the sun, and went forward. They met cautiously, and he felt uncertainty as well as warmth in his father's contact. He was astonished at the fact his father looked older. His face was deeply lined now, the skin loose, his hair dark grey instead of the true black of the shadowkin.

"Something changed you a great deal," his father said. He still had a hunting bow and an arrow in his hand although they weren't joined. This was as close to effusive warmth as his father got, Zal knew. His spirit touch was much more affectionate than his stance or his expression. It felt no more fragile than it ever had, and Zal was grateful. "I barely recognised you."

Zal moved forward, dripping, into the deepening shadows under the branches and stopped a metre away. "I got the shit kicked out of me a few times."

His father's eyes narrowed. "But not the manners." The merest flicker of a smile on his flint-edged mouth came and went.

"No fear," Zal said, ducking his head. "That's what you always told me."

"I hope one day you forgive me," came the reply, quietly. "What is on your mind?"

Zal grinned. His father always said that, no matter how obvious or awful the situation. "Well, I found your name in this book here. . . ." He pulled out the object from inside his dry jacket as his father looked at his armour very closely but without saying anything. The Saaqaa coughed slightly and cocked its head.

"He says your friend has gone."

Zal guessed that they meant Unloyal. "Yeah well, he's not much use on the ground."

"So I see." He took the papers in his hand without looking at them and beckoned. "Come this way."

Within a moment Zal was alone on the bank. The night birds, the frogs, and the insects filled the darkening air with sound. He followed the two into the purple, blue, and inky tones of the underforest and felt himself slide from view, not only from the huge open eye of the sky, but from other kinds of eyes. His trace in the rich energy currents of the forest ocean was all but lost to the most experienced senses. He could only follow his father because they had not let go of each other yet. Through the contact, Zal felt the years of isolation and withdrawal that had been his father's life, a hermithood of sorts, straying further and further from civilisation. He tasted how difficult it was for the old man to form sentences though his spirit touch was effortlessly sure.

Presently they stopped and sat down. There was nothing to mark the place as special except their presence. Zal realised that his father had no home at all and felt a wry correction pressed upon him—his father was at home *everywhere*. He thought he saw the man smile, but it could have been a moving leaf shadow.

"Your name is in the list," Zal said. He didn't know if he would have to explain the book but apparently not.

"It is your great-grandfather's name, not mine, though we share it," came the reply. The book was handed back to him. "I am scarcely so old, nor will be, and he is long dead."

Zal was relieved, so much so that he just sat for a moment, holding the papers. "Do you know where my mother is?"

"No."

He had expected as much. They both thought she was dead but had never said so. That was a relief too, in a way. There were fewer people to concern himself with now. "Do you know what's happening in the rest of Alfheim?"

"You mean Wrath's coming," his father said. "Yes I know about it. I guessed that is why you are here. Again you manage to be at the centre of our greatest scandals."

Zal frowned. "What happened to the ones at Delatra?"

"She took them for power and as punishment for her exile," came the reply. "No doubt she came for the book. The other book, I should say."

"What book?"

"The book of binding. Do you have that one also?" There was an edge in the voice now that was unmistakable, even though Zal felt no shift in his father's touch. Against his chest the second book pressed itself, uncomfortable under the armour.

"No."

"Good. She will not stop until she has it."

"What for?"

"The names of the phantoms, perhaps some other knowledge she has forgotten."

The venom in Zal's blood pulsed suddenly, causing him to fall onto his knees as a wave of longing and sweet loyalty to Xaviendra filled him. It smothered all awareness. He started getting to his feet to rush to her, and then the Saaqaa's solid stave hit him and knocked him down again. The armour deferred only some of the impact and used the impetus to jolt him with a nerve shock of its own, across his entire skin. Lila was slapping him. The pain briefly cleared his head.

There was a pause, filled in by the world's cacophony, and Zal realised what an idiot he'd been. He'd assumed that Xaviendra was there on some foolish mission related to what had happened before, or because Malachi had sent her, or Sarasilien maybe, to save the library. He'd assumed that his father had been talking about Wrath when he said "she." But now he saw it wasn't so. To save the library. Sure. Of course. That's exactly it. She wasn't heroically trying to save elvish culture; she was here to destroy it. It was not Wrath who had consumed the living. It was Xavi.

On cue the wound in his neck pulsed, and a wave of longing washed across him, undisguisable in all of its awful detail.

"Poisoned," his father said after a moment as though he had just noticed a bee sting. "Come, let me get rid of it for you."

As poultices were sourced and made and magical incantations muttered, Zal called Unloyal to ask for a pick up. His father bent over his neck, applying hot, vile-smelling mud. He slapped some leaves on the top of it and ordered Zal to lie still. "Is the offending demon dead?"

"Yeah," Zal said, distracted by a sudden and horrible sensation of pulling at the wound site. He winced and put his hand up—it was firmly taken and moved away. "Lila axed it."

"Lila?" said his father.

"My . . . wife," Zal said. "We really are out of touch, aren't we?" He thought of introducing them, but given Lila's present condition he couldn't actually imagine himself doing it. For once he was lost for words and gestures.

"What beautiful armour," his father said, careful not to touch it in any way, and then Zal felt himself a double fool because he could feel the old man laughing at him.

"Is that what you were doing all this time? Hiding in the woods to build up your psychic superpowers?"

He didn't get an answer. He didn't expect to. His father placed his hand on top of the leaves. "Hold this in place. If it stops hurting, you need a new one."

"How long is this going to take?"

"Not fifty years," came the reply.

It took about two hours of constant, nagging, inescapable pain which even Lila the armour could not undo. At the end of it Zal was sure he had ground half a millimetre off his own teeth. Then, to his disgust, he fell asleep.

When he woke up, it was full night. His *andalune* body had spread out completely, as it used to when he was young. His father was nearby, the old Saaqaa with him, sitting. They had eaten some mushrooms to enhance their night sight, but Zal didn't need these. In Alfheim, in the dark, he was less substantial but much more alive.

He communicated with them by the soul energy alone, and they got up and moved with him in silent passage through the hooting, humming forest.

Wrath approaches, his father told him, and the Saaqaa showed him the burst of grey that was the spirit plane in which the phantom moved. It was nothing more than a kind of cloud. He felt it looking, but it passed over him when it came close, rising to the surface of Alfheim's teeming fullness like a carp coming from the depths of a still pool. With a flick it checked them and was gone. It could not find Xaviendra, because she had the power to hide herself—after all, her soul wasn't here. She had no presence in its plane.

They led him to the wall of the canyon to a place where he could climb up to meet the drake.

His father asked him where he was going to go, and what he was going to do.

Zal asked to be shown the spirit plane again, to call Wrath.

Through the shadow bond they shared he was allowed to move through his father's journey. He waited, saw shapes, moved forward, and was stopped by his father's strong presence.

No further. If you're lost here, you won't return.

Zal had to wait. Meantime beneath them in the thin aether of the plane hungrier things gathered, flashed their shining scales, the blades of their fins. Then the cloud returned, shark-sleek this time on the scent of something that knew its name.

An age ago, when he'd been a junkie making Zoomenon circles in the woods to ease his habits, when Lila had been a cute girl chasing him up the mountain, when Solomon's Folly had been visited by ghosts as a matter of mystery, Zal had fallen down and a ghost had sucked his hand empty of spirit. He had thought it was junkie's bad luck, chalked it up to stupidity and greed on his part. Now he knew it wasn't any of those things.

Zal offered Wrath his empty hand, and like a snake coiling into a crack in a rock the form of Wrath wound into it and fastened there.

In the night forest the insects sawed. They heard the heavy flap and shudder of Unloyal's precarious landing on the cliff high above, and then Zal was up and climbing with the armour's warm embrace on him humming an ultrasound song that filled his body with strange pleasures as it power-assisted him up the sheer face so that he felt he was flying.

"Junkie," the drake murmured as he came up on it, laughing drunkenly, strap-hanging again like a teenager on a late date.

"Time to go," Zal said. He thought of the girl he'd left on the island, but she was better off there.

"Delatra?"

His father released him. He felt the old elf and his companion subside into the forest. The spirit plane closed. There was only night, the drake, the armour's burring love.

"Fire first," Zal said. He needed all the power he could get. And even then it wouldn't be near enough, but he had to try. "I need fire."

"I am not an igniter," the drake said. "And nothing here is dry enough."

"Find a place," Zal said. "Somewhere rocky. I'll do the rest."

It was cold when they got to the dry desert of the mountains and landed on the raw scarp, and colder yet when Zal stripped the plate and clothing off his top half. He was shaking as he took the book of names and ripped out the pages, scrunching them up and wedging them between some stones. Unloyal sheltered the spot with the bulk of his wiry body and half-unfurled wings. Lila played the music Zal requested, and the night stopped to listen to the unprecedented sound of the most intense bass that had ever come to that part of the world. He needed it to start the fire.

The paper was protected from ordinary flames. Zal allowed his demon's wings to unfold from his back to ignite them. They were blazing already with the characteristic orange colour of his personal flare, brought to instant heat by the energy of the soundtrack. It was a fire that existed on several planes at once, and it was sufficient to start the process of disposing of the twin books.

"You didn't say you could fly," muttered the drake.

"Never tried it," Zal confessed, seeing their shadows thrown into stark shapes across the flickering yellow rocks.

Zal crouched down close to the small, smokeless pyre and added page after page, turning to the second book that his father had said she had to have and shredding it with his fingers before feeding all the bits into the flames.

He supposed it was a kind of sacrilege, but he wasn't prepared to run the risk of allowing them to survive. This was the last record of all those people who had died and what had happened to them and how it had been done. He was disposing of knowledge that had been bought with thousands of lives, with incalculable suffering. It was his own history. Some would say, maybe Tellona would say, that he was disposing of the past and dooming them to repeat the horror that even his generation had already forgotten.

They could say it if they liked. He turned to the final pages then and pulled them free, made sure they were well alight, then started to rip the rest at random, counting on luck to make sure the job was done right in case he was interrupted. At no point did he attempt to find or read the names anywhere. He just tore and burned and listened to Ska on the empty hillside with the drake in between him and the wind, a bitter grimace on his face; a two-tone funeral at high volume.

At last both the books were ashes. He rubbed these into dust and then he and the drake stood back and watched the wind blow it all away. Both of them felt slight misgiving, but not for what Zal had done; because they knew that it might still be possible to remake the books. Perhaps one or two beings in the universe would be able to, though he doubted they'd care to.

"Be bloody hard though," Zal said after a minute.

The drake agreed.

Zal picked up the chestplate of his armour and put it on next to his skin under his elf jacket. "Funk it up please," he said to her, and she obliged though she kept the beat steady and heavy and he could feel the bass resonating in his heart. The demon wings had no trouble passing through either Lila or the clothes without setting them alight. They were almost immaterial and caused no trouble to the drake either. Zal liked the way they made him look, even though he knew he was no match for Teazle on that score.

"Delatra?" Unloyal asked.

Zal brushed the last of the ash off his hands and tightened up the saddle straps one more time over his stiff legs. He longed for a hit of something strong, but he guessed he'd be better off with a clear head for once. "Thought you'd never ask."

When they arrived in Delatra, it was almost morning and a heavy rain was falling. The elves upon whom Xaviendra had fed and visited her personal ire were all sheltering in the ruins or had run off into the lowlands. Everything was clad in a filthy, low light, grey and sliding. The smell of wet rottenness lay all over.

The one thing Zal couldn't get out of his head was Tellona. She had read the books and she was still alive, castaway or not. Leaving her alive was a gamble of stupendous proportions, and most of the risk lay in his ability to conceal the fact.

In his hand Wrath lay dormant—a promise of malice to come. He flexed the fingers, but they felt no different. Rain lashed the parapets and the wind howled its lonely notes through the tunnels. He squelched forward and began to retrace his steps to the library. Behind him in the streaming mud the drake sat back on his haunches and tuned his wires to Lila-armour's direct frequencies. At his back and given the circumstances, Zal didn't know if that counted as an extra stupidity or not. Any connection could be used against you.

Water sizzled and spat as it passed through his wings. He hoped their light and the memory of demon hunters past would keep the savages at bay, but he was disappointed.

He heard a scrape of stick on rock, the mutter of something going crazy with fear, as he approached the open doorway of the library staircase.

"Get lost," he said. "I'm not interested." At the same moment he drew out the dagger from his belt and felt himself lighten as his body moved into a defensive posture. "Really. Run away and no hard feelings." There was a snicking noise that took him aback because it was so close to his ears, and in the glimmering winglight he saw that his armour had grown rills of blades on its outer edges. Steam billowed around him. He didn't fancy moving into the enclosed space, but he had no choice. Nobody came out, so he went in.

There were two. One leapt at him without weapons and screamed horribly as it sliced itself open on the armour. He saw, in a blur, a spear come stabbing at his face at the same moment, and he ducked aside. It passed his neck and through one wing but the thrower, perhaps distracted by the incoherent gibber of the other, cowered down in the corner with filthy arms over its head and seemed to be fighting itself.

Then as the bloodied one tried to come forward, Zal, disbelieving, saw the terrified one get up, moving with the jerky forced twitches of a marionette, and realised that they were animated by a will other than whatever was left of their own. He put his dagger in the throat of the first, ending it as quickly as he could before wrenching the blade out and spinning around. The spear-thrower faced him with total panic in its eyes. They were oval and white as the moon. The orange torch-flicker of winglight showed him a pretty girl. His wingtip had set her hair on fire, but she barely noticed. She was openmouthed, streaked with filth and blood, her teeth broken as her lips parted in a helpless grimace. Her hands lifted, gripping muck and rocks from the floor, and Zal jumped forward and headbutted her as hard as he could, hoping he didn't crack her skull. She went down in a heap without a sound, and he bent down for a second to put out the fizzling damp embers of her hair before he jumped over her on the way up the first flight of stairs.

His anger made the wings burn hotter still, now well manifested in the heaviness of Alfheim's material plane. They lifted him so that he skimmed across the ground. In the halls there were more of these living zombies coming to delay him, but he was ready and the fact that they were turned against their will made them slow and easy to incapacitate. Perhaps it would have been kinder to kill them. He thought so, but he let them lie and told himself that he could always kill them tomorrow if nothing changed. There was nothing like looking on the bright side.

At the library's greater doors, undamaged and ajar, he saw the first light that wasn't his own.

He pulled the nearest door wide open and looked inside. The light was bluish-violet and it was coming from an enormous bonfire, parodic in its size, a mountain of books, scrolls, and objects crawling with the aetheric flames of a consumption that wasn't combustion.

Xaviendra was standing at the side of it, a stack of fresh volumes at her side balanced on one of the library's carts. The writhing fire covered her as well, and snaked across the floor in a lazy oxbow to the bonfire. She checked a title and riffled the pages, shook it, and then tossed it over her shoulder onto the heap.

"Read any good books recently?"

He didn't even know that was going to come out of his mouth until it did, as laconic and dry as if he'd planned it. The landing book dislodged some from their places, and they came slithering down and slid across the polished stone floor towards him. He angled his head to look at its pages and wasn't surprised to see that they were blank.

"Mmn," Xaviendra said and held out her hand, waggling it. She wasn't the least surprised to see him. "I really need a recommendation, I think. Is that why you've come back?"

He ignored this. "My, here we are at the book depository. It's not the way I pictured the end of the world."

"Well, you have to take what you can get," she said, throwing several more slim volumes on and then taking hold of the cart's handles and dragging the whole thing to the fire where she clumsily upended it and then righted it again, the cargo dumped and downloading into her.

Zal thought of Lila and in return he felt her vibrate against his skin, maybe laughing. "You won't find what you're looking for."

"It wasn't the only copy I'm sure," she drawled. She gave the cart a push, and a figure darted out from the darkness in the stacks and grabbed it with bloody hands.

"Zombie minions," Zal said. "Classy."

"Can't you think of any cracks about late returns and fines or something?" Xaviendra said, as though she was already very bored of him.

"Fresh out," he said, wondering how this was going to go down. Wrath showed no sign of waking; it was waiting for something else and he had no idea what. "What are you trying to do?"

"Well, when you and your friends and lovers have finished bringing the phantoms here, I'm going to eat them all up," she said, skimming a huge leatherbound and hand-gilded atlas into the fire.

She rubbed her eyes and sighed. "Very kind of you. I wonder if you'll be able to try to kill me as effectively as I've tried to kill you. Curious thing that ink and that book. You'd think I'd have recognised it, but apparently there are some artefacts that are still beyond me. And then I had to drink all the vile beer with you and all you could do was talk nonsense about dragons . . . ah ha . . ." she laughed, a tinkly, merry sound of girlish amusement.

"Imagine that," Zal said, finding himself more than able to dislike her. "And after you eat these phantoms, what are you going to do?"

"I don't know," she said, unrolling a huge, handpainted history scroll and squinting at the illuminated names of aeons past, arrayed with the pictographic details of their personal histories. She let it reroll itself and then wanged it end over end into the conflagration. "Having missed out on getting the mantle I might try for it again, although the Bloody Sisters have probably hidden or lost it by now."

"Yeah," Zal said, walking forward to see what it was that the keepers were handing her now as they kept coming out of the black stacks, dumping vases, caskets, more books. He picked up a thin, wide, illustrated children's story and flicked through the pages. "But what for? Where are you going?" He turned to the inside of his wrist as he read the book and tapped his finger there. Lila showed a playlist. He cued, started the music, and this time it played for the room as clearly and loudly amplified as if he had an entire tour's worth of gear in place for a concert of thousands.

Xaviendra actually jolted with shock. Her glare at him was pure poison. The shuffling in the stacks stopped abruptly.

Zal moved his head and shoulders to the beat of the old-style country rock—all goodtime swing beats and boot kickin' riffs—and began to sing quietly along, "aw-uh-uh-oh. . . ." Inwardly he was smiling. At last they were on familiar ground. He glanced up innocently. "What?"

Xaviendra strode over to him and ripped the children's book out of his hands before throwing it on her blazing heap.

He looked at her without interrupting his groove. "And how is *The Velveteen Rabbit* part of your master plan?"

She bared her teeth. "To have to somehow feel a bond with you is so aggravating—I can't tell you just how much I HATE you! Trivial, pathetic, feeble little . . ."

He held up his hand. "Ramp up the B-movie script darling. After studying all this, I think you'd be up to something more eloquent."

He wondered if she could literally explode from anger, but it seemed not, unfortunately. "But seriously, to get back to the subject at hand. Don't you think you deserve some kind of reward for creating a subrace, beginning a race war, and torturing thousands of people to death? I mean, it does seem like a whole big list of achievements in one sense but . . ."

He pulled his dagger out and stabbed it into her just above the collar bone with accuracy and force. Her eyes widened and then she took hold of his hand on the hilt and yanked it out. There was no blood. She glared at him and then let go, pushing his hand away forcefully.

"You're a moron," she said and went back to heaving the collected works of ages onto her fire, apparently brushing him from her consciousness.

Zal put the dagger away. "I didn't think it'd work."

"Treachery was always your strong suit," she retorted though she seemed halfhearted, he thought. She beckoned, and the trailing not-yet-dead resumed their haulage from the library's dark recesses. Then she paused and looked up. "Ah ha," she said. "Your robot girlfriend and her lackeys have arrived. Good. I won't have to listen to this dreadful cacophony much longer."

He knew she could kill them, and there wasn't much he could do about it. Still, he had a minute or two left.

Zal looked at the fire. He walked across to the edge of the tumbled pile and crouched down. His orange wings and the blue creeping witchlight combined to form an ugly, smoglike colour on the covers of the books and the blank faces of the scrolls. He weighed up the chances of surviving what he was about to do versus it being an effective distraction and felt the armour quiver subtly as it connected to the Lila prime. She was nearly there. Malachi was shot in the shoulder, but it had only made him mad. He figured that if Xavi could suck the power from the books, she could suck it out of him too, but he could suck back—junkies have their uses after all.

Xaviendra seemed to have thought along the same lines because she dropped the book she was holding and fixed him with a stare across the flames. "Don't even think . . ."

Zal put his hand into the fire. Their aether bodies merged.

"Oh, you *filthy* . . ." Her disgust hit him like a blow.

Zal felt them connect, felt himself exploding into his full demon form, shadow and fire, the armour melting around him into its own liquid shapes as the music roared into deafening decibels and mixed up with all that Xaviendra was trying to pull out of the scripts. He didn't know how long the music archive would last, or him after it, but she was going to have a tough time chewing him up because he was going to taste as nasty as possible, he was going to make sure of that.

"Gonna getcha good . . ." screamed the vocal—Zal's own cover. He grinned into her face and gave her his best glam-rock wink.

Orange fire and blue met. The dry, heated paper beside him immediately burst into yellow flames. Zal felt Xaviendra scream as the orange fire of his demon flare burned her, and then he felt her gather herself and *pull*. It was like a millstone dragging on his heart. His strength began to drain inexorably away.

"Oh," he was surprised. It was much, much worse than he had

imagined. He realised he was an idiot of course. He should have used the other hand, where sleeping Wrath slept on. Trust a junkie to forget the important bit.

Then the violet fire of Xaviendra's consumption filled his entire aetheric form, and the coil opened in his hand.

"Pull back," it said to him. It's voice sounded like a child's. It anchored him in his hand.

Xaviendra was going to stretch him out like cartoon toffee, but however much she tried, she wasn't going to get him after all.

Wrath wasn't angry. That surprised Zal too. Wrath was calm.

"Don't worry," it said. "The others are coming. We will take her away and then we will die."

That wasn't as comforting as it might have been intended to be, he thought, hoping that he wasn't included. He pushed as much clear focus into the demonic music as he could, forcing Xavi to slow down what she was doing, grinding at her concentration. Lila would be pleased, he thought, to find that the game wasn't just chance and determinism. Skill had something to do with it. And just when you didn't expect it, the rules changed. He thought he would have to fight this Titan, but it was going to fight for him.

The tug of war went on, Zal losing steadily, slowly, as the music ran through him and into her and was destroyed.

Lila felt the rain running down her face, at her side the beast in the darkness breathing heavily and Zal's life flowing away from her like sand through her fingers.

She snapped the two AI units shut regardless of the sensory distortion that resulted from being in two places at once, and let the black android Sandra Lane move ahead of them through the open doors. The sopping rags that bound her torso, legs, and head with their black dripping burnwater tightened like steel boning. She was dead, but walking. She knew it. She was dead, but not crossed over, because Tath was standing in the way.

This understanding had come to her in the office at some point when she understood how the phantom called Nemesis was able to cross over. The collapsing house at Solomon's Folly had fallen on her and the quantum forge had done the rest. Maybe the faery dress had pulled a divine intervention at its own cost. She didn't know, but she did know that she'd lost interest in Xaviendra's story around the time Sarasilien had been talking about the this and that of it, the organisation, the time, the game, the stake, because simultaneously she'd been with Zal in this vile place, reading the names, watching the papers burn, feeling the poison of the demon's last curse leaving him, and listening to the insane dub of his endless supply of music, and it had come to her that she could place bets wherever she liked but when it came to play there was only one way—forward. It was her move.

As she came around the door's heavy block on Lane's tail, she saw the inferno that the room had become, a war of lilac and orange fire in which the elven figures of a man and woman could just be discerned. One had wings and was on his knees. One had a tail and stood over him in a position of power.

Lila commanded her secondary body to release Zal and reattach. There was nothing she could do for him anymore.

Shards of metal flew out of the conflagration towards her as she did something she hadn't tried to do since she and Bentley had spent a few hours revising the plans and working bugs out of the systems: she activated her battle systems.

Lane stood, taking in a scene Lila was already on top of. From behind Lila the dark slinking shape of Nightbane oiled forward, strangely flat and two-dimensional as if he were no more than the bad dreams of children seeing shadows in their room at night. He leapt on Xaviendra's back, and the blue fire faltered. She staggered but only for an instant. The fire itself coiled around the catlike body, immobilising it and pulling it away in a web of force.

Malachi screamed.

"Clear," Lila said to Lane, and watched the android perform an inhuman leap sideways out of range as she let two shatter grenades rip free of her arm and into the detonation point of Xaviendra's partially material rib cage. Fragments of super-hot, depleted plutonium reactor core charged with a faintlife aether frag capacity exploded in the confines of the shell's split-second forcefield, their violence contained within a three-metre radius well clear of Zal.

The elf's small body flew apart.

She knew it wouldn't kill Xavi. Nothing that Lila had would kill her, but it would buy some time.

Then the blue fire snapped back to its mistress with a single, back-draft surge, and it let go of Malachi and of Zal.

"Suppressing fire," Lila said to Lane, who was in position now, on one knee, her arms opening up into the huge silvered fans of radiant reflectors as she shielded herself from the backwash of the light pulses coming from her fingertips. Super-focused beams sliced the blue fire into strips, strobing with a speed no eye could match.

Lila watched as Xaviendra, pulled herself together. Zal was much slower to do the same. They were almost out of delaying plays.

The light hit Xaviendra and for a few moments the form shuddered and seemed as if it shrank. Then with a pulse much brighter than before there was a returning bolt of purple violence and Lane was knocked backwards with a sharp cry, her reflectors wrapping and crunching around her. She did not get up.

From the white-hot burning cyclone that stood where Xaviendra had been, came a sharp pissed-off voice.

"Where is that damned book? You can save a lot of time and life if you just give me what I want, Lila. Then you can be free of that pathetic spirit and we can all go our lovely amicable ways."

Lila reloaded the shell launcher in her arm. It was her last shot. She watched Zal, an agonised figure of light and shadow getting up, but so slowly. She willed him to move, but she could see he'd taken too much damage. He might be able to fuel himself on firelight or darkness, but Xavi could fuel herself on him much more effectively.

A line of blue-white flame licked out towards him. He fell down, agonised, and the coil began to draw him towards the whirling tornado of energy. She guessed it was too hard for Xavi to return to a physical form now, required too much of an effort to reconfigure all that detail, all that information. She waited as Zal clawed the floor, trying to escape, but was dragged relentlessly back by the white-lilac flares of Xavi's hunger. Cries of pain came from what was left of his mouth.

Lila shot the second grenade when she knew he was still safely outside the blast radius and watched Xaviendra falter and flicker. Zal breathed again for an instant.

Pop a few more of those and she'd collapse the local instability enough that there wouldn't be much of anyone left to worry about. She measured the time it took for the mage to pull it together. Not much longer than the first time. Meantime Zal hadn't moved an inch.

Lila backed a step and reached down to Lane. The android gave off no signals. When she touched the body, there was no response. She tried hacking a port, but there was no resistance in any channel. Lane was blown. Even her reactor core had shut down.

"Too late," Xaviendra's voice said. The coil and the cyclone were back. Zal was unconscious now, the orange fire dying out quickly all across the dark form of his body. Lila picked this for a bluff, but she didn't know for sure.

Then there was a light behind her and a burst of quantum particles flaring their unpredictable tracks.

She turned and saw an angel behind her, radiant with white blazing wings and a halo so intense it burned out several photo receptors in her head. There were hints of metal feathers in its wings, razor-edged and gleaming with jewel glints of blue and yellow, and in its face two red eyes stared straight at her.

Zal woke up. He got to his feet slowly, swaying like a drunk and pointed accusingly at the angel. "You're late," he slurred, falling to his knees.

Teazle held out a plastic food carton towards Lila.

Xaviendra saw the huge, spiked form of the armoured cyborg turn, glimpsed what was behind it, and then saw the carton. It was blue, scratched, uneven, unmistakable. Inside it was a single playing card. She didn't need to see it. She knew it. The Queen of Cups.

In those days she had liked a joke, and storing her soul in something that mimicked the fey queen's own tricks pleased her enormously, a perfect twist of fate. She felt sick, giddy. Her head was full of music and a sensation as if she had feet and was dancing, dancing, unable to stop.

She reached out and saw the cyborg's black metal gauntlet close on the plastic carton, crushing and melting it so that the running plastic and the card inside caught fire.

Strange, she thought, that you cannot feel a spirit, even when it is within. Strange, she hadn't expected to see so many moves turn out this way as she watched the machine open its empty fist and receive the angel into it in the form of a sword, a blazing shard of impossible light, existing equally and fully in all dimensions, the axis of the world at that moment.

Rooks, she thought. He said it would be like rooks. And he wasn't even here to see the victory of his one Titan in her revenant rags and scattered bodies.

Friends, she thought.

The possibility had never occurred to her after so long and all that was done. Lila's face was emotionless, impassive. Xaviendra wished for something else, anything but indifference. If she had had eyes, they would have cried.

Lovers, she thought, watching the blade swing free of the air, free of everything. Why wasn't he here? They had all come for each other. Not for her. He'd loved her once. Lovers. Why hadn't he come?

"It's not for you," she said to Lila, meaning no and how could this happen and it isn't supposed to end this way and no. No. No. How could the blood that bound her all this time not hold this sword and this arm back? Friends. Lovers.

"It's my name," Lila said, and her expression changed in that instant as the blade cut. "Friendslayer." There were tears in those mirror eyes. And then they weren't mirrored, they were blue.

Mercy, thought Xaviendra, I . . . but then Render had her and she was no more.

Zal felt Wrath leap through him, a flash of power.

"Goodbye, friend," said the child's voice, strangely exultant.

He heard other voices, an argument, stilled by that childish tone that said they all must go now, yes, time to go, long past time, it was late. And then he knew no more.

Teazle stood as Hellblade shed him. He felt all that power leaving him, all the ability, all the knowledge. It took some of him with it as the ghostly figure of the elf child standing over Zal's body held out its hand. He saw a tall elf and a huge demon for an instant, each touching their hands to that small one, and then they were gone. Wrath had consumed them, transformed them. In front of Teazle, Lila's huge armoured form locked into position with a solid, machinelike finality and moved no more.

"Nemesis, you cannot stay," said the child's ghost. "Come away now."

"Wait," Teazle said.

But a tall shadow peeled away from Lila's body and paused. It looked back at him, dark pits for eyes. "It's been too long," she said. "She cannot come back so far. I'm sorry." She moved forward, a graceful curtain of darkness, touched the child's hand, and vanished.

Teazle stared at Lila's empty body in disbelief.

"Hello, angel," said the boy, turning to him. The small face was peaceful and a little sad. "Because I am the Eater, I cannot eat myself. Only your blue sword can end me. The others are gone now. No more pain. No more tears. Don't worry."

Teazle stared at him. He looked at Lila's immobile wreckage. Zal was a heap, almost invisible beneath the boy's glowing outline.

A scrape of claws made him turn around. He saw the strange drake Zal had ridden and was about to turn back when suddenly it wasn't there anymore. An old dwarf had taken its place and came hurrying across the stone, almost tripping on a discarded book.

"Do as he asks, boy, do as he asks; it's not done to make such as he is wait for their mercies, you know that."

Teazle looked back at the boy. He looked at the dwarf with suspicion, a slow conviction growing on him, and then when he had the dwarf's attention he glanced at Lila. "You have to pay me if you want me to serve."

The dwarf, an old man, bearded and clothed in green, glared fiercely at him with a yellowing eye. "Don't test my patience boy."

"Don't 'boy' me, granddad. You want me to serve. So you give me my favour."

The dwarf stuck his thumbs in his belt and frowned, pushing his lips forward. He tapped his heels on the floor, but he wasn't wearing any boots, only striped socks, and this looked comical. Teazle wasn't fooled by appearances, however. He knew what, if not who, he was facing down.

The dwarf surveyed Teazle and then the entire scene. The book bonfire burned with ordinary fire now. The dwarf flicked a finger and the fire went out. Smoke rose in ugly clouds. He flicked a finger and the smoke vanished. He blew out between his lips and flapped them with a horsey sound, his attention coming to rest on Lila's motionless body. He narrowed his eyes and peered sideways at Teazle.

The ghost boy waited patiently meanwhile.

"Love," the dwarf said with a snort, "you would hold a soul to ransom what's already waited lifetimes for peace, for this, would you?"

"I am no slave," Teazle replied, folding his arms. He knew the fire and smoke were demonstrations of what could easily happen to him. "You pay me for all our service, old man. You pay us good." He drew both the swords easily.

The dwarf eyed him, turning his head but not his body. "You threatening me?"

"Preparing to defend myself."

"You know what my name is, boy?"

Teazle shook his head. "You know mine, I expect."

"I do. So put your sticks away. Though they'll do for me when the time comes, it ain't now."

"I thought you wanted me to finish this sad story?" Teazle looked at the elf ghost, which gave him a distant kind of smile.

"It's your duty, Lightbringer. Do this and the last of your demon days are over. Then you will be free to choose."

"Free to serve," Teazle said.

"Aye but free to choose a name," the dwarf assented. "They call me Mr. V. That help you any?"

"I heard it," Teazle said. "I still won't do it, unless you bring her back."

"Not my power that one," the dwarf said.

"You were sent to see this finished. If he lives on, it's not done. I think that the *geas* isn't paid out. Is it?" Teazle asked. He rested the swords' points on the ground and leaned on them.

The dwarf took a snorting breath and puffed it out with blown cheeks. "Damn junkie elf forgot to call Miss Arie too. So there's another loose end. What a goddamned mess." His gaze darted suddenly to Teazle, and it was slitted and gleaming for a moment.

"Is she for the chop as well?"

"Well now, she's what you might call the full house," the dwarf said. "If she'd been here, I don't doubt you'd have grabbed her and he'd have killed her. Leaving her alive's trouble indeed but killing her in cold blood . . ." He turned to the ghost boy. "This creature's right. You're one short of the number. Surprised the others let you take them."

The elf ghost Wrath looked up at the dwarf and shrugged. "Dead's forever and nobody pays. Some stories need ending. Others might have twists and turns worth leaving in. When I die, the whole is ended. No *geas*. Except yours, old man."

"Hmmm," the dwarf muttered. "Do you expect me to kill Arie with my own hands then?"

"You did not when you had the chance before."

"Eating's not my business," the dwarf said, but he looked deep in thought. "Killin' neither." He looked darkly at Teazle. "And now held to ransom, both of us, by this pipsqueak invention here. Death asks for life, for love." He turned to Teazle again. "Why'd you love her, boy? She's not your type." He pointed at Zal's body. "Him was the one. Not you."

Teazle looked down from his greater height, leaning on the swords. "That's my business. Pay me, or we're done here."

The dwarf scowled even deeper. "And then what? You go rampaging until someone stops you in your petty vengeance?"

"It won't be petty," Teazle reassured him.

"You must not leave me," the boy said then to Teazle, his face serious. "My existence here in this plane is anathema, and anathema will be the end. Anathema is the cracking and soon nothing will hold."

Teazle glanced at the dwarf. "Hence your *geas*, Mr. V? This is your duty, to ensure the survival of the worlds? Then I know you rightly. I want her," he hesitated for a moment and then pointed across at Zal, "and him too."

The dwarf sighed. "Very well. I grant your payments. Don't bloody ask me anything again, though?"

"Summon the King and Queen," Teazle said, smiling without humour. He straightened and flipped both swords up into his hands. He put away the yellow blade and stood waiting.

The dwarf clicked his fingers three times, and two people appeared beside him. One was a tall elf with white-blond hair and a dog, the other a small, black human girl with messy dreadlocks. Both looked surprised. "Deal's good," Mr. V said. He turned to the ghost boy. "Bless you on your way, lads."

"Goodbye," said the boy.

Teazle gave the dwarf one last, long look that promised much if this did not go well, and then stepped forward and cut through all the enchantment that held Wrath to that or any world.

There were no lights, or explosion or sound.

Wrath disappeared, and Teazle put the sword back in its baldric.

Mr. V looked up at Sassy and at Ilyatath. "I've got a favour to ask you," he said to them both.

Behind them they heard a scrabble of claws and a yawning sound as Malachi rejoined the world of conscious things.

"Wha' did I miss?" he said, trying to get up.

"Nothing," Teazle said, rubbing his chest as if easing a slight twinge and smiling at Mr. V.

CHAPTER TWENTY~ONE

Lila stood on the doorstep, flowers in hand. She'd been there five minutes and they were starting to wilt in the noon heat. Finally she knocked. She heard the footsteps and the creaky board and the opening door pulled her through into a hallway that smelled of paint and garlic.

"Late," Max said through a mouthful of something, turning to let Lila show herself in.

She went through into the kitchen and looked around in surprise.

"Tiles," she said.

"Yeah well, they were on sale," Max said dismissively, and gestured at the table. "Sit down." She took the dying roses out of Lila's hand and put them into a vase.

Lila sat down obediently. Zal and Sassy glared at her from the other side of the table, pointedly. She cleared her throat. "You can stop worrying, Max. He isn't coming for you."

"Who isn't?" Max turned around and leaned on the sink, hands wet from the water. "Oh. Ilya. You can say his name, you know. Well, he came for everyone else."

"Not everyone," Lila said, reaching for a piece of garlic bread.

Lila opened her eyes. She was still in the library at Delatra. She felt like someone had run the mains grid off her for a few hours. In front of her the body of Sandra Lane was cold and silent.

She could barely move. With effort she pulled her hands in front of her. She saw human skin, and her own fingers and thumbs. She pushed up to sit, a slow and painful business that made her head spin. She heard whimpering, but it was the elves that Xaviendra had enslaved, hiding in the stacks.

"You sit still now," said an unfamiliar, business kind of voice, and she felt a hand on her shoulder. She saw a dwarf standing beside her looking concerned, his chubby hand patting her with fatherly ease. "You've had a big scare."

She looked around for the others. Everything was black. Then she realised everything was coated in ash and soot. "Who the hell are you?"

But the dwarf had gone off and was busy pulling at a sack. She saw that it was Zal. Beside him a beastman, all fangs and claws, was on his hands and knees, panting in a fixated, self-controlled manner. Malachi.

"Don't . . ." she started to say, but then she realised that under the dwarf's persuasion Zal was moving.

"Fire, I said it didn't I? I said it. Fire is the path I said," the dwarf was muttering as he hauled Zal into a sitting position and began to pat his hands. "One good turn deserves another, don't it, boy? Come on now. Come back to Mr. V."

The wind howled and Lila winced. She looked for Teazle, or a sword. Nothing.

Under the dwarf's ministrations Zal began to babble, "Does it stand for Value?" she heard him say, his cracked lips smiling. "Is it Vainglory? Is it Visible?"

"No no no, 't'ain't none of those," the dwarf said briskly.

Zal opened one eye, looked for Lila, saw her, and let it close again, lying flat. "Vermiform."

"No."

"Vanquish."

"No. I wish it were though, lad. There. You'll be right now." The dwarf moved back and dusted off his hands. He glanced at Lila, and for a moment his eyes might have been slitted and glowing gold, his skin a scaled green. Just for a moment.

"And it's definitely not Unloyal," Zal rasped.

"That was just a cover."

"Nice."

"Rather have me eyes." The dwarf stood back and surveyed them. "You'll do. I got to go."

"Wait," Lila held up her hand. "Are you . . . Mr. V, the dragon?"

"It's possible," the dwarf said. He lifted an imaginary hat. "Good day."

She saw him walk out of the doors. Her head hurt. "Zal?"

"Still here," he said and groaned.

She dragged herself across the floor to him and lay down beside him. He felt warm, and solid and alive. Mal lay down with them, and they all slept for a short time. This time when Lila woke she saw light, very bright. "Teazle?"

But then she heard a dog bark, and the figure that came towards her from the light wasn't the demon but a tall elf with blond hair. His clothing was white and his face was younger than she'd ever seen it. "Ilya," she said, realizing what this meant.

He crouched down beside her, and she reached up to him and saw her arm, suddenly translucent, fading as she watched it rise towards him. To her surprise he pushed it back down and held his hand out towards her. His eyes were clear as crystal; she found them compelling to look at, so pure. . . .

"Lila," his voice brought her back to the moment. She looked at his opened palm. A single snowflake lay there, and then there was a smaller, darker, and more impatient figure bending next to him.

"For heaven's sake!" Sassy said. She grinned at Lila and gave her a thumbs-up. "Look, you found my mirror!" She held up a pink plastic compact with a white daisy printed on the back of it, which Lila had picked up in the empty land beyond Last Water just before they were flung here. "How did you do that? Lost for ages it was. Anyway, what he means to say is that you can go back if you like."

Lila peered slowly at Sassy. Yes it was the same girl.

Sassy flipped the mirror shut and slid it into her jeans pocket as Lila watched. Lila looked at the snowflake in Ilya's hand. It hadn't melted. In the crystal surface she saw her young self, her father, her mother, Max, the dogs, Zal, but they were just fragments. At the heart of the flake something shone with a steady, cool light. "Am I . . . dead?"

"Surely," Sassy said. "I mean, if you want to be. But who'd want that?" She reached down and picked something off Lila's destroyed clothing with interest. It was a small card from a tarot deck of the elves, but Lila recognised it—Queen of Cups. "Like, aces win over queens any day, right?"

In the girl's fingers the card moved, the colours changed, the picture redrew itself and became a single shining cup, overflowing. "Ace of Cups. Look at that!"

"Is this . . ." Lila began, realising her mouth wasn't moving and that confused her. "Are you . . . ?"

"A one-time offer," Sassy said. "Yes. But no strings attached, cross my heart and hope to lie." She made as if writing the letter x with her hand over her chest. She grinned at Lila, an unstoppable, toothy curve. "I won big today. Big."

Lila could see around them all, she realised. She saw herself from above—a crumpled, broken, blackened shape. Zal beside her, not much better but breathing, only sleeping. Beside them Malachi also lay. He was prostrated flat on his belly in front of Sassy like the worshipper of an ancient god. Ilya knelt at their heads, and the single snowflake from the soulfall lay in his hand.

"Come on," Sassy said, getting to her feet. "No more games. I promise. Only on your terms anyway. Probably. What do you say?"

Lila looked away from the challenging gaze of the faery queen into Ilya's clear eyes. She thought of the flicker of a possible future that she'd seen a moment before—a phase gift courtesy of the quantum flux.

Under her cheek she felt Zal's heart beating.

Lila listened for a few moments to its steady rhythm that paced out the measures and the memories and bound them briefly to the world.

What else could she say?

"Yes."

EPILOGUE

"**O**f course strange things can happen to people who've crossed over," Sassy's voice was saying. "They don't always see straight."

Malachi growled something.

Lila frowned and crossed her booted feet on the table, looking at the cards in her hand. "Stop trying to cheat, Sass. I count cards you know, and you ain't got no fours."

Sassy stuck her tongue out. "Where's that angel got to?"

"Here," said Teazle's voice from the kitchen. He emerged, looking very much like his old self, Zal trailing him carrying both their drinks and saying, "Yes I did go back for her, what, you think I was gonna forget and leave her on that island for the rest of her life?"

"The dragon should have gone."

"Yeah, he should have, but librarians weren't his thing, apparently."

"It's your go," Lila told Teazle.

They sat down with the rest of the group. Teazle pulled his hand of cards out of his sleeve and looked at the betting. "I'm out."

"Me too." Max threw her hand down carelessly and picked up her beer before getting up to go outside onto the decking. It was early evening and the temperature was blissfully cool. Cicadas burred.

Below them and across the lake the glittering lights of Bay City were bright and the moon was full and low over the sea.

In the middle of the table, amid scattered plastic chips and inside a pool of spilled whiskey, a grass doll held court, its own tiny set of cards in hand. "Myeh," it said. "I see your pathetic four and raise you ten. Eat that, shortcakes."

Zal pushed all his remaining chips forward. "I'll see those cards."

"Me too," Sassy said, pushing her stake in.

"Out," Malachi muttered, tossing his cards onto his chair as he got up. He smoothed his sleek fur and became cat to curl by the log fire.

"Hey, Lila," called Max from the deck. "He's here."

Lila got up, flipping her cards together, and putting them face down on the table. She pushed her stack of chips forward to the grass doll. "Seeya," she said, and went to answer the door just as she heard soft footsteps on the stairs leading up from the drive. As she passed Teazle he got up too, a man getting off his chair and a wolf as he started walking beside her, one step behind. She put her hand on his head. "It's all right."

He still followed her as she picked up an oblong parcel from the kitchen counter and then went to open the door before the knock. She found herself facing Sarasilien in the porch light, the moon behind him like an onlooker. Moths circled above him and then, casting dust, blundered off into the darkness. For a moment they just looked at each other.

"I said she didn' wanna see ya," said a voice from behind Sarasilien's back, and there was Mr. V in his socks, sitting on the porch rail.

Lila smiled and stepped back, holding the door open, "Come in." She left it open and padded back into the candle and firelight of the house's big interior in her bare feet. Teazle's claws tacked on the wooden floor as he followed them all, circling around. He sat down pointedly in the middle of the rug.

At the table the grass doll began laying out its cards.

Sarasilien and Zal shared a look, of recognition and wariness. Lila held the gift-wrapped object out to Sarasilien. "For you."

Mr. V slipped past them and took a beer off the side table on his way to the fireside. Their only recliner was free, and he climbed up into this and sat there, producing a pipe from somewhere and beginning to fuss with all its tools and accessories.

Sarasilien took the present and looked at it awkwardly. It was clear that after the invitation he'd expected to find Lila alone, but since everyone carried on regardless of him and Lila was watching him expectantly, he eventually pulled off the blue ribbons and carefully undid the seals on the glittery paper. He stared at his present for a few minutes, holding the cheap frame with his fingertips and then looked at Lila over the top of it with a puzzled frown and the smile of someone who detects a joke but isn't sure where it's being played.

"It is a picture of dogs, in a bar, playing snooker."

Lila nodded and her smile at him was shy. "Nobody in this family ever had any taste. I thought you'd be needing it."

His expression became unreadable and he was about to speak, but she waved him off with a sniff and then beckoned him to the table. "Look, card game's finished. Let's see who won."

". . . the Knight of Barbarians and the King of Diamonds!" the grass doll said triumphantly. "I think that concludes the—"

"You haven't seen Lila's cards," Zal said, putting his hand out and slapping the table just as the doll reached towards the large pile of chips.

"Right . . ." Sassy said, leaning across to turn Lila's cards face up. "And look. Six of Furies, Three of Elves, Nine of Dragons, Nine of Fools, Ace of Conundrums, Prince of Dark Gods, Ace of Blind Walkers, Ace of Ruins, Ace of Spades. Charmed Flush. She wins."

The doll stamped a fraying foot. "Hell's teeth have no fury like a damn bad hand!"

"Pay up," Lila said. "You promised one question, one answer."

"Yeah, yeah," it flung itself down in its whiskey slick. "Shoot."

"Who are you?" Lila asked before anyone else could speak, although they'd been thinking of questions every night for months just in case they ever got to win.

Suddenly every eye in the room, even Mr. V's, was focused on the table.

The doll lay back with its head on its arms and wiggled its feet as if swimming in a luxury pool. "Heh, always the easy ones," it said, and cleared its throat. It raised one arm and made a few conductorly sweeps of its malformed hand. In a rich and husky voice that made the whiskey shimmer it began to sing.

"There may be trouble ahead . . ."

Then without pause, the white wolf opened his mouth and sang, "But while there's moonlight . . ."

". . . and music . . ." Zal added, looking startled.

". . . and love . . ." Lila sang, equally surprised.

". . . and romance . . ." Malachi purred, batting at his own mouth with his paw.

"Let's face the music and dance!" sang the doll in its stolen voice, leaping up and bowing deeply around to everyone. It laughed. "I da Hoodoo. Hoo you? Hm? Hoo you? One answer, one question. Debts paid and rest laid. Adios, Maestros!" It leapt up and fell apart into shreds and pieces of old, drying grass.

"Nat King Cole," Lila said, sharing a look with Zal, who returned her gaze with affection and remembering.

"Dar loved Nat King Cole," he said.

"Who doesn't?" Malachi sighed.

Sassy was looking at the grass pile. She poked it with her fingertip. "Never saw it do that before. Usually you have to pull its head off."

A rich smell of pipe tobacco furled across the room just as a car pulled into the driveway.

"Not too late am I?" called a loud, male voice as feet came

stamping up the outside stairs. There was a chink of bottles as a case of beer was put down, and then they saw Temple Greer come in, accompanied by the nearly silent grey form of Bentley.

"Never too late," Zal said, and hooked Teazle's chair by the leg to offer him a place at the table. "I'll deal. Poker your game?"

"It is now." Greer sat down and took an inventory of all the faces around him. "You wouldn't know anything about these vigilante reports happening all around town now would you?"

Lila shrugged. "No."

He peered at Sarasilien, but the elf just raised his eyebrows and showed Greer his picture.

Greer winced. "What the hell is that? Dogs?"

"Playing snooker," Sarasilien said. "In a bar."

"What'll they think of next?" Greer looked at the grass, the chips, the drink. "Come on then, let's see what you're made of. Who's in?"

In the end only Mr. V did not play. He said that cards wasn't his thing.

Later there was music, and food cooked by Max, and the moon fled across the sky and slipped behind the sultry veils of clouds at the horizon. Zal and Lila found themselves overlooking the city and the stars, Teazle at Lila's other side in his most human form, his tail almost hidden in his robe.

"Three never works out," Teazle said conversationally.

"Three's the heaven number," Zal replied.

"Three's the charm," Lila said. "Let's get married again. Only this time, we stay here. I mean, it's not like we're ever in at the same time anyway. Zal has his music. You've got . . . what you do. And I . . ."

They both turned to her and asked at the same time, "Yes, Lila, what is it that you do?"

"Me?" she shrugged and made an innocent face. "I mess around with bikes." She pointed down to the driveway where, next to the inert forms of the taxis parked there for various return journeys, sat the unearthly form of a genuine original parts-made V-Rex.

"Just one seat," Teazle said, admiring the machine.

"Yep." Lila held up her hand and the keys jingled on her finger. "One seat, one key, one ring, one ride." With a smooth motion, she put her hand to the porch rail and hopped over, landing silently on the drive some thirty feet below where she turned and hollered up to them, "But I'll let ya ride it if you're sweet to me!"

They saw her spring, light as a feather, into the saddle. She turned the key, and the thing growled into life with a deep bass tremor that made the porch support vibrate.

"She looks like a faery on that thing," Teazle said, referring to the fact she was wearing only a short sundress. Her bare legs and arms were pale in the porch light. She flicked her wrist and the monster roared.

"You'd better thrash it before I crash it!" Zal yelled down to her.

"See you in the morning!" she called back and blew them kisses with both her hands. "Byeee!" and all the way down the mountainside, through the woods, and into the city they heard her roar.

ABOUT THE AUTHOR

JUSTINA ROBSON was born in Yorkshire, England, in 1968. She studied philosophy and linguistics at university. After only seven years of working as a temporary secretary and 2.5 million words of fiction thrown in the bin, she sold her first novel in 1999.

Since then she has won the 2000 amazon.co.uk Writers' Bursary Award. She has also been a student (1992) and a teacher (2002, 2006) at the Arvon Foundation, in the UK. Her books have been variously shortlisted for the British Science Fiction Best Novel Award, the Arthur C. Clarke Award, the Philip K. Dick Award, and the John W. Campbell Award.

In 2004 Justina was a judge for the Arthur C. Clarke Award, on behalf of the Science Fiction Foundation.

THE NO SHOWS VS. CYNIC GURU

Through the agency of arcane powers beyond imagination, Zal's band, The No Shows, has been in collaboration with real-world band Cynic Guru, so that together they are able to bring you a free track for your entertainment. Listen live to "Doom,"* at www .thenoshows.com.

This page is dedicated to **Cynic Guru** as a thank you for allowing themselves to be temporarily possessed by beings from beyond. They are:

Roland Hartwell (vocals, violin, guitar)
Ricky Korn (bass)
Oli Holm (drums)
Einar Johannsson (lead guitar, vocals)

They also write and record many great songs entirely their own that have nothing to do with channelling the mystical aether of imaginary space-time. More information about them, their tour dates, and their music can be found on their websites: www.cynicguru.com and www .myspace.com/CynicGuru.

*For the composition of this track, Roland took his inspiration from the highly addictive computer game of the same name, while Zal swears it's all about the thrills of fighting alongside and falling in love with Lila Black . . .